Anonymous

Biographies of successful Philadelphia merchants

Anonymous

Biographies of successful Philadelphia merchants

ISBN/EAN: 9783743358768

Manufactured in Europe, USA, Canada, Australia, Japa

Cover: Foto ©Raphael Reischuk / pixelio.de

Manufactured and distributed by brebook publishing software (www.brebook.com)

Anonymous

Biographies of successful Philadelphia merchants

BIOGRAPHIES

OF

SUCCESSFUL

Philadelphia Merchants.

PHILADELPHIA:

PUBLISHED BY JAMES K. SIMON,

No. 33 South Sixth Street.

1864.

INTRODUCTION.

During the years 1860 and '61 the *Commercial List* of Philadelphia, published a series of sketches, giving a lively account of the personal and private history of the Bank Presidents of that city, and also, in the same connection, some notice of the antecedents and career of the cashiers of the same institutions. The record was generally a fair one, though a few of the officials came off with drooping colors and a reputation far from enviable. As, however, no effort was made by the writers to suppress truth, and as there was much intrinsic merit in the sketches, they attracted a wide circle of readers, and were the subject of much attention among those interested in banks and banking, and in many classes of the business community who have heavy financial relations. These sketches, of so much interest to the banking community, would have been published in book form, for permanent preservation, profit and interest, both historically and locally, had it not been for the earnest protest, with but one exception, of the entire body of whom the sketches were the chronicle. Their value would have been considerable, as we know from experience. Think how interesting it would be to have a full, reliable local account of the operations of the great financier, Robert Morris, written all fresh and glowing with life, at the very time when Morris was carrying the financial burthen of the United States as he walked through the streets of the Quaker City.

Of course maturer views come later than contemporaneous

impressions; but there are certain facts and incidents in the
lives of all distinguished men, which, if there is no Boswell at
hand to record, perish beyond the reach of the historic pen.
Though as fleeting and evanescent, they are far more characteristic than the snow flake on the river, or the bubble on the
fountain, to which they have been likened. As Shakspeare
has it,

> " There is a history in all men's lives,
> Fig'ring the nature of the times deceas'd;
> The which observed, a man may prophesy
> With a near aim, of the main chance of things
> As yet not come to life."

Mr. Girard's gig, his peculiar coat and his characteristic
walk, might have been sketched by any habitue of Third
street thirty years ago; and yet, at this date, how few there
are who remarked him sufficiently well to give a correct pen-
portrait of the great financier, or one even half as accurate and
satisfactory as the marble statue which stands in the glorious marble edifice by which his name has become renowned
throughout the country. Hence we see the importance of
treasuring up what appears to be gossip now, for it may become history hereafter. Let us keep an eye on our nascent
leaders of finance, and our youthful generals of the business
world, for we know not who may be the master minds and
mighty men of the future.

In addition to the Bank Presidents, the Commercial List
published, in later issues, choice sketches of successful merchants, who have earned and spent their capital in Philadelphia, and whose lives, thus written, have also attracted attention and interest in business circles.

The approbation which both sets of sketches have met
with, in the circles for which they were written, determined
the production of the present work, the character of which is
indicated by the title. In pursuance of the plan upon which
they were started the sketches take a wide range, and care has
been taken to have them accurate and readable; not only
containing lessons for practical use, but such personal gossip as
indicates character or will interest the reader. Broad traits

are outlined with a liberal hand, while narrow and petty characteristics have no courtly veil thrown over their deformities.

> "An absolute historian
> Should be in fear of none: neither should he
> Write anything more than truth for friendship,
> Or less for hate."

Little things go further than many of us think toward making
up the character of all humanity, and frequently much can
be learned by watching how a merchant signs his name,
handles a bank note, or gives an order. Magnanimity and
meanness have each their set marks, by which the thinking
eye and the quick intellect detect them, be they ever so ob-
scure to the idle brain or the foolish vision of the indolent and
silly.

The interest of the work will spring partly from the fact
that in Philadelphia there is more real, solid, enduring wealth
than in any city in the Union. Financial crisises, which have
swept like a tornado over the land, have touched Philadelphia
with gentle wings. Ups and downs are common to all business
communities, but our city claims a greater immunity than any
other. There are, however, in Philadelphia, perhaps, a number of mean men in business equal to the proportion in any
other metropolis. This class is marked by its selfish unwil-
lingness to assist in the promotion of the general interests of
the community, unless they can see without an opera glass
that the stream of direct pecuniary profit is to percolate and
trickle into their capacious pantaloons pockets. We have
expounded, for general edification, glimpses we have obtained
of the contemptible characteristics of this class of men, and
thus, perhaps, do some good in the prosecution of our general
plan. There is a wide field for such elucidation, and in the
dry goods line it especially exists. It is with pain that we
have time and again observed that merchants, after a prosperous career of twenty, thirty or forty years in this line, and
after having accumulated a handsome competency, make up
their minds to retire, and cut loose absolutely from all connection with their partners, clerks and other employees. After
a profitable association with young and struggling men, these
curmudgeons vanish from the stage of active business, leaving

all their employees to shift for themselves, when, by a little
timely liberality, they might assist them to enter on a career
of honor and usefulness. In New York a much more liberal
idea prevails. On retiring, the Gothamite merchant frequently
leaves a large portion of his capital in the house to which he
has been attached, and thus benefits a wide circle who have
become endeared to him by hourly association, and whose
sterling qualities he has learned to respect and honor. Many
who fail to act this just and generous part were mean in their
active life, and are still meaner in their retirement; meanness
is a component part of their character, and particular attention
should be paid to their ignoble qualities. It may be that our
disclosures will hardly comport with their present apparently
dignified seats in the social synagogue, but the lesson of their
lives may be made a jewel of value to others who are about
entering on a career, and need landmarks by which to avoid
rocks, quicksands and shoals. The achievement of wealth
and position is accomplished in ways as various as the idio-
syncracies of the seekers after money and honor; God has
gifted some men with liberal minds and hearts; in other cases
a coarse-grained and illiberal nature struggles through all the
cultivation or courtly veneer which the instincts of selfish prudence induce men to throw over their moral deformities.
Some men are benevolent, charitable and kindly natured by
as simple a process as the sun shines, or the flowers bloom, or
the glad waters run. Kindness is a law of their being, and
they shed as chivalrous and noble an influence around them
as those knights of old shed opulence by the scattering of
largess or the dropping of pearls from their jeweled garments.
A room is cheerful because such generous men are in it, and a
kindly action seems ten fold more kindly because they have
so large-hearted a way of going into it.

Philadelphia is remarkable for the number of self-made
merchants and manufacturers in it; men who feared not

> "Those twin-jailors of the aspiring soul,
> Low birth and iron fortune,"

pushed right onward over difficulties which would appal
any heart less stout, and energy less powerful and untiring.

To the American, whose country is a living epistle, known
and read by all men, as to the capacities of the entire human
race for elevation, honor and usefulness, such lives are the
most inspiring of lessons. They teach patience, boldness, prudence, energy and daring; and they should also teach us that
every man can help his brother, if he will only set about it in
the right spirit, and with a generous determination to act as
fairly by others as he would wish to be dealt with himself.
We can find many bright and striking contrasts in the lives of
such men as Stephen Girard, John Grigg, T. P. Cope, John
Welsh, J. W. Claghorn, Richard Wistar, Jos. R. Evans, Adam
Steinmetz, J. W. Myers, J. B. Lippincott, John Macrea,
Richard Ashurst, Samuel Grant, I. Cornelius, S. Morris
Waln, John Stitt, and a host of other noble Philadelphians, who have built up the fabric of their fortunes, and now
hold, or have held while living, positions of influence or
honor by the title of their own intellect. It is from this class
that liberal subscriptions to enlightened public improvements
come, and they are constantly performing disinterested and
high-minded acts, of which the world knows but little, because they are not done for the sake of mere ostentation or
self-glorification, but from a sincere and wise conviction of
the justice and sagacity, as well as liberality of such actions.
We do not know what we would do without such atlas-like
men to uphold the commercial and manufacturing interests of
Philadelphia; they sustain grandly the projects which have
built up our beautiful city, and genius and patriotism, literature and the arts, never look in vain to them for recognition.
Visit their mansions, and behold how our merchants are
princes; see the graceful appreciation awarded to genius and
intellect in the works of art which adorn their walls and
drawing-rooms; scan their rich libraries and delicate and fragrant conservatories. Then go to the abodes of the humble,
and learn how many of the rich and honorable recognise their
duties to humanity and shed the bright light of generosity
over places which would else be dark and desolate.

Let us, without at this time revealing the name, tell the
simple story of the career of a manufacturer, who has long

2

been an honor to the circle in which he moves. It is as follows:

About thirty years ago, an Irish lad of eleven years of age, arrived in Philadelphia. He was fresh from the Emerald Isle, and was probably rough, awkward and untutored. But he had the stuff in him of which men of grit are made. He entered a counting house at a weekly stipend of one dollar. Patiently and slowly he won his way. By promptness, quickness, energy and industry he won on the regard of his employer, and ere long the post of assistant clerk rewarded his zeal. A vacancy occurring after he had shown his trusty qualities, he was awarded the position of first clerk. Then he became cashier, and then a partner in the business. He is now sole proprietor of one of the largest manufactories in Philadelphia, and he may be set down as worth $200,000. All of this sprung from his one dollar per week, together with his sterling qualities of head and heart. He is just the same modest, simple, unassuming man to-day, as he was a lad of eleven when he came to Philadelphia. He has his oddities of manner and peculiar eccentricities about other minor matters, but his heart is as sound and his brain as clear as a silver bell. He is ever ready for a work of real benevolence, while abhorring humbug and cant, and he can always be appealed to on behalf of any extensive improvement, irrespective of the question whether his own personal bank account is to be increased or not. His life has been honorable and useful, with not a few of the elements of greatness mingling with its warp and woof.

As the pole suggests the tropics, such a career brings to mind other and meaner lives. There are some men, wealthy and influential ones, too, who commit acts which, if they were done by the poorer classes, would result in their incarceration within the walls of the Eastern Penitentiary. We have a case in point, which is calculated to make an honest man blush. The *gentleman*(?) who is the hero of the narrative—for he is recognized as a gentleman in society—has been in the frequent receipt, by mail, of remittances in large and small sums. Not long since he made his appearance at the desk of the Chief

Clerk in the Post Office, and alleged that he had just taken from his box a letter from which a draft on a city bank, for about one hundred dollars, had been fradulently abstracted, and as the point from which the letter had been mailed was but a short distance from Philadelphia, he was confident that the draft had been abstracted by some one in the Post Office here. This imputation on the character of the office nettled the chief clerk, and that functionary determined to sift the matter to the bottom, and ferret out the criminal, if such there was. He made the necessary inquiries as to the day the letter was due here, closely cross-examined the clerks, and after a diligent investigation, proceeded to the bank on which the draft was drawn. He found that *it had been paid*, and bore the endorsement, or seeming endorsement, of the loser. He borrowed the draft, and brought it to the office. On comparing the apparently forged signature of the loser, on the back of the document, with the hand-writing of a certain night clerk, a remarkable resemblance was discovered. Several experts were called in, and declared that the hand-writing of the clerk and the chirography of the "forger" were one and the same. A clerk in the bank was privately shown the suspected clerk, and he identified him as the man *to whom the money had been paid!* The net-work seemed to be closing around the poor night clerk, and it was determined that he should be arrested. The Chief Clerk, jubilant at his discovery, sent for the merchant who said he had lost the draft. While the Chief Clerk and the merchant were closeted in the Postmaster's private office, and the former was detailing his success to the merchant, he observed, as he proceeded with the recital, that the merchant began to wear a livid hue ; his countenance assumed a pallid aspect, in which a guilty conscience seemed to come to the surface to horrify and disgust the beholder. Trembling lips, too, were seen, and as the truth, in all its damning meanness, flashed across the mind of the Chief Clerk, he at once boldly charged the merchant with having written his own signature *in a feigned hand,* so as to secure the spoils of his own guilt, and ruin an innocent man. The guilty, miserable creature, overwhelmed with confusion, confessed his guilt and im-

plored mercy.   He acknowledged his criminality in the whole
transaction—a transaction which was about to stain forever
the reputation of an honest, hard working man, whose only
capital was his skill as a scrivener and his integrity in his cle-
rical position.   The Chief Clerk, determined that the reputation of the night clerk should be vindicated, threatened to have
the guilty merchant exposed and punished, unless he proceeded
to a magistrate at once, and made an affidavit confessing the
crime in all its details.   The merchant humiliated himself by
signing and swearing to the odious confession, and the matter
there rested.

Look on this picture and then on the one given before it.
Contrast the character of the two men, and read the moral
which stands out so plainly.

In the line of our sketches we enliven our recital by such
incidents as appear instructive to the young and interesting to
the old.   Personal gossip, when reliable, is not disdained, nor
graphic pen-portraits omitted.   We all know how John Jacob
Astor peddled the figs in the streets of New York, and Stephen
Girard retailed the fragrant orange in Philadelphia; and yet,
these facts only make more instructive the subsequent career
of these great men, one of whom blessed mankind when he
founded the Astor Library, and the other set an example for
all future ages when he endowed the college which bears his
name.   All men cannot leave such towering monuments to
their memory, but all can do something that will leave "foot-
prints on the sands of time," so that after they are dead, the
recollection of their elevated qualities will be grateful to their
descendants, and instructive to all who learn the story of their
lives, with their toils, trials, struggles, successes, downfalls and
victories.

> "No age hath been, since nature first began
> To work Jove's wonders, but hath left behind
> Some deeds of praise for mirrors unto man,
> Which more than threatful laws have men inclined:
> To tread the paths of praise excites the mind;
> Mirrors tie thoughts to virtue's due respects;
> Examples hasten deeds to good effects."

TO

EDWARD G. JAMES,

THE FOLLOWING PAGES ARE

𝕽𝖊𝖘𝖕𝖊𝖈𝖙𝖋𝖚𝖑𝖑𝖞 𝕯𝖊𝖉𝖎𝖈𝖆𝖙𝖊𝖉,

AS

A TRIBUTE TO ONE OF PHILADELPHIA'S MOST SUCCESSFUL MERCHANTS,

AND ONE WHO STANDS FORTH AS A TYPE OF

THE SELF-MADE MAN,

THE LARGE-HEARTED PATRIOT,

AND

THE TRUE FRIEND;

With the ardent wishes of the author, that the biographies recorded in these pages may incite the young generation of mer= chants, now growing up around us, to a career as honorable and as successful as that of him to whom this work is affectionately inscribed, by

STEPHEN N. WINSLOW.

CONTENTS.

JOHN GRIGG

AMERICAN BANK NOTE CO.

BIOGRAPHIES

OF

SUCCESSFUL PHILADELPHIA MERCHANTS.

JOHN GRIGG.

THE history of the book trade in the United States is yet to be worthily written. Beginning in the smallest way, amid the contemptuous sneers of the egotistical foreigner—continued under circumstances of the most discouraging description—illustrated during the progress of its development by noble examples of resolute energy, daring enterprise and successful tact, this department of American industry has reached such a degree of importance and perfection that we need have no fear of comparison. As late as the year 1786, book publishing was still in its infancy in this country, and we depended almost entirely upon England for literary pabulum. Four publishers of that period held a consultation in regard to the probability of their being remunerated for the labor and expense involved in the production of an American edition of the New Testament. But not many years afterwards, thanks to the efforts of such men as Matthew Carey and Ebenezer Hazard, our own publications obtained decided success, and amply rewarded their projectors. Carey, particularly, distinguished himself by issuing an edition of the Bible, at a cost of about fifteen thousand dollars—a bold enterprise at that day. Nearly all the standard educational works were imported, and the prices of some of them were so high that they were beyond the reach of the masses. Philadelphia was then the principal centre of the book trade, and, as

3

the business of the dealers increased, branch establishments were founded in the leading cities of the South. It was not until the West began to loom up in importance as a market, that New York could maintain a respectable rivalry with the city of Penn in supplying the literary wants of the nation. Book trade sales were inaugurated in Philadelphia in 1824, and have been continued with great success ever since. Boston and New York now enjoy the superiority in the publication of light literature; but Philadelphia publishes more medical and educational works than any other city in the Union, and can boast of containing the most extensive book distributing concern in the world. The latter was founded, and raised to the summit of prosperity, principally by Mr. John Grigg, whose career we now propose to sketch.

Mr. Grigg began life at the foot of the ladder of fortune. He was left an orphan at a very early age, and compelled to gain his bread by the severe drudgery of a farm. But while still a lad he was remarkable for restless activity and self-reliance; and we find that he soon left the plough to try the roving and adventurous life of the sailor. The sea has often an irresistible charm for bold and sanguine youth. The desire of seeing strange lands and people—the anxiety to behold the wonders of the deep—the thirst for thrilling exploit in the face of deadly peril—send thousands of boys to encounter trials which their fancies clothe with wild romance. Young Grigg remained long enough on shipboard to gain a thorough knowledge of a seaman's duty—to enlarge his acquaintance with the world and to discipline his own character. Ambitious, industrious and energetic, his earnest desire to acquire all the knowledge and advantages of his position, enabled him to resist many of the temptations that assail youth in all circumstances and places. Leaving his seafaring life, he took up his residence in Richmond, Va., and devoted thirteen months to arduous study; his ability and application attracted his relatives, who offered him some assistance; but his main reliance was upon his own quickness of apprehension and unwavering industry in acquiring knowledge. The West, then opening bright pages of promise for enterprise, next won the attention of the young student, and he left Virginia for Ohio. Here he established himself in Warren county, where he was appointed Clerk of the Court of Common Pleas and Chancery. This was an arduous and exacting office, but Mr. Grigg mastered all the details of the business, and displayed such extraordinary industry that his friends became alarmed for his health. While thus employed he won the esteem and cordial friendship of some of the first men in Ohio—among whom were Hon. John McLean and Hon. Thomas Corwin. With the latter gentleman his friendship was of the closest intimacy, each holding the other in that loving esteem which is founded on congeniality in tastes and habits. Writing of him, Mr. Corwin says: "I can say of him, with entire confidence in the opinion, that he was, from boyhood up, through every change of place, occupation and fortune, an earnest, frank, sincere, honest man. After entering the Clerk's office, he very soon made himself master of every detail, and became, in fact, clerk of the court. I know he often wrote from fifteen to eighteen hours, every twenty-four, for weeks together." The intimacy thus begun has continued until the present day.

The trying industry of his life began to show itself upon the young overtasked frame, and Mr. Grigg was compelled by claims of health to leave his situation and again seek a new sphere of action. He found no difficulty in procuring a less trying and harrassing situation, being well known and highly esteemed in a large circle of influential friends. At that time woolen manufactures were engaging much attention in Kentucky. The business had been encouraged by the prevalence of a war between this country and Great Britain, and new proprietors were commencing the lucrative pursuit with much zeal. Mr. Joel Scott had a prosperous factory in Scott county, Ky., on the Elkhorn Creek, a region renowned for its beauty, fertility and salubrity. In 1815 Mr. Grigg entered Mr. Scott's establishment, as superintendent, bringing to bear upon his new employment the same resolution to conquer all its difficulties that had already given him insight into the mysteries of his former vocations. Many times his best energies were sorely tasked; on one occasion he found himself unexpectedly left with the entire charge of the establishment resting upon him; but his ability proved equal to every emergency, and Mr. Scott bore willing testimony to his value in his new capacity. From the most minute details of sorting wools, to the enlarged comprehension of the duties before him as a whole, he proved himself competent, willing and untiring in his position. Mr. Scott writes of "his uncommon industry, activity and efficiency in business," and of "his exalted and honorable feelings and principles." He says: "Mr. Grigg won the entire confidence and most cordial attachment not only of myself and family, but also of all with whom he had been associated in business. This attachment was fully reciprocated by his own warm and generous heart, and was evinced not only by the manifestation of feeling, but also by the bestowal of some memorial to the various members of the family when he took leave of us." Again Mr. Scott writes: "Still (1851) the warmth of his noble heart is unabated. Not a single year has been allowed to pass without the receipt of some substantial and cherished memorial of his abiding friendship, not only to myself, but to my children and grand children, all of whom he seems to embrace in the wide scope of his generous affections, although he has never seen but a single individual of them."

But Mr. Grigg had not yet reached the vocation in which he was to achieve a great name and a great fortune. Although he was pleasantly situated in Kentucky, his ambition increased as he became more conscious of his natural aptitude for extensive business operations. He desired a broader field for exerting his abilities. In 1816 he determined to go to the city of Philadelphia—then the commercial metropolis of the country—and seek a situation in a wholesale dry goods house. But when Mr. Grigg arrived at his newly chosen theatre of action, he discovered that the dry goods trade was much depressed. He found himself in a large city, comparatively without means, and with but few friends. It is stated that he was about to abandon the plans he had formed for the future, and return to Kentucky, when a fortunate circumstance occurred, which rendered it necessary that he should remain a citizen of Philadelphia. He made the acquaintance of Mr. Benjamin Warner, a bookseller, who was a remarkably keen judge of character. Mr. Warner was quick to appreciate Mr. Grigg's good qualities, and immediately gave him the situation of clerk. This was the commencement of John Grigg's connection with the book trade. The business was entirely new to him; but so the woolen manufacture had been. The young clerk acted upon the principle that energy and perseverance will enable a man of ordinary intelligence to master any mercantile or mechanical occupation, and applied himself to the book trade as if he had never been trained to any other branch of industry. Among the clerks then in the house were John Bouvier, who afterwards became eminent as a Judge and legal writer; our venerated citizen Uriah Hunt and John B. Ellison, all of whom became the life-long friends of Mr. Grigg. One of the great advantages enjoyed by Mr. Grigg was a remarkably tenacious memory. His first achievement in his new employment was to fix in his mind the name, character and price of every book in the establishment, so that he could promptly put his hand upon the article wanted by a purchaser. His evident superiority not only awakened the admiration of his employer, but kindled the jealousy of an older clerk in the house. Mr. Warner apprehending that trouble would arise from this circumstance, resolved to maintain peace and yet gratify his young clerk's ambition, by sending him to Virginia, to settle up the affairs of a firm with which the Philadelphia concern was connected, and which had been dissolved by the death of a partner. This duty was gladly undertaken, and performed in such a manner as to strengthen the young man in his employer's good opinion. A few years later, Mr. Warner closed his noble and useful career. One of the latest acts of this estimable gentleman was to recommend John Grigg as a suitable person to continue the extensive business of the concern, writing in the memorandum of his wishes, that "one or two young men, in whom confidence can be reposed," should undertake the charge, adding, "I consider John Grigg as possessing a *peculiar* talent for the bookselling business. *Very industrious,* and from three years' observation (the time he has been employed in my business) I have found nothing in his conduct to raise a doubt in my mind of his possessing correct principles."

It was during the time he was with Mr. Warner (1817) that Mr. Grigg visited almost every part of the State of Virginia, for the purpose of replacing by a *correct* map, the defective one then published, and so successfully attained his object that the map became the best, and the State Legislature cordially acknowledged its great value. The original map, with the corrections in Mr. Grigg's hand writing, now hangs in his counting house.

Mr. Warner's executors, taking that gentleman's own advice for their guide, confided the settlement of the affairs of the firm to Mr. Grigg, as the individual in whom the deceased reposed most confidence. These affairs were found to be complicated and widely ramified. Mr. Warner had large dealings with firms in the South and West, besides a branch house in Charleston, S. C., and various agencies in the West. This caused Mr. Grigg's labors to be very heavy and harrassing. He had also to encounter the difficulties of traveling slowly, by primitive conveyances. But habits of rigid punctuality in meeting engagements, and determined energy in the performance of duty, enabled him to work through the business with infinite credit to himself. On one occasion (in Dec. 1825) he was in Charleston, and had promised to be in Philadelphia upon Christmas day. There was but a brief interval, considering the character of the travel to be undertaken, but, resolved to fulfill his promise, Mr. Grigg accomplished one of the most remarkable journeys on record. He pushed forward by day and night, through a week of stormy weather, and succeeded in reaching Philadelphia on Christmas morning, almost exhausted by fatigue. If that journey had been performed by a soldier, the man would have been crowned with laurel. This was the peaceful triumph of a tradesman. On another occasion Mr. Grigg was taken sick at Lexington, Ky. He was unable to stand, but he ordered himself to be carried to the stage coach, and thus made a wretched, jolting journey back to the city of Philadelphia. But such energy and punctuality are certain to win for a business man general confidence in the end. At the close of the first year a statement of the affairs of the concern, as conducted by Mr. Grigg, was exhibited by that gentleman to the executors of Mr. Warner, who expressed the highest commendation of the skilful management displayed. In November, 1823, the affairs of the house were entirely settled, to the satisfaction of all interested parties.

Once more without a fixed occupation, Mr. Grigg was undecided what course to pursue. He had some means and much experience in a difficult branch of trade. The advice of a Baltimore friend, Mr. Joseph Cushing, was, "Rely on yourself; you cannot fail to succeed. You will yet astonish yourself and the book trade of the whole country." Acting upon this advice Mr. Grigg took a store, with lodgings in the rear, on Fourth street, above Market, and opened the store, which afterwards became so renowned. He began prudently, and without attempting extravagant display. He economised his resources, was always attentive to business, and only enlarged his sphere of operations when he was assured that it could be done with safety. The rapid extension of the public school system creating a great and steady demand for educational books, he devoted much attention to such publications, for which he found a ready sale in all parts of the Union. As the business increased and the establishment was enlarged, Mr. Grigg found it expedient and necessary to take into partnership individuals in whom he had confidence. Young men, trained under his own eye, were preferred, for he valued energy, capacity and integrity, more than the possession of wealth. The firm was long known as Grigg & Elliott, and then as Grigg, Elliott & Co.

During the year previous to withdrawing from the book trade, Mr. Grigg wrote the scorching letter to the President and Directors of the Bank of Pennsylvania, whose subsequent career proved the justice of his reproaches. Seeing with clear forsight the illegitimate and irregular method the bank was pursuing, looking upon the deposits as sacred trust funds, and bravely daring to speak the truth, Mr. Grigg wrote to these gentlemen one of the sharpest letters ever penned.

In 1850 the firm was dissolved. Mr. Grigg felt the necessity of withdrawing from the concern, as age was stealing on and he had accumulated what he considered a sufficiency, the care of which, alone, would give him sufficient employment. January 1st. 1847, Mr. Henry Grambo. Edmund Claxton and George Remsen were taken in as partners. the new firm styling themselves Grigg. Elliott & Co., afterwards Lippincott, Grambo & Co. In 1850 Mr. G. retired. Joshua B. Lippincott purchased the interests of Messrs. Grigg and Elliott, and. with the junior members of the old firm, established the present house of J. B. Lippincott & Co. The general business includes that of publishers, printers, bookbinders, and wholesale booksellers and stationers. The premises of the old concern, where Mr. Grigg commenced with a small store. proved to be too contracted for the vast operations of the new firm, and they have erected a large six story building, in Market street, between Seventh and Eighth streets—a wonderful tree, grown from the original seed planted by Benjamin Warner's indefatigable clerk.

Mr. Grigg has always been distinguished for caution and foresight. Indeed we have heard complaints of him as being rather too cautious. He has preferred to be safe in his investments, and not endanger the fruits of many years of toil in hasty experiments. He foresaw the financial crash of 1836-7, and skilfully provided against the day of trial. Although his business was of vast extent he had not confined his operations to the book trade. He was largely interested in stocks and other property, which a period of depression was likely to depreciate. He promptly changed his investments in stock to real estate, and bought immense properties in Mississippi, Illinois and Philadelphia. When the shock of the storm broke over the country Mr. Grigg was ready, and he stood unscathed, while the majority of those engaged in all branches of trade were forced to succumb. The rapid appreciation of real estate in Philadelphia and Illinois has contributed to swell the fortune of this gentleman. He was an early friend and a large subscriber to the stock of the Pennsylvania Railroad Company, and that could scarcely fail to be a remunerative investment. He is represented to be worth a million of dollars.

In activity, firmness of purpose, economy, punctuality, foresight and general capacity for trade, he was always a shining example. No man had ever a more complete knowledge of the book business, although several have made a more ostentatious display, claiming to be "Napoleon's of the realm of print." We may add, that John Grigg is particularly deserving the remembrance of Philadelphians for having labored so successfully to prevent the complete transfer of the book trade to New York.

JOHN JORDAN.

THOSE familiar with the history of the men who, during the last century, gave to Philadelphia the enviable and well deserved reputation of being a city whose merchants were alike remarkable for industry, enterprise and integrity, will scarcely have forgotten Godfrey Haga, the founder (ninety years ago) of the well-known house of Jordan & Brother, wholesale grocers, now doing a flourishing business at No. 209 North Third street. Mr. Haga was one of that oft quoted, though rare class, known as "self-made men." Like many of his countrymen, poverty compelled him at an early age to leave his native place, Isingen, in Wirtenberg, and seek a new and better home in America. Being sorely straitened in circumstances, he left his native town with little save an earnest and unflinching determination to win success in the land, which at that period offered special inducements to the energetic and persevering. Not having funds sufficient to pay his passage across the Atlantic, he became a "redemptioner," or, in other words, pledged himself to the captain of the vessel that his labors should be at his (the captain's) disposal, after his arrival here, until it yielded a sum equal in amount to the passage money. His allotted term of service was disposed of to a tailor in Philadelphia, named "Beck," whom he faithfully served until his obligation was fully cancelled, earning in the meanwhile sufficient by overwork to enable him to contribute materially to the comforts of a kind widowed mother, whom he left behind in Isingen. The honorable manner in which the young "redemptioner fulfilled his contract with his purchaser (Beck) is one of the brightest spots in Mr. Haga's character, clearly foreshadowing the uprightness and persevering industry which marked his after life. Having accumulated a small capital, he commenced the grocery business at what is now No. 239 Race street. In a comparatively short period, by dint of untiring industry and economy, coupled with a scrupulous regard for promptitude and integrity in all his transactions, he amassed a splendid fortune, and in 1793 retired from the business he had so successfully established, leaving it in the hands of his two principal clerks, John Jordan (the subject of our present sketch) and Frederick Boller.

In referring thus somewhat at length to the history of Mr. Haga, our object has been not to present a sketch of his life, but simply to show the prominent characteristics of the man under whom John Jordan received his mercantile training, and to whose counsel and example he was doubtless largely indebted for the eminent success which crowned his career as a merchant, as well as for those higher traits of character which marked him as a gentleman and a Christian. There are few persons who properly appreciate the immense influence for good or evil which the master exerts upon the mind and character of the apprentice or clerk. "Like master like man," is a trite but truthful maxim. Mr. Haga was remarkable for industry, enterprise, integrity and sobriety, and in all of these estimable traits were developed in a special manner in the conduct and character of John Jordan.

The Jordan's are of German descent; the grand parents of John Jordan having emigrated to this country about the year 1698. His parents were both born in America, and the family may therefore be regarded as thoroughly American. Frederick Jordan, the father, was born near Trenton, N. J., 1744, and Catherine Eckel, the mother, near the same place, in 1750. The elder Jordan was a well-to-do farmer and mill owner, managing his business with shrewdness and frugality, and securing for himself and family a comfortable independence.

John Jordan was born at Frenchtown, Hunterdon county, New Jersey, September 1, 1770, at a place known as Mount Pleasant. Having at an early age manifested unusual aptitude for business, it was his father's earnest desire that he should lead a mer-

4

cantile life. This desire was carried into effect shortly after his father's death, which occurred early in 1784; and in October of that year young Jordan, then only fourteen years of age, was sent to Philadelphia, and placed under the guardianship of his uncle, Godfrey Haga. He was employed as a clerk, being assisted in his labors by Frederick Boller, with whom he was after associated in business, as a partner of the firm of Jordan & Boller, successors to Godfrey Haga. Untiring in his attention to business, faithful to his employer's interests, polite and obliging to all, and possessed of that indomitable spirit of enterprise which strongly character- ized the merchants of his day, his uncle could safely entrust to young Jordan the control of the business with which, for nearly eleven years, he had been so closely identified.

The new firm commenced business March 23, 1793, under the title of Jordan & Boller, in the store No. 123 North Third street, where Mr. Jordan resided, and where he continued to reside until the rapidly growing business of the firm demanded more commo- dious store rooms. Mr. Boller, who was a brother-in-law of Mr. Jordan, died in 1802, but the firm continued without change of title until 1807, for the benefit of Mr. Boller's widow. In 1809 the widow's interest was withdrawn, when a new firm was established, under the title of John Jordan & Co., with Samuel Worman a junior partner. This partnership continued until Mr. Worman's de- cease, in 1813, when the business was transacted by John Jordan alone until 1828. On February 21, of that year, William H. Jor- dan, eldest son of John Jordan, having attained his majority, be- came associated with his father in business, under the title of John Jordan & Son, which partnership was continued until July 1, 1832, when the father retired, having, in the course of thirty-nine years, secured the fruits of an active business life.

Upon the retirement of the father, Edward Jordan, a younger brother, was associated with W. H. J., under the title of W. H. & E. Jordan. The business was most successfully managed by the brothers until 1835, when it was interrupted by the death of the elder brother. William H. Jordan was a most estimable young man, possessed of all the requisites of a successful merchant, and combining with them the nobler traits of open handed generosity and uprightness, he won the entire confidence of those with whom he transacted business as well as the golden opinions of all who knew him. Although but thirty years of age at the time of his death, he filled with honor and ability the responsible position of

Treasurer and Director of the Philadelphia City Savings' Institution. This institution subsequently wound up its affairs with great credit to all concerned.

After the death of W. H. Jordan, in 1835, the firm was changed to Jordan & Brother, being composed at various times of Edward, John and Francis Jordan, until 1842, when Edward Jordan died. The business was then continued by John Jordan, Jr., & Francis Jordan, until 1854, when the arduous duties connected with his position as President of the Manufacturers' and Mechanics' Bank compelled the senior partner, John Jordan, Jr., to withdraw from the active duties of the firm, leaving the business in the hands and under the special management of Francis Jordan and his brother-in-law, Thomas J. Woolf, whose connection with the firm fifteen years previously was then admitted as a partner January 1, 1855, the name of the firm remaining the same. From that period until 1862 John Woolf Jordan, a son of Francis Jordan, the senior partner, was added to the firm, the title remaining the same, Jordan & Brother.

And we may also make record of the fact, that the sterling and meritorious George Francis Clay, drayman, who commenced his career with the elder John Jordan, still continues in the employ of his sons and grandsons—now a period of half a century.

In thus briefly summing up the various changes of partners in this well-known house during a period of *ninety years*, it is a fact worthy of special note, that during the whole of that long period, although the financial crisis of 1794, 1804, 1815, 1822, 1837, 1842, 1857 and 1861 occurred, in no single instance was its paper dishonored or its credit in the slightest degree impaired. It is not less worthy of note, that all the persons connected with the house as partners, from its first establishment down to the present time, were members of the Jordan family, either by blood or marriage ties.

The business relations of the house continue as when first established, (wholesale grocers and dealers in East India saltpetre,) principally with Pennsylvania, Tennessee, North Carolina and Virginia. Intimate business relations were established between this house and Moravian settlements and mission stations in the West Indies, Russia, Greenland, Europe and the Indian tribes of this country, and up to this time these relations continue unimpaired. The firm of Jordan & Brother are the principal disbursing agents of the Moravian Church, and also act as agents for those time-honored seminaries located at Bethlehem, Nazareth and Litiz, in this State.

John Jordan was a prominent, active and consistent member of the Moravian Church. He was what may be emphatically termed an honest man and an humble and devoted Christian. At various periods of his life he contributed liberally to the support of the church, and for a period of more than thirty years he was treasurer of the church in Philadelphia, (which position is now held by his youngest son, Francis Jordan.) At his decease he bequeathed a handsome legacy to the congregation with whom he had been so long associated, to be applied to the support of the Moravian ministers in Philadelphia.

The high estimation in which he was held by the Moravian denomination, is shown in the almost unlimited confidence reposed in him, in placing the funds of the church in his hands, and this confidence has been extended to and is fully maintained by his successors, as we have already shown.

In business Mr. Jordan was always distinguished for his clear perception and sound judgment. His almost uniform success attests this; while his transactions were always characterized by prudence and good fortune, his ventures were not unfrequently of a bold and dashing style. Less clear-sighted men predicted failure, where he felt perfectly confident of success. His spirit of enterprise was always made subject to the control of that practical, clear common sense judgment for which he was remarkable. As a mutual sequence, wealth flowed in upon him surely and rapidly, so that, after an active business life of nearly forty years, he was enabled to retire with a handsome competency. As a man of such notable business traits, he was naturally sought for as a fitting person to fill places of honor and profit; but with a firmness in striking keeping with his modest and unassuming nature, he invariably declined all the public positions offered him.

In politics he was a Federalist, though never actively engaged in political life. His duties as a good citizen were faithfully discharged by regular voting, but beyond this he never ventured in politics. An idea of his tastes may be formed from the character of his intimate associates; prominent among these were Paul Beck, Jacob Ridgway, Lewis Clapier, Captain Daniel Man, John Welsh, (the father of the present firm of S. & W. Welsh,) Stephen Girard, the Willings and the Latimers, nearly all of whom were regular visitors at Mr. Jordan's house or store. From these associations the natural inference would be that he was a perfect gentleman of the old school, and such, in fact, he was. Although making no pretensions of a literary character, he was, nevertheless, thoroughly versed in the current literature of the day and conversant with the standard authors.

In his domestic relations he was peculiarly happy; his family idolized him, while his friends were devotedly attached to him, not less for the many amiable and admirable traits of character displayed in his intercourse with others, than for his uniform kindness and gentleness towards those of his own household. An indulgent father, he was nevertheless a thoughtful and considerate parent, counseling his children always to tread those paths which alone could lead to usefulness, honor and happiness—illustrating his advice by his own example.

He was married in 1804, to a daughter of Judge William Henry, of Northampton county, Pa., son of one of the members of the second Continental Congress. His happy union was blessed with six children, five sons and a daughter; of these only three survived him—John, Francis, and the daughter Antoinette.

Mr. Jordan died February 18, 1845, at the advanced age of seventy-four years. His wife died two months previously. Their remains were interred in the Moravian graveyard, at Franklin and Vine streets, but subsequently removed to Woodland's Cemetery, and were followed to their last resting place by a large number of his old and distinguished associates.

Thus ended the career of a man who was an ornament to his profession and an honor to his native city; his example is one which should stimulate the young men of the present day, and especially those engaged in mercantile pursuits.

John Jordan won his way to affluence and respectability by close attention to business, unspotted integrity, Christian-like liberality, strictly temperate habits, and gentlemanly associations. The same principles, properly carried out, will, in almost every instance, lead to like happy results.

HENRY BUDD.

A MAN'S reputation is the property of the world. The laws of nature have forbidden isolation. Every human being submits to the controling influence of others, or, as a master spirit, wields a power, either for good or evil, upon the masses of mankind. Therefore, while a sense of delicacy and honor would deter us from invading the sanctity of strictly private life, there can be no impropriety in justly scanning the motives and acts of any man as they affect his public and business relations. If he is honest and eminent in his trade and profession, investigation will brighten his fame and point the path that others may follow with like success; but if dishonesty has marked, and ruin closed his career, then let the warning be proclaimed, that it may be carefully heeded.

It is not presuming too much to assert that the course of every man is guided by one predominant sentiment, that overrules all other feelings—ennobling or degrading every transaction—a single bright, or else discolored, thread running through the tissue of existence. This individuality of spirit is felt in the first aspirations of boyhood; it nerves the energies of the man, and takes its parting flight as hope's last glimmer leaves the face of age. It is difficult, indeed, to find this key-note of destiny.

In the subject of this sketch, Mr. Henry Budd, we are enabled to form some judgment of a picture which charmed a youthful fancy, and principles which seem to have directed his aspirations. A diary of this gentleman contains the following memorandum, which we copy verbatim:

" PHILADELPHIA, April 1, 1828.

"This day I commenced living with Messrs. T. Latimer & Co., for the purpose of learning their business; and, to receive as a compensation for my attention and service $200 per year, for the first two years, and $250 for the third year of my stay with them.

"This day, perchance, may be a memorable date of my life's history. Being nearly eighteen years of age, I may be said to commence the action of my life, when a desire for forbidden things is strongest and indulgence most dangerous. Now, when in the midst of temptations and dangers, may the Father of Mercies guide me through the sea of life—teaching me to avoid the shoals and rocks on which has split the happiness of thousands. And may my mind never soar to unattainable objects; may a sober and friendly disposition be the means of gaining me many friends; and, may my path in the business of life be marked with justice, precaution and upright dealing."

How far the sentiments thus early expressed have been fulfilled in his subsequent acts, the community in which he has passed to the present time all his days, can best determine. Certainly such resolution and piety as the diary evinces, were very remarkable in a man of his years. It is seldom that we find a young man surrounded with the temptations of city life, exhibiting such strength of will and devotion to the right path as we discover in the early career of Henry Budd. A diary is an aid to discipline. In making a daily record of our proceedings, we are compelled to review them, and we cannot do this without exercising a certain degree of criticism, which must have a wholesome influence upon the character.

Mr. Budd attained his majority in the house of Thomas Latimer & Co., and he remained there afterwards until the decease of Thomas Latimer.

Wm. B. Potts, the surviving partner, continued the business, and Mr. Budd remained with him until the first of January, 1836. This house was a fine school for merchants. Mr. Latimer and Mr. Potts were among the best business men that this country had produced, and those who were in their employment enjoyed the advantages of their tact and experience. Mr. Potts, especially, we have had occasion to commend as a man of great skill and energy in his peculiar line of business.

On the first of January, 1836, Mr. Budd commenced the flour business, in company with Mr. Thomas Ridgway, who, before that time, was a member of the house of Ridgway & Livezey. The title of the new firm was Ridgway & Budd. The subject of this sketch was a junior partner, but he soon became extensively known in the business world.

During his connection with this firm, Mr. Budd found occasion to serve his fellow citizens in the exercise of a public spirit, which is a feature in his character which affords him a pleasure to indulge. The trade of the Susquehanna and Juniatta rivers, at that time, was of great importance to this city, and was threatened to be diverted to Baltimore by the completion of the tide-water canal. At this juncture Mr. Budd was active in aiding the establishment of a line of tow-boats between this city and Havre de Grace, which converted the dreaded canal from an injury to a benefit, and re-invigorated the declining energies of the Chesapeake and Delaware Canal Company. On this occasion, as upon several others, Mr. Budd showed that he had a generous regard for the public weal, and could rise above considerations of selfish profit.

About this time, animated by public spirit, Mr. Budd gave what time his regular business permitted to the duties of a Director, and afterwards to the Presidency, of the Beaver Meadow Railroad and Coal Company, exhibiting abilities that convinced everybody of his thorough competency for the most responsible positions.

On the first of January, 1846, Ridgway & Budd associated with them Mr. Roland Kirkpatrick, a young gentleman who had been brought up with the house. The firm was then Ridgway, Budd & Co., and continued until 1849, when Mr. Kirkpatrick withdrew from it.

Thomas Ridgway and Henry Budd continued the business until the first of August, 1850, when Thomas Ridgway retired. The great conflagration of the 9th of July of the same year, destroyed the entire stock of Ridgway & Budd, and afforded a favorable opportunity for a dissolution of partnership. Henry Budd, upon the retiracy of Thomas Ridgway, formed an association with Mr. S. J. Comly, and the firm of Budd & Comly was then established. This is one of the most distinguished firms engaged in that department of trade. The number of flour and grain houses had now greatly increased, numbering, perhaps, from fifty to sixty, of various grades in the commission business. The trade, lacking system and proper understanding among those engaged in it, was at once unpleasant and unprofitable. As the results of an ungoverned competition, jealousies approaching in degree almost to hatred, had nearly crushed out every friendly and manly feeling, and the compensation was reduced to a point altogether inadequate to the capital and labor employed and the risk encountered. Necessity demanded a reform. At this period Mr. Budd invited to his house some twelve gentlemen engaged in the trade and occupying antagonistic positions, (as near as their interests could be determined by their locations and the character of their respective business,) for the purpose of organizing the business. Here it was resolved to effect the object, if possible. Meetings were held from time to time, and in due course the "Corn Exchange of Philadelphia" took its place among the institutions of this city, a living and useful reality, of which its members have cause to be proud for its efficiency in drawing them near each other in the bonds of friendship and interest. This organization gives a position to the flour and grain trade which could not have been obtained by any other means. It renders the flour dealers influential at home and abroad. Mr. Budd deserves at least local renown for his efforts to place this organization upon a proper basis.

Mr. Budd has been very successful in the management of his private affairs. In energy, tact and industry, we cannot call to mind a man who is superior in this community. But, as we have intimated, Mr. Budd has not limited his attention to transactions in flour and grain. He has been connected with the Northern Liberties Gas Company ever since it was started, and has been President for five years. He has been a member of the Board of Trade for many years, and has always taken an active part in the proceedings of that body. For more than ten years past he has been an attentive Director in the Bank of Penn Township; and is now the Vice President of that substantial and time-honored institution, "The Fire Insurance Company of the County of Philadelphia."

In social life, Mr. Budd is amiable, intelligent and always agreeable. As a citizen he is full of public spirit, and ever anxious to advance the general welfare. The city of Philadelphia has urgent need of a few more merchants as liberal in heart and mind as Mr. Budd, who, ever prompt in the honorable promotion of his own business, and the faithful discharge of all its obligations, has never suffered the slothful consideration of personal ease to find a place between his matured convictions of utility and ready actions, when required in aid of a worthy cause.

Mr. Budd has never entered the field of politics. The claims of party have been too weak to enslave his independence of thought and expression. His morals are simple, for they are founded upon the eternal and immutable principles of nature—unsophisticated, pure from the hands of the creator—controlling the relations of man, social, political and religious—dispensing justice to every creature—bestowing gifts and blessings according to the manifest capacity of each recipient; and when these are invaded by private interests, political factions, or specious doctrine, he claims the right, sanctioned by our own beneficent government and by the

5

" divinity that stirs within" every honest heart, to resist such en-
croachments, as leading to the ultimate destruction of the earthly
happiness and liberty of mankind.

SAMUEL CARPENTER.

THE curious view of Philadelphia, by Peter Cooper, which hangs
in the Philadelphia Library, and is supposed to have been painted
about the year 1714, contains as a conspicuous object the storehouse of Samuel Carpenter, situate upon the wharf, below Chestnut
street. " Carpenter's stairs," nearly opposite, was a passage from
Front street to what was then called King street, but which since
the Revolutionary war has been called Water street. Carpenter's
wharf was a well known land-mark among the drab coated men
who came over with Penn, and Samuel Carpenter has literally the
the distinction of having been one of our *first* merchants. It is
impossible, at this time, to give much information in relation to
the state of our commerce during the period between the settlement of the city, in 1682, and the death of Samuel Carpenter, in
1714; but all accounts agree that Carpenter was the most successful merchant of his time. Commerce was then mostly confined to
coasting trade, with greater voyages occasionally to the English
West India Islands. Barbadoes and Jamaica were the principal
points of intercourse, and from these islands came many of the
settlers whose blood still courses through our Philadelphia families. Our exports were mostly agricultural products, in which
grain, flour and tobacco held a large proportion. Skins and furs
were important articles of trade also. Our imports were fruits,
spirits, and many articles of British manufacture, which were
thus brought through second hands, in preference to the risk of
voyages to England. Ships were then more plentiful than they
are now, but these ships were small craft of from one hundred to
two hundred tons burthen. There was much danger from pirates,
even in the short voyages which those vessels made. The names
of Kidd and Blackbeard are yet remembered, and their exploits in
sea robbery were quite as daring, considering the amount of commerce and the perils of encountering the king's cruisers, as those

of the Florida and Alabama at this unhappy day. The pirates frequently came to the capes, and at times landed and came to the city, where they spent their ill-gotten money in drinking and revelry, which greatly shocked the sober prejudices of the Quakers.

In 1700. to enforce the laws against piracy and illegal trade, it was declared that strangers should not travel without a pass; that inn keepers should give notice to some neighboring magistrate when strangers came to their houses: that ferrymen and boatmen should not carry strangers or suspicious personages *on the water*. unless each passenger produced a good testimonial under the hands of a magistrate. The old law, a part of the original frame of government of Pennsylvania. that no person should leave the province without fastening a notice of his departure on the court house door thirty days before he left the province, was also declared to be enforced.

Samuel Carpenter, writing. in 1708. to Jonathan Dickinson. says: "I am glad thou didst not come this summer, for craft from Martinico and several other privateers. have been on our coast. and captured many. Our vessels here have been detained some time in fear of the enemy. and now. by this conveyance to Jamaica. they are hurrying off sixteen vessels, to join convoy at the capes under the York man-of-war."

Vessels were at that time generally armed with small cannon, and occasionally they made so much noise when in port. by firing salutes. that they not only wounded the peaceful ears of Friends, but produced political disasters thereby. A curious evidence of this fact is preserved in the minutes of the Council of the Province, under the date of August 7, 1700.

"Complaints having been made to this Board by some of ye Members of Councill, that ye late firing of Gunns, from on board some vessels lying before Philadelphia. hath not onlly frightened some women and children, but hath also occasioned some of the Seneca Indians, that came hither to treat with this Government, to depart, as believing ye fireing of sd Gunns to have been signs of hostilities intended against them: It was yrfore ordered, that no vessel lying before Philadelphia shall fire aney Gunns, but att coming in and going outt, as a sign of yr arrivall and departure; and yt James Logan give notice to mrs of vessels of this order, at their entree of their vessels in his office.; Ye Gov'r, also in open Councill. informed ye three Seneca Indians that stayed behind the rest, that it was the custom of ye English to fire gunns, as a sign of joy and kind entertainment of ye friends, coming on board, and was in no manner of way intended to frighten or disoblige ym, that they were and should be ever welcome to this Government. And in token of amitie and friendship with ym, ye Gov'r gave ym a belt of wampum by ym to be showen to ye other Seneca Indians, yt went away upon fireing of ye sd gunns, which they kindly accepted of. The Gov'r also desired ye Members of Councill to go on board Capt. Sims' vessel, with ye sd three Indians, and their interpreter, that they might see ye manner of ye English on board ye vessels, which was accordingly done to yr great satisfaction."

In 1707, Isaac Norris says, in a letter: " The Province consumes annually of produce and merchandise of England, £14 to £15,000 sterling. The direct returns are in tobacco, furs and skins. The indirect are in produce and provisions, via the West Indies and the southern Colonies. In 1706, about eight hundred hogsheads of tobacco went from Philadelphia, and about twenty-five to thirty tons of skins and furs."

But whilst Samuel Carpenter was an enterprising merchant, and actively engaged in commerce, it was as a citizen and improver of Philadelphia that he deserves a prominent place in our memory. " He was the Stephen Girard of his day in wealth, and the William Sansom in the improvements which he suggested and the edifices which he built."

He owned a crane, bakery, granary and mansion house near the wharf, above Walnut street; a storehouse, wharves, warehouses, a tavern called "The Globe," and a large vault adjacent; the coffee house and "scales" in Front street, near Walnut. He erected, together with William Penn and Caleb Pusey, the third mill in the Province, which was built at Chester, in Upland. He owned the Bristol mills, in Bucks county, where the present town of Bristol is situated. This property was valued at £5,000 sterling—a very considerable sum of money in those days. He built, for his own use as a residence, the fine old mansion, now sadly dilapidated but still standing, at the southeast corner of Second street and Carpenter's alley, afterwards called Norris' alley, and now bearing the barbarous name of Gothic street. This mansion was considered, when built, the greatest house in Philadelphia, and it maintained that eminence until the Revolution. James Logan wrote to William Penn, in relation to it: " There is nothing in the town so well befitting a governor." The grounds extended south to Walnut street, and eastward half way to Front street. Here, in 1696, the

Assembly of the Province convened, and in 1700 Samuel Carpenter gave it up to the use of William Penn, upon his second visit to the Province. In 1703 Carpenter sold it to Judge William Trent, the founder of Trenton, and from Trent it came into the possession of the Norris family, in which it still remains, having lately fallen to the heirs and devisees of Sally Norris Dickerson, a descendant in the female line.

This house became the official residence, and was known as " The Governor's House," and later as "the slate roof house." John Penn, afterwards Governor of Pennsylvania, was born here. Lord Cornbury, Governor of New York and New Jersey, was feasted at this house with great ceremony, in 1702. Governor Hamilton lived in it. General Forbes, the successor of Braddock, also boarded here, after it ceased to be the government house. Baron De Kalb was at one time its inmate. John Adams, and other members of the Continental Congress, resided there when in Philadelphia, and the eccentric and it is now said traitorous General Lee died under its roof.

Of landed property Carpenter was an extensive owner. Besides the Darby mill, in which he had one-half interest, he owned a saw mill and large pond of water near by. He was the owner of the Sepviva estate, adjoining Fairhill, in Philadelphia county, containing three hundred and eighty acres. Besides the above, there was land at Poquinny creek, five thousand acres, with large tracts in New Jersey and elsewhere.

It must have been with regret that a merchant of so much ability and experience felt himself compelled to withdraw from active participation in trade. James Logan, in writing to the proprietors of Pennsylvania concerning Samuel Carpenter, says: "He lost by the war of 1703, because the profitable trade he before carried on almost entirely failed, and his debts coming on him, while his mills and other estate sunk in value, he could by no means clear himself, and from the wealthiest man in the Province in 1701, he became much embarrassed."

Isaac Norris, in a letter dated June 10, 1705, says of him: "That honest and valuable man, whose industry and improvements have been the stock whereon much of the labors and successes of this country have been grafted, is now weary of it all, and is resolved, I think prudently, to wind up and clear his encumbrances." He carried out his intentions, disposed of considerable portions of his property, and retiring to the Sepviva estate, which was near enough to the city to be of convenient access, devoted his leisure time exclusively to public affairs. In 1689 he was a Trustee for the Quaker school and a member of the Assembly. In 1701 he was appointed a member of the Provincial Council, the official advisers of the Governor. Subsequently he became the Treasurer of the Province, a position which he held at the time of his death, in 1714.

Samuel Carpenter left three children—Samuel, John and Hannah. Samuel married a daughter of Samuel Preston, a grand-daughter of Governor Lloyd. There are many descendants of Samuel Carpenter yet among us who bear other names, in consequence of the partial failure of the male lines. Among them were the late Col. Charles F. Ellet, the civil engineer, the builder of the bridge at Niagara Falls, and the originator of the ram fleet now operating upon the western waters. His sons are officers in the Union service. Prof. Ellet, formerly of Columbia College, N. Y., the husband of Mrs. E. F. Ellet, somewhat known as an authoress; Charles P. Smith, ex-State Senator, New York, and Wm. J. Wainwright, of this city. Hon. Thomas P. Carpenter, formerly Judge of the Superior Court of New Jersey, is a descendant of Samuel. John Carpenter married a daughter of Reece Meredith. Hannah married William Fishbourne, who was Mayor of Philadelphia in 1719 and 1720. From that branch of the family are descended the Whartons, Clymers, and Fisbournes, names once proudly registered among those of the best families of Philadelphia.

Whilst it is impossible to give much information concerning our early merchants, it is equally proper to make this record of the few items gleaned in relation to Samuel Carpenter. A member of the Society of Friends, and associate of the founder of the State, he entered into business immediately upon his settlement among us. He built up our commerce, gave comfort to the doubting and timid, encouraged the emigration of industrious mechanics and tradesmen, founded the business of ship building, and directed the course of trade. His successful ventures for many years, gave him the means of expending his wealth in decorating and improving the town. The memory of such a man is entitled to preservation and respect. He was literally, as well as figuratively, the *first merchant of Philadelphia*—the predecessor in whose footsteps have since walked hundreds of eminent mercantile characters, whose tact, ability, integrity, and enterprise have made Philadelphia a magnificent city.

WILLIAM MUSSER.

IN the various branches of the leather manufacture no city in the Union has attained greater distinction than Philadelphia. The tanneries of the Keystone State, in which a capital of about four and a-half millions of dollars is invested, find their principal depot in this centre of wonder-working industry. Immense quantities of the leather tanned in the interior, among the forests of white and chestnut oak, are brought to the city in a rough condition, to be transferred to the numerous establishments of the curriers. There are also about a dozen tanneries, within the limits of the city, which are extensively engaged in the production of sole leather, belting leather, and calf skins. The finer kinds of leather manufactured in Philadelphia are beyond all competition in this country; and, upon the other side of the Atlantic, are admitted to be equal to those for which the French are so renowned. The number of deer, sheep, lamb, and goat skins, consumed by the firms engaged in this department of industry, might induce a morbidly sensitive Cowper to weep over the incidental sacrifice of animal life. The noble buck of the grand old woods of Pennsylvania, the bleating sheep upon a thousand hills, and the leaping goat among the mountains of Hindostan, are made to contribute their valuable articles to supply the steady and increasing demand of our manufacturers. It is stated that three-fourths of the whole number of goat skins imported into the United States from the East Indies are brought to Philadelphia; and, in addition, a large number of very superior goat skins find their way here from Tampico and Curacoa. The morocco produced here is in demand throughout the country. The total value of all ramifications of the leather manufacture in this city cannot be precisely ascertained, but the following is an approximate estimate:

Leather, exclusive of Morocco	$1,610,000
Morocco and Fancy Leather	1,158,000
Boots and Shoes	4,142,000
Saddles, Harness, &c.	1,500,000
Hose, Belting, &c.	180,000
Gloves, Buckskin and Kid	150,000
Trunks and Portmanteaus	313,000
TOTAL,	**$9,053,000**

The finer varieties of leather are also used in the manufacture of porte-monnaies, daguerreotype cases, and in book binding; so that if we say the leather interest is valued at nine and a-half millions of dollars we shall not be accused of exaggeration. Lynn, Mass., is renowned for its enormous production of course boots and shoes. But Philadelphia is still more celebrated for the fine workmanship bestowed upon our pedal coverings. The ladies' shoes produced here are unrivaled in tasteful style and durable quality.

It is our purpose in the present article to sketch the career of a self-made man whose name has long been associated with the leather trade of Philadelphia. There are few men engaged in the business who have not heard of William Musser. For more than fifty years he has been identified with this important interest. Mr. Musser was born in the ancient town of Lancaster, Pa., August 17, 1789, and came from one of the numerous German families which originally peopled that beautiful portion of the State. He received but an ordinary education, such as the times and the country afforded; but he inherited the qualities of energy, self-reliance and thrift, which have always distinguished the German element among the American people. In July, 1803, when young Musser had reached the age of fourteen years, he came to Philadelphia, then still recognized as the commercial metropolis of the Union, and entered the counting-house of his brother-in-law, John Singer, wholesale dealer in hides and leather, who was located at 137 Market street, but in 1808 removed to 263 Market street. This branch of trade was comparatively in its infancy. Our domestic manufactures were of small account. The business was to be developed and men of the right stamp were needed to accomplish that desirable object. By close application, rigid integrity, and the display of practical talent, the young Lancasterian soon won the confidence of his employers, and was entrusted with responsible duties. But the clarion of war was destined to break in upon all peaceful avocations. In 1812, the "second war of independence" was declared. The British invader was expected at all points along the seaboard. On account of the position and importance of Philadelphia, it was thought that this city would be one of the first objects of attack.

A patriotic spirit pervaded the whole population. Old and young men prepared to shoulder the musket and defend their beloved firesides. Individuals of all classes, of all trades and professions, came forward promptly at the call of their country. A number of those who have since became very distinguished in public life were then in the ranks by the side of clerks from the counting-house and artisans from the work-bench. Among the first volunteers was no less a person than James Buchanan, late President of the United States. William Musser was filled with patriotic ardor. He joined the force raised in Philadelphia and its vicinity, and accompanied the troops to Camp Dupont. The service performed by these volunteers was not at all varied by excitement and adventure. It was a tedious routine of duty. But the spirit of all in the camp were cheered by the consciousness of the important protection they extended to a populous region of the Republic. The British made no attempt to reach Philadelphia. At the close of the war the volunteers returned to the city and received the honors earned by their protracted and patient service, and their sacrifice of private interests in behalf of the general weal. Mr. Musser was so highly esteemed that he was readily admitted to partnership in the firm of John Singer & Co. in 1814. His attention and talent for trade soon made him the leading member of that firm—the pack-horse and the manager of the business. All kinds of domestic manufactures had been greatly stimulated by the war which had the effect of a prohibitory tariff, and the affairs of the house had risen in importance. Upon the retirement of Mr. John Singer, senior, in 1829, the style of the firm was changed to John Singer, Jr. & Co., who continued the business with great success until the year 1836. Then Mr. Singer's ill health compelled him to give up the cares and anxieties of trade. The firm was then reorganized under the title of Wm. Musser & Co., as it has been known ever since. In the meantime, the subject of this sketch had steadily advanced in mercantile reputation, in knowledge of the leather trade, and in pecuniary means. He had chosen to climb slowly and surely, and when he reached the height of which he had dreamed while a boy in the counting-house, he felt that noble pride of position which leads a man to endeavor to honor the standing he has so laboriously attained. In 1846, an amiable, intelligent and very active gentleman—Mr. A. Ruth, also of Lancaster County, was added to the firm. Mr. Ruth justified the good opinion formed of his abilities at the commencement of his career, and he has always been considered, since that time, as one of the substantial pillars of the house. Mr. Richard M. Greiner, also an efficient young man of business, is the third partner of Mr. Musser. The three members of this firm constitute, in the phrase of the day, "a strong team," which the mercantile classes have learned to respect.

Mr. Musser accumulated an ample fortune. But in 1848, the calamity which always hangs over commercial operations, and which, in many instances, even consummate foresight and prudence cannot avert, fell upon the firm, and it was announced, to the general regret, that the house had suspended. Mr. Musser's reputation, however, was now worth to him a mint of money. The creditors were convinced of his strict integrity and capacity for recovering from the severest strokes of disaster. They promptly granted an extension, and the firm continued the business with more energy than ever. And now we have to record a fine example of mercantile honesty, which fully substantiates all the claims that have been put forth by the friends of Mr. Musser, as to the sterling worth of his character. The trade in hides and leather having been unusually prosperous and profitable, and the firm having more than regained the ground it had lost during the lapse of four years, Mr. Musser called upon all their creditors in 1853, *and satisfied to the cent all their just demands.* From that period until the present day, no house in the country has stood higher in credit and general esteem than that of William Musser & Co. It is notorious that there are men engaged in trade who "make money by failing," and they are usually considered but little better than "respectable" swindlers. But there is an honorable way of making money out of a failure, and that is by paying creditors as soon as possible and thus establishing a reputation for integrity. This policy is wisest in the end, and perfectly justifies the venerable saw concerning the wisdom of honesty.

Mr. Musser has no children, but has adopted and educated a number, who have since made their mark. The junior member of the house is among the number. Mr. Ruth married a Miss Martha Glenn, a most intelligent and estimable lady, who was another of Mr. Musser's adopted children.

Mr. Musser is about seventy-five years of age. His career has been one of constant activity. His means are ample to secure comfort and luxury in his declining years. He is hale and well preserved. In gaining a knowledge of men and things in the busy world of trade, he has not found the truth of the selfish maxim of Rochefocauld, or learned to be misanthropical. A more benevolent man in an unostentatious way does not exist. He never omits to aid the deserving unfortunate if it is in his power to lend a helping hand. In private life, as in commercial relations, he is irreproachable.

Mr. Musser has been much sought after to lend the weight of his name to corporations, and has been invited to preside over the affairs of various coal companies, a railroad, and one of our principal monied institutions. But he has invariably declined, not from any defect of public spirit, but from the inherent modesty and diffidence of his nature. This is the age of "brass," and modesty ought to be honored according to its rarity. Mr. Musser was one of the founders of St. John's Lutheran Church, and has long been President of its Board of Trustees. As trustee for a number of large estates, he has discharged his onerous duties with admirable fidelity and skill. Such is the history of a Lancaster boy, developed by his own industry and tact, into a wealthy and influential merchant in a great metropolis.

JOSEPH H. SEAL.

"THERE is a tide in the affairs of men, which, taken at the flood, leads on to fortune," according to the immortal Shakspeare; but how many are there who drift about wildly, and never get into the strong current. And how many there are whose desperate exertions carry them into eddies, from which they sometimes fortunately escape, but are more frequently whirled round in the same unquiet circle. The secret of success in business is to *try*, and the best of all qualities to a merchant is indomitable perseverance, with a steady determination, and a disposition which is undaunted by reverses. We shall endeavor to show the applicability of these maxims to the mercantile career of Joseph H. Seal.

Born in Birmingham township, Chester county, Pa., on the thirteenth of December, 1792, Joseph H. Seal seemed destined by nature for the life of a farmer. His parents were farmers—plain, honest people; and their son was given that sturdy and practical education which the country furnished in his youthful days, the great rule then being that labor was better than book learning. The country school was not much of an institution fifty years ago. Farmers thought that their boys were wasting time in conning lessons—and

duty to society. He has invested his money as a special partner in several firms, and is thus the means of assisting worthy young men to improve their own condition and add to the business of the city. In 1840 he became a special partner with E. S. Burnett. In 1842 he was a special partner with Tanguy & Bringhurst; afterwards with Erringer & Pease, and then with Pease & Foster. In 1854 he engaged as special partner in the wool business, with E. L. Reece and Wm. H. Seal, his son. Wm. H. Seal died in 1857. He was a most estimable young man, with fine business qualities. The same assistance was extended after his death to Reece, Seal & Co., composed of E. L. Reece, J. Howard Seal and Alfred Seal, who still occupy the honorable position as leading wool merchants, at No. 20 North Front street, a situation at which they have been located for fifteen years. He is also a special partner with John Zebley, Jr., at No. 17 North Fourth street, and since his retirement from business has been thus associated with seven firms. Few of our retired merchants can show a similar record of usefulness, and the example of Mr. Seal is one which is worthy of being extensively followed.

Mr. Seal has kept himself aloof from politics, and has never held public office. He was an "old line Whig," and supported that party as a citizen and voter. He has been a Director of the Penn Township Bank and of the Manfacturers' Bank for the last twenty years. He was for three years Director of the Schuylkill Navigation Company, and he has been a Director of the Delaware Mutual Insurance Company since it has been established. He is a quiet and unassuming gentleman, and has proved himself to be an honorable and useful citizen.

EDWARD C. KNIGHT.

FROM among the ranks of quiet, persevering, steady going citizens, whom we meet in the walks of everyday life, there are but few more deserving of a place in these pages, than the subject of the present sketch.

Mr. Knight was born upon a farm, in Gloucester county, N. J., in December, 1813. His parents were members of the Society of

Friends. His father (Jonathan Knight) died in 1823, when Edward was but ten years of age, leaving his mother, with three children—two daughters, in very narrow circumstances.

But the boy was healthy, stout hearted, and industrious. Animated by affection for his mother and sisters, he exerted himself to the utmost of his ability, doing such farm work as generally falls to much older persons. In 1828 he was fortunate enough to obtain a situation in a store at Kaighn's Point, N. J. This was his first introduction into business life. Here he remained four years, steadily devoting himself to the interests of his employers, and improving his acquaintance with men, and the manner of transacting business.

In 1832, when but nineteen years of age, being anxious to improve his circumstances, he obtained a situation in the grocery store of Atkinson & Cuthbert, at the foot of South street, in Philadelphia. In this house Mr. Knight toiled as a clerk until 1836, when he adopted the resolution of going into business on his own account, and, in connection with his mother, (Rebecca Knight,) opened a wholesale and retail grocery store in Second street opposite Almond. There he continued for ten years; at the end of which time, in 1846, his mother having some time previously withdrawn from the business, he removed to the southeast corner of Water and Chestnut streets, and entered upon the wholesale grocery, tea, and commission business. After being here some years, Mr. Knight associated with him in the business, under the firm of E. C. Knight & Co., Mr. Charles A. Sparks, who had been with him, as principal clerk, from his removal there.

In addition to their wholesale grocery business, they are also the sole agents of the grocers' sugar house of Messrs. Kusenberg & Bartol, the celebrated refinery, on Passyunk avenue below Carpenter street. They are also extensively engaged in shipment to and from California, Valparaiso, Cuba, and New Orleans. The business of the concern is very extensive, and its reputation for healthy prosperity is not exceeded by that of another house engaged in the same trade. During the crisis of 1857, a number of the wholesale grocery houses in this city were prostrated. Mr. Knight was not only able to weather the storm, but to assist several establishments which were in a tottering condition. He came out of that terrible ordeal with greatly increased distinction as a merchant and a man.

Mr. Knight was interested in the barque Onioto, that sailed from this port in 1849, for San Francisco, when she took out on deck the small steamer "Islander," and which was the first steamer that plied upon the waters above Sacramento City. Mr. Knight was interested in the building of the ships Morning Light and John Trucks. He built a block of stores on Penn street below South, also, the Corn Exchange Bank building; both of which he still owns, as also several other properties in different parts of the city. As an active and useful member of the Board of Trade, as an efficient Director, successively, in the Southwark Bank, the Bank of Commerce, and the Corn Exchange Bank, he has continually evinced his capacity for dealing with matters of finance, and has rendered good service. He has exhibited a warm interest in all the great railroad enterprises, which have contributed so much to the prosperity of our trade, and was an earnest friend of the Pennsylvania Central Railroad, when that magnificent project had need of support. And in this connection, we may mention that he is the inventor of a railroad sleeping car, which is being introduced on many of our railroads, and bids fair to be largely appreciated by the various railroad companies, and the traveling public.

Mr. Knight is no politician. He has no relish for the intrigues and excitements that characterize the strifes of parties at the present day. Still, like all intelligent Americans, he has political opinions, and these are of the kind asserted and vindicated by the great Clay and Webster. In 1856 the People's Party of the First District, in which Mr. Knight resided, nominated him for Congress by acclamation. This nomination was entirely unsolicited on his part. There being a decided Democratic majority in the district, Mr. Knight was defeated, although running far ahead of his ticket. Probably if we had a few more such practical men at Washington, instead of the inveterate wranglers, the interest of the nation would gain by the change.

P. S.—Since the above sketch was written in April, 1860, Mr. Knight has been engaged as a Director in the Pennsylvania Railroad Company, elected by the City of Philadelphia, for two years. He is at present a Director in the North Pennsylvania Railroad Co., and the Insurance Company of the State of Pennsylvania. He is also a joint owner, with Messrs. Kusenberg & Bartol, of the Southwark Sugar Refinery, a new and extensive establishment lately erected by them on Shippen street wharf, of which E. C. Knight & Co. are the sole agents. He is interested in other enterprises, among which are the development of an extensive and valuable coal property at West Pittston, in Luzerne county, Pa., and the erection of the Camden Woolen Mills, on Cooper's creek, Camden, N. J. He is an active member of the National Union League, of Philadelphia, and, in connection with many of his colleagues therein, has rendered material aid and valuable services in support of the government of the United States.

HUGH CRAIG.

It has been observed that the sons of green Erin get along rapidly everywhere except at home. We find them earning fame and fortune in all quarters of the globe. In Ireland, until quite recently, Irishmen seemed to groan under a kind of nightmare; all their worldly hopes were centred in leaving that emerald sod upon which they played in childhood. Our country must acknowledge a heavy indebtedness to the Celtic element of her population. From the earliest colonial times until the present day, Irishmen have been conspicuous actors in the drama of our republican life. When the storm of battle has swept over the land, brave and chivalrous sons of the Emerald Isle have bared their breasts to the foe; and when we have enjoyed the sunny days of peace, sons of the same soil have shown their capacity for civil station and for success in trade. Irishmen, and the children of Irishmen, now swell the ranks of our self-made men. A native quickness of wit, cheerful humor in the midst of difficulties, and a healthy activity of body and mind, are the characteristics of this portion of our people, and the most ingenious and indefatigable son of Yankee land will frequently meet his match among them in the negotiations of bargain and sale.

Hugh Craig, the subject of this sketch, first saw the light at Coleraine, Ireland, in 1817.

The well known charms of his native town, as set forth in the ballad of "Kitty of Coleraine," were not sufficient to enchain the youth, for he was only fifteen years of age when he sailed for the United States. In 1832, on the day after landing in the city of Penn, Craig entered the store of Robert Fleming, dealer in flour and grain, at Seventeenth and Market streets. The Irish lad be-

7

gan at the foot of the hill, but he began with the determination to reach the top. Mr. Fleming's business was very extensive. Craig could not have found better opportunities than this house afforded for learning everything relating to transactions in flour and grain. Mr. Fleming retired with the comfortable sum of a million and a-half of dollars. Craig must have advanced very rapidly in his knowledge of commercial affairs, for in 1838, when he had just reached his majority, he ventured to commence business on his own account, at the northwest corner of Broad and Cherry streets, where, after the lapse of twenty-two years, he still remains. Mr. Thomas Bellas was the principal partner of Mr. Craig, and the firm was styled Craig, Bellas & Co. In 1845 the firm was changed to Craig & Bellas; but Mr. Bellas retired about five years ago, having secured a fortune.

The prosperity of the concern is chiefly due to the industry and practical talents of the senior partner. The reputation of Mr. Craig among mercantile gentlemen has remained unsullied during many severe ordeals, and no man engaged in the same branch of trade has risen more rapidly in the social scale than he who came to us a poor boy from Coleraine. After the retirement of Mr. Bellas, Mr. Craig carried on the extensive business of the concern alone for a time, when he took into partnership a young man named William Wilson, who had been for eighteen years a clerk in the house, and who was distinguished for industry and integrity, commercial talent and pleasant manners. This is what may be called the immediate history of this well known firm.

In 1845 a very destructive conflagration occurred at Broad and Cherry streets, and before the flames could be extinguished the warehouse of Craig, Bellas & Co., that of James Steel & Co., on the opposite corner, and several other buildings, with nearly all their contents, were consumed or ruined. Consignors of produce had no legitimate claim for a dollar's worth of the loss: but Craig, Bellas & Co. acted on this occasion in a highly liberal and honorable manner. They immediately issued a circular, containing the following remarkable feature: "Those having claims against this firm for produce destroyed by the late fire, will please present the same at once for payment." This was no mere flourish of a promise never meant to be fulfilled. Every dollar of such claims was promptly paid upon demand. There was nothing lost by this generous method of doing business. Indeed, considered as a sagacious stroke of policy, nothing more effectual could have been devised to ensure the concern a future career of heavy patronage and prosperity. Such a course demonstrated the entire soundness of the house, and gave the business community the greatest confidence in its operations. From that very day there was a steady increase in the profits of the concern. But the conduct of Craig Bellas & Co. stands in marked contrast to the policy pursued by other produce houses under similar circumstances. The latter refused to recognize the claims of consignors, and have been involved in almost interminable litigation, the natural consequences of which is a wholesale depreciation of their business.

The energy of the firm of Craig, Bellas & Co., was brilliantly displayed in another way. They immediately set about the erection of one of the most spacious and convenient produce warehouses that the city could boast—the building we now see at the corner of Broad and Cherry streets. This structure has three fronts—one of one hundred feet on Broad street, but a second of one hundred and eighty feet on Cherry street, and a third of one hundred feet on King street. It is in this establishment that the immense business of the firm is now transacted, and an admirable system prevails in all the arrangements. The warehouse is the property of Mr. Craig himself.

There are two brothers of Hugh Craig now engaged in business in this city. They, also, are remarkable for their industry and tact. Andrew C. Craig, the elder, is now about forty-seven years old. He commenced the liquor trade in 1831, at Sixth and South streets. Afterwards he associated with Mr. Catherwood, and the firm was known as Catherwood & Craig. Their store was located at Thirteenth and Market streets. After the dissolution of this firm, Andrew entered into partnership with his brother Joseph, and they are now largely engaged in the liquor business in Front street, above Walnut. Both brothers have been successful in achieving wealth.

Hugh Craig is esteemed very rich, and able at any time to retire from the active pursuits of trade. He is in the prime of life and the full vigor of manhood. Activity, shrewdness, enterprise and liberality, have marked his whole career since boyhood. The success that has crowned his labors in his own private affairs, has recommended him to the good opinion of the financial circles. Mr. Craig has been a Director of the Delaware Mutual Insurance Company, and has also held the same position in the Corn Exchange Bank. In all these positions he has shown himself a capable, attentive and upright officer. He still cherishes a warm regard for the land of his birth and her representatives among us. He is a prominent member of the Hibernia Society, and serves faithfully as the chairman of its committee on charity. But no deserving sufferer in our midst, no matter what may be his nativity or creed, ever appeals to this large-hearted Irish merchant in vain. Generosity is one of his most conspicuous traits, and we have reason to believe that his success in life, and the universal esteem in which he is held, are as much due to his broad liberality as to his earnest devotion to business and skilful management. He seldom neglects an opportunity for aiding enterprises of public importance and unquestionable advantage, and is worthy to be entrusted with any responsible position demanding strict integrity and consummate financial ability. This is not eulogy; it is but a transcript of the general opinion that this community entertain of Mr. Hugh Craig.

Mr. Thomas Bellas, who retired in 1854, was eighteen years in business. He always enjoyed an enviable reputation for integrity, and carries with him in his retirement the esteem and respect of all his fellow merchants.

THOMAS RIDGWAY.

In writing the name of this successful merchant, we are reminded of the Society of Friends, of which he is a member, and the members of which have always enjoyed power and wealth in this city. At the first settlement of Philadelphia, "the people called Quakers" were at the head of the community, and they have retained a considerable proportion of their ancient prominence up to this time. They have given to this city many of its peculiar features, and the name of "Quaker City" is a testimonial of their influence, which is as widely known as the name of Philadelphia itself. The reputation of individuals like the Copes, Townsends, Davises and Prices, with many others whom we might name, has been completely identified with Philadelphia, and the extent of their business operations has justified the identification of their names with that of the "City of Brotherly Love."

Thomas Ridgway is a native of New Jersey, and was born near

Walnford, Monmouth County, on the fifth of May, 1797. His father, John Ridgway, an elder brother of the late distinguished merchant, Jacob Ridgway, was a highly respected farmer, who, after a long life of usefulness, died in 1845, at the advanced age of eighty-nine years, esteemed and beloved by a large circle of friends and acquaintances.

It may not be inappropriate to mention here that Jacob Ridgway was also a native of New Jersey. He was born in 1768, and came to Philadelphia at the age of sixteen. He had some capital left him by his father, which he rapidly increased by merchandising. He was most successful as a shipping merchant, and lived abroad many years, for the protection of his interests in that line. While in Europe he constantly remitted sums to be invested in real estate in Philadelphia, and on his return to this country, he devoted himself exclusively to the management of his real estate. Eventually the rise in this description of property made him enormously wealthy, and when he died, in 1843, he was justly accounted a millionaire.

When about thirteen years old, Thomas was placed by his father in a commission house on the wharf below Chestnut street, where he remained till 1816, when he entered into the flour and grain commission business with his brother Jacob, under the firm of J. & T. Ridgway. The senior partner retired in 1821, when Thomas took into partnership his cousin Benjamin Ridgway, and the business was continued under the firm of Thomas & Benjamin Ridgway. In 1823 Mr. Benjamin Ridgway retired, when a co-partnership was formed with Mr. John Livezey, under the firm of Ridgway & Livezey. In the year 1825 this firm was in full and successful operation, and many business men who have since become prominent were just making their way into active life. At this date, Henry Budd, Esq., was a clerk with Messrs. Latimer & Murdock, on the wharf near Arch street; James Steele, whose silvered locks and smiling countenance are now seen daily at the Corn Exchange, was a clerk in the same house; Alexander Derbyshire was a clerk in the flour house of Timothy Paxon; Henry Sloan was a lad in John R. Neff's office; Charles Camblos, the broker, was clerking for Amos W. Butcher, and subsequently for Scull & Thompson, and it would be interesting to follow their futures, if we had time at present. Mr. Livezey retired January 1, 1836, with an ample competency, which he has since largely increased by fortunate operations, and is now one of the rich men of our city.

On the first of January, 1836, Mr. Ridgway, with Mr. Budd, formed the firm of Ridgway & Budd, and the circle of their business was greatly enlarged. At that date Mr. Roland Kirkpatrick, quite a lad, was in their employ, and he remained with them until 1846, when he was taken into the firm. In 1850, just after the great fire of the ninth of July, the firm dissolved, and the style of the house was changed to Budd & Comly, Mr. Ridgway retiring. Mr. Kirkpatrick, we may here remark, is quite a character; he came to Mr. Ridgway's store in 1835, when a mere lad, and was employed at a salary of fifty dollars for the first year. He remains unmarried, and has been quite cautious in disposing of his accumulating means (and they now amount to a handsome sum) so much so, that we believe that some of his original salary still remains in his possession as originally invested. He is quiet, retiring, and unassuming; minding "his own business," and never intermedling with that of his neighbors or his competitors in business, which is more than can be said of many others in the breadstuff trade. He never mingles in convivial assemblies; he is never—

> "With weariness and wine oppressed."

He commenced without a dollar, and by his own untiring industry and economy has built himself to his present position. In 1816, the year Mr. Ridgway began his business career, there was frost in every month, which injured the wheat crop so seriously that flour advanced in 1817 to $14 and $14.75 per barrel, and wheat $3 per bushel. In 1821 flour declined to $3.75 per barrel and wheat to 75 cents per bushel.

The store now occupied by Messrs, A. Derbyshire & Co., No. 126 North Delaware avenue, is the oldest "flour house" in Philadelphia. In 1780 it was occupied by Mr. Samuel Smyth. In 1782 Timothy Paxon succeeded him, and continued there for *forty-five* years. He was succeeded by Mr. A. Derbyshire, who has now been in the same store *forty years*. In the days of Smith, Paxson, Lattimer, Hollingsworth and Potts, business in breadstuffs was conducted on far different principles than at the present period; then trade was slow and sure, now it is fast and uncertain. This remark will apply equally well to all other branches of business.

> "All sects, all ages smack of this vice."

How differently different people consider opulence and influence? How few have the moral courage to resist the temptation to spread themselves with pride and *hauteur* after having secured a competency? A man's riches do not consist in his having more gold, silver or "green backs," but in having more in proportion than his neighbor.

Mr. Ridgway's means were not large when he began business, but his prudence in the care of his "sinews of war," as well as his energy and enterprise, have enabled him to accumulate quite a large fortune. His character is quite a marked one, and his acquaintances can never misunderstand his peculiarities. When engaged in any transaction he unites every energy of his mind upon the single object before him, and holds fast to it until his object is thoroughly secured. He has no sympathy with anything that is not entirely practical and which does not present a surface for common sense operations in the legitimate line of business. In politics he is a decided Republican, having sympathized with that party through all the exciting events which have culminated in the present war for the integrity of the Union. In religion he inclines to the Hicksites branch of the Society of Friends. His residence is at No. 911 Arch street, where he has lived for the past fifteen years in a comfortable, though not ostentatious style. He talks well when he chooses, but except on business subjects he is usually taciturn; and, though taking an active interest in public matters, he is never seen at banquets or other gatherings of this character. In his business career he has always been too shrewd to be caught in any "wild cat" operation. His fortune was made in the commission business, and it has been built up slowly but surely.

The Hon. Benjamin W. Richards died in July, 1851; by his death, the office of President of the Girard Life Insurance, Annuity and Trust Company became vacant, and Mr. Ridgway was unanimously chosen by the Directors his successor, and still continues President of that substantial and prosperous institution. Its office is located at 408 Chestnut street. With one exception, this is the oldest Life Insurance Company in the State, having been chartered in 1836. From the day this Institution went into operation, it has always enjoyed, and justly so, the confidence of the public, but under the skillful and prudent management of its President, Mr. Ridgway, assisted by the accomplished Actuary, John F. James, Esq., and an able Board of Directors, it has assumed the very front rank among Life Insurance Companies, and is regarded as one of the strongest and most reliable Institutions that our city or country can boast of.

Mr. Ridgway has always been a warm advocate of our common school system, and we believe the only office he ever consented to accept from the public, was that of school director. In this capacity he served several years, and gave much of his time and attention to its duties He has also, for years, been a liberal contributor to our various public libraries, in several of which he has taken an active interest—serving as manager, treasurer, &c.; among others, in the Friends' Library, at Fifteenth and Race streets, and the Apprentices' Library Company, in the free or fighting Quakers' church, at Fifth and Arch streets. This library company, by the way, has about eighteen thousand well selected volumes, which are loaned out, without charge, to persons of both sexes, and deserves a more liberal support from the public than it has heretofore received. It is supported by individual donations and bequests.

Mr. Ridgway has also been, within a few years past, one of the visitors to the convicts of the Eastern Penitentiary.

During the alarming ravages of the yellow fever, in 1820, and of the cholera, in 1832, when many of our citizens fell victims to these dire diseases, and many fled in fear and dismay from the infected city, Mr. Ridgway, with a devotion to duty characteristic of the man, remained, faithfully attending not only daily to his business as a merchant, but exerting himself to calm the fears of the timid, and ministering, so far as he was able, to the relief of the suffering and the destitute. Through both of these fearful periods, owing, doubtless, to his abstemious and methodically correct habits, he escaped from all disease. To these same careful habits he is, no doubt, indebted for his almost entire exemption from sickness, for we think he has never been confined to his house by sickness more than a couple of weeks in his life.

In concluding our brief sketch of some of the prominent events in the life of Hr. Ridgway, we would direct the young, and especially the young merchants, to his career, as worthy of their study and imitation. When he began business his means were limited, and his difficulties great; but he determined to succeed, and he did so. By undaunted perseverance and untiring industry, by the closest application and attention to his business, and by the prompt fulfilment of every engagement, he soon became a prominent and rising merchant, and thus was the circle of his operations enlarged, so that in the prime of life he was enabled to retire from active pursuits, with ample means—a reasonable portion of which he has always conceived his duty to appropriate to religious, benevolent, and other institutions useful to society. No truly benevolent object ever appeals to him in vain. May his life of usefulness be prolonged, and may the evening of his days be passed " in *otium cum dignitate.*"

ALEXANDER ELMSLIE.

WITHIN the past few years we have lost from the mercantile community many of those who may be called the *old merchants* of Philadelphia. Those who began their career early in the century, maintaining honorably their own position, and forming the basis upon which the future generations of merchants do and will work. Among the most prominent of such men stands the name of Alexander Elmslie, who in his life held his position in the fast thinning circle of the father merchants.

The career of a successful merchant is not only interesting to the contemporaries with whom his life is pleasantly familiar, his memory green. But it has another and deeper interest for the young aspirant for mercantile honor and position. In the struggle for a start, the early encouragement or draw-back, the successful ventures or disastrous failures, the young merchant finds a guide-book by which to steer his own bark through the ever varying current of trade, may learn the whirlpools and safe deep waters, and how best to avoid the many temptations that lead to ruin. "Experience keeps a dear school," but those who have bought their tuition may offer the more lenient mistress—example, for the sons following in their footsteps.

Mr. Elmslie was born in Scotland, about the year 1768, and came to this country in 1780, when he was only twelve years of age. Eight years after this date he embarked in business on his own account. Soon after this the firm of Olden & Elmslie was formed, and located at No. 35 Chestnut street, where they were very extensively engaged in the importation and sale of foreign dry goods, and did a larger business than any other firm in that branch of trade. He was brought- up in Mr. Olden's store. Mr. Elmslie then resided at No. 311 South Second street, below Lombard, where he continued to reside until his decease, a few months

8

ago. In 1806 the firm was dissolved, and James Olden & Son went into business on their own account. The son, in 1811, became inflated with the idea that coffee would soon rise to a fabulous price. He built a large warehouse in the rear of No. 33 Chestnut street, and bought up an immense quantity of the article on speculation. It did not go up; his stock was sold out at a ruinous loss. He failed, and soon afterwards died quite poor, at No. 19 Crown street.

Among the prominent merchants, in 1800, were Joseph Sims, Robert Waln, Willing & Francis, Gurney & Smith, Eyre & Massey, John Wilcocks, Robert Ralston, Edward Thomson (the great tea speculator), Chandler Price, Maris, Evans & Welsh, Nicklin & Griffith, Joseph Clark, Montgomery & Newbolds, Henry Pratt, John Mease (father of Dr. James Mease, and paternal grandfather of Pierce Butler), Robert Smith, John Donaldson, and Elliston & John Perot, who did business at 43 North wharves, and at the date of their dissolution formed the oldest firm in the Unite States. Ellison Perot died in 1834, and John Perot in 1841. Mr. Olden came from New Jersey, and died in 1801, only a few years after his son became associated with him.

Mr. Elmslie was a Quaker, and attended the Pine street meeting until 1830, after which period he attended the "Orange street" meeting, on Washington square. He retired from active business pursuits in 1824, and during the past thirty years has occupied many positions of honor. He was a Manager of the Pennsylvania Hospital and of the Humane Society; a Director of the Philadelphia Insurance Company, and of the Philadelphia Charity School. For several years past the principal companions of Mr. Elmslie were Joseph Jones, of the Commercial Bank, Alexander Derbyshire, the retired flour merchant, and James Carstairs the father of Charles S. and James Carstairs, No. 126 Walnut street.

The fortune of Mr. Elmslie was made entirely by his regular business, by his knowledge of trade, and by his judgment in regard to the value of mercantile paper, and of the credit of those entitled to consideration at his hands. He was content with profits, however small, and was economical, saving, and extremely industrious. These great qualities, exercised during many years, have made, and will make every other man who possesses them, very wealthy. Mr. Elmslie was no believer in the rich velvet carpets, costly furniture, and brown stone residences of the west end. He dressed plainly, and wore his clothes carefully. He resided in the same building, occupied the same parlor, slept in the same chamber, and occupied the same seat at the same table for upwards of thirty years. So far as we can learn, he never threw away his money on beggars, nor squandered it on institutions of a doubtful character; and never permitted his name to be placarded in the public prints, in connection with acts of charity, yet he gave freely. But few merchants in this city have possessed so correct a judgment, and so rarely erred. He never ventured upon outside hazardous and reckless speculations. He left, at his decease, about $400,000, of which sum $25,000 was in gold in his house, and $25,000 in bank.

While upon the dry goods trade we will refer to John Robins, of New York, one of the richest merchants of that city, who commenced his career in Philadelphia. He was born in 1779, in Monmouth county, New Jersey. When a lad he wandered to Philadelphia. Congress met here at that time. They were considering the propriety of rejecting or confirming "Jay's" treaty. Meetings were held in different parts of the city, and young John Robins attended them to hear what was going on. On one occasion, Mr. Dallas, the father of the late minister to England, was speaking. He had a copy of the treaty in his hand, and after venting his indignation in the most fiery language, he flung it from him and exclaimed "kick the d—d thing to hell." The boys picked it up and made a bonfire of it, in front of the British minister's house.

Where John was born there was game. He caught a muskrat, skinned it, and took the skin to Philadelphia on his first visit. He bartered the skin off for two books—one was Robinson Crusoe, and the other a bible. He keeps the bible yet.

John was idling about Philadelphia, waiting for something to turn up, when the whiskey rebellion broke out. A proclamation was issued to raise troops. There had to be notices served upon the military privates raised. He did this business, and received seventy-five cents, the first money he ever earned.

Not long after this, John Robins went on to New York, then quite a town, but not so large as Philadelphia. He had an elder brother, named Enoch, who kept in Old Slip.

Enoch Robins owned several vessels, and was quite a shipping merchant of those days. He loaded his vessels with all sorts of assorted provision cargoes, pork, beef, onions, etc., and sent them to the West India islands. He owned no vessels larger than 150 tons. In fact, the largest ship owned in New York, in 1796, did not exceed 250 tons burden.   One of 200 tons was an uncommonly large ship.

Enoch owned one brig called the Mary, of 150 tons burden. He loaded her with staves for wine casks, dried codfish, and other truck, to make up the assorted cargo, and despatched the "Mary" from New York to Bilboa, in the Bay of Biscay.   He sent his brother John out as supercargo.   At that time the United States was at war with France, and the brig "Mary" had a narrow escape from a French privateer.   She lay at Bilboa three months, selling cargo.   Then the "Mary" went to Lisbon, disposed of her staves, and took on board a quantity of gold and silver for New York. The exportation of silver was prohibited by Portugal, but Mr. Robins had a belt made, and every trip he made on board his vessel he would take a thousand Spanish dollars.   In this way he got on board $16,000.

At that time the British fleet was anchored at Lisbon, and among the vessels was the sixty-four gun ship, "Asia," that had given the city of New York so much trouble in the dark days of the Revolution.

Finally the brig "Mary" went to St. Ubes, loaded with salt, and got back safe to New York, making a splendid voyage.   The salt sold for a dollar a bushel.   The supercargo had saved several hundred dollars, which he put away in a safe place.   On his return, in 1797, he made another voyage to the West Indies as supercargo. When John Robins got back he did not go to sea any more.

He made up his mind to go into the dry goods business.   He fancied he should like it, but, of course, it would be necessary to learn the business before attempting it on his own account.

Now I come to the reason why John Robins came to start a dry goods store in that particular part of Pearl street, near to Chatham, No. 446.   John was passing along Pearl from Chatham looking at the various stores, and the tasty manner in which the dry goods were temptingly displayed in front and in the windows.   Young John Robins stepped in at one of these dry goods stores and asked if they wished to get a young clerk.   He had no success.

Finally, he halted at the door of 430 Pearl, where was kept a large stock of dry goods.   It was a wholesale as well as retail store.   Robins asked the owner the usual question:

"Do you want a clerk?"

"What to do?"

"I want to learn the dry goods business."

"What wages do you expect?"

"None. I want to learn the dry goods business."

The proprietor of the store looked at him. He was earnest and honest. He liked his appearance.

"Very well, you may come; I'll try you."

That merchant was the celebrated Henry Laverty, who in after years became a renowned merchant and very rich. After the year or eighteen months for which he was engaged was up, he told Mr. Laverty he should leave him. Mr. Laverty was not ready to part with him.

"Oh, yes, John, you'll stay. I'll give you a good round salary."

"No, I know how to handle goods. I have acquired a good deal of knowledge, and I will try and do something for myself," said John.

Mr. Laverty offered a still more tempting salary. John still said "No." Then he was offered a partnership. John still said "No." His mind was made up. He was astonished at the partnership offer, but he firmly declined it. Mr. Laverty parted with him regretfully. He had found out his sterling integrity, and his industry and care made him invaluable to anybody who was doing so large a business as Mr. Laverty.

After leaving the employ of H. Laverty, John Robins started a dry goods business on his own account, and finally retired with a competency.

SAMUEL BRECK.

ONE of our most honored and beloved members of the mercantile world, a man whose strict integrity, active benevolence and warm sympathies endeared him to all companions, was called to his last home, August 31, 1862, at the advanced age of ninety-one years. This long term of usefulness contains many points both of interest and instruction, being that rare and beautiful object, a well spent, useful youth, manhood, and old age.

Samuel Breck was born in the city of Boston, on the seventeenth of July, 1771, and it is a memorable fact that his infancy and childhood, his old age and death, have both occurred during the periods

of the great national struggles of the country of his nativity—
the country he loved with a devoted ferver. It is a well authenti-
cated fact that, as a child, held aloof in his nurse's arms, he saw
the great dawning of American Independence, the battle of Bunker
Hill.   Lexington, too, the scene of the first revolt from British
tyranny, was the town where his first years were passed, until in
his fourth year, he, with the wondering unconsciousness of childhood, witnessed the great battle of Bunker Hill. The natural pride
felt in his more mature years at this event of his childhood, seems
to have been the firm foundation upon which was built as strong
and fair a structure of patriotism, loyalty and devotion to country, as ever dwelt in the breast of man. It was the key of his
heart, the ruling passion of his life, this pride and love of country.

From a very early age Mr. Breck took a delight in occupying
his leisure time by keeping a minute and copious diary, which at
his death filled about twelve closely written volumes. Having
much leisure time, and passing a great portion of it alone, this occupation grew into a delightful habit, and these pages are filled
with the recollections of the men and events of his long life. They
contain, in a familiar and agreeable style, much that is instructive
and pleasant about the master minds of the age, with the opinions
of a keen, well educated intellect on the events passing around him.
It is a proof of the kindliness of the old gentleman's heart that he
left with the manuscripts a strict injunction to the legatee to ex-
pugn from his diaries any lines that can possibly be painful or
offensive to others.   In the many contributions which his pen has
given to the literature of the societies to which he belonged, he
referred to and quoted from his diaries, feeling certain of the
correctness of information written as the event or opinion recorded
was passing under his own eye, or within his own knowledge.
Such information must be as reliable as it is interesting and freely
offered.   Without waiting for invitation, his unusual fund of useful
knowledge was contributed readily and frankly wherever he saw
an opportunity for making it useful or available. As a man of
strong literary tastes, and a good amateur artist, his pursuits were
naturally such as led to the accumulation of information, and his
search was chiefly directed towards historical anecdotes and events
which his pen clothed with all the charm of a retentive memory
and keen perceptions.

In the year 1782 an opportunity occurred for sending Mr. Breck,
then a lad in his twelfth year, to complete his education in France.

Several military and naval officers, friends of his father, were returning to France, and it was determined to send the lad, under their protection, to a college in that country. On the twenty-fourth of December he sailed from Boston in the frigate Iris, sharing the cabin of the commander, Marquis de Traverse. The College of Soreze, in Lower Languedoc, was recommended to his parents by the French admiral, and one of the officers in Rochambeau's army, residing at Toulouse, within twenty-four miles of the college, undertook to see him safely placed in the charge of the principal. Provided with letters from the admiral to the principal, the Very Reverend Dom Despaulx, and others, he entered thus, in very early life, upon a career removed from all home influence, parent's care, or any but new friends around him.

During his residence in college, his opportunities for instruction were excellent. The teachers who had the care of the pupils were attentive and efficient. Languages, both ancient and modern, scientific studies, music, drawing, fencing, dancing, and drilling were all within reach, and all actively studied. Joseph R. Ingersoll, in his "Memoirs of Samuel Breck," says:

"It is a proof that he became thus endowed at this seminary, that his education in reality began and ended there. It was pursued no further, either abroad or at home. A mind sufficiently intelligent, industry and application sufficiently faithful, and a disposition sufficiently ambitious, were all kept in order and employment by a moral principle and rectitude that appear to have been his guardians at all times. Habits of occupation were formed which were always afterwards ready for exercise. All exercise, or rather indulgence of them, was a pleasure and a pride. While they brought him knowledge, they made it easy for him to impart its fruits on suitable occasions in after life."

During his residence in France, Mr. Breck became so strongly interested in the tenets of the Roman Catholic Church, that he requested the principal of the college to appoint for him a confessor. Having been educated at home in the most rigid and intolerant form of Presbyterian worship, it is not strange that his young heart was captivated by the beautiful outward forms of the religion of the country in which he now found himself; he frankly acknowledges that no attempt was made by the monks in the college to influence his religious views; but an intimate friend, to whom he confided his desires, advised him to confess, as the first step in the new belief. The principal showed no eagerness upon the subject, advising the young convert to reflect a week before taking so important a step. At the end of that time, his wish never changing, a confessor was appointed, to whom he went at stated times during his residence at the college. On Easter Sunday, being in Lyons, he attended mass, confessed and communicated.

Upon his return home his religious views, now that his mind was more matured, again changed, and he joined the Episcopal Church, of which he was a member until his death. His moral principles were always remarkable for their soundness, and his life was free from any taint of intemperance or dissipation.

After an absence of four years and a-half, he left Havre for his return to America, in one of the monthly packets. Paul Jones, the celebrated sea captain, at that time an admiral in the Russian service, is mentioned in his diary as one of his fellow passengers. On the second of July, 1787, he landed at Boston, to leave a student's life for one of greater activity. His appearance at that time is described as very prepossessing. Mr. Ingersoll says:

"Before his departure from that country (France) he visited its great capital. A kind temper given to him by nature, was here adapted to gentleness and grace of manner, and personal accomplishments must have been almost unconsciously cultivated among those to whom they were then still familiar, under a yet undisturbed government. This was combined with the fact that he found Boston, on his return in 1787, crowded with well educated Frenchmen, driven there by disturbances in St. Domingo. It made him still more closely acquainted with the habits, and accustomed to the politeness of a people the most polished and refined. The great revolution in France was yet some years ahead. His knowledge was increased by the elegant literature of France, and he is not supposed to have been contaminated by the surrounding tendency to religious scepticism. His deportment naturally assumed a finished air, which did not leave him during his long life. No one could have known him, however slightly, without being struck with these peculiarities, which were marks of cultivated kindness, without undue affectation. He was a thorough gentleman of the old school—courteous, animated, affable and kind."

Shortly after his return home, having expressed his desire to enter upon the life of a merchant, his father, at a cost of one hundred guineas, obtained for him a position in a counting-house, where he remained until 1790. In his journal he speaks with indignation of the principles of trade as taught him in these three years; they were, he says, "of the most immoral character, owing chiefly to the disturbed and feeble state of the old Confederate Government, and in execution of the revenue laws of the Commonwealth of Massachusetts. On the arrival of a vessel one-half the cargo was placed in the upper part of the store, and the other half only entered at the Custom House, and thus they were initiated into the secret of smuggling." "To ask," he says, "one hundred guineas of young gentlemen, educated in honorable principles, to teach them low fraud and disreputable course of trade, showed the times to be sadly out of joint." The laws were a dead letter; the states, collectively and individually, were bankrupt; the public debts at ten or twelve dollars on a hundred. Each state was pulling against the other, and the fruits of our seven year's war for independence, did not then appear to be worth gathering."

He felt and wrote, expressing his strong patriotic interest in the machinery of government that changed this melancholy prospect to such unrivalled brightness. In speaking of the "Constitution adopted in 1798," he says, it "carried this great nation, in the course of forty years, from a fearful state of poverty and disorder, to high station and unrivalled prosperity."

In 1790 Mr. Breck again visited Europe, remaining one year abroad. Upon his return, having received from his father a capital of ten thousand dollars, he entered upon a mercantile career, but did not establish himself permanently until 1792, when the family removed to Philadelphia. He himself states the cause of the removal from Boston to have been a most iniquitous and unjust system of taxation which drove many of the richest inhabitants from the city. After rating an inhabitant for watch where there were no watchmen; for lighting streets where there were no lamps; for municipal regulations in general where there was almost an entire absence of police, they put down under the head of "faculty," just what they pleased—*guessing* this man to be worth so much, and that other so much—thus laying a heavy tax upon him who lived liberally, and spent his income among his fellow-townsmen in acts of hospitality to them and to strangers, while the rich miser who kept his money out of circulation was deemed poor, and scarcely taxed at all. This long corrected injustice was not to be patiently borne when in full operation, and Mr. Breck was only one of many who left the city solely on that account.

In September, 1792, the family removed to this city, and three months later Mr. Breck followed them. His first year was one long to be remembered in our city records, when the yellow fever thinned the population fearfully.   The fall, however, removed the disease; and although in the heart of the worst region (near Walnut street wharf), Mr. Breck escaped the contagion.

The family residence was situated in what was then the centre of fashion, the "court end" of the city.   It was 319 Market street, above Eighth, where now not a private dwelling is to be found.

During the progress of the whiskey insurrection, in the interior. of the state, Mr. Breck joined the Macpherson Blues, which embodied most of the ardent young men of the city.   There is, however, no mention of his ever having served his country in a military capacity.

In 1823 he was elected to Congress, and was the only one of the Pennsylvania delegation who voted for John Quincy Adams, when the votes of the people failing to elect the President, and he was chosen by Congress.   He was in this body for two years.

In 1825 he was elected a member of the Historical Society of Pennsylvania, in which he continued to occupy a prominent position until his death, being at that time vice-president of the society. His interest in this association was warm and untiring, and at one period his zeal was all that saved it from dissolution.   The lukewarm indifference of many of the members was so clogging the operations of the body, that it was proposed to abandon the attempt to maintain it.   Mr. Breck, in a letter to Mr. John Vaughan, in which was enclosed a list of the members, says:—"You will see that the deaths are twenty-two, the resignations are fifty-five, and the number remaining as members is fifty-three.   Perhaps several of those who have resigned may be induced to rejoin.   At any rate, even with our present number, there is no occasion to dissolve, or think of any such thing.   Should you be of this opinion, please to return me the list after conferring with Mr. Leaming. I will draw up a report upon the subject.   March 15, 1838."   Upon his death Mr. Breck bequeathed a portion of his library to the Historical Society.

This was only one of the many societies to which Mr. Beck gave his time, means and influence.   He was a Trustee of the Pennsylvania University; one of the Directors of the Philadelphia, Wilmington and Baltimore Railroad; one of the Common Council; President of the Institute for the Blind, and one of its founders. Mr. Ingersoll mentions an interesting incident connected with Mr. Breck's interest in the Institute for the Blind.   He says:

" Soon after the attack on Fort Sumter he was at a concert of the pupils of this institution, and occupied a seat on the platform. He here availed himself of an opportunity, as he had done on a former occasion, to manifest his deep interest in the events that have been crowded into the months elapsed since the opening of the Southern rebellion. At the close of the concert a call was made for the Star Spangled Banner, and it was sung with great spirit. At the last chorus, Mr. Breck sprang up in view of the audience, (about seven hundred persons,) and waving his hat over his head, called for three cheers for the Union and the Constitution, *one and indivisible*, adding, ' I was a man when they were formed, and God forbid that I should live to witness their downfall.' The cheers were given with *three times three*, to the great wonderment of the blind pupils, who knew not what it all meant. This relation is given by a gentleman who was present."

Mr. Breck's residence was at Sweet Briar—a lovely villa on the West bank of the Schuylkill, not far from the city. He resided here for thirty-eight years, having a strong love for farming, botanical pursuits, horticulture, and indeed all country pleasures.

On the twenty-fourth of December, 1795, Mr. Breck married the daughter of Mr. John Ross, one of Philadelphia's prominent merchants. She died in 1859, at the advanced age of eighty-six years.

Mr. Breck's fondness for research and literary pursuits was proved by the number of articles that he has contributed to the many societies of which he was a member. While a member of the Pennsylvania Senate he published a work on the prosperity and prospects of the State, which passed through two editions. Among other productions may be mentioned " The recollections of Samuel Breck, Sweet Briar, in the township of Philadelphia, state of Pennsylvania, removed to the city of Philadelphia, in December, 1835, having resided at Sweet Briar about thirty-eight years;" a " Discourse before the Society of the Sons of New England of the city and county of Philadelphia, on the history of the early settlement of their country;" a "Sketch of the benevolent services of the late Jacob G. Morris; a "Biography of Robert M. Patterson;" "An address to the pupils of the institution for the blind;" a speech on the "Abolition of slavery in Pennsylvania," delivered in the Senate; a "Historical sketch of continental paper money, presented by him to the American Philosophical Society;" an "Address made when President of the Athenæum, at the laying of the corner-stone of the new hall, in 1845," with many other reports, speeches and addresses.

One of the most prominent points in Mr. Breck's character was his love of occupation. He was never idle. Study, literature, microscopic investigations and scientific research were varied by active out-door pursuits.

In July, 1828, he lost his only surviving child, who died in his arms, at the age of twenty-one. He writes of this sad event to his sister in these terms : " Thus is my greatest hold on this earth dissolved, and she whose future comfort and happiness was my great study, and a source of anxious thought, is snatched from me. No worldly transactions of mine took place that had not 'reference to that dear child's future life. I am now without solicitude, it is true; but I am also without her society, her companionship, and I may add without her counsel, which was generally the dictate of good sense and mature judgment." Again he writes: " One subject is forever uppermost in my thoughts. It seems often as if I took a melancholy pleasure in nourishing my grief. In spite of myself I have her before my mind's eye in my .solitary walks * * * until the last sad week of her existence rushes on my mind, and makes, by its most painful recollection, my heart move within me. An effort to shut the whole scene out follows, and succeeds for a time, when the dear image recurs again, and so twenty times a day. But I trust time will weaken, without wholly obliterating, these sad recollections."

On the twenty-second of August, 1862, an illness which had troubled him for some months, resulted in an attack of paralysis, and on the thirty-first, at noon, he breathed his last, at the advanced age of ninety-one years, one month and fourteen days.

Mr. Ingersoll says: "He was correct in deportment and honorable in conduct; of amiable temper and lively and affectionate feelings; quick in perception, and of tenacious memory and sound judgment; industrious when he had anything particular to do, and looking out for it when he had not; of strict punctuality; a good Christian and husband, father, neighbor and friend, and a patriotic citizen; domestic in habit and temperate in living—yet well inclined to social intercourse."

Again he says: "A pious spirit, however, seems to have chiefly aided him in his departing hours. He had habitually manifested a more than common respect, which was real and devout, for religion and its institutions and practices. For many years he had been a communicant at St. Luke's Episcopal Church; he was an active member of the vestry, and at all times present at the meetings; and he persevered in his attendance on public worship. He was visited, at his own request, after his fatal attack, by a distinguished clergyman, and expressed to him with great clearness his trust in his Saviour, and his readiness to depart. He desired prayers to be offered, wishing the attendance of all the family, and specifying the prayer for the sick on the point of departure. His utterance was imperfect, but all was calm and clear. It is attested by one who knew him best in this respect, that his piety did not render him morose or severe in manner, but just chastened the natural gayety of his disposition into a beautiful and most attractive cheerfulness. He was lively and buoyant, and retained an interest in passing events, it may be literally said to the day of his death. After he was stricken with paralysis, and one hand was entirely disabled, his patriotism was still manifested. On learning from a friend some cheering news respecting his beloved country, he raised his eyes and his hand in an attitude of prayer and thanksgiving, and moved his yet remaining vigorous hand above his head, and waved it three times around—a silent but cheering expression of his joy. The medical gentleman who attended him also informs us that the ardor of his patriotism was extinguished only by death.

THOMAS LEAMING.

In the course of these sketches we have, in a certain degree, illustrated the variability of the American temperament. The adaptability of our countrymen to the circumstances which surround them; the ease with which they accommodate themselves to social and business changes; the handiness with which they lay aside old habits and engage in pursuits entirely new to them, are peculiarities which have frequently engaged the attention of intelgent foreigners, who endeavored to make themselves acquainted with the characteristics of the American mind.

In the career of Thomas Leaming it will be shown that a classic education, a course of legal studies and practice at the bar are not impediments to the making of a good merchant; and, that a mercantile experience and success are no barrier to a resumption of the profession of an advocate and counsellor.

Thomas Leaming was born in the city of Philadelphia on the twentieth of August, 1748. His parents were in comfortable circumstances, descendants of a wealthy and respectable English family, some of the members of which came to this country about the year 1688. They had prospered in the colony of Pennsylvania, and they had the means and the will to procure for their son an education equal to the best that the literary and scholastic resources of North America could furnish. They obtained for him in childhood solid and judicious instruction at Philadelphia, and when he had attained sufficient age they placed him in the college at Philadelphia, at that time one of the most noted institutions of learning on this side of the Atlantic. Having graduated with credit, his fancy, or the wishes of his parents, led him to the profession of the law. He was entered as a student by the celebrated lawyer John Dickinson, whose professional reputation has, in the regards of posterity, been eclipsed by his patriotic essays in "the times that tried men's souls," known as the "Farmer's Letters."

About the year 1769 Mr. Leaming was admitted to the bar, and he commenced the practice of the law amid a talented but small circle of professional brethren, many of whom were soon to make their names celebrated in the history of their country. When the troubles with Great Britain, which had been growing more serious during his minority and early manhood, became so threatening that it did not seem possible to avert hostilities, Mr. Leaming was found arrayed upon the side of his country. He joined one of the "association" companies which were formed in Philadelphia for the purpose of preparing for the conflict. He devoted himself to the acquisition of the infantry drill, and made it his business to study military tactics. Having thus accomplished himself in this practical school, he determined to make his knowledge valuable in organizing military bodies elsewhere. He was in good circumstances, and owned, in the right of descent, a handsome landed property in the colony of New Jersey, upon which it was his custom to reside during the warm season of the year. As a natural consequence, he made many friends in that colony and was considered as a citizen. Repairing to his estates, he exercised his influence among his neighbors for the purpose of raising military companies. He was exceedingly successful, and not only in raising companies but in forming a battalion, which he instructed in military exercises. Whilst engaged in these patriotic duties his energy and enthusiasm naturally attracted the attention of the people of the county, and he was chosen to represent them in the convention which assembled June 10, 1776. Its labors were completed by the second day of the ensuing month, and among the resolutions passed by it, with the support of Mr. Leaming, was one calling upon Congress to declare the Colonies free and independent States—a request which was complied with two days afterward.

Relinquishing further residence in New Jersey at that time, he returned to Philadelphia to find that his own profession had ceased to exist. "*Inter arma leges silent.*" The sentiment of the Latin poet was fully exemplified throughout North America during the American Revolution.

In this condition of affairs his active spirit induced him to engage in mercantile adventure. The field of commerce was not large, but it was prosecuted by some adventurous spirits. With Andrew Bunner, who before the Revolution had been a merchant in successful business, Mr. Leaming associated himself, furnishing a most important assistance in capital. Andrew Bunner & Co. prosecuted their business under constant risk of loss from captures of their vessels by British ships of war. Their transactions were of the utmost importance to the American cause. They imported ammunition largely, and frequently in the hour of necessity the Continental troops were indebted to them for the means of meeting the enemy. They also put their capital into vessels intended to retaliate upon the British. They built several privateers, which made havoc in the commerce of the "mistress of the seas." One of these privateers, the schooner Mars, Captain Yelverton Taylor, took, in three vessels, five hundred English and Hessian soldiers. During the war the privateers of Bunner & Co. took one thousand prisoners, for whom American prisoners, languishing in the "Old Sugar House" and the "Jersey Prison Ship," at New York, were exchanged. Fifty prizes were also captured by the privateers of this firm. The house was patriotic, and ready at all times to aid the government. The firm of Bunner & Co. subscribed to the amount of £6,000 to the fund of £260,000, raised among a few citizens of Philadelphia, in 1780, for the support of government in an hour of great need.

Mr. Leaming joined the "First Troop of Philadelphia City Cavalry," in 1775, and was a spirited and active member of that honorable organization until his death. He was one of the twenty-six members of that company who served at Trenton and Princeton in 1776-7, during which time their services were so valuable that they received the special thanks of Gen. Washington upon their discharge. During the Revolution they performed other duties, when called upon by the executive of Pennsylvania or by high general officers in the Continental service, and their record of the congratulations extended to them for these actions remain a proud legacy to the members of this volunteer association.

The house of Andrew Bunner & Co. was dissolved shortly after the close of the Revolution, and Mr. Bunner was appointed vendue master. Mr. Leaming resided at No. 152 South Front street, next door to the store of the firm.

His withdrawal from mercantile affairs naturally took him back to the law. In 1791 his office as counsellor at law was at his old residence, but he did not long remain there. He removed to the corner of Vine street and Cable lane, (New Market street,) where, during the yellow fever of 1797, he fell a victim to that dread disease.

Mr. Leaming's sons—Thomas Fisher Leaming and Jeremiah Fisher Leaming—devoted themselves permanently to those mercantile pursuits which their father temporarily followed. They were in partnership for many years. Descendants of Thomas Leaming still keep up the family connection with business affairs. J. Fisher Leaming and Robert W. Leaming, at No. 30 South Front street, maintain a name which, among merchants of the Revolution in the same locality, was known and universally respected.

JAMES McHENRY.

THE name of the subject of this sketch is as familiar on both sides of the Atlantic as that of any man who for generations has created reputation and fortune by the pursuit of an exclusively mercantile career. Perhaps there are a few instances, like that of Roscoe, the banker and historian, of Liverpool, (whose eulogy was so gracefully pronounced by Washington Irving, in his "Sketch Book,") who have acquired an equal reputation in both

mercantile and literary life. Charles Sprague, too, the president of a Boston bank, and an eminent poet, may also be cited as
an example of wide fame resulting from the blended exertions of
the study and the banking-house; but still we reaffirm that the
reputation of James McHenry is unsurpassed by any case of strict
devotion to business life.

The elements of Mr. McHenry's greatness are finely mingled, yet
we can point them out for imitation so clearly as to prove that his
large fortune and the honor in which his name is held, are the natural outgrowth of the noble qualities of the man. He is a native
of Ireland, and in his early life his mother was the proprietor of a
retail dry goods store, No. 36 South Second street, and he was employed as a clerk on Market street. He grew up amid the busy
scenes of these wonderful streets, and we can fancy that the ceaseless activity which was ever before his eyes exerted a large influence over his subsequent career. Second street, as most of our
readers are aware, stretches for seven or eight miles through the
most populous part of Philadelphia, and is almost exclusively devoted to retail trade. Market houses dot its extent in very many
places, while venders from wagons by thousands cluster around
them. Dry goods stores, drug stores, groceries, hardware establishments, fancy goods shops, iron mongers, factories, furniture
warehouses, foreign fruit stands, book stores and stalls, stationery
establishments, clothing dealers, glass and china warerooms, hotels,
restaurants, intelligence offices, and every class of place where the
wants of an immense city are supplied, range themselves side by
side along mile after mile of pavement. Crowds upon crowds of
buyers, sellers, and gazers at the busy scene who throng the side-
walk from daybreak until long after dark, also present a thousand
characteristics as worthy of the pen of the novelist as any scene
on the Strand or in the London Cheapside. It was amid the busy
scenes of such a thoroughfare that James McHenry, as a youth,
mingled, and we doubt not that even now he turns from the scenes
passing before his eyes in London, and recalls the active life of his
youth in Second street.

In London he has so ably managed his affairs that he has secured
an ample fortune, which he controls and uses most nobly and generously. To Americans, and particularly Philadelphians visiting
England, his hospitality is unbounded, and to make his acquaintance there, is, to a native of the Quaker City, like "brother meeting
brother in a foreign land." To Mr. McHenry the recollection of

10

Philadelphia is a pleasant memory, and he keeps it alive by generous deeds. Nor are the claims of kindred less powerful with Mr. McHenry. He has with loving affection gathered comforts and luxuries around his mother who resides in this city. Nor are the claims of patriotism less strong with him. When this accursed rebellion broke out, his sympathies were at once aroused for the stars and stripes, and he affirmed his detestation of treason. He contributed five hundred dollars to the equipment of the Corn Exchange Regiment, and as a testimonial of his love for the City of Independence, he sent the Whitworth gun battery as a gift to our municipality. A warm rich character like this contains the seeds of all successful and noble designs within it, and we cannot wonder that the name of James McHenry is honored wherever patriotism and all manly qualities are revered.

James McHenry was born in Larne, Ireland, May 3, 1817, and came with his father to Baltimore in 1818. At this place he remained a short period, when his father removed to Pottsville, in this state, and afterwards to Butler county, where he remained from 1819 to 1824. About this time his parents removed to Pittsburg, and early in the year 1826 came to Philadelphia. During a greater portion of the ensuing twelve years, from 1826 to 1838, Mr. McHenry resided in Philadelphia, where he received his education. From 1835 to 1838 he was employed by Messrs. Trevor, Spering & Mixell, an extensive dry goods jobbing house, on Market street above Fourth. In 1838, at the suggestion of his brother Alexander, he went to England, where he remained about a year, at the expiration of which time he became the junior member of the firm of A. R. & J. McHenry, who were engaged in the commission business up to the close of 1846, when the copartnership was dissolved, and Mr. McHenry was taken into the firm of Messrs. Allen & Anderson, one of the largest provision, grain and flour commission houses in Liverpool. This association was a most unfortunate one, for at the expiration of eight years the firm failed, and was unable to pay but a very small per centage of its indebtedness. In 1855, Mr. McHenry associated with a Mr. Crow, of Liverpool, and commenced business again under the firm of James McHenry & Co. This association was a most successful one, resulting to the pecuniary advantage of both members of the firm. In the ensuing year, Mr. Ward, of Ohio, and Mr. Doolittle, of Germantown, went to Liverpool, and succeeded in engaging this firm to negotiate the bonds of the Great Western and Atlantic Railroad Company, amounting to the sum of £3,000,000. This arrangement was consummated through Salamanca, the great banker of Madrid. Independent of this, Messrs. McHenry & Co., were largely engaged in the provision and breadstuffs commission business, in which they were very successful in accumulating for both members of the firm a handsome competency.

Dr. James McHenry, the father of James McHenry, died in this city, in the year 1845. He resided for many years at No. 36 South Second street, where Mrs. McHenry superintended the management of a dry goods establishment. Dr. McHenry was a gentleman of great literary abilities, having written a number of works, among them, "The Wilderness," "O'Halaran," "Mysteries of Mischanza," "Pleasures of Friendship," and others. He was also the author of the Irish tragedy known as the "Usurper," which had quite a successful "run" at Weym's & Warren's old Chestnut street Theatre, in this city.

Mrs. James McHenry, wife of Dr. McHenry, is still alive, and lives in elegant style at No. 1902 Chestnut street. The McHenry family consists of four children:—Alexander McHenry, now engaged largely in the petroleum trade in Philadelphia; James McHenry of London; George McHenry, formerly of this city, but now in London (sympathizing with his Southern friends), and Miss Mary McHenry, a most estimable and patriotic lady, who still resides with her mother.

Last year Mr. McHenry paid every dollar—principal and interest—of the indebtedness of the suspended firm.

COLONEL WILLIAM B. THOMAS.

THE subject of our sketch was born in Upper Merion township, Montgomery county, Pa., on the twenty-fifth of May, 1811. He is now, therefore, about fifty-two years of age. In early youth his attention was attracted toward the manufacture of flour. The neighborhood of his home boasted many fine mills; at this early day the use of steam was resisted, on the plea that it drove the stones too rapidly and heated the flour too much; but this, like the old fogy prejudices against gas, railroads and telegraphs, has.

been dissipated by increased intelligence. Flour manufactured in our city by steam mills is now generally preferred in this and other markets. Within the past thirteen years an extraordinary impetus has been given to the business.

Immense quantities of grain are now brought to our city which formerly sought other outlets. Our increased and constantly increasing railroad connections are enabling the miller to bring the products of the teeming granaries of the great and fertile West to his door, without breaking bulk; and the wonderful and rapidly developing resources of our great throbbing artery, the Pennsylvania Railroad, promise bright hopes for the future to our goodly town.

The energies of young Thomas were early devoted to the flour business, and in 1832, upon attaining his majority, he commenced the business, at the "Gulf Mills," where, with the interval of a year, during which he made an experiment in storekeeping at Lyonsville, Pa., he continued till 1843. Mr. Thomas now wished for a larger field for his activity and enterprise, and accordingly he came to Philadelphia, determined to begin business in a small way. Very soon, through the efforts of clear sighted men, like Mr. Thomas, the use of steam power in the manufacture of flour became not only tolerated, but recognized by all as a necessity, and was found perfectly practical in its workings. He commenced in a diminutive mill, at Thirteenth and Willow streets, starting with but twenty horse power; but such energy, industry and sagacious management as that of Mr. Thomas could not fail of its reward, and he soon ranked as one of the most successful manufacturers of this community. The power of his mill was raised from twenty to eighty horse. Still the demand increased so rapidly that Mr. Thomas found it imperative to increase his facilities for manufacture; and to effect this, secured another mill at Thirteenth and Buttonwood streets. Time rolled on, and again such was the popularity of Wm. B. Thomas' flour, that another enlargement was called for, and he has within the past year increased his capacity for manufacturing by the introduction of an additional engine, of three hundred horse power, which propels sixteen pairs of mill stones, making, in his entire establishment, three engines, with an aggregate power of four hundred horse and twenty-four pairs of mill burrs, which are capable of manufacturing twelve hundred barrels of flour per day; requiring to feed them five thousand bushels of wheat daily, or a grand total of three hundred and sixty thousand barrels of flour, requiring one million five hundred thousand bushels of grain annually. The manufactory of Mr. Thomas, it is believed, will produce more flour, and consume more wheat per annum, than any other milling establishment in the world. Where the demand, and the consequent increase to meet it, will cease, it is futile to attempt to predict, as there is no appreciable limit to energy, coupled with clear, sound judgment.

From very small beginnings, Mr. Thomas has steadily battled his way to wealth and distinction as a manufacturer of fine flour, second to none in this or any other market.

Mr. Thomas has not limited his activity to the private pursuits of trade; "no pent up Utica confines his powers." Possessing liberal views on all subjects, and great public spirit, he was not content to hide his light under a bushel, but has sought to make himself useful to his country and his fellow citizens. He was one of the founders of the Corn Exchange Association—an organization full of vigor and patriotism, and keenly on the alert to everything that promises to advance the interests of commerce and promote the welfare of the nation. Appreciating the advantages to be derived from a fraternal union among those engaged in a kindred pursuit, and desiring to stimulate that feeling and that local pride so essential to the development of a true metropolitan spirit of enterprise, he strove to establish this association on a firm basis; how he succeeded, let the record of the Corn Exchange Association, in peace and war, answer. He was chosen first President, and at the expiration of his term was reëlected unanimously, and was only allowed to leave that highly honorable position by his peremptory declination of any further service as President. He has, however, continued one of its leading men ever since. Mr. Thomas is also a prominent member of the Board of Trade. He is always prompt to assist in and contribute to any measure which his clear judgment sanctions as being of real advantage to Philadelphia. He is one of the few among us who have the practical talent to enforce their views of public policy. No man in the Board of Trade is more prompt with wise suggestions, or more earnest and impressive in pleading for what he believes right and beneficial. We need more men of this stamp, as examples and shining lights to point the way to true mercantile success for young and unwary feet. When we add that he is a director of the Manufacturers' Insurance Company, and that his reputation is very high among business men as a high-toned, honest, liberal merchant and manufacturer, we have said all that is necessary of Mr. Thomas in connection with trade. But this gentleman is widely known in other relations of life.

Mr. Thomas was originally a member of the "GREAT" Democratic party; but when still a young man he formed decided opinions on the subject of slavery, believing it to be the sum of all villainies, and also denying the right of any man to hold his brother man in bondage; and becoming convinced that the Democratic party had swung from its old mooring, and drifted under the dangerous rule of the fire-eating oligarchy of the South, he cut loose from that organization and united himself with the then hated and despised Republicans, and became a warm and sturdy champion of free labor, free soil, free speech and free men, when to espouse that cause—now so dear to the hearts of the American people—was to be shunned and branded as a fanatic and disorganizer.

Mr. Thomas, in common with other kindred spirits, struggled on, bearing the heat and burthen of the strife, striking heavy blows against error from a few brave and valiant arms, knowing that truth is mighty and must prevail. The nomination of Van Buren and Adams was the first great evidence of a radical change in the North. Defeated in that strife, but never conquered, we again find Mr. Thomas true as steel to his convictions of truth and the right, supporting and voting for John P. Hale in the memorable year 1852.

During the administration of Franklin Pierce the firm foundations of the great Republican party of to-day were laid. Mr. Thomas was one of those who led that great crusade against the damning sin of the nineteenth century, in this section; and contributed not a little, by his wealth and position in this community, to give the young giant of freedom, just rising in his strength and bursting his bonds, prestige and respectability. He participated in the preliminary arrangements of the campaign of 1856, and took a very active and influential part in that determined struggle. Although the Republicans were defeated, they demonstrated their strength to such a degree that it was an object with politicians to conciliate them. Upon the general union of the opposition in this state, under the name of the People's Party, a number of prominent Republicans were honored with official positions. Mr. Thomas was elected to the Common Council: here, as everywhere, his great qualities shone forth. The ever memorable and stirringly eventful year of 1860 dawned upon the land, and we find Mr. Thomas in the foremost ranks of the champions of freedom, and opponents of the further extension of the one blot upon our bannered stars. He participated in the nomination of Abraham Lincoln, at Chicago, and, on returning to his home, entered heart, hand and purse into that absorbing contest, marching to victory beneath that glorious banner inscribed, "No further extension of human slavery." His were some of the few keen eyes which early discovered the little cloud, no bigger than a man's hand, rising on the Southern horizon, and his ears could distinguish afar off the muttering of the coming storm of secession, so soon to burst in all its terror on our heads. Holding firm to his faith in God and the triumph of the truth, he passed undaunted through the trying hours of the winter of 1860; utterly refusing to lend his aid to any scheme of conciliaiion or compromise, to fritter away the dearly bought and hard won victory of truth over error, and right against might; or to "crook the pregnant hinges of the knee, that thrift might follow fawning;" nor would he bow his head to the threats of incipient treason, and begging pardon for having dared to vote and act like a man, place his neck beneath the Juggernaut of Southern slavery—that whited sepulchre, without full of rottenness, and dead men's bones within; whose figure-head of the golden calf so many of our Northern men fell down and worshipped—promising, if taken again to the horrible ogre's embrace, never to venture to think and act, except as it dictated.

As the eventful year of 1861 drew nigh. the dark shadow of treason settled thicker and thicker o'er the land. Men held their breath at the terrific coming of the tempest, and looked anxiously in their neighbor's face—longing, but not daring, to place confidence even there; not venturing to hope for the peaceful inauguration of a chief magistrate legally and constitutionally chosen. The time that tried men's souls was upon us, and we find Mr. Thomas, with many more brave hearts, wending his way to the nation's capital, to stand by that President in his hour of extreme peril, and carry him safely through the expected fray; for he realised that on honest old Abe hung the hopes of a great free people and the freedom of a continent. Happily the storm burst not then; a kind and merciful Father watched over us, and Mr. Lincoln quietly took his seat. Louder, and still more loud, roared the gathered wrath of the tempest. State after state joined hands with impudent and treasonable South Carolina in her mad dance toward the yawning gulf of

disunion. Not yet could the North realise that the South was in
deadly earnest, but thought it only the rantings of a spoiled child,
to be appeased by the appetising tit-bit compromise. But " man
proposes and God disposes." While the North was hugging " the
delusive phantom of hope," athwart the Southern sky flashed
the fire and rolled the smoke of rebel guns opened upon devoted Sumter, the echoing boom rolled over the hills of the sturdy
Northland; then did we realise that " grim visaged war had un-
masked his wrinkled front ;" and from every hill and valley, where
had been heard the story of Sumter's doom, rushed out armed thousands to do battle for their country and her unity. Mr. Thomas,
being in Washington when the mad waves of secession rolled over
Baltimore, and our capital seemed doomed—being cut off from present succor—enrolled himself as a volunteer in Hon. C. M. Clay's
company, and, musket on shoulder, paced the city, keeping watch
and ward over the centre of our nation's hopes and fears. On that
dark and gloomy night of early April—that night so sombre, without a single star, and illumined only by the flashes of the trusty
muskets of our gallant volunteers, fighting their way through Baltimore—terrifying was the then condition of our country. Soon
was heard the joyful sound of the steady tramp of our glorious volunteers surging in billowy masses about Washington, throwing
around her the protecting arms of her brave sons, the soldiers of
the republic.

The President and his counsellors, recognizing the gravity of
the events by which they were surrounded, determined at once to
apply rigidly that blockade which has proved so singularly effective, and deeming it of immense importance that so important a
point as Philadelphia should be made secure, and that none but
men of proved loyalty should be put on guard in high places as
well as low, called Mr. Thomas to them at dead of night, when the
world was clothed in slumber as a garment, and offered him the
collectorship of the port. He accepted ; not a seeker after office,
but as one recognising the gravity of the President's reasons, and
at once left for his post, to reach it ere the blockade was pronounced—passing round the gap in the ironway in Baltimore, and
through the dangers that there environed the path, undaunted and
unscathed. Arrived in Philadelphia the necessary arrangements
were soon completed, and Mr. Thomas took possession of the office
he so worthily occupies—in his official acts vindicating the wisdom
of the President's choice. Not content with guarding vigilantly

the great trust consigned to his care, he frequently—as the lurid light of conflict shone with brighter glare over our beloved land—offered his services in a military capacity to the government; but the President, wisely, thought him invaluable in his official position, and courteously refused, desiring him to continue at his post.

We find Mr. Thomas always actively engaged in advocating and supporting the war measures of the President, and stoutly upholding him in his efforts to crush this infamous rebellion; advocating a sharp, short and speedy eradication of the evil, by sending into the defenceless portions of the South a large army, to march into the interior, liberating as it went; whose term of service should be short and during the winter, thus avoiding the pestilential vapors of the Southern clime; earnestly asking for the decree of emancipation, and ably seconding that great instrument when issued, in immortal words from the inspired pen of the great liberator Abraham Lincoln.

The autumn of 1862 found the arms of the republic generally unsuccessful, and gloomy forebodings were manifested throughout the land; but Mr. Thomas never fainted nor grew weary in well doing; so we find him—after McClellan's and Pope's defeats, and the red mist of war came rolling dim and heavy on the Southern wind—with that rare foresight for which he is remarkable, preparing, notwithstanding the ridicule of many wiseacres, for the invasion of his native state, which he saw was sure to happen. He saw the imperative necessity of an organization that could be rendered effective in case of need; and believing it the particular duty of men in government employ to support that government with sword as well as pen, he, in August, set about placing the Custom House employees on a war footing. A meeting was called, and a military company formed—the Revenue Guards—of which Mr. Thomas was unanimously chosen captain. Although then comparatively unskilled in military matters, he manfully accepted the position, and immediately equipped the company out of his private means, in the most complete manner possible. No pains or expense was spared by him in his endeavor to produce an organization worthy of our city. Scarcely had the arrangements been completed ere Captain Thomas was called upon to march to the defense of his state and nation, against an insolent and triumphant foe. Promptly answering the Governor's call, on the fourteenth of September he marched his company to Harrisburg, the first thoroughly equipped organization to report to Gov. Curtin. Ere

11

leaving he made ample arrangements to equip the second company
of Revenue Guards, who followed the first almost immediately.
Upon the arrival of the second company, the twentieth regiment
was formed, from seven Philadelphia companies and three from
Reading, of which Captain Thomas was chosen Colonel. Com-
pleting the organization of the regiment he immediately marched
to the front, reaching Hagerstown the Saturday following the
bloody battle of Antietam, his being one of the few regiments who
hesitated not at crossing the border, but were willing and ready to
go where duty called. Here the regiment went into camp, but
soon were ordered to Green Castle, and took up their line at night
fall. After a toilsome and dangerous march, in which Col. Thomas' noble nature shone out with added lustre, scorning to ride
while others walked, devoting his horse to foot-sore private or
weary drummer boy. They reached their new encampment, but
owing to the imperfect arrangements, consequent upon the calling
out of so large a body of men as rushed to repel the invasion, the
commissary department was in a sad condition, and the rations
very sparse and irregular; but Colonel Thomas' liberality prevented
suffering among his men, as he furnished them with food from his
own private purse.

Not without death and wounds was the regiment permitted to
reach home. When in sight of Harrisburg an accident occurred,
so terrible as almost to paralyse. Amid the crash of colliding engines, the noise of escaping steam, the groans of the dying and the
shrieks of the mangled, Col. Thomas moved a very ministering
angel, binding up wounds, soothing the dying, and pouring the
balm of consolation into many an ear listening its last to earthly
sounds, while tears coursed his manly cheeks at sight of sorrows
he was unable to prevent or alleviate.

At request of Gov. Curtin the organization of the twentieth regiment was preserved, regular drills established, and the regiment
kept on a war footing. Early in the winter of 1862–63, with that
perspicuity to which we have before made allusion, Col. Thomas
predicted a second and more formidable invasion of the state, and
so important did he deem the emergency that he wrote the President and the war department that, in his opinion, such an invasion
would take place, in comparison with which the former one would
sink into utter insignificance; that all signs and known facts in regard to the rebel army pointed plainly at the extreme probability
of such an event; the scarcity of food in the region infested by that

army; the tempting bait of the teeming granaries of Pennsylvania; the clamor of the Southern populace, urging the transfer of the war from their soil to that of the North, thereby relieving them from the devastations of the armed hosts of both combatants, and the depleted and enervated condition of the Army of the Potomac, the aid promised by Northern traitors to their infamous scheme, all indicated that such an attempt would speedily be made. In this view he urged upon them the complete and ample protection of the border by a volunteer force of at least fifty thousand, called out for six months—offering himself to raise ten thousand good and true men for that purpose.

Unfortunately the government could not believe the danger so imminent, and, thanking him for his warning and patriotism, declined the offer.

Still of the same opinion, strengthened by every day's record of events, he prudently and wisely determined to place his regiment on such a footing that it, at least, could be ready when called upon. To this end, he called for all his employees to join in the movement, and was nobly seconded by them; and also sent a circular, embodying the facts, as he believed them of imminent danger, to all the loyal leagues and organizations in the city. The response to this circular was not such as he expected. So earnest was he in this work, that by some he was called a military monomaniac. But soon had Philadelphia cause to rue the hour when she paid not heed to the watchman from the tower, and gave no listening ear to his warning. Well do we all remember the dark days of early June, when the air was full of rumors of the coming tempest, when that portentous cloud of desolation rolled nearer and still more near our borders, and there was none to stop its coming—neither horsemen nor footmen; and the Southern horizon grew black with its gathering gloom; when white lips whispered words of ill omen in the trembling ears of quaking, shivering fear—"Lee has marched over the mountain wall, and holds Maryland."

> "While nearer still, and nearer,
> Did the red whirlwind come;
> From underneath the whirling cloud
> Is heard the trumpets war note proud,
> The trampling and the hum."

Then rang through our state the clarion call of the President and Governor. Now was the proudest hour of Col. Thomas' life. While others hesitated and shrunk back, knowing not what to do, and urgent appeals for armed men came with every beat of the telegraphic pulse, thanks to his energy, foresight and determination, Col. Thomas answered promptly, and without an if, a but, or a question as to pay, bounty or time of service, mustered in and marched his regiment, twelve hundred strong, to Harrisburg, forty-eight hours after the telegram asking his speedy appearance reached him. Immediately upon his arrival there he reported to Gen. Couch, and was by him assigned to the important and dangerous service of guarding the Northern Central Railroad, that great connecting link between Harrisburg and Baltimore. This was looked upon by the authorities at Washington, and by Gen. Couch, as of grave moment, as the free travel of that railway facilitated the movements of the pursuing army of the Potomac, and rendered easy the transmission of supplies and information from headquarters to the department of the Susquehanna. Not disguising the danger, the General told Col. Thomas that he expected nothing less than that his regiment would be sacrificed to the urgent necessities of the case. The next forty-eight hours found the twentieth scattered for twenty miles, above and below York, along this thoroughfare, busily engaged in fortifying their different positions. From his headquarters, at York, where the details of his responsible command were worked out, the keen eye of the Colonel was over all, and a general personal supervision exercised. Scarcely a day passed but he made the regular circuit of his extensive lines, and every company felt his fostering care and fatherly interest. Fortifications were erected, rifle pits constructed, and careful preparations made for the coming of the foe. On the third day preceding the commencement of the bloody contest at Gettysburg, the rebels appeared in very large force along the line of the Northern Central Railroad, menacing York with seven thousand men. Col. Thomas finding the place untenable by the force at his command, ordered that portion of the regiment in and about York to fall back to the river. So sudden was the appearance of the foe, that the portion below York (five companies) was cut off from the rest of it, and knew not their present danger. The wisdom and correct judgment of his retreat at that time, is amply sustained by the following telegraphic correspondence between Major Haller, chief of staff, and Gen. Couch, but which failed to reach Colonel Thomas until after the object had been effected. On the twenty-seventh June Major Haller telegraphed :

"I think Colonel Thomas' troops hopelessly exposed. Sought for him, but he was absent; so could not discuss the question..

York must fall, and the bridges follow of course. He might, perhaps, withdraw to-night."

The reply of General Couch came next morning, viz:

HARRISBURG, *June* 28, 1863. To MAJOR HALLER:—"When you find it necessary to withdraw the main body of Frick's command from Wrightsville, leave a proper number on the other side to destroy the bridges, and use your own discretion in their destruction. Keep them open as long as possible. with prudence. Send one (1) or two (2) secret messengers with dispatches to Thomas to withdraw if he has not already done so."

Col. Thomas had already fallen back, and the messenger arriving at York, ascertained the fact, but it must be borne in mind that Col. Thomas did not leave York until after the surrender of that town by the chief burgess, which event took place at three o'clock on Saturday, the twenty-seventh June. The companies at and above York leaving just in time to prevent capture. Reaching Wrightsville, the portion of the regiment mentioned took part in the spirited engagement at that place, and suffered a considerable loss in wounded and prisoners, and were ultimately forced to retreat across the Susquehanna, burning the bridge at that place to prevent pursuit. The companies below York were also attacked, but succeeded in beating off their assailants, and forcing their way to the river, reaching the Lancaster county side in safety; from their point of crossing they rejoined the regiment which had been ordered to Bainbridge, and where they labored night and day on fortifications and rifle pits on the mainland, and also on the islands in the river, at the fords at that place, and by their efforts and determined aspect, prevented the threatened crossing of the river by the rebels at that place. The Colonel was placed in command of all the forces; thus did General Couch show his confidence in and reliance upon Colonel Thomas. By his orders all the flat boats at the different ferries had been brought to the Lancaster county side, thus compelling the foe to try a crossing at the only accessible ford on the river, which was foiled by this admirable arrangements. After the battle of Gettysburg, the regiment, in common with other militia, was thrown forward into the Cumberland valley, making forced marches through mud and rain, through storm, and the summer's heat, to join General Meade, that he might be enabled with this reinforcement to drive Lee into the river and destroy him, but reaching within co-operating distance of that army, only to participate in its chagrin, felt so keenly, at the escape of that wily rebel.

The twentieth now laid in camp for some weeks, perfecting themselves, under the leadership of their gallant Colonel, to do with honor any duty they might be called upon to perform, until ordered to return to their homes. In all the arduous duties of those trying times, in rain, sun, or the dampness of night, on the wearisome march, or lonely bivouac, everywhere was visible the evidences of the love and kindness of Colonel Thomas; did rations fall short, his ready hand and purse supplied the needed food. Always soldierly in bearing and discipline, stern and exacting, requiring that ready and prompt obedience from his inferiors, that he so willingly accorded to his superiors; just in all judgment of cases, kind and benevolent to a fault, when the stern duties of the soldier did not conflict. We can point with satisfaction to Colonel William B. Thomas as a pattern man in all relations of life, and ask the young to look to such as he for their models by which to form and shape their own courses. Colonel Thomas is still in the enjoyment of robust health, the result of temperate living and wholesome activity, and entire freedom from those vices that do enervate. His wealth is spread with lavish though discriminating hand upon objects of real worth. He is a born philanthropist. His heart is "open as day to melting charity." He gives largely to benevolent institutions, and contributes lavishly of his ample means for the benefit of our sick and maimed heroes. Just as he is benevolent, he long ago conceived the idea of a community of interest in his milling operations, and carried it into practical working by giving every man in his employ a share of the profits of the concern, while he furnished the capital and requisite means to carry on the business; this system has been found to work with very beneficial results, and has assisted in procuring for Colonel Thomas his present enviable and highly honorable position before the community of which he is so bright an ornament ; long may it be ere Philadelphia has to morn her model merchant, miller, patriot, and high-souled gentleman.

QUINTIN CAMPBELL.

THOSE persons who remember Quintin Campbell during a whole generation, as the Cashier of the Philadelphia Bank, an institution in which he held vast trusts, and discharged them with industry and fidelity, can have but little suspicion of the simple and humble incidents of his early career. A sketch of his life will show that the secret of success is good conduct, and that integrity and attention must in all cases lead to honor and wealth.

Quintin Campbell was the son of the Reverend John Campbell, minister of the Parish of Glenfairn, in Gallowayshire, Scotland, where he was born, in the month of November, 1774. His father occupied the manse and glebe lands, which were beautifully situated upon the river Ken, which empties itself in the Loch of the same name, near New Galloway. In the year 1780, the Reverend John Campbell died, leaving three children—Quintin, Ivie and Agnes. His death of course produced a great change in the circumstances of the family. His mother removed from the manse to the village of St. Johnstown, in the adjoining parish of Dalry, where she took a house next door to that of her mother, Mrs. Hair. Here she lived economically, her principal means of support being £21 per annum, which she received from "the fund for the widows and ministers," at Edinburgh. This small sum, however, had at that time a purchasing power equal to six times the amount at the present day; and by frugality, Mrs. Campbell managed to live upon it, and with assistance from her mother, to bring up her small family. Quintin was sent to the free school of the parish, where, under the direction of James Buchanan, a type of the flogging schoolmasters of the time, he gained those rudiments of education which were to assist him through life. At the age of sixteen, the young Scotch boy naturally began to consider what course it would be necessary for him to pursue in order to relieve his mother of the burden of his support. The country offered him as the only occupations, the life of a farm laborer, or a shepherd, and the prospect of following these pursuits was distasteful to him. James Douglas, a boy companion, and himself, frequently conferred upon those subjects, and the result was a youthful resolution that they would join their for-

tunes, and go out into the world together associates and friends.
Their relatives were consulted upon the subject, and finally gave
their consent.   The boys were of opinion that the navigation of the
sea offered them inducements, and they left home determined to
seek employment in a principal seaport town.   In the month of
April, 1790, Quintin Campbell and James Douglass, with their
little wardrobes tied up in their handkerchiefs, and with a small
stock of money, (Quintin Campbell was the owner of forty-two
shillings,) left St. Johnstown forever.   They walked to Kircudbright. where they stopped the first night with a relative of Campbell's, who treated them kindly.   They took with them letters of
introduction to persons of standing in Liverpool, from Miss Dick, a
benevolent maiden lady, who for many years had made St. Johnstown
her home.   This assistance was of great advantage to the young adventurers.   On the fifteenth of April, 1790, the boys sailed from
Kircudbright, in a small sloop, bound for Liverpool.   They experienced a severe storm during the passage, and the vessel was
forced to put into Whithaven.   They reached Liverpool a few days
after, and having been consigned to Sandy Reed, a canny Scotch-
man, took lodgings with him until the gentlemen to whom Miss
Dick had recommended them, could do something for them.   These
strange friends succeeded in getting a situation for Douglas upon
board of a ship in the Guinea trade, and for Campbell they secured
an apprenticeship to Captain Andrew English, master of a small
ship called the "Hope," which was bound to Baltimore.

Thus, these boys, who had so bravely resolved at St. Johnstown
to unite their destinies, were separated forever.   What became of
Douglas, Mr. Campbell never heard.   On the twenty-fifth of April,
1890, the ship "Hope" sailed from Liverpool, and after a narrow
escape from stranding on the Irish coast, reached Baltimore, after
a passage of forty-nine days.   The incidents of the voyage completely disenchanted Quintin Campbell of the romance with which
his young imagination had imbued the idea of sailor life.   As the
youngest apprentice and cabin boy. he not only had to perform
many repulsive duties, but his religious training and principles
were shocked by the rough and brutal character of his associates.
His ingenuous young mind was pained by the profanity and blas-
phemy which prevailed on board of the ship, and the idea of continuing in his situation was so horrible, that he formed the design
of abandoning it at any risk.   To escape from the ship was not an
easy matter—but fate favored him.   He was instrumental in saving

the life of the ship's carpenter, who, whilst bathing in the basin at Baltimore, was in imminent danger of being drowned. This service secured the gratitude and friendship of the man, who being informed of the intention of Quintin to run away, engaged to assist him. He procured for him an asylum upon shore, to which the boy succeeded in escaping. From this place he finally emerged to take passage in the packet-boat for Philadelphia, sailing directly by the dreaded ship "Hope," upon the deck of which Captain English seemed to be in command, preparing to sail from the port.

Quintin Campbell landed at Market street wharf, Philadelphia, about the middle of September, 1790, and walked up that street with the same feelings which Benjamin Franklin experienced when he left the packet-boat and proceeded to explore his new home, with a loaf of bread under his arm. Campbell's forlorn appearance was no recommendation to the landlords of different inns to whom he applied for lodgings. After some rebuffs, he was taken in at a tavern in Front street, near Callowhill, where he got to bed and slept soundly. The next morning he inquired for Ive Porteus, his cousin, a flour dealer, who had lived at Philadelphia, and in whom he expected to find a friend and protector. The people at the tavern did not know Porteus, but they sent the boy to Levi Hollingsworth, as one likely to know, being extensively in the flour trade. He was the father of the present Pascall Hollingsworth, and the store was at that time at No. 61 South Wharves. Mr. Hollingsworth was standing at the door when the little Scotch boy approached him. He did not remember Porteus, but upon reference to Maurice Kennedy, his chief clerk, the latter said that he had dealt with Hollingsworth, but that he understood that he had died some months before, at Norfolk, Virginia. This intimation must have been a terrible blow to the hopes of the boy. There was some gleam of sunshine, however, in reference to Thomas and Peter Mackie, at No. 42 Front street, who had been friends of Porteus. To these gentlemen the runaway sailor boy told his simple story, and fortified it by the only evidence in his possession, a certificate of good character, from the Rev. Alex. McGowen, of Dalry. The Mackies promised to befriend him, and told him to call the next day. Promptly he repaired there at the appointed time, and was astonished and gratified at unexpected news.

It seemed that Mr. Hollingsworth was in want of an apprentice, and liking the apparent artlessness of the boy, he called upon the Messrs. Mackie to ascertain what they knew about him. They

12

could only give Campbell's own story; but Mr. Hollingsworth, satisfied by his looks and manner, and having a favorable opinion of the Scotch, offered to take him in his store for his victuals and clothes. The offer was munificent to Quintin, and he gladly embraced it. Perhaps no occurrence in the life of Mr. Campbell was of more importance than this. The revulsion in the feelings of the boy upon so suddenly finding friends and an agreeable employment, in a city in which he had only landed the day before, can be imagined, but cannot be described.

Quintin Campbell went into the family of Levi Hollingsworth, and was well provided for. He was diligent and trustworthy. He served a faithful clerkship, disturbed by no adventure; but meeting with his old master, Captain English, who, however, treated him well, and did not seem inclined to enforce the obligations of his indentures, even if he could have done so in a foreign country. He gained the good will and esteem of Mr. Hollingsworth, and when, after five and a-half years of service, his indenture expired, he was not turned out upon the world without employment. Mr. Hollingsworth exerted his influence in his favor, and procured for him a clerkship in the bank of Pennsylvania, at a salary of $600 dollars a year, which seemed to be an independent fortune to the young man.

In this situation Mr. Campbell remained for five or six years, when he was induced to resign, in order to undertake a commission for Gurney & Smith, to act for them as supercargo at Havana for several ship loads of flour, sent there from Virginia. Having by these means obtained some knowledge of the West India trade, he determined to establish a commission house at Havana. This project was suddenly defeated by the peace of Amiens, in 1802, and the closing of the ports of Cuba against foreigners. He then returned to Philadelphia, where he was out of business for some months, but was finally engaged by the Pennsylvania Insurance Company to go to the Island of Guadalope, to inquire into the circumstances attending a supposed wreck there, which was thought to be a fraudulent attempt to cheat the underwriters.

Upon his return to Philadelphia, in 1804, the Philadelphia Bank was about being organized. He applied to the directors for a situation in the institution, and was appointed first teller. In 1806 the cashier, James Todd, died, and Quintin Campbell was chosen his successor. For thirty-one years the name of Quintin Campbell as cashier of the Philadelphia Bank was known and honored

throughout the community. In the sixtieth year of his age he resolved to withdraw from the active and responsible duties of cashier, and retire to private life. But his fellow citizens, who had
confidence in his business capacity, were not willing that he should
resign all interest in business affairs. In 1840 he was elected President of the Pennsylvania Fire Insurance Company, a position
which he resigned, in consequence of ill health, in 1853. From
that period until his death, March 2, 1863, he was active and useful as a citizen. His career is a fine example of the benefit of early
moral training and of good habits. No one could have been more
forlorn than the runaway sailor boy who entered Philadelphia to
seek his fortune in September, 1790. No one could have been more
respected in consequence of his worth and a long life of probity
and usefulness, than the citizen who departed this life March 2,
1863.

DANIEL H. ROCKHILL.

THE progress of the tailor's art is coeval with the progress of
civilization. The difference between the bear skin of the savage
and the delicately fitted and tasteful coat of the elegant gentleman
who appears upon our fashionable promanade, is typical of the
difference between humanity in a condition, but little removed
from that of the brute, and mankind refined, polished and enlightened in cultivated society. The history of clothing, from the
days of the fig-leaves, to those of the Raglan and Talma, is a most
curious and instructive study. Even the comparisons of the styles
in vogue in the various countries at the present day, would afford
matter for an entertaining volume. The primitive simplicity of
dress among many nations; the picturesque attire of others, who,
for centuries, have retained the same costume; and the fleeting
fashions of people who claim to be the foremost representatives of
the highest refinements of civilization, may furnish the philosopher
with food for thought, and the artist with fanciful suggestions. In
styles of clothing, we are generally content to receive instructions
from Paris, but we doubt whether the Parisians ever dreamed of
such a wholesale manufacture of costumes for the millions as that
which has been developed in America.

Let us glance at the tailoring business in this city alone, as an illustration of our rapid improvement upon industrial operations of the Old World, and of our own people in by-gone days.

About twenty-five years ago, the tailors' craft was entirely confined to the production of what is called customer work—that is, to the supply of single garments, of single suits, for special orders. Every individual who desired to renew an article of clothing was required to be regularly measured and fitted, and their garments were made to suit them, whether in accordance with the fashion of the time or otherwise. But this was at length considered too slow a system for a fast and changeable people, who cared less for the excellence of workmanship than for the promptitude and sufficiency of manufacture. Ready-made clothing establishments were started; at first their patronage was neither extensive nor of the most desirable kind. But as more capital was gradually drawn into the business, and the garments improved in style and quality, the sales of these stores so largely increased as for a time to threaten the "customer" tailors with ruin. The cheap labor of women and indigent foreigners enabled the dealers in ready-made clothing to under-sell their rivals, and to not only supply a heavy local demand, but to send their goods to all parts of the country. This business has increased to such an enormous extent that the great clothing establishments of our principal cities may be said to clothe the whole nation. The capital invested here in this branch of industry is estimated at $3,500,000 annually. The wages paid annually, amounted to about $3,000,000. There are sixty-seven firms, whose aggregate production is valued at $6,050,000 annually, while others, who are engaged in a smaller way, produce garments to the value of $3,500,000 annually. About ten millions of dollars per annum will barely cover the whole production of ready-made clothing in this city. It is worthy of note, however, that certain "customer" houses here do a larger and more profitable business than any tailoring establishment of the period before the commencement of the wholesale manufacture. With the increase of aristocratic refinement and the cultivation of taste in dress, the masters of the customer's mystery have endeavored to keep pace, and the result is, that they enjoy a kind of patronage which those who manufacture for the masses cannot hope to gain. The old tailor "shops" of our fathers have given place to palatial stores, in which the fashionable gentleman may lounge, look over the latest styles of goods, select patterns and give orders, with exquisite satisfaction. These resorts are not inferior in attractions to any of those which are patronized by the *beau monde* of any European capital; and we may point to one of them—that of Messrs. Rockhill & Wilson, on Chestnut street, above Sixth, as unsurpassed in reputation for taste and elegance. This house is also worthy of particular notice on account of the character and career of its founders, who is entirely the architect of his own fortune.

Daniel H. Rockhill is a native of New Jersey. He was born at Columbus, in that state, in 1801. His parents were in humble circumstances. He enjoyed but little educational advantages, and was destined for a life of toil. He became an apprentice to the shear and the needle, and his only hope of rising in the world was based upon his becoming a thorough master of his trade. While still a mere youth, Mr. Rockhill came to Philadelphia, and resided in West's alley, while he obtained employment from Mr. Joseph Ridgway, whose establishment was located in Third street, opposite to the Mechanics' Bank.

He was careful, industrious, economical and self-reliant; but it was not until the year 1829 that he thought it expedient to commence business on his own account. He then opened a "shop" on Second street, below Callowhill. Here he labored early and late to secure a reputation for excellence of workmanship, and a consequent increase of patronage. Business flowed in upon him as the reward of his toil, as a natural result of his endeavors to please all customers. He remained in the same locality for fifteen years, or until the enlargement of his means and the popularity of his establishment induced him to display his energy, taste and enterprise, in a more fashionable neighborhood.

Mr. Rockhill had in his employ a young man named Franklin S. Wilson, whom he had taken as an apprentice in July, 1834. Wilson was remarkable for his intelligence, active and attentive business habits and pleasing manners; and having fully tested the capacity of this young tradesman, Mr. Rockhill determined to take him into partnership, at the commencement of tailoring on a more extensive scale. Accordingly, the firm of Rockhill & Wilson was formed in 1843, and in August of the same year they opened what was then considered a commodious establishment, on Chestnut street below Third. A number of concerns in the same line were located in that bustling portion of the city. The rivalry was keen, and the struggle for supremacy aroused the energies of the competing clothiers. Some attempted to dazzle the public by glaring display, or to delude by alluring misrepresentations. But Rockhill and Wilson mainly relied upon their prompt fulfilment of orders, their taste and liberality in the selection of material, and the style and perfection of their work. They succeeded beyond their first anticipations. They gained a large and extremely valuable custom, and their establishment became the resort of the devotees of fashion and the judges of elegance in garments. Their profits were satisfactory, and the poor knight of the needle of West's alley became a successful merchant In May, 1856, they removed to a new, spacious and splendid store, on Chestnut street above Sixth, where they are located at present. Their business is larger than that of any other customer retail concern in the same line of trade in this city. Their patrons are of the class who generally lead the mass of people in their styles of dress, and who recognize this store as the resort of all who are anxious to obtain the latest and most fashionable article of male attire. Their profits are immense, reaching in one year $300,000! They are large operators in real estate, owning the handsome brown stone store on Chestnut street; four brick dwellings on Seventh street above Green; three on Old York road above Noble; two on Green street between Third and Fourth streets; and two brown stone dwellings on Arch street above Eighteenth street, which cost $75,000.

Mr. Rockhill, now in his sixtieth year, is still active and full of enterprise. He has never held any official position, being of rather a retiring disposition and devoted to business. He has taken a lively interest in that great philanthropic movement, the temperance reform, and has given much time and money for the advancement of the cause. In his opinion intemperance is the source of the most frightful evils that afflict the land; and he has felt called upon, from a conscientious desire to benefit mankind, to do all in his power to check the fiery flood that annually sweeps away thousands who might be the pride and ornaments of society. He has held the highest position in the order known as the Sons of Temperance—the most efficient organization ever formed for the rescue of humanity from the degradation of drunkenness. Mr. Rockhill is said to be in very comfortable circumstances. To a sound and practical brain he unites a warm and generous heart, which is never closed against the appeals of the suffering. He is one of those examples which we would especially commend to the attention of our working men, as proving that industry, cultivation of skill in a particular trade, and economical management, will, under Providence, raise the humblest to a social position, which may be the envy of men who were born with a golden spoon at their lips.

DR. DAVID JAYNE.

THE infusion of new blood into the veins of the commercial body, is, in this country, a continual process. In some of our large cities the principal merchants who control the business character of great communities are natives of other sections of the country, and many of them never saw the localities which they were finally to develope and manage, until they were well grown, and until some of them had long passed the beginning of manhood. New York and New Orleans illustrates this fact more generally than other American cities. The industry, enterprise and success of New York is in a small degree due to native New Yorkers. New England men and Jerseymen are its merchant princes—men who left their humble homes to seek their fortunes, have found them in the Empire city; and whilst the descendants of the Dutch have slumbered away in the drowsy comfort that made their venerable ancestors respectable and dull, adventurers have seized the helm of their affairs and contributed their quota toward making New York the wonderful metropolis which it is. Philadelphia is indebted for its present attitude very much to the enterprising persons who have engaged in business here; and although our proportion of native merchants is larger than it is in New York, we cannot shut our eyes to the fact that some of the most successful business men in the city came to us from other portions of the country.

Among the strangers whose settlement here have been of equal advantage to themselves and to Philadelphia, few have been more successful or more useful, as a citizen, than Dr. David Jayne. Born in Monroe county, Pennsylvania, on the twenty-second of July, 1799, David Jayne was perhaps more fortunate than the sons of the majority of his neighbors, in having intelligent parents, who knew the value of education, and used their endeavors to secure to their children as thorough instruction as was possible in that wild region. His father, the Rev. Ebenezer Jayne, was a Baptist clergyman, a pious and intelligent man, and the son received home tuition and counsels, which exercised a happy influence upon his future career. He availed himself carefully of these advantages, and after having learned all that was possible in Monroe county, went out into the world to learn more. Fate directed him toward Cumberland county, New Jersey, where he commenced his active exertions in the arduous business of earning his own living, by engaging in the troublesome and unremunerative occupation of keeping school. This fact alone, shows that David Jayne had received a fair education at home. He enjoyed the confidence of his scholars, and while he held the birch of the pedagogue his success was sufficient to bestow honor upon the ancient profession. But whilst engaged in this drudgery, school-master Jayne had a higher ambition. His tastes led him toward the study of medicine, and while yet supporting himself by the profits of his school, he was preparing for a wider sphere of usefulness.

In the year 1821, he commenced the study of medicine, under the control of Dr. E. Sheppard, of Cumberland county, New Jersey. He was a faithful and close student. His mind was fitted for analysis and reflection; he progressed rapidly in his investigations, and in due time passed through his collegiate course, and received a diploma, conferring upon him the degree of Doctor of Medicine. Having thus gained the great object of his ambition, Doctor David Jayne established himself in Salem county, in 1825, and devoted himself to the laborious and badly paid duties of a country physician.

His practice led him over a wide region of the surrounding country, to the farm and the hamlet. His patients were plain people, who appreciated his kindness and skill, but were slow to testify their gratitude by liberal appropriations of the *quiddem honorarium*, for which physicians, as well as lawyers, are ambitious to work. For twelve years, Dr. Jayne tested the discomforts and disappointments incident to the career of a country doctor, and by the end of that time, his experience was sufficient. He felt that he had the energy and knowledge which fitted him to conduct more extensive interests than those to which he had been hitherto devoted. Accordingly, in the year 1837, with but a small accumulation of profits to show for the twelve years of his life spent as a Jersey doctor, he came to Philadelphia resolved to try his fortune upon a more extensive arena. Upon his arrival, he sought advancement by every legitimate means. As early as April, 1837, he was at No. 32 South Third street, at which place he offered "his professional services to the citizens of Philadelphia," and hoped "to receive a share of their patronage."

In this location Dr. Jayne remained for many years, but he soon gave up the uncertain remuneration of the consulting and practicing physician for the regular and steady profits of the druggist. Engaging in the drug business with a small capital, his shrewd mind and business qualities rapidly won for him a profitable set of customers, and a steady trade. Being a thorough pharmaceutist, having closely studied the materia medica, and having beside twelve years actual experience as a practicing physician, Dr. Jayne soon aspired to be something more than a mere buyer and seller of drugs. There was no reason why the physician's prescription, so useful to the afflicted, should be withheld until those who needed it could obtain (sometimes not easily procured), the advice of a regular practitioner. Dr. Jayne saw that much good might be done by placing within the reach of the people those simple compounds, the foundation of the practice of medicine, which are sufficient, in a vast number of cases, to arrest and conquer the progress of disease. He accordingly become something more than a druggist, and was, if we might use the term, a merchant physician. His preparations were the results of his own experience and observations. They were compounded with precision and accuracy, and they were accompanied with such descriptions of disease, and directions for use, that they were available to intelligent persons without the necessity of consulting a regular physician. In a country like this, such means of placing the safeguards of health in the hands of the pioneer and planter, the hunter, trapper and denizen of the prairie and forest, are absolute manifestations of humanity.

Dr. Jayne's preparations soon became popular, not only in this country, but throughout the world. His business, from the line of home commerce, soon flowed into the channels of foreign intercourse. The West Indies and South America were his regular customers; Europe did not reject the medicinal preparations of the Philadelphia druggist; and in time, China and Asia were added to the numerous countries which steadily imported Dr. Jayne's medicines. At No. 32 South Third-street, Dr. Jayne remained until about the year 1845, when he removed to a larger establishment, at No. 8 South Third street. This was but a temporary expedient.

13

Dr. Jayne knew the necessity which existed that he should occupy more extensive quarters, and he determined that the new establishment should be a monument to his wealth and liberality.

The massive eight-story granite building, at Nos. 84 and 86 Chestnut street, is, as our readers well know, one of the most solid and costly business edifices in the United States. The main building, with its extensive wings on either side, and the adjoining eight-story building, running from Carter street to Dock street, lately occupied by the United States Post Office, form together a magnificent proof of the business capacity and success of one man.

About the year 1850, Dr. Jayne took possession of this splendid store. Since that period, he has in other ways proved his taste and liberality as an improver of the city. The splendid granite building on the North side of Chestnut street, once known as "Jayne's Hall," now occupied by Decoursey, Lafourcade & Co., and with others, was succeeded by the more magnificent block adjoining, constructed of rich white marble, in which Yard & Gilmore, M. S. Hallowell & Co., and others are now located; and to that succeeded the "Commonwealth Building," a rich specimen of ornamental brickwork, which shows the architectural capacity of that style of material in an elegant example. As an improver of the city of Philadelphia, no man of the present generation has done as much as Dr. David Jayne. His wealth and extraordinary profits from his business enable him to spend handsomely upon the real estate which he purchases. His fine taste is shown in the erection of first class buildings, ornaments of the city, and enduring testimonials of the liberality and judgment of this most successful among all the drug merchants of Philadelphia.

ALEXANDER G. CATTELL.

THE grain trade of Philadelphia is a most important branch of its commercial interest, and for many years has been steadily increasing in magnitude. The principle cause of this increase is undoubtedly the extension of our great system of railways, which brings to us not only the cereal products of the rich valleys of our own state, but also those from the fertile regions of the extreme

West. The iron horse now bounds over the Alleghenies, and we are connected by the most direct routes with the father of waters and the great lakes of the Northwest. These facilities must insure to Philadelphia an increasingly liberal share of the produce trade of the country. But in the development of this trade much credit is due to the enterprise, energy and sagacious management of the men who have engaged in this business. The Corn Exchange Association is composed of many of the most liberal and wealthy merchants in the community; indeed, the general policy of that body shows it to be rather in advance of our other business boards in public spirit and fidelity to the interests of the city. It stands ready to exert its powerful influence in favor of any measure that has for its object the advancement of the prosperity of the city, whether pertaining to their branch of trade or any other. They are also a pre-eminently loyal body of citizens. When the treason and rebellion of the South culminated in the attack upon Fort Sum. ter, the echoes of the cannon had scarcely died away when the Association, assembled for their daily business, laid aside their "samples," and raising the flag of our country in front of their Hall, pledged themselves to keep it floating till the rebellion should be subdued and the honor of that flag vindicated. The Association has been ever since faithful and zealous in the support of all measures for the suppression of the rebellion. They have contributed largely of their means to aid in the enlistment of men and the support of the families of such as have gone to fight the battles of their country. There have been enlisted and organized under their auspices fully two regiments, and they have not exhausted their liberality or abated their zeal.

Prominent among the members of this association, and one of its early Presidents, is the subject of the present sketch, Mr. Alexander G. Cattell. He was born in 1816, at Salem, New Jersey, where his venerable father still resides, after an honorable career as a merchant for more than half a century. At the early age of twenty-four Mr. Cattell was elected to the legislature of his native state, and in 1844 was honored with a seat in the convention called to revise the state constitution. Although the youngest member of that body, which embraced the leading men of the state, he was second to none in ability or influence. Distinguished for sound common sense, a choice command of language, a graceful and forcible delivery, he never rose to speak without commanding the respectful attention and generally securing the conviction of his auditors.

In 1846 he removed to Philadelphia, and engaged in business at his present location, No. 26 North Wharves; first in connection with Mr. E. G. James, (now of the firm of T. Richardson & Co.,) and afterwards with his brother, Mr. Elijah G. Cattell. Although honored with seats in both branches of the municipal government, and fully sustaining his previous reputation as a judicious and eloquent representative, it is as a business man that he has won his present enviable position in our city. No house has stood higher in the confidence of business men for integrity, enterprise, and all that forms the basis of mercantile success.

The traits of character which Mr. Cattell exhibited in his private business could not fail to make a deep impression on business circles at large, and consequently his services have been constantly sought for in various responsible positions. Formerly as a Director in the Mechanics' Bank, and now as President of the Corn Exchange Bank, he has proved himself to be an able financier, fully meeting the high expectations which were formed from his character and talents as well as his previous career.

We have spoken of the loyalty of the Corn Exchange Association. As might have been expected, Mr. Cattell has been among the foremost in this work. His private purse, always open to every legitimate object of benevolence, was not closed now, when the claims of the soldiers and their families were presented. While, as chairman of the regimental committee of the Corn Exchange, he devoted his time and talents to aid in raising, organizing, equipping and sending forth the men who have done themselves such honor and the country such service. As showing the esteem in which Mr. Cattell is held by his associates in this work, we may say that when the old flag-staff at camp "Union," around which the gallant 118th Regiment had been rallied, was taken down, it was voted that it should be removed to the grounds of his handsome residence, at Merchantville, N. J. A magnificent flag was then purchased and presented to him, with interesting and appropriate ceremonies. (See the Daily Press, Dec. 10, 1863.)

In conclusion we would add, that Mr. Cattell, always fluent and graceful as a public speaker, is never more felicitous than when called upon for "special duty" at the various meetings, public and social, of his fellow citizens. We might refer to his eloquent response to the Hon. Montgomery Blair, Postmaster General, on the opening of the new post office building, in Chestnut street; and also to the following introduction of Miss Anna Dickinson to one of the largest and most intelligent audiences ever assembled in Philadelphia. We quote from the Evening Bulletin, of Jan. 29, 1864:

"Ladies and gentlemen: The distinguished lady," said Mr. Cattell, "your own gifted townswoman, who is to address you to-night, needs, I am sure, no formal introduction to you. The gushing words of passionate eloquence which well up from her patriotic heart, have been heard in this hall, and the presence to-night of this large and graceful audience is a speaking evidence of your appreciation of her worth and power, and of your sympathy with the cause she so nobly advocates—the cause of our common country, and the flag which is the emblem of its dignity and power.

"When the pestilent theory of secession, and the latent treason of the haughty slave power, that would crack its whips over the heads of Northern freemen, culminated into open rebellion, and the paracidal hand was raised to strike at the life of the nation, the loyal heart of the great North resolved that it would stand by our time-honored flag, and maintain its supremacy or perish in the attempt.

"Determining from the very outset, with a unanimity unbroken save by the ignoble few who would

> 'Crook the pregnant hinge of the knee,
> That thrift may follow fawning,'

that the rebellion should perish, and those who first took the sword should perish by the sword, we have been driven by the inexorable logic of cause and effect, and the eternal principles of truth and and justice, to the further determination, that slavery, the pestilent cause of all our woes, the very root and groundwork of the rebellion, should perish with it, and the twain be entombed together.

"Prominent among those who have nobly advocated this sentiment—a sentiment approved alike by reason and conscience, by patriotism and humanity—is the gifted lady who is to address you to-night. Her eloquent appeals for the right, and her scathing invectives against the wrong, have been heard and approved by large and intelligent audiences in nearly every loyal state of the Union; and while thus battling for the right, the resources of those beneficent institutions, the Sanitary and Christian Commissions, for whose benefit she has so often spoken, have been largely aided.

"She comes to-night, by invitation of many citizens, to repeat in this, her own city, and before you, her friends and neighbors. almost within the shadow of that Hall wherein the nation had its birth, the eloquent address delivered recently at the National Capital, in the hall of the House of Representatives, crowded to its utmost capacity—the honored President, the Vice President, and members of the Cabinet and of Congress, being among her auditors.

"And here the agreeable duty delegated to me should end— but the circumstances of the occasion, the simple fact that it is a lady who is to speak to us to-night, should awaken a deeper sense of our obligation to the loyal women of the North for their steadfast patriotism in this hour of our country's peril. True, they have no call to the tented field—it is neither fitting nor needful they should be there. There are enough of just such brave boys as grace this amphitheatre to-night, to crowd into that mythical last ditch, all the boasted chivalry of rebeldom.

"But their undying sympathy for the soldier, their ceaseless, untiring efforts to promote his comfort and his welfare, the ten thousand works of love and kindness which are daily emanating from their hands and hearts, make up the silver lining to the dark cloud of war that overhangs our land. They bear this great army on their loving hearts, and follow the soldier, with their generous contributions for his comfort and their personal deeds of kindness, to the camp, the field, and even to the prison-house.

"How surpassingly beautiful are their kind and gentle ministrations to the wounded, or sick and suffering heroes! Their feet press the wards of our government hospitals, where many a gallant hero lies upon a bed of pain and anguish, far, perhaps, from home and kindred. They bind up his wounds, lave his throbbing temples, anticipate his every want, and cheer him with words of kindness and sympathy. And when the flickering pulse and filmy eye tell too plainly that the soldier's last conflict is well nigh over, they whisper in his ear the consolations of our Holy religion, and watch by his couch till

> 'They see in death his eye-lids close,
> Calmly as to a night's repose,
> Like flowers at set of sun.'

God bless the loyal women of our country! And may He reward them abundantly in this life, and still more abundantly in the life which is to come.

"It only remains for me to say, when this roll of honor shall be written up, composed of those who have made their names forever illustrious by their prominence in these works of love and mercy, high upon that immortal scroll shall be found names known and honored, and loved, in our own goodly city, and conspicuous among these the name of her who is to address you to-night will forever stand.

"Ladies and gentlemen I have the pleasure of presenting to you Miss Anna E. Dickinson."

CHARLES MACALESTER.

PHILADELPHIA has hitherto boasted of one "merchant and mariner," in the name of Stephen Girard. Whilst there can be no dispute as to the propriety of the application of the title to that distinguished man, it is just to say that Philadelphia might boast of other "merchants and mariners" if any care were taken to enlighten its citizens in relation to its commercial history. We have chosen for the subject of the present sketch one who was much more of a mariner than Girard, and who, if not as successful as a merchant—if the acquisition of vast wealth is the test of mercantile talent—was at all events a merchant of honor and integrity, and prosperous in his affairs to a reasonable degree.

Charles Macalester first saw the light in the village of Campbellstown, in Argyleshire, Scotland, on the fifth of April, 1765. He was born in a strictly Presbyterian community; Campbellstown itself enjoyed the distinction of being the seat of a Presbytery, and its population was composed of godly people. Connected with religion, in the minds of the Scotch Presbyterians, the interests of education are invariably associated—an education which shall strengthen religious principles and restrain young people from a departure from the correct line of action. Charles Macalester received at these schools a solid and stern tuition, which, while it insured the scholar full and systematic instruction in the most useful branches of human knowledge, never permitted him to forget that high moral principle and integrity of purpose were the surest means of rendering knowledge profitable.

After receiving as much schooling as fell to the portion of children of the villagers, the question of a business avocation was presented to the boy. It was natural that he should evince a preference for the sea. Campbellstown was a sea-coast village. It was situate upon the mull of Cantyre, a promontory of Western Scotland, which stretches into the Irish Sea. It had a fine harbor, was a noted refuge for coasting vessels, and was the seat of an extensive herring fishery. Sea-going men were its permanent and transient inhabitants, and sea-going matters were the great materials for town talk. To become a sailor, therefore, seemed to be the natural destiny of Charles Macalester. At a proper age he entered into the calling, and learned the practical duties of seamanship among the crews of vessels belonging to his native town. Having thus instructed himself in navigation, his ambitious mind impelled him to seek a wider sphere of action. When he arrived of age, his thoughts turned to the United States. It was a young country which had just emerged from the struggles of the Revolutionary War, and to enterprise and industry it offered a most tempting reception. Mr. Macalester, at the age of twenty-one years, arrived in the United States a young Scotch sailor. So pleased was he with the prospects of the country, that he determined to become a citizen, and under the liberal naturalization laws which then existed, he was admitted to that privilege in the year 1786, establishing his home in Philadelphia. In October of the same year, he gave a new pledge of the sincerity of his citizenship by entering into marriage with Miss Ann Sampson, of Baltimore, a young Scotch lady, whose virtues and affections were his solace during a long life. The young pair established their humble home at No. 78 Union street, at which location they remained for many years. The sound education and intelligence of young Macalester soon enabled him to rise in his profession. He had attracted to himself the confidence and good will of respectable merchants, and it was not long before he was the master of a ship, entrusted not only with the safety of the voyage, but entitled, as supercargo, to dispose of the merchandize on board, to the best advantage. His fidelity in these trusts, and the good fortune which attended his management, added to his gains in double measure, and in a short time he began to accumulate portions of his savings. These were invested in the vessels in which he sailed. Commencing with small interests, he gradually increased them until he became a sole owner. One of the ships acquired by him, in this way, was the George Barclay, a very successful vessel. This ship was armed with twenty guns, in order to keep off privateers, and those sea desperadoes who at that time preyed extensively upon American commerce. With a picked crew, this daring captain ran the gauntlet of the seas, and notwithstanding frequent dangers, the ship was navigated safely from port to port during a season of peculiar peril.

Captain Macalester next commanded the Fanny, one of the fleetest vessels of her day. This beautiful vessel was built by Grice, a ship carpenter of Philadelphia, from plans of his own, and she proved a model of beauty, safety and speed. Her first voyage was made from Philadelphia to Cowes in seventeen days—the quickest passage ever made up to that time between the United States and Europe. The Hon. William Bingham was a passenger with Captain Macalester in this trip, and from the incident, Captain Macalester subsequently reaped the advantage of the acquaintance, influence and friendship of Alexander Baring, (afterwards Lord Ashburton), who was a son-in-law of Mr. Bingham. This connection introduced him to the confidence of the house of Sir Francis Baring & Co., long among the most influential of the English bankers.

When the Fanny reached London, she was chartered for a voyage to Batavia and back, which was performed in seven months and twenty days, a shortness of time which was so astonishing, that when Captain Macalester presented himself at the counting-house of the charterers in London, they supposed that the voyage had been broken up, and that the captain had returned unsuccessful. During this trip, the Fanny was chased for sixteen hours, by the fastest frigate in the British navy. When overtaken, the boarding officer remarked—"Sir, you have a very fast ship." To which Captain Macalester replied—"I thought so until to-day." "Our frigate," continued the officer, "is reputed to be the fastest in our navy, and we never had such a chase."

After eighteen years sea service, Captain Macalester longed for the quiet of the life of a landsman. His family was growing up to maturity. His wife had, in consequence of his frequent absence, the care and responsibility of the education of his children. He had made money, and had sufficient capital to establish himself in business. His resolution to do so was made in the year 1804. In the succeeding year he established himself as a merchant at No. 51 South Wharves, and removed his family from the old homestead, in Union street, to more capacious and comfortable premises, at No. 142 Arch street. He established an extensive correspondence, and enjoyed the advantages of business relations with Baring & Co., of London, Hope & Co., and Insinger & Co., of Amsterdam, and numerous influential merchants in China, India, Surinam, Ceylon, and other Eastern places. His business was chiefly as a shipper and importer, and consequently he became much interested in improvements in marine architecture. He built several fine vessels, which were successful in increasing the commerce of the city and in spreading the fame of American ship builders. In 1810, Mr. Macalester removed his store and counting-house to No. 5 Dock street, and two years later he located himself at No. 66 Dock street, where he remained until, at the age of sixty, he felt himself justified in retiring from active business. During his commercial career, he was for a long time one of the Directors of the Bank of North America. His early religious training led him to connect himself with the Second Presbyterian Church, of this city. He was Treasurer of the Marine Bible Society of Pennsylvania. He was an active promoter of the erection of the Mariners' Church, which was eventually built in Water street, below Walnut, and was for many years under charge of the "sailors' friend," "Sosey Eastburn," as he was affectionately called. Mr. Eastburn was not a regular minister. He was a cabinet-maker by trade, but being a pious, earnest man, his attention was called to the want of spiritual instruction among the seamen transiently in port, and he exerted himself to obtain for them instruction and religious counsel. Failing in obtaining the assistance of the ordained clergy he took upon himself the task of lecturer, with such acceptability to sailors and to citizens, that when the "Mariners' Church" was finished, general opinion declared that it was the right and duty of Joseph Eastburn, the fervent and devoted cabinet-maker, to continue in the position of teacher.

In 1825, the Insurance Company of Pennsylvania was in trouble. It had encountered serious losses, and required energy to stem the tide of disaster. In this emergency, Charles Macalester was called upon to take the helm. So successful was he, that in two years the danger was passed, and the Company was once more in a successful course of business. The danger had been great, the service important, and the gratitude of the stockholders was commensurate with the occasion. In 1827, they presented to their President a service of plate, a gratifying testimonial of their esteem and thanks. He remained President of this Company until his death, which occurred at Willow Grove, Montgomery county, on the twenty-ninth of August, 1832. His body was interred in the burying ground of the Second Presbyterian Church, Arch street, above Fifth.

The family is now represented by Charles Macalester, the eminent banker, of the firm of Gaw, Macalester & Co., a gentleman whose sterling integrity and generous character are proud certificates of the influence of an honorable descent. Another son, Edward Macalester, is, or lately was, a resident of Lexington, Kentucky.

JOSEPH R. EVANS.

It gives us especial pleasure, for several reasons, to open this sketch with a slight memorial of this eminent merchant, who died some years since. His high personal character well befits eulogy, and his generous relations towards those in his employ while engaged in active business, also merit more than passing notice.

Joseph Russell Evans was born on the fourteenth of July, 1783, in the two story stone building, yet standing, situate near the foot of Dock street, some thirty yards west and north of the western terminus of the city tobacco warehouse. He was at an early age placed in the best school of the times, which with a natural intelligence, the teachings of his devoted mother, and subsequently the superintending care of an affectionate aunt, soon developed the path of future usefulness and prosperity to which he was destined. Shortly after leaving school, he entered the counting-house of Nixon & Walker, on Penn street, who at that period were actively engaged in the West India trade. During his apprenticeship, Mr. Evans became an accountant and book-keeper of the first class, quick and correct in calculations, and always prompt to exhibit a balance sheet to his employers. During the latter period of his term of apprenticeship, the late Mr. John Stewart, former President of the Insurance Company of the state of Pennsylvania, was a junior clerk, between whom and Mr. Evans an intimacy and warm friendship continued through life.

Mr. Evans was married in this city, by Mayor Robert Wharton, the twenty-ninth of October, 1805, to Miss Margaret Maris. This lady was born in Springfield, Delaware county, Pennsylvania, in the same year with her husband, (1783.) Her older sister was then the wife of the distinguished merchant John Welsh.   Shortly after Mr. Evans' marriage, he entered into commercial business with his two brothers-in-law, John Welsh and William Maris, under the firm of Welsh, Maris & Evans, at No. 31 South Wharves, the site of the present building immediately adjoining the Smith property, on the north side of Tun alley (not Ton alley, as our present City Fathers have it).   The firm pursued an active and prosperous business in the West India and European trade for some years, when the senior partner, Mr. Welsh, withdrew with an ample competency, and in consequence of impaired health, we believe, removed for a brief period to Charleston, S. C.   This eminent merchant sebsequently returned to this city, resumed his wonted active business life, on his own individual account, which he conducted with untiring energy, skill and prosperity, for many years, in fact until a short time previous to his decease.   Mr. Evans, then the real active partner, associated with Mr. Maris, under the firm of Maris & Evans.   Their correspondents became augmented, consequently the business of the new firm lost none of the vigor of its immediate predecessor.   Mr. Maris having in prospect a new field of operation, in the erection of mills for manufacturing purposes, the firm of Maris & Evans was dissolved.

Mr. Evans purchased of his former partner, Mr. Welsh, the stores and wharf property so long occupied by the several firms, and continued business under his own name, and with his own capital. Gradually, yet cautiously, he extended his correspondence, which at one period embraced several of the West India Islands, London, Liverpool, Dundee, Bordeaux, Rotterdam, St. Petersburg, and most of the ports on our Atlantic coast.   Mr. Evans was really cautious in all his business operations.   After nibbing his quill-pen, in order to test it, his undeviating word was " caution," and caution could be seen written from top to bottom and crosswise on the slips of paper retained on his table for ready calculation.

Early in his individual business career, he had several ships in the London trade; two of which, the Electra and Thames, he had constructed by Philadelphia mechanics.   The late Captain George Robinson, of Southwark, was the successful commander of the Thames.   The New York and London line of packets, formerly under the management of the late John Griswold, now conducted by Captain Morgan, had a warm, zealous and financial friend in

Mr. Evans. He had a special interest in several of these ships, the last of which, the " Margaret Evans," is yet a staunch, sound vessel. The original share of which belonged to the father, and is retained by his son, the present Joseph R. Evans.

Mr. Evans possessed a happy style of mercantile correspondence, clear, explicit and condensed; to the captains in his employ, though the ship might be engaged in a regular trade, it was his custom to deliver written instructions on starting on a voyage, which were regularly recorded in the "Letter Book." So, in his frequent business absence from the city, if only of two or three days' duration, special written directions were left with his chief clerk. Here were caution and command.

He was well posted in *maritime* laws, frequently called upon to pass judgment on general average and partial loss statements; in numerous instances he has also acted as sole arbitrator in matters of difference between mercantile friends. Mr. Evans was a Director in the Philadelphia Bank for upwards of twenty years, and rarely missed a daily visit there, unless absent from the city, until the unfortunate position of the late Bank of the United States, in 1837; which, in the opinion of a majority of the directors of many of the city banks, it was deemed expedient to aid in its resuscitation. In this, Mr. Evans differed in opinion with his colleagues, and temporarily withdrew from the meetings of the Board; notwithstanding, he was returned a member at the ensuing election of the stockholders.

In politics, Mr. Evans voted with the old school Federalists, when, upon a re-organization of parties, he associated with the Democratic party. He took a lively interest in the election of General Jackson, whose administration of the affairs of the government he approved, especially the firmness of the President in arresting the Calhoun-Hamilton South Carolina rebellion, of 1833, and his anti-tariff views. He was often the Democratic candidate either for Select Council, State Senator, or Congress, from the old city proper. Mr. Evans was an active member of the celebrated Free Trade Convention, which assembled in this city in the year 1834, of which Judge Barbour, of Virginia, was President, and the late Condy Raguet, of this city, was Secretary. In the year 1846, Governor Shunk appointed Mr. Evans a member of the Commission, authorized by an act of the Legislature of Pennsylvania, to dispose of the Delaware Division of the State Canals, which, though not then accomplished, has been since happily consummated. Mr. Evans was made Chairman of the Commission.

On the eighth day of September, 1848, Mr. Evans left in the early P. M. train for New York, where he arrived in due time, and proceeded to his usual lodgings, the old City Hotel, on Broadway. While in the office conversing with a friend, the clerk of the establishment registered Mr. Evans' name, who, on inspection, discovered some discrepency in the record, and while in the act of its correction, fell back in the arms of his friend, and died in a few moments, from heart disease. His widow survived him but a few years.

Mr. Evans left one son, the present Joseph R. Evans, and one daughter, the wife of Samuel Welsh, Esq. Also, as legatees under his will, the widow and three daughters of his deceased son, Edward Russell Evans. As an evidence of the caution displayed through life by Mr. Evans, it may be well to note that the only son of the late Edward R. Evans, who had been kindly remembered in the will of his grandfather, died in the month of August, 1848. A few days after, Mr. Evans made a codicil to his will, devising the portion intended for the lad, between the sisters.

In opening this sketch, we alluded to Mr. Evans' noble conduct towards his clerks and employees, and we will be borne out by all who knew him, in eulogizing this admirable trait in his harmonious and well balanced character. In February of the year 1831, Mr. James Stuart came into Mr. Evans' employ as a clerk, when the latter was located at No. 31 South Wharves. Mr. Stuart succeeded in that capacity Mr. C. W. Churchman, who for six years had been Mr. Evans' book-keeper. On leaving Mr. Evans, Mr. Churchman went into the dry goods trade, in Market street, and subsequently, moved into Front street, where, being quite successful, he accumulated a large fortune. But, with many other merchants, he "went down" in a heavy financial crisis, and gave up his accumulated property. In this affliction he had the hearty sympathy of all who knew him, for his character, like that of his early employer, was elevated and generous, and his reputation was as spotless as snow. He is now attempting to retrieve his disaster, and he has the good feeling and assistance of all who respect integrity and high toned honor. Mr. Stuart, however, continued in Mr. Evans' employ for seventeen years, when the latter died, as above stated, and the affairs of the firm were closed. The son of Mr.

Evans then formed a copartnership with Mr. Stuart, which continued for some six years, when the firm dissolved, and both parties retired.

Would that we could record more of such cases of just appreciation of long and true devotion! Such things brighten the pages of history, and elevate mercantile life to noblest point of dignity.

JOHN T. RICKETTS.

SINCE these papers were commenced we have been asked, "What, in a general sense, is meant by a self-made man?" The reply is easy. A man who, without any extraordinary family or pecuniary advantages at the commencement of life, has nevertheless battled earnestly and energetically in the walks of trade, commerce and manufactures, and by indomitable industry and unwavering integrity achieved both character and fortune. The whole story is thus told in a few words: Stephen Girard, the founder of the college that has become one of the leading moral and intellectual ornaments of our city, was a self-made man. He advanced step by step, little by little, and through the magic power of industry and enterprise, he rose from comparative obscurity, and became one of the most eminent bankers and capitalists of modern times. Dollar by dollar he accumulated at first, until, long before his decease, he was the possessor of millions. And yet this extraordinary man, as we are told, at one time peddled oranges through the streets of the city of Brotherly Love. We might refer to another instance, in one of the best and most useful of our living citizens, a native of the interior of Pennsylvania, who commenced his career in a similar manner. But this is no new thing. The builders of cities, the founders of states, the pioneers of civilization, are, in the great majority of cases, self-made men.

It is so ordered, wisely and beneficently, by a superintending Providence. Affluence is in many respects desirable. When properly appreciated and employed it constitutes a blessing not only to the possessor, but to the many who are assisted through his means or are the recipients of his bounty. But when abused or misapplied it is a curse, for it hardens the heart, embitters the feelings, chills the genial sensibilities, and neutralizes the kindly sympathies. This is too generally the case with those who inherit wealth, who have been reared in the lap of luxury, and have never experienced the caprices of fortune or realised the noble compensations of toil. It is, therefore, that a self-made man—one who started from a comparatively humble position, and ascended step by step, day by day, year by year, is better able to understand the trials of others, and to feel for the multitude who have not been successful. He is thus able not only to realise the true uses of affluence, but to remember that he was at one time among the hewers of wood and the drawers of waters.

> "Oh! who can tell how hard it is to climb
> The steep where fame's proud temple shines afar,"

And so with the hill of fortune. Its ascent is a work of infinite difficulty. The struggle and the competition are always keen. Many falter and fail by the wayside. A single blow overwhelms some, while others persevere for years, but succeed at last. And hence it is that more honor and more glory are due to those who, despite the difficulties and dangers, the rugged paths and the many pitfalls, press on, still on, and in the end achieve a triumph. Time, faith and energy are almost invincible, especially when associated with truth and integrity.

The subject of our present notice is John T. Ricketts, and he may be referred to with confidence as a fitting illustration of what is understood by a self-made man. Mr. Ricketts was born at Tuscarora, Loudon Co., Va., October 19, 1805, and commenced his business career in Philadelphia, in 1834, as a manufacturer of ship bread and crackers, in Front street below Race. A that period the ship bread manufactories of the United States were in a primitive and limited condition, as compared with the existing order of things. The consumption by a single establishment of fifty or sixty barrels of flour per day was considered quite an extensive operation; but by the introduction of steam power and machinery this quantity gradually increased, until four or five times the amount could be baked within the same space of time. The factory and warehouse owned and occupied by Mr. Ricketts are models of their kind. We enjoyed the pleasure, a few weeks since of walking through them, and were at once surprised and gratified. The most perfect order exists throughout, and every department has a distinct superintendent with an adequate number of subordinates. The verting it into crackers or bread goes on as regularly as clock-work, and the visitor cannot but experience pleasure at the regularity, system and good management that everywhere prevail. The building is one of the most substantial in the city. It occupies eighty feet on Front street and extends forty feet in depth, to Water street, being four stories high on Front and six on Water street. It is of brick, with extensive and admirably constructed vaults, which are used as storehouses. The machinery is propelled by steam power, an engine having been introduced for the purpose in 1847. This establishment employs from fifty to sixty hands, and the wages per week amount to several hundred dollars. An important feature in the business is exportation, and thus in the year large amounts of ship bread and crackers are sent to the West Indies, South America and the British provinces. In some cases the goods are shipped per order, and in others at the risk of the manufacturer, who thus unites the two occupations of merchant and manufacturer.

The bakery of Mr. Ricketts is capable of converting two hundred barrels of flour into bread per day, and is perhaps the most complete and extensive in the United States. Slowly but surely this work has progressed under the eyes and the mind of the enterprising proprietor, and those with whom he has been associated, until it has become a prominent feature in the industrial establishments of Philadelphia, and an important element in the commercial world.

The fact that we have in the very heart of our city a ship bread bakery that is capable of consuming, in the particular objects to which it is devoted, fifty thousand barrels of flour per annum, is one that speaks volumes upon the subject. The intelligent reader may readily form an idea of the amount of labor in-doors and out that is constantly engaged in the various occupations, the extent of capital that is employed, and the usefulness to the community at large of the individual who controls and directs so laudable an enterprise.

And yet a more modest and unaffected man than John T. Ricketts may not be found in Philadelphia. Of retired habits and unostentatious disposition, he is rarely to be met with out of his counting room or his dwelling, except when called upon to discharge the duties of a member of the Common Council, having last year, without the slightest solicitation on his part, been elected by his fellow citizens as one of the representatives of the Sixth ward.

We have known Mr. Ricketts long and well, and therefore speak of him with warmth and confidence. Integrity is his leading characteristic. He realises, to the fullest extent, the beautiful sentiment of the poet, that "an honest man is the noblest work of God." In all the relations of life he is frank, manly, upright and honorable. Liberal in his views, feelings and opinions, he is tolerant and charitable in relation to the errors and prejudices of others. Although not in the enjoyment of robust health, he is cheerful, nay, even joyous, in his disposition, and is as ready to join in a laugh or to participate in a harmless scene of merriment or festivity as the lightest hearted in the crowd. As a father he is generous and indulgent, yet decided; as a husband he is devoted and affectionate; as a citizen he is patriotic and public spirited; and as a manufacturer and merchant he is at once clear headed, direct, high-minded and honorable. Such, then, is one of the self-made men of Philadelphia. Virginia may well be proud of him as one of her sons, and the city of Brotherly Love may point to him with pride and pleasure as a bright and shining example of the force and beauty of industry, integrity and fair dealing.

Mr. Ricketts died in November last. His remains were interred in the Woodland Cemetary.

WILLIAM CUMMINGS.

SOME of our readers may not be aware that the African trade of Philadelphia is, and has been for a number of years, quite extensive, and that in the person of William Cummings, Esq., our city boasts the oldest merchant in that line of commerce. For over thirty years, Mr. Cummings has been actively engaged in trading to Africa, and he has built up a fine business and accumulated a handsome fortune by his efforts. He has, during that period, also displayed a liberal interest in everything relating to Philadelphia and her trade, while he has been quiet and unobtrusive in a remarkable degree. The African trade flourished 'in the quaint old seaport of Salem, Massachusetts, for several generations, and even yet the ancient town claims a very large share of this kind of commerce, which is destined, when Africa becomes more subject to the developing force of civilization, to grow to an extent we little think of at this period. That mysterious continent abounds in rich natural productions and precious metals, and it may be called the region *par excellence* of animal life, since there are more than twice the number of animals in it according to late explorers, than there are in the other quarters of the globe. Its kingdoms have been great and powerful—Egypt and Carthage, for instance—and in modern times we see Liberia and other colonies striking for commercial and political control of the continent. The trade of Sierra Leone, Liberia, the Ivory Coast, Cape Colony, and the islands along the coast, is large, and is participated in to a very considerable extent by the United States. Of a single article, (Palm oil,) in the year 1856, American importers drew from Africa 1,149,547 gallons, valued at about half a million of dollars, while the trade in ivory and other articles is increasing. Philadelphia's share in the trade is handsomely represented by Mr. Cummings. He is a native of this city, and was born February 6, 1806. He entered into partnership with his uncle, bearing the same name as himself, in 1828, and in 1832, thirty-one years ago, he went into business on his own account, on Delaware avenue, below Pine street. About the same year he embarked in the African trade, which he has prosecuted with such success that he is acknowledged, even by the best known Eastern importers, to be the *oldest established merchant* in this line in the country. This is a distinction he may well be proud of, when it is recollected how many rivals he has had, and what flourishing houses have risen and fallen since 1832. His operations have been conducted on a sound basis throughout his career, and he has built and owned the following vessels:

Schooners—Kathleen and John McCrea.

Brigs—Baron, Stranger, Pennsylvania, Norris Stanley, Delaware, Jos. Cowperthwait, Emily Cummings, Clara, Huntress and Calvert.

Barques—Mary Irvine, Emily, Cora, Linda, Fairmount, A. I. Harvey, Ann Elizabeth and Margaret Hugg.

Ships—Frigate Bird and Wm. Cummings.

Among the merchants of 1832, we notice the names of such men as Thomas P. Cope, Samuel Grant, Dexter Stone, John Welsh, Andrew C. Barclay, Jos. R. Jenks, (who lived until his 94th year,) William S. Smith, Nathan Bunker, Matthew Bevan & Porter, Samuel T. Lewis, Jacob S. Waln, John Siter, John Coulter, John F. Ohl, J. Neuman, Smith, Ridgway & Co., Jonathan Leedom, Timothy Paxton, Lewis Clapier, Lincoln & Ryers, and others. How few of these still live? How few have escaped the financial crisis of the times? How few now continue in active mercantile pursuits? How many have been swept away by the current of adversity? Death has blotted from existence the most of them. How different the rich men of the old time from the opulent men of the present. One would suppose that the attaint on the hands of many of the latter who have attained to sudden affluence, were enough to chasten their haughtiness, and keep their arrogancy within moderate bounds. But, notwithstanding, these abjects carry the marks of their baseness on their brow, and their character is charged with the ill-odor of unfair advantages, artful concealments, plausible misrepresentations, barefaced falsehoods; of injustice, wrong and oppression; they exact obeisance from integrity and virtue, and frown if they refuse to do them honor. They are the dupes of a foolish delusion, for though the needle of the widow remind her of their villainy, and their suffering victims cease not to load them with reproaches, they fancy that they have turned the key upon their crimes. Emboldened by this strange infatuation, these possessors of ill-gotten gain carry their heads high in the presence of honor and purity, and glancing about with eyes of pride from the seat of ther gilded chariots, they would not hesitate to drive over the orphans they have robbed.

The conceit that some persons show, excites our amazement as often as we witness its manifestations. They have no name wherein they may glory; they carry their fortune upon their persons; their wit is small, and all their knowledge is under their tongue, and yet their self-sufficiency is boundless. Beholding their fine forms and remarking their elegant carriage, in the absence of any other claim to notice, failing to discover any ground for their conceit of themselves, we are forced to the conclusion that the looking-glass has turned their head.

Mr. Cummings is not one of this sort. He is remarkably modest, retiring and unassuming. His capital was but small when he embarked on the sea of commerce, and he has worked his way upwards to liberal and liberalizing fortune by steady application to his particular line, and by the manifestation of all those qualities which mark the safe, sure business man. He has been a member of the Episcopal Church almost all his life, and while as rigid in the performance of his duties as a citizen as those of a merchant, he has never mingled in politics, prefering the more useful pursuits of his profession. For a number of years he has served as a bank director, a member of the Board of Trade, of the Corn Exchange, as a manager of an insurance company, and he has also been prominent in other mercantile organizations. As a liberal and public spirited Philadelphian, he stands high, as may be seen from the positions of honor and trust he has held; and time, while it has ripened his judgment, and made his sagacious counsels sought after by business friends and associates, has not altered his quiet demeanor or his carefully formed habits and opinions. He has recently associated with him his son, Norris S. Cummings, a young man of amiable disposition and excellent business qualifications. His undeviating devotion to the African trade, while so many of the business community have been vascillating from one branch to another, fully indicates his turn of mind and comprehensiveness of vision. The details of his operations, the successful voyages of his vessels, the fortunate "hits" of his cargoes each way, would make an interesting chapter of commercial life in Philadelphia, had we leisure to chronicle them. As it is, we leave them to the imagination of the reader, who can fill up the outlines we have sketched, and then affix to the picture the legend "Success."

A. J. DERBYSHIRE.

It is remarkable that many individuals who are pre-eminently successful in the management of private business have, or appear to have, but small capability for public office. Whether the narrow calculations of trade have a tendency to contract certain minds, or absorption in counting-house pursuits, render them timid and diffident, when brought prominently before the community, we are unable to decide; but we know that some of our ablest merchants and manufacturers are extremely loth to accept any position of public trust, requiring them to exercise the voice or pen. This ought not to be the case. Every business man, however eager he may be in search of gain, should remember that he is a citizen, and has duties to discharge beyond those of private concern; that he is interested in the prosperity of all enterprises that will contribute to the wealth and influence of Philadelphia, and that if men of his class keep in the background, either the work will not be done at all, or it will fall into incompetent hands. We know of nothing this metropolis has in more urgent demand, than a body of earnest, practical, well-educated merchants, who will

even condescend to become politicians, if they cannot otherwise
serve the public interest.   Probably there are but few of our business men who think themselves qualified for such a career. We
have seen even a railroad meeting, of great importance to the city,
where not a merchant could be found who would venture to
express his views, and the addresses were delivered by a western
judge and a Harrisburg borer.   The debating school of our present
Board of Trade may prevent the repetition of that humiliating
display; but reference to several bright examples of public-spirited
merchants, will not be without its effect.

In Alexander J. Derbyshire, our city has an illustration of that
enlarged capacity for business which cannot be limited to individual affairs—which can achieve success in the ordinary operations
of trade, and yet rise above them, to push forward works of improvement that will conduce to the general advantage of the community.   We regard him as one of that progressive and vigorous
generation of merchants who are destined to infuse into Philadelphia the true metropolitan spirit.   Let the record of his career
speak for him.

Mr. Derbyshire was born in 1808.   At fifteen years of age
(1824) we find the future merchant an apprentice boy in a flour store
of Timothy Paxson.   But the boy was prompt, intelligent and industrious, and he was soon promoted to the more responsible position of book-keeper.   The business of the concern was favorable
to the acquisition of a thorough knowledge of the trade in flour.
Mr. Derbyshire appears to have improved the opportunities thus
offered; for in 1836, when Paxson retired, a partnership was formed
between the former errand-boy and Mr. Watson Jenks.   This firm
continued the business of the old house, with increasing profit,
until 1846, when Mr. Jenks retired, and Mr. Derbyshire went on
alone, enlarging the business of the concern and increasing his own
reputation for tact and fortunate enterprise.

In January, 1850, Mr. John Derbyshire, cousin of the subject of
this sketch, was associated in the business, and the firm is now
known as A. J. Derbyshire & Co.   The operations of this house
are moderate, but under vigilant and skillful control—its credit
stands as fair as that of any other firm in the same trade.   Mr.
Derbyshire erected and owns the two spacious and imposing warehouses, Nos. 108 and 110 North Delaware avenue.   His parents
were Quakers, and Mr. Derbyshire is of the same persuasion.
This brief chronicle is sufficient to show that Mr. Derbyshire has
attained great success as a merchant, rising by dint of industry,

prudence and intelligence, from a very humble situation to the foremost rank among the men engaged in the same branch of commerce. Another portion of his career is still more worthy of attention and emulation.

As a member of the Board of Trade, Mr. Derbyshire earnestly strove to render that organization practical, efficient and public-spirited in its deliberations. Although a modest and unassuming man, he appreciated the fact that the Board was generally regarded by our citizens and strangers as behind the demands of the times; and he therefore took an active part in the proceedings, as an advocate of various improvements. We are persuaded that it is due to the influence of such progressives as Mr. Derbyshire, that the organization of the Board has been enlarged and improved within the past few years. That body is now in a condition to be of vast service to the city, and if the spirit of old Rip Van Winkle is entirely banished from its deliberations, we may look upon it as an excellent school for young men who are just commencing a mercantile life.

The men who devoted their energies and means to the completion of the Pennsylvania Central Railroad, are entitled to the lasting gratitude of every citizen who has the interest of Philadelphia at heart. That highway has more than realised the promises of its projectors, and yet its future business must inevitably cast the present great transportation into the shade. The construction of that road opened to us the trade of the teeming West, and brought us directly into competition with an arrogant rival, who was accustomed to sneering at our lack of enterprise. A more powerful impetus has not been given to the trade of a city by any improvement since the completion of the Erie Canal. Mr. Derbyshire, Colonel G. C. Childs and others, warmly advocated the construction of the Central Road before the Board of Trade, and were very active in collecting subscriptions for that purpose. Mr. Derbyshire fully comprehended the immense importance of that work. He also gave expression to the general regret that we had so long delayed this magnificent enterprise. The energy and success of this indefatigable merchant's labors recommended him for the position of Director of the Central Railroad, and, accordingly he was selected, and served faithfully and intelligently for two years. Taking abilities and means into consideration, no man did more for the completion and success of that highway to the West, than Mr. Alexander J. Derbyshire.

Mr. Derbyshire also found time to serve his fellow citizens for three years in the City Councils. In that body he was an active and useful member, losing no opportunity of pushing whatever improvements he considered practicable and conducive to the general welfare. Compared with the petty politicians who now occupy the seats in our municipal legislature, Mr. Derbyshire was an invaluable member.

Philanthropic motives induced this active gentleman to accept the position of Secretary of the Humane Society—an organization which accomplished a vast amount of good in its day by saving life and encouraging deeds of genuine heroism. This Society was subsequently merged in the Pennsylvania Hospital, and Mr. Derbyshire is now a Director of that noble institution. The only other position of importance he holds at present is that of Director of the Mine Hill Railroad, a work in which he is deeply interested, and President of the Little Schuylkill Railroad Company.

During the past three years Messrs. Derbyshire & Co. have given much of their attention to the development of the railroad and mining interests of this and other states.

When Mr. Derbyshire commenced his mercantile career the principal firms engaged in the breadstuff trade were Willis & Yardley, P. Hollingsworth, Bunker & Starr, Ridgway & Livezey, Timothy Paxson, Wm. S. Smith & Co., J. Fen Smith & Co. and Thomas Latimer & Co. The two first named in this list failed; Timothy Paxson retired with $80,000; Mr. Bunker left that firm with about $30,000; Mr. Smith, with a competency, and Mr. Ridgway with a fortune estimated at $120,000. Thomas Latimer's estate at his decease was small—only about $10,000. These men, with a single exception, have passed away.

> "All that live must die,
> Passing through nature to eternity."

The subject of this sketch is now about fifty years of age. He is in the prime of life, full of energy, fond of active employment, and has at his command a worldly independence. His career deserves to be studied by all who would be successful in business or useful to their fellow men. In his character are happily blended unflinching purpose, quick intelligence and stern integrity, with mild, genial and winning manners.

ISAAC R. DAVIS.

A PECULIARITY of American business men, which has done more to develop the resources of the country than any other quality, is the adaptability of individuals and communities to changing circumstances, and the ready provision which is made to meet the requirements of the time. The unswerving routine of precedent is not followed in slavish subservience in the United States, if it is apparent that advantage is to be gained by the substitution of new principle for old rules of action. In business here, it may be said, that—

"Each man, in his time, plays many parts."

From merchandize to manufacturing, from manufacturing to farming, from farming to navigation, from the ship to the locomotive engine, and from the railroad to the painter's easel, might be the erratic course of one man in the United States, attracting scarcely any attention among his friends. In noticing the career of Isaac R. Davis, we shall not be called upon to record a wide range of employments to which he was devoted, dissimilar in object. But an experience turned from merchandize to manufacturing, brings him partially within the range of American changeability.

Isaac Roberts Davis was born in the year 1809, in Montgomery county, Pennsylvania, near the estate of Isaac Roberts, in honor of whom he was named. His parents were in moderate circumstances. They had no hereditary estate to offer him when he should become of age, but they secured him the foundation of wealth and honor by obtaining for him a sound education, which he received at Friend's School, Westtown, Chester county. John Cook, a Quaker merchant, whose store was at the northwest corner of Front and Walnut streets, was a friend of the Davis family, and took some interest in young Isaac. The latter was, after leaving school, an intelligent and well behaved boy, and friend Cook addressed himself to the task of finding an opening for him in some reputable mercantile establishment. Henry C. Corbit was in the dry goods business in 1825, and for some time afterwards, at No. 40 South Second street. Mr. Cook procured for Isaac R. Davis a situation in that store. Mr. Corbit shortly afterwards relinquished the dry goods business, and took out license as a wholesale auctioneer, at No. 39 North Front street. Davis went with him, and from selling dry goods by the yard, he became an adept in selling them by the package, to the music of, "going, going, one, two, three—gone." This avocation was, perhaps, not entirely to the taste of young Davis, but he served his apprenticeship faithfully, and was his own master in the year 1830. He was anxious to acquaint himself more thoroughly with the mysteries of the wholesale dry goods trade, and, accordingly, he accepted a position in the importing house of E. & C. G. Fehr & Co., No. 28 South Front street. The Fehrs did a large foreign business, and the opportunities of Davis in this house for becoming thoroughly acquainted with the theory and practice of the wholesale trade, were very important, and they were fully embraced by him. The Fehrs lived at this time at No. 3 Comptroller street, and Davis resided there with them.

In the meanwhile, he continued a favorite with the Corbits, so much so that he succeeded in inducing one of the lovely members of the family to give him her hand and heart, a union which was attended with happiness and prosperity. This connection brought him more closely to his old friend, Henry C. Corbit, and when the firm of Fehr & Co. gave up business, a new partnership, including Henry C. Corbit, Isaac R. Davis, and others, under the firm of Corbit, Davis & Co., was formed about 1838, and located at the southeast corner of Second and Market streets, up stairs. This partnership with one brother-in-law, led him shortly afterward into a new field of action. Jos. Corbit was for some time a member of the firm of Jos. S. Lovering & Co., sugar refiners, at No. 27 Church alley. Mr. Lovering commenced business in a small way, some years before, at No. 101 North Seventh street, but business increasing, he removed to the old sugar house in Church alley, where his means were enlarged by the capital of partners. Mr. Davis left the firm of Corbit, Davis & Co., and became a member of the firm of J. S. Lovering & Co., in 1841. Having already had experience as an auctioneer, and in the wholesale and retail dry goods business, he became interested in one of the largest manufacturing establishments in the city.

Once enlisted in the interests of this firm, the energies of Mr. Davis became also engaged in the subject of manufactures and their encouragement. Up to this time he had been a faithful and close servant of business, paying but little attention to public affairs, other than that regard which in this country is given to them by every intelligent citizen. But his active mind was now directed to the great subject of the manufacturing industry of the country, and the best means of encouraging it. He believed that it was the duty of the government to sustain labor in its endeavors to support itself against foreign competition. As a merchant, his interest might have been in large importations and the widely spread commerce for which free trade sighed. But as a manufacturer, his aims were different. He became a warm advocate of the doctrine of protection. As such, his position as a principal partner in a large manufacturing house naturally placed him in the advance, and although never ranked as a professional politician, he was forced into public notice as an influential friend of the old Whig party. Earnest in his nature, a thorough going and faithful man in all that he undertook, Mr. Davis was soon called upon to take a prominent part in the affairs of the country.

In Philadelphia he was considered a standby in the organization of every meeting, convention or consultation, which might be necessary for the good of the cause. His excellent judgment, judicious tact and experience, were frequently called upon in the party movements of the day. His integrity of character, calm and careful attention to every subject which engaged his attention, recommended him as a person who was to be relied upon on occasions when responsibilities were to be met. And yet, with those qualities which naturally placed him in the line of political preferment, Mr. Davis shrunk from the actual occupation of public office. He assisted in obtaining office for many men, but he could not be induced to give his own service in official station. *That* was a business which he was contented to leave to others, satisfied that his duty was well performed when he lent the influence of his counsels to the choice of good candidates.

In private life Mr. Davis was a warm and useful friend. He was ever ready to bring the benefit of his experience to those who consulted him upon their own affairs, and to add, when necessary, something more than advice. He was liberal and kind, and never hesitated at the proper course when the subject was worthy. He enjoyed a large circle of friends, whose admiration of him was the natural expression of their sentiments towards a worthy and honorable man.

Commencing life without a single dollar, by his talent and industry he amassed in a few years a large fortune. When he beame sufficiently able to enjoy a country life, his mind reverted to the scenes of his childhood in Montgomery county, where he purchased for himself a fine plantation, and established his country seat. At this retreat he died on the fourth of February, 1857, in the forty-eighth year of his age, cut off in the prime of life, at a period when his experience as a merchant and manufacturer was ripened, and when he was in a position to have made the labors and successes of his life more useful to others than he had ever been able to do before.

GEORGE W. CARPENTER.

THE wholesale druggist is a modern associate among merchants. The apothecary, until about the commencement of the present century, was able, out of his small stock, to supply the wants of his neighborhood and of places more distant. The merchant was the importer of large quantities of drugs, among the miscellaneous goods and fancy articles of an unclassified commerce, and the apothecary procured his supplies from the general importer. It was not until after the Revolutionary War that drug merchants in the United States began to create the elements of what is now an extensive business.

The house of the Wetherills was among those in Philadelphia which led off in this trade. The Lehmans gave to the business an important impetus. Caleb North, an early druggist, gave way to Thomas Cave, and Cave & Schaffer for many years were among the principal drug houses of Philadelphia, with A. S. & E. Roberts and others. Among the earliest to engage in the wholesale drug business in this city were the descendants of one of the oldest apothecaries in Philadelphia, the representatives of Christopher Marshall, who, a hundred years ago, kept his apothecary shop in Chestnut street, between Second and Third. It was Christopher Marshall, Jr., a son of the original Christopher, who, during the Revolution, scandalised Friends by taking the patriot side, and was "turned out of meeting" for his unquakerly behavior. It was the same Christopher who, while an active member of the "Committee of Inspection and Safety" of Philadelphia, kept a minute diary of the daily transactions occurring in the city, the historical value of which is recognized by every student of American history as very great. Christopher Marshall was succeeded at the old stand, No. 56 Chestnut street, by Charles Marshall; and a son of the latter, Charles Marshall, Jr., established himself in the wholesale business, at No. 310 Market street, near Eighth, about the year 1814, having removed there from No. 226 Market street.

It was with this Charles Marshall, Jr., at No. 310 Market street, that George W. Carpenter was entered as an assistant, in the year 1820, for the purpose of learning the drug business. He was then eighteen years old, having been born at Germantown, in the county of Philadelphia, on the thirty-first day of July, 1802. He was educated at the old Germantown academy, that venerable establishment which gives the name to "School House Lane," one of the most beautiful of our suburban avenues. At this school he attained the rudiments of a classic and substantial education, which fitted him in after life for the scientific pursuits to which he devoted his spare time.

His salary at Marshall's was small, and he had no hereditary fortune to help him along, but he was prudent and saving, and in a few years had accumulated sufficient to justify him in undertaking business on his own account. He had also laid up for himself a much more valuable capital in a scientific reputation, which, when he entered into trade, brought him at once friends and valuable customers. Shortly after entering the store of Mr. Marshall, he became acquainted with the distinguished naturalist, Thomas Nuttall, who was at that time a resident of Philadelphia. Nuttall was a simple hearted enthusiast, whose devotion to natural science was unconquerable, and whose frank and genial character won for him admiration and esteem. The friendship of such a man naturally developed young Carpenter's taste for natural history, and in a short time his studies were bent in that direction.

While yet an assistant in Marshall's store George W. Carpenter was elected an associate of the Academy of Natural Sciences—an institution of which every American may be proud—an institution which ranks among its members eminent men—an institution which has the most extensive scientific museum in the United States, and in some departments is better stored with rare specimens than any museum in the world. Mr. Carpenter was a regular attendant of this society, and while enlarging the sphere of his knowledge he made many valuable acquaintances. Mineralogy became his favorite study, and he devoted his time to the collection of such specimens as were to be procured within the field of his visits. His cabinet soon became large, and was continually increased by his own acquisitions and by exchanges. Professor Cleveland, in his valuable treatise upon mineralogy, availed himself of the extensive cabinet of Mr. Carpenter, and his descriptions were in many cases relied upon by that eminent philosopher. "Silliman's Journal of Science and Art" was also enriched by Mr. Carpenter's contributions. But mineralogy was with Mr. Carpenter a pastime. In his attention to that science he did not neglect the more important studies connected with his business. It was his duty to understand the qualities and uses of the drugs which he handled daily, and he applied himself so faithfully to the study of pharmacy, that from a student he soon attained to proficiency, which entitled him to the position of a professor. He contributed a number of papers upon various medical subjects to the " American Journal of Medical Sciences," then edited by Dr. Nathaniel Chapman. His first *book*, "Carpenter's Essays on Materia Medica," soon passed to a second edition, and it has since become a text book.

· With these advantages to assist the young shopman, he entered into business for himself with a fair prospect of success. It was in the year 1828 that he opened at No. 301 Market street, next door to the corner of Eighth street, north side, the small drug store in which, with a limited capital, the results of his savings, he launched out upon the sea of business. But, in doing so, he found numerous eager friends. His policy in the management of his concern was the most judicious that could have been adopted to secure success. He resolved to keep the best quality of drugs, and to sell none of an inferior nature. He gave to his business his close personal attention. Knowing that in a country as large as ours, embracing vast districts thinly settled, and affording but small inducements to the physician, there were certain diseases of periodical appearance, which required only the prompt application of simple medicines, he applied himself to the preparation of a set of family medicines for home use, which might be employed in case of emergency, without the necessity of regular prescription. By this means Mr. Carpenter's medicines were introduced throughout the South and West. They were found effectual and reliable, and there were thousands of families who, on the prairies or in the forest, needed no other attendant than the far-distant druggist, whose admirable medicinal preparations were to them as useful as could have been the prescription of a regular doctor difficult to have been made up at the nearest village, many miles away. Carpenter's "Medicine Chest Dispensatory," a popular treatise on the properties of the medicines most commonly used, with a concise description of diseases, and directions for treatment, was intended for the use of parties who could not procure the attendance of physicians, and it has been a most important means of relieving pains and suffering in thousands of cases.

From the moment when George W. Carpenter went into business for himself, in 1828, until the day of his death, his success was extraordinary. Riches flowed in upon him with an undeviating current. In eight years he had accumulated enough, beyond all necessities upon account of his capital, to purchase a farm in the upper part of Germantown, which, under the influence of his taste became one of the most splendid country seats in the United States. The taste and elegance shown in this mansion are too well known to need particular detail. The place was, during Mr. Carpenter's life, open at all times to visitors, and thousands are familiar with it. One of the features of "Phil Ellena," for this was the name given to the place by Mr. Carpenter, in honor of his wife, was a mineralogical cabinet and museum, a choice and valuable collection.

A Germantown boy, it was the pride of Mr. Carpenter to be useful as a Germantown man. He forsaw the splendid future of this quiet village, and put his spare profits into the purchase of Germantown property wherever he could find an eligible investment. The quiet and sleepy burghers, who had not the foresight of Mr. Carpenter, gladly availed themselves of his liberal offers, little dreaming that the prices which he paid would in a few years be increased fifty and a hundred fold. Long before his death, Mr. Carpenter was the owner of over five hundred acres of ground in Germantown, and he bought whenever an opportunity presented itself. The present value of this property, in comparison to its cost, is immense. Before he died, Mr. Carpenter was the owner of over four hundred houses in the city and county of Philadelphia, the income from which was very large, and the expenses heavy; yet with all these immense interests to manage, and the care of his extensive drug business upon his mind, so methodical was he that he rarely allowed a day to pass without having all his affairs thoroughly posted up until the last moment.

Mr. Carpenter was one of best friends that the Philadelphia,

Germantown and Norristown Railroad Company ever had. He went into the management when the Company seemed to be help-lessly bankrupt. With others, he devoted his time to the resuscitation of its credit and the restoration of its reputation. These efforts were so successful that the creditors have all been satisfied, and the stock, which at one time was worth only seventy-five cents per share in the market, is now selling at fifty-nine dollars, and but little for sale at that price.

Mr. Carpenter was a Commissioner to organize the Pennsylvania Central Railroad Co., and for many years a Director. So extensive were his operations, that at one time he was a director in six railroad companies, one bank, one insurance company, and a member of several private societies, beside being the executor and administrator of several estates, with his own immense interests to take care of.

Mr. Carpenter early in life adopted several rules which helped him along in life—some of these we may concisely state thus:

1. To rise early. He was always up between 4 and 5 o'clock in the morning, and did almost a day's work before other people were awake.

2. To employ method and system in everything, whether of study, pleasure or labor.

3. To never undertake any enterprise without being thoroughly prepared for success as well as failure.

4. To purchase for cash, instead of credit, causes the purchaser to be prudent and careful, and not to overload himself with stock, besides being an advantage in the discount for prompt payment.

5. To go into business entirely upon credit is dangerous, and likely to swamp the young beginner.

6. Never sell to a person who purchases entirely on credit. To meet his payments he will, in eight cases out of ten, be compelled to sacrifice goods for which he promised to pay full prices.

Upon these principles, George W. Carpenter acted, and when, on the seventh of June, 1860, he was called upon by death to leave his affairs, we will venture to say his accounts were posted, and that he left to his family a clear record of his worldly career, free from doubt or intricacy.

For many years before his death, Mr. Carpenter was assisted in the drug business by Wm. C. Henszey, a gentleman whose knowledge of the trade was gained in the establishment, and who worthily succeeded to a partnership. Mr. Henszey was brought up in Mr. Carpenter's establishment, and was first employed in 1833. He was admitted as a partner in 1842, and is now the senior member of the firm.

ROBERT WALN.

THE Walns are of an old and well known Pennsylvania family. If there is any merit to be ascribed to the fact that one can trace his ancestry for five or six generations, the Walns may boast of that distinction. But as the Walns are of Quaker stock, and pride of birth is not a vice of Friends, the fact is only worthy of mention as being somewhat notable in a country in which the majority of inhabitants have very confused ideas of the social positions which were held by their grandfathers.

Nicholas Waln, the first of the family that came to America, belonged to an English family of respectability, who resided near Settle, in Yorkshire. As early as 1654 the Walns espoused the doctrines of the Society of Friends. Nicholas was an early companion of William Penn, and when the Quaker founder devised the plan of his colony in the wilds of the West, Nicholas Waln was one of the trusty friends who resolved to seek America with him. He came to Pennsylvania in 1682. Having been a purchaser in England of one thousand acres, he located his ground near Penn's Manor, at Bristol. He was a representative of the county of Bucks in the General Assembly of 1683, a position which he occupied until 1695, when he removed to Philadelphia. Holding other offices of trust and honor, his life was spent usefully until his death, in the year 1721.

A grandson of this Nicholas Waln, was Nicholas Waln, the third son of Nicholas and Mary Waln, who was born at Fair Hill, near Philadelphia, on the nineteenth of September, 1742. His father died in 1750, and he was reared by his mother, formerly Mary Shoemaker, and his uncle, Jacob Shoemaker. He was educated at Friends' school, at Fourth and Chestnut streets, in Philadelphia. On arriving at the proper age he commenced the study of the law, under Joseph Galloway, afterwards notorious for his toryism and treason during the Revolution. Nicholas practiced in the

17

courts of Chester county as early as 1763, and before he was twenty-one years of age. But not satisfied with his acquirements he withdrew from practice, and went to London, where he was entered at the Inner Temple. After a year's study at this fountain of the law he returned to Philadelphia, and practiced for several years. But the law was not to his taste, and it is said that after having gained an important cause for a client, who, according to his judgment, ought to have lost it, he determined to withdraw from a profession which occasionally demands services which his conscience declared to be wrongful. He devoted himself henceforth to the propagation of the principles of his sect, and became an eminent preacher among Friends. He traveled extensively upon religious errands, and preached throughout America and Europe. The career of this good man was closed in 1813, on the twenty-ninth of the ninth month, when he had passed his seventy-first year.

Robert Waln, a great-grandson of the original Nicholas Waln, and a nephew of Nicholas Waln the preacher, was born in Philadelphia, in the year 1765. Being descended from wealthy parents, he might have spent his life in inglorious ease; but his education early taught him that industry was the best safeguard of virtue and happiness. Himself and his brother, Jesse Waln, prefered mercantile pursuits, and they acquired the necessary knowledge of trade in commercial houses of eminent standing. In the year 1785, when Robert Waln was but twenty years old, he was in business for himself in Front street, between Arch and Race; whilst Jesse Waln was similarly employed upon his own account in Vine street, betweeen Second and Third. The brothers were not satisfied with their separate fortunes, and a short time afterward they entered into partnership. In 1791 the firm of Jesse & Robert Waln was located at No. 57 South Wharves.

The commercial prospects of Philadelphia were at this time exceedingly promising, and the foreign trade of the port exceeded that of any other in the United States. Jesse Waln had his residence at No. 183 South Water street, and Robert Waln at No. 46 South Front street. In 1800 Robert Waln lived at No. 136 South Front street, and Jesse at No. 115 South Third street. Jesse and Robert Waln went largely into the shipping business. They commenced with the West India and English trade, but as time passed on, they gradually concentrated their attention upon the East India and China trade. In this traffic, they engaged largely, and at one time were scarcely surpassed by Stephen Girard in the comprehensive character of their commercial enterprises.

In the good old times, when the business of politics was respectable, the efforts of the adherents of the various parties were unlike those of the "leaders" in this unfortunate age. The desire *then* was to get the "best men;" now the effort seems to be to choose the *worst*. The integrity, fine business capacity, and intelligence of Robert Waln, marked him as one who was worthy of the confidence and trust of his fellow citizens. He was elected to the State Legislature for several years, and in 1798 was elected to Congress, as a representative of the city of Philadelphia, a proud distinction at that time. Being a Federalist, Mr. Waln happened, during the contests which marked the latter end of the administration of John Adams, to be on the weak side, but he discharged his duties with fidelity, and gained the respect of his friends and opponents. Leaving Congress at the end of his term, Mr. Waln returned to Philadelphia, to become the honored trustee of many civic interests. He was a member of Councils for many years, and at one time President of the Select Council. He was President of the Chamber of Commerce, of the Mercantile Library Company, and of the Philadelphia Insurance Company; a Director of the Bank of North America, of the Pennsylvania Hospital, and of the Philadelphia Library Company, and a Trustee of the University of Pennsylvania.

During the last war with England, Mr. Waln turned his attention to domestic manufactures. He built a cotton factory upon his property near Trenton, New Jersey. It was, for its time, an extensive establishment. He took, also, a large interest in the development of the iron business, and was a heavy stockholder in the works at Phœnixville, in Pennsylvania. He was a friend and advocate of a protective tariff, and wrote some essays and treatises in reply to the theories of the free-traders.

As a Quaker, Robert Waln maintained the principles of his ancestors. When the Hicks' schism disturbed the peace of the Society, he took strong ground on the Orthodox side, and during the controversy he published "seven letters to Elias Hicks," in which the tenets of the new apostle were warmly attacked.

When, in the year 1836, Robert Waln, then in the seventy-first year of his age, died, he left as an example to his successors, a character, as a merchant, both honorable and useful.

The firm of Jesse & Robert Waln was dissolved some years before the death of Robert, by the demise of the senior partner. The business passed into the hands of Jacob S. Waln, likewise a descendant of the first Nicholas Waln, who was brought up in the counting-house of his relative. Jacob was born in 1776. He was a man of brilliant intellect and thorough education. He was versed in science and law, the latter being with him a favorite study. He served the state and city in their councils, and held many offices of trust, responsibility and honor. He died in the year 1850, after a short illness.

The business of the Walns has descended from Jacob S. Waln to S. Morris Waln & Co.—the firm being composed of S. Morris Waln, Wm H. Pile and C. W. Cushman. They have given up the shipping business, as ship owners. They are importers and commission merchants, and are located at No. 128 South Delaware avenue. The high character of the house established by Jesse and Robert Waln, and continued by Jacob S. Waln, has descended to able and consciencious representatives. S. Morris Waln & Co. are rated among the most influential and successful of the merchants of Philadelphia.

ALEXANDER HENRY.

ALEXANDER HENRY was born in the North of Ireland, in the year 1763. His father was respectable and well established, but his death, when the young Alexander was but two years old, wrought an important change in the circumstances of the family. There were five children who were orphaned by this event, the youngest of whom is the subject of our sketch. An elder brother took charge of the interests of the boy, and brought him up with the intention of giving him an university education, as a means of securing him admission to one of the learned professions. In consequence of this kindness, the boy was enabled to acquire such an advance upon the ordinary studies of youths of his own degree that he experienced the beneficial results throughout his life. The intention of his brother was interfered with, however, by the death of the tutor of Alexander, which incident disarranged the plans which had been determined upon in the family. Alexander, who had now arrived at an age in which he was entitled to have some voice in the settlement of a question of the utmost importance to himself, already felt dissatisfied with the prospects which were before him. His tastes were not such that a professional life seemed to him to be a great object to the accomplishment of which he ought to dedicate his energies. His thoughts inclined to trade, and he fancied that in the life of a merchant he discovered the elements of a congenial occupation, and the certainty of respect, final success and competence. But there was a difficulty in establishing himself in business in the North of Ireland, which resulted from the political condition of the country. The British domination over Ireland was severe, and the encouragement of Irish enterprise was repressed, as much as was possible, by adverse English laws and by hostile English influence. There was no space for an increase of business or for the enlargement of commerce. The local demand for merchandise was circumscribed by the local wants. The population of the North of Ireland, instead of being constantly swelled by new comers and by the natural increase among families, was diminishing by emigration and the want of stimulus to improvement. To an ambitious youth, like Alexander Henry, home, with all its familiar attractions, was not the place for enterprise or success in business, and, therefore, as thousands of his countrymen have since done, he turned his hopes to America. His mother could only give him an outfit and her blessing. A brother resolved to try his fortune with him; but, after having made every preparation, his resolution faltered, and he discovered that there was a tie at home which he could not break. The "girl" whom he would have "left behind him," he could not leave. Love proved stronger than the hope of success abroad, and the young man relinquished the adventure and allowed his brother to go alone, whilst he solemnized at the altar the vows which were to make him happy.

In the year 1783 Alexander Henry left Ireland, to seek the land of promise. In comparison to the style in which thousands of his countrymen have since sought the friendly asylum of the United States, he came in comfort and endowed with importance. He was a cabin passenger, and what was better, the consignee of a stock of dry goods—a matter which gave him position and importance on board of the ship, and was a valuable means of introduction to strangers when he reached his destination. He arrived at Philadelphia, and having disposed of the goods under his charge sought employment. He had with him valuable letters of introdection, and these procured for him a small clerkship in a mercantile house, at an annual salary of $250. This trifling sum was but the beginning. In a short time it was wonderfully increased in amount. The young Irishman applied himself to his business with a diligence, ready tact and success which were surprising. He soon succeeded in convincing his employer that they had taken in an assistant of much more than ordinary capacity. They found employment for his talents in a more responsible sphere than a clerkship, and in a short time a special branch of the busines was established, of which Alexander Henry was made the superintendent, at a salary of $1,300 per annum. In this position he was equally fortunate, not only gaining the good-will of his employers, but laying up such portions of his earnings that he soon began to consider what he should do with his capital. He felt justified in undertaking to go into business upon his own account, and believed that he could command sufficient confidence among the merchants of the North of Ireland to render the commencement of a commission business a prudent undertaking. He accordingly addressed his friends in England and Ireland, soliciting consignments, and was soon honored by gratifying proofs of the confidence which was felt in his integrity. Invoices rolled in, and in a short time he found himself at the head of a successful business. In the year 1790 he was established at No. 17 South Second street; but his consignments increasing, he removed to a more successful locality for the wholesale trade. He rented the store No. 42 South Front street, and removed there about the year 1792. In 1793 he increased his facilities by entering into partnership with Mr. James Boggs. The firm of Henry & Boggs continued at No. 42 South Front street until the year 1800. The store was then removed to No. 225 Market street, where, in a short time, the parties dissolved their connection. Mr. Henry remained at No. 225, where he had also his residence. Mr. Boggs entered into a new firm, Boggs & Davidson, which was established at No. 229 Market street, next door but one to the old store. The situation was between Sixth and Seventh streets, considerably West for those times, but a popular place of business in consequence of its proximity to the headquarters of the Western trade, which was then chiefly performed by wagons.

In 1805, Mr. Henry removed to No. 192 Market street, between Fifth and Sixth, and occupied the house next to that which had been the residence of General Washington, whilst he held the office of

President of the United States. The property was spacious and comfortable. It extended through to Minor street, upon which avenue, at No 25, Mr. Henry afterwards established his counting-house. After seventeen years faithful application, in which his integrity and prudence had been most successfully applied to the management of his commision business, as well as to the direction of his own adventures in the importation of British and India goods, Mr. Henry found himself, in 1807, perfectly independent, and justified by his good fortune in retiring from trade, and devoting the remainder of his life to those pursuits which were congenial to his tastes. He accordingly resolved to relinquish active participation in business.

He had, while yet an active merchant, sent to Ireland for his nephew, Alexander Henry, Jr. The habits of the youth were excellent. He proved himself to be possessed of admirable commercial qualities, and so won upon the confidence of his uncle, that the latter determined to place him upon the foundation which he had already securely built. Alexander Henry, Jr. & Co., succeeded to the business at No. 192 Market street, whilst the original of the name confined his attention at his counting-house, No. 25 Minor street, to the winding up of his affairs. A few special matters of new business occupied his attention between 1807 and 1818; but in the latter year he addressed a circular to all his correspondents, apprising them of his determination to relinquish an active participation in commercial affairs. This resolution he was compelled to partially relinquish by subsequent events. Alexander Henry, Jr., was sent to England, where there was an opportunity for extensive mercantile operations. His uncle freely supplied him with capital, and as a result, the Manchester house of Alexander Henry is now one of the most extensive and influential in England. It was, therefore, necessary for the subject of our sketch to partially resume business as a matter of prudence, and as a correspondent and agent of his nephew, and also to furnish the ready means of establishing in life his own son, John S. Henry, who afterwards took in hand the business at No. 192 Market street.

Having by early success achieved for himself a handsome fortune, the great pleasure of Alexander Henry, for nearly thirty years of his life, was to dispose of his surplus in such a manner as to render it useful to others. He was a large hearted, generous man. He had a liberal disposition and a kind heart, and never was deaf to the call of affliction. He was a friend and assistant to the needy and the distressed. His ear was ever open to the narratives of the needy, and his hand was ever ready to solace their afflictions. He used his opulence with a due regard to the best interests of those who applied to him. The merchant struggling against bankruptcy, to whom a present loan might be the means of preserving his mercantile honor, found in Alexander Henry a ready friend, who was ever willing to assist those who deserved it. The widow reduced to despair, the young clerk whose hopes of meeting with employment were unsuccessful, found a true friend and counsellor in Alexander Henry. His private benefactions are known to have been extensive. In generosity and affability he had few equals. No one, however humble his situation, applied to him without receiving from his words and manner the comfort and satisfaction which ever must flow from the slightest intercourse with the Christian gentleman.

Mr. Henry was distinguished also in what we may call "public charities," those benevolent efforts which call for open assistance, and which are aided at all times by the examples which individuals afford to each other. His name is to be found upon almost every subscription for a worthy object which was originated during the latter part of his life. He was always expected to subscribe to every project, moral, religious or benevolent, which called for assistance from citizens, and he never refused to give aid to a worthy object. He was one of the founders, in 1817, of the "Philadelphia Sunday and Adult School Union," over which he was President until 1824. In the latter year the society was merged into the "American Sunday-School Union."

Mr. Henry was elected the President of the latter, and held that office uninterruptedly until his death. He was also the President of "The Board of Education of the Presbyterian Church," President of "The House of Refuge," and President of "The Magdalen Society," beside being a manager of many other benevolent, religious and literary institutions.

He died at his house, No. 254 Arch street, on the thirteenth of August, 1847, leaving behind him a spotless reputation, and causing that sincere regret which pervades every community upon the demise of an unselfish man.

Mr. Henry married about the time that he entered into business. His son, Thomas Charlton Henry, D. D., was born in September, 1790, and accomplished his theological studies at Princeton College.

He became the pastor of the Second Presbyterian Church, in Charleston, S. C., and died there in 1827. He wrote "Letters to an Anxious Inquirer," and an "Inquiry into the Consistency of Popular Amusements with a Profession of Christianity." He was an effective and brilliant preacher. A daughter of Alexander Henry married Silas E. Weir, auctioneer and commission merchant. After the death of the latter, Mrs. Weir gave her hand to the Rev. John Chambers, pastor of the Independent Presbyterian Church in this city. She died some months ago. The male branch of the family is worthily represented by Alexander Henry, our present Mayor, who is a son of John S. Henry, and has proved himself by his integrity of character and industrious attention to the duties of his position, to be a model magistrate, and worthy of the position of chief officer of the great city; and another son, T. Charlton Henry, wool merchant, No. 10 South Front street, is an upright, unostentatious and estimable gentleman.

JOHN PRICE WETHERILL.

HEREDITARY succession in business pursuits is not in this country, as in Europe, almost a matter of course. The son of the laborer may become a lawyer, doctor, or preacher; and the sons of the lawyer, doctor or preacher may turn out to be merchants, surveyors, or sailors. In Europe the father hands down to the son the shop, the warehouse, or the factory. Generation after generation follow the same business with a fidelity to caste only to be excelled by the Hindoo. In this country one son may succeed to the business of his father, but the chances are even that he will abandon it, and before his death try something else.

The Wetherill family, for four generations, have been manufacturers and venders of drugs and chemicals. Accident threw them into this business, but choice has confirmed them in it. Samuel Wetherill, the grandfather of John Price Wetherill, was the son of Christopher Wetherill, who settled in New Jersey as early as the year 1682, near the town of Burlington, where he gave to Friends the ground upon which their meeting-house is built. Samuel Wetherill, his son, was born near Burlington, in April, 1736, but he came to Philadelphia at an early age. His occupation was a carpenter, an employment which he fo'lowed until the rising disputes with Great Britain turned his attention to new pursuits. At the breaking out of the Revolutionary War, Samuel Wetherill, the carpenter, took a strong interest on the patriot side; an interest which led him to such length that the Orthodox Quakers, who, in addition to their dislike of wars and fighting, were intensely toryish in their sympathies, disowned him. Samuel Wetherill was a shrewd, practical man, and he early foresaw that the great want of America was independence of England in the matter of supplies derived from manufactures. He was one of the promoters and managers of "the United Company of Philadelphia, for the Establishment of American Manufactures," which was formed in the year 1775. This association did much good, but Wetherill added to his weight and assistance as a member thereof, his personal assistance in the cause. He embarked his whole soul in the business. He set up at his dwelling-house in South alley, between Fifth and Sixth streets, which was on the lot of ground extending from Market to Arch street, once called Hudson's square, a manufactory of jeans, fustians, everlastings and coatings. In order to prepare these properly, it was necessary that they should be dyed. There were no dyers in Philadelphia at that time equal to the work, and as a matter of necessity, Samuel Wetherill was compelled to undertake this branch of the business. Furthermore, the proper dyestuffs were scarce, and to carry out his plan, the carpenter turned weaver, was compelled to turn chemist, in order to prepare the necessary coloring stuffs and dyes to finish them. This circumstance no doubt explains the reason why Samuel Wetherill abandoned carpentering, and weaving, for the manufacture of chemicals, and it shows why the family are manufacturers of drugs and chemicals to this day. Wetherill was one of the few Quakers who were Whigs, and he did not scruple about entering into a contract with Congress to furnish cloth for the uniforms of the patriot troops. This was an unpardonable offence in tory eyes, and for the violation of rule, Samuel Wetherill, with other "fighting Quakers," was deprived of his "birthright." These disowned men afterwards petitioned the Legislature for relief, a consequence of which was the determination to build a meeting-house for themselves, and the citizens of Philadelphia furnished them with funds to purchase the lot at the southwest corner of Fifth and Arch streets, upon which was erected the Free Quaker Meeting House.

A grant of the lot on the east side of Fifth street, below Prune, for a burial ground, was also made by the State, and for many years the Free Quaker Society, composed of such men as Samuel Wetherill, Colonel Timothy Matlack and others, who had stood up for their country in preference to their sect, worshipped there. Samuel Wetherill became one of the preachers. In civil life he was a Vice-President of the Yellow Fever Committee of 1793, a member of City Councils, and a member of the Watering Committee. He died in the year 1816.

His son, Samuel Wetherill, Jr., was the active man of the concern, and assisted his father in all business matters. The enforced experience which was pressed upon them during the revolution, concentrated their attention upon the manufacture and sale of chemicals, and they went into the drug business. In 1785 Samuel Wetherill & Son were located in Front street above Arch. Here, for many years, "Wetherill's drug store" was an old landmark, and the place at which sons and grandsons were brought up to the business. The Wetherill's were the pioneers in the manufacture of white lead. They established it before the year 1790. They erected extensive white lead works near Twelfth and Cherry streets, which were burnt down in 1813, but afterwards rebuilt.

John Price Wetherill was a grandson of Samuel Wetherill, and son of Samuel Wetherill, Jr. He was born in Philadelphia, on the seventeenth of October, 1794. He was, at an early age, an enthusiastic student, and gave to chemistry all the powers of his mind. He became a member of the Academy of Natural Sciences in 1817, and was its Vice-President for many years. In 1827 he became a member of the American Philosophical Society. With other learned and scientific societies he had an extensive membership. He was elected a member of the Geological Society in 1832. In 1837 he was chosen an honorary member of the Boston Society of Natural History. In 1844 he was elected a member of the Mineralogical Society of St. Petersburg. In 1848 he was elected a member of the American Society for the Advancement of Science, and in 1848 he was elected a member of the New Jersey Society of Natural History. Inheriting the tastes of the "Fighting Quakers," John Price Wetherill was also a military man. He was the Captain of the Second City Troup for several years, and the title by which he was generally known, "Colonel John Price Wetherill," was legitimately obtained.

Whilst, however, devoting his time to scientific affairs, rendering himself a superior chemist, and maintaining the supremacy in the drug business, which the Wetherills had kept up since the Revolution, it was as a public man that John Price Wetherill was best known to his fellow-citizens. He was elected to the Common Council of Philadelphia in 1829, being the third Wetherill thus honored. In 1832 he was made a member of Select Council, in which body he served until his death, a period of nearly twenty-four years. In that position he exercised more influence than any of his contemporaries. A firm Whig, and a devoted friend of Henry Clay. His uncompromising fidelity to his party gave him an influence which his strong will, activity of mind, and indomitable resolution enabled him to maintain. He was in his purposes, as in his personal appearance, opposed to shame. He disdained ceremony and hollow form, and was devoted to simplicity and substance. He was uncommonly industrious, resolute and persevering. What he took hold of he held on to, and never relaxed his grasp until his purpose was accomplished. There was in his character a feature of remarkable energy and determination. Once he assumed a position he was unbending and stern; neither argument, opposition nor ridicule could move him. He rarely abandoned a position, but fought on until the last. In his public career he made some mistakes. As Chairman of the Watering Committee, before consolidation, his opposition to the just claims of Spring Garden and Kensington, that they should be allowed the use of the Schuylkill water at the same rate as city consumers, led to the building of opposition works in these districts, and produced a decision from the Supreme Court which nullified the monopoly of the water for which the city had paid dearly. This was a misfortune it was thought at the time. But the consolidation of the city and districts, the actual necessity that the Spring Garden works have since proved themselves to be, have long since obliterated all feeling upon the subject. In the course taken by Mr. Wetherill he was undoubtedly honest, but in error. Time has long since obliterated all feeling in consequence of the error.

John Price Wetherill died in July, 1853, after a short illness, contracted whilst acting as a member of the committee to receive President Franklin Pierce on his visit to Philadelphia.

THOMAS SPARKS.

THE word "plumber," in these modern times, conveys to the mind of our people ideas essentially different from those which would have attached to it seventy-eight years ago, when Thomas Sparks was born. A plumber, as we understand it, is a worker in lead, but in a very circumscribed degree. His business is almost entirely confined to the fixing up of apparatus connected with hydrants and water pipes, to which he has latterly joined the iron and brass work connected with the introduction of gas into dwel- 'lings and houses. In the year 1785, when Thomas Sparks saw the light in the city of Philadelphia, a "plumber" was a maker of leaden vessels. The arms of his trade, derived from the venerable Plumbers Company of London, were a mallet, sable and two plum- mets azure, with two soldering irons between a cutting knife and a shave hook, with the motto, "In God is all our hope."

In the year 1797 there could not have been more than two or three plumbers in Philadelphia. They made plates, waiters, mugs and flagons, occasionally a leaden coffin, as the last resting place of some member of a wealthy family, and in addition the leaden work for ships and vessels, mercantile and naval.

Of these plumbers, one of the busiest was John Cousland, who, in the year we have named, lived in South or Cedar street, between Front and Second. The introduction of the Schuylkill water into Philadelphia, in 1799, gave to the plumbing business a great im- petus, and Cousland moved, in 1801, to Farmer's Row, which run east from Dock street, below Second, in the exact position now occupied by Godley's Row, upon Granite street. About the same time there was another plumber in the city, John Bishop, who lived at No. 194 Pine street. These gentlemen formed a partner- ship about the year 1803. With this firm Thomas Sparks became an apprentice, probably as soon as it was established, as he was then seventeen years old. He was an earnest and faithful young man, and served Cousland & Bishop so well that they took him into partnership the day after he had arrived at age. The firm had their principal establishment at No. 49 South Wharves, and it is probable that the admission of Thomas Sparks into the firm was due to the fact that they determined to add the manufacture of shot to their business.

On the fourth of July, 1808, the corner-stone of the Southwark shot tower, in John street, between Front and Second, was laid by the firm of Cousland, Bishop & Sparks, and the building was pressed forward rapidly to completion. Thomas Sparks paid particular attention to this branch of the business, and in a short time the patent shot of the firm became celebrated throughout the country. So long as this article was used by sportsmen and hunters, there seemed to be no difficulty about the propriety of the manufacture in the firm. But when the war of 1812 broke out, the firm then being Bishop & Sparks, the senior partner, who was a consistent member of the Society of Friends, felt conscientious scruples as to the rightfulness of continuing a manufacture which the United States now demanded should be turned to the production of munitions of war. John Bishop, therefore, withdrew from the firm, and retired from business. He still lives a quiet and peaceful life in Burlington county, N. J., having reached his eighty-eighth year.

Thomas Sparks, therefore, continued the business for several years alone. In 1818 he took into partnership his brother, Richard Sparks, and the firm continued at No. 49 South Wharves, as Thomas and Richard Sparks, the shot tower operations being in full play. It was necessary that they should reside near the tower, and accordingly Thomas had his house at No. 476 South Front street, and Richard at No. 478. This partnership did not last very long. Richard Sparks fell a victim to the yellow fever in the year 1821, and for many years Thomas Sparks continued at No. 49 South Wharves, and at the shot tower, without a partner. In the year 1838 he took in with him his nephew, Thomas Sparks, Jr., a son of Richard. The business was then conducted under the firm of Thomas & Thomas Sparks, Jr., at the old stand, which from No. 49 South Wharves had become No. 49 South Delaware avenue.

During his active and useful life Thomas Sparks held some offices of public trust. He was a commissioner of the district of South-wark for many years—a firm Democrat, but at the same time an honest and independent one. He always supported the Democratic ticket when the ticket contained the names of worthy men; but he would not vote for a bad man merely because he had been nominated by a party convention. In this integrity of principle Mr. Sparks followed a line of conduct which should be a rule of action with all good men. He was one of the commissioners appointed by the commonwealth of Pennsylvania to superintend the erection of the Eastern Penitentiary, in connection with\Robert Vaux, John Bacon and other eminent citizens, and was President of the Board. He was a director of various railroad and insurance companies, and for many years the President of the old fashioned, reliable and admirably managed institution, the Southwark Bank. The integrity and prudence which characterized that bank in the time when Thomas Sparks presided at the directors' board, have descended as legacies to the present officers, and are faithfully followed and remembered.

On the first of February, 1854, Mr. Sparks relinquished active business—a preparation, as it seemed, for his final departure from this world of care. He died May 15, 1855, at his residence, No. 278 South Third street, above Spruce, universally regretted as a representative of the honor and good character which have prevailed among the manufacturers of Philadelphia, and given them a reputation throughout the country. He had never been married, and his large fortune, the result of honest industry—for he was a self-made man—was mainly bequeathed to his two sisters, (now Mrs. H. W. Flickwir and Mrs. W. C. Donaldson,) and other relatives, and to his nephew and former partner.

Thomas Sparks, Jr., who succeeded his uncle at No. 49 South Delaware avenue, was born in the year 1817, at his father's resi- -dence, South Front street. At the age of sixteen years he was taken into the store of his uncle, and instructed in the details of the business which his father and uncle had established. The latter was perfectly willing to put the young man in the place of his father when he reached the proper age, and upon his attaining his majority he was accordingly taken into the firm. Since he bought his uncle out, in 1854, he has conducted the large operations of the business with care and integrity. He has been identified with many public enterprises. He is Vice-President of the Southwark Bank, and is one of its largest stockholders. He is Treasurer of the Pennsylvania Salt Company, in which he has taken a lively interest for many years. He has been a director of insurance companies of substance and success. He was one of the projectors of the Philadelphia and Darby Passenger Railway Company, a very useful improvement.

As a liberal citizen no better man can be found than Thomas Sparks, Jr. For objects of charity and improvement he gives not only hundreds, but thousands of dollars. He has never withheld assistance from any object which has been worthy of care and encouragement. Since the outbreak of the rebellion no one has been more hearty and enthusiastic in support of the government. He has shown this not merely by words, but by deeds. He has given freely to every plan of benevolence designed for the comfort and assistance of our suffering soldiers. He has been ready to aid in fitting out troops, and has given enough for this single purpose to assist very materially toward equiping a regiment. Philadelphia has many such patriots, but among them few can excel in devoted loyalty, readiness, and free and generous contributions, Thomas Sparks, Jr.

MATTHEW CAREY.

As THESE sketches are devoted to "the merchants and manufacturers of Philadelphia," we had some hesitation as to whether our present subject was strictly within the limit. But when we consider that a printer is, in truth, a manufacturer of books and newspapers, and that a bookseller, who buys and sells books, is as much a merchant as the man who buys and sells dry goods, or any other material, our scruples are relieved. Matthew Carey was a manufacturer of books, in the most literal sense of the word, for he not only wrote extensively himself, but he printed and sold what others had written; so that his case fully satisfies the most rigid requirements of our readers, if any of them should be inclined to hold us to a strict accountability. In presenting the claims of his career to attention and respect, we are performing a task which is pleasant, and which we trust will be profitable to our readers.

Matthew Carey was born in the city of Dublin, on the twentyeighth of January, 1760. His father had been an army contractor, and had in that capacity amassed considerable wealth. He was enabled to give to each of his five sons a liberal education, which not only comprised the useful English branches, but embraced French and Latin. At the age of fifteen the father of Matthew Carey permitted him to make a choice of his future employment, out of twenty-five trades. He selected the profession of a printer, with which, at that time, was associated, by those who could command the capital, the vocation of the bookseller. This union now combines in the book publisher, who is not a general printer, but prepares and sells those works in which he has a special interest. The father of Matthew did not particularly admire the selection of his son, and opposed it as strongly as he was able without using coercion. But young Carey was firm, and his parent finding remonstrance useless, withdrew his opposition. The boy was placed in the office of an eminent Dublin printer, where he assiduously devoted his time to the acquirement of his profession, and was noted as a diligent and promising youth. Being of a literary turn of mind he attempted authorship at the early age of seventeen years, in a treatise entitled "An Essay upon Dueling," which was published in the Hibernian Journal. This was followed, in 1779, by a pamphlet upon the necessity of repealing the penal code against the Roman Catholics. The advertisement announcing this treatise was "spicy and sensational," and it occasioned much alarm. The Irish Parliament, then in session, denounced the intended publication, and offered a reward for the apprehension of the author. Mr. Carey's father sent him to Paris, to escape a prosecution, and whilst there he made the acquaintance of Franklin and Lafayette. Returning to Ireland after the excitement in relation to the Roman Catholic pamphlet had subsided, Mr. Carey established, in 1783, the Volunteer Journal, devoted to Irish rights and Irish interests. In this paper he was boldly fearless, and the publication soon attracted the attention of the British government. An article, published April 5, 1784, brought down upon the publisher the indignation of the Irish government. Matthew Carey was arrested and brought before the Parliament at Dublin, where he was subjected to examination. He refused to answer some of the interrogatories propounded to him, and for his obstinacy was imprisoned until May, 1784, when, Parliament having adjourned, he was liberated. Being still subject to prosecution for libel, his friends advised his withdrawal from the country. His thoughts and hopes directed him to the New World, and in accordance with his resolution he left Ireland, September 7, 1784, on board the ship America, Captain Keiler, bound for Philadelphia.

At this port he arrived November 1, 1784, with very little means, and basing his hopes of support upon remittances expected from Dublin, the proceeds of the sale of the Volunteer establishment. At that time the Marquis de Lafayette was in Philadelphia, and hearing of Mr. Carey's arrival he sent for him. Inquiry was made of the young Irishman concerning his prospects, and he frankly informed the General that upon receiving funds he intended to establish a newspaper. Lafayette interested himself in his behalf with the leading men of Philadelphia, and what was more to the purpose, sent him next day four hundred dollars. Carey had not solicited nor expected a loan, and he was profoundly impressed with this generous act. Upon his offer to secure repayment, Lafayette intimated that he could best do so by extending assistance thereafter, when in his power, to others in distress and upon the same terms—thus making this loan an instrument of good to many, inasmuch as the only requirement was that they, when in affluence, should extend their assistance to others. Mr. Carey solemnly fulfilled this trust in after years, and he took special delight in seeking out and relieving Frenchmen in distress. Besides this, he afterwards paid Lafayette in full.

With the small capital thus strangely acquired Matthew Carey & Co. established the Pennsylvania Herald, the first number of which was published January 25, 1785, in Front street, between Market and Chestnut. In this paper he introduced the then novel feature of publishing reports of the debates in the House of Assembly—a circumstance which secured to the journal immediate attention and assisted the circulation. The Herald did not last very long; but during its continuance Mr. Carey managed to get into a controversy with Colonel Eleazer Oswold, of the Independent Gazateer, which led to a duel, in which Carey was wounded so severely that he was confined to his house in consequence for sixteen months. In the meanwhile he was in partnership with one Stewart, as Carey, Stewart & Co., printers, at No. 22 North Front street. Upon his recovery he joined with several persons in the establishment of the Columbian Magazine, an illustrated serial, which in excellence was ahead of all the cis-Atlantic periodicals of the day. But the expenses of this work were heavy, and the profits were to be shared among too many persons. This fact led Carey to withdraw from the concern, and he established, upon his own account, Carey's American Museum, a periodical which accorded with the tastes of the public at that time, and which even yet is of considerable value to historical students. The American Museum was published for six years. At the end of that time, and in the year 1793, Mr. Carey relinquished the publication, and established himself at No. 118 Market street, as a " printer, bookseller and stationer."

During the fever of 1793 Mr. Carey was a member of the Committee on Health, and history is indebted to him for a clear and interesting account of the appearance and progress of the epidemic in that year.

Cobbett made Carey one of the subjects of his unsparing attacks, and the latter fought the testy Englishman with gallantry. He retorted upon him a satyrical effusion, "The Porcupined, a Hudibrastic Poem," the novelty of which was that the greater part of the strong language which it contained was Cobbett's own, quoted from his attacks upon others, and now turned upon himself. Carey was the promoter of a plan for the establishment of a "Sunday School Society in 1796, an institution of which Bishop White was elected President He brought out, in 1802, a quarto edition of the Bible, the type of which, as stereotyping had not yet become common, was kept standing for a long time to supply the demands for new editions. In 1801 Mr. Carey wrote several essays upon the propriety of uniting the booksellers and printers of the United States in measures necessary for the preservation of their interests, and in imitation of the German book fairs. The first meeting was held in the city of New York, and an association was established, which was kept up four or five years, during which time it exercised a very beneficial effect upon the trade. In 1803 Mr. Carey removed his shop and printing office, from No. 118 to 122 Market street, where he remained for ten years. In the meanwhile his active pen and voice were busy in discussing and suggesting measures of public benefit. He was one of the first persons in the United States to call attention to the inequalities in taxation, by which real estate was compelled to bear nearly the whole burden, whilst personal property escaped contribution. In the discussions which took place in the United States upon the policy of rechartering the first Bank of the United States, Mr. Carey bore an active part in writing pamphlets and communications for newspapers. He favored a recharter.

During the war with Great Britain, which commenced in 1812, Mr. Carey was impressed with feelings that the warm partisan discussion of the friends and enemies of the war were injurious to the best interests of the country. He therefore projected his most successful book, "The Olive Branch, or Faults on Both Sides." It was a calm and impartial review of the follies and errors of both parties, so clearly stated that conviction followed the appeal to the common sense of his countrymen. This volume had an extraordinary circulation. It passed through ten editions, and besides the

Philadelphia editions, it was reprinted at Boston, Middlebury, Vermont, and Winchester, Virginia. It was an important and useful work. This was followed, in 1818, by "Vindicæ Hibernicæ," which was devoted to a vindication of the people of Ireland from the slanders of English writers of what is called "history."

In 1819 Mr. Carey came out as a pamphleteer upon the question of the protection of American industry. He took strong ground in favor of the system, and wrote voluminously upon it. Between 1819 and 1833 he wrote and published no less than fifty-nine different pamphlets upon this subject, numbering in the aggregate two thousand three hundred and twenty-two pages. His industry was immense, and his influence wide-spread and respected. In 1832 he again came before his countrymen in opposition to the nullification doctrine set up by the state of South Carolina. He was an able opponent of the detestable theme of state rights, which of late years have been used to inflame the minds of the people of the South, and to bring the conspiracy of 1837 to a head in 1861.

Mr. Carey was indefatigable in his literary pursuits. He undoubtedly wrote more than any man of his day. He was constantly at work at some political, economical or patriotic subject, and he never allowed his faculties to rust in idleness.

In 1814 his shop and printing office were removed from 122 Market street to No. 121 Chestnut street, on the north side. In a short time the store at No. 124, on the south side, was also occupied by him. In 1818 he took his son, Henry C. Carey, into partnership with him, and No. 126, at the southeast corner of Fourth and Chesnut, was added to No. 124. Shortly after this time Mr. Carey retired from business, which devolved upon his two sons. Henry C. Carey entered into partnership with Isaac Lea about the year 1821. Carey & Lea afterwards confined their attention specially to the publication and circulation of their own publications. Edward L. Carey, another son of Matthew Carey, succeeded to the general bookselling business at the corner of Fourth and Chestnut streets, and he took into partnership with him Abram Hart. Carey & Lea occupied the lower part of the building on Fourth street. E. L. Carey and A. Hart did a large business as publishers and booksellers. The death of Mr. Carey left Mr. Hart sole proprietor of the trade. He had been lucky and successful, and gave up the establishment to Mr. Parry. The firm of Parry & McMillan was not successful, and was, after a few years, dissolved, and thus ended the valuable bookselling business which Matthew Carey nursed by his care and industry into a valuable trade.

Mr. Carey died September 16, 1839, in the eightieth year of his age. His death was mourned as a public calamity. He was a faithful citizen, and from his career is to be deduced the great lesson that industry and integrity are the safeguards of fortune and honor.

DAVID FREED.

OF the crowd of hopeful lads who annually find their way from their rural homes into the thronged and busy metropolis, how many discover that they have entered upon a race in which the chances of their ultimate defeat are as ten to one. If they happen to be endowed with a courage not easily daunted, uncommon intelligence and facility in winning influential friends, they may succeed, even if they are without pecuniary capital. But the majority soon become sick of the fierce rivalry and constant demand upon their energies, and yearn for the quiet, steady pursuits of the farm, where they are at least certain of food, clothing and shelter, as the reward of physical and by no means anxious toil. We never see one of these young adventurers in the streets of our city without wondering what sort of fancies have lured him from his home, and speculating upon the career that is before him. Perhaps, at the old homestead, he has grown weary of the monotonous and unexciting labor, though surrounded with every comfort, and has dreamed of becoming one of those great merchants whose names are weighty in the mart, and who reside in princely mansions. But he knows nothing of the thorny paths these men have struggled over, and the wear and tear of body and brain they have experienced upon the road to fortune. Nor has he heard of the thousands who, in attempting to overcome the same difficulties, have fallen by the way. Only a sad and bitter trial of the reality of commercial life in a large city can teach these country boys the fearful task that is before them, if they are resolved to plunge into the strife. To all such we have some encouraging examples to offer, which may serve to cheer their hours of gloom and disappointment, by showing them what they may accomplish by honest perseverance and judicious enterprise. One of these examples shall be David Freed, the venerable flour merchant.

Mr. Freed was born in Montgomery county, Pennsylvania, in the year 1792. He was bred to rural pursuits, but in 1808, when he was only sixteen years of age, he determined to mingle in the bustle and turmoil of city life, and seek his fortune in a business career in Philadelphia. He had a hardy robust frame, industrious habits, and considerable self-reliance. Obtaining a situation in a grocery store, he was soon initiated into the toil and anxieties of daily trade. Among those who were boys in humble employment about this time, and who have since become prominent in the commercial world, were Alexander J. Derbyshire, Henry Budd, James Steel and Hugh Craig, of whom we have already given biographical sketches. These gentlemen remember the youth of Freed, and take pleasure in recalling instances of his steady devotion to business and manifest resolution to work his way upward to ease and independence. In 1812, when there was much apprehension in the public mind that the British forces would attempt the capture of Philadelphia, Freed, who was filled with patriotic ardor, joined the rifle corps, commanded by Captain Uhl, and went to camp Dupont, where he performed tedious and wearisome duties throughout the uneventful campaign. At this period the total amount of funds at the command of the young volunteer, consisted of a small sum in silver coin, which he accidently discovered remaining in a pocket of some old clothes. After the excitement of the war fever had cooled young Freed returned to business. It is still mentioned by his intimate friends as a noteworthy instance of the small beginnings of men of subsequent distinction, that when Freed commenced, he bought a single barrel of flour, and wheeled it home. Previous to this he formed a partnership in the grocery business with Richard Austin. They took up a lot on the east side of Fourth street, below Vine, and built a store. Here the firm prospered until Mr. Freed's partner became dissipated, and this unfortunate circumstance caused a separation. Mr. Freed left the store. Two years afterwards we find him engaged in the flour business, at the corner of Third and Noble streets. Here he remained until 1829, when he returned to the old store, and continued retail dealing in flour there until 1836, at which period he was enabled to virtually withdraw from active participation in business pursuits.

Mr. Freed was personally active in the retail trade during the protracted term of twenty-eight years. Such was his untiring devotion to the business, and his popularity, that his sales by retail averaged for several years twenty-five thousand barrels per annum. He was a careful and an economical manager, with all his enterprise. His profits were large, and they were so judiciously invested that the aim of pecuniary independence, which he had proposed to himself at the start, was attained while he was still comparatively young. One feature in his business policy was observed by all persons who had dealings with him: he always paid promptly, according to his engagements, and never allowed himself to be dunned for a bill. By the early adoption of this course, and a persistent adherence to it under all circumstances, Mr. Freed never had a load of debt to carry or to vex his mind, and always knew precisely where he stood. But though the subject of this sketch had realized a competency from personal activity in trade, he did not give up his connection with mercantile affairs. In 1838 Mr. Freed purchased the interest in an old established flour store, in Market street near Thirteenth, for the exclusive benefit of his son and sons-in-law, giving them his valuable services and means, solely for their advancement. Shortly afterwards the wholesale house of Freed, Ward & Freed was founded. In 1849, at the suggestion of Mr. Freed, the son and sons-in-law bought a portion of the estate of Paul Beck, on Market street above Eighth, and improved the property. The partners in this concern are Mr. Samuel L. Ward—recently Treasurer of the Corn Exchange Association—Mr. Joseph M. Freed and Jacob Umstead—clever and estimable gentlemen and energetic merchants, who are calculated to maintain and extend the reputation of the firm. Mr. Ward is quite as popular as any other man engaged in the same line of trade, and has been honored with many trusts of the highest responsibility. Mr. Freed is entitled to great credit for the establishment of a house which has been so successfully managed upon his own upright, straight-forward and exact system of doing business, and having implicit confidence in the upright and prudent management of the latter gentleman, has allowed his name to appear in the firm to the present day, without any pecuniary advantage to himself.

Mr. D. Freed is now seventy-three years of age. His declining days are made pleasant and comfortable by the possession of a competence, which enables him to live in good but not ostentatious style, at No. 508 North Sixth street. His career has fulfilled every anticipation that may have been formed in his boyish days. He began life as an humble toiler, and has never been too proud for employment of any honest description. From the smallest kind of a commencement he struggled on hopefully, manfully— paying as he went—living within his income, and laboring early and late, with one object kept steadily in view.

Mr. Freed has never taken any active part in political movements, as far as we are informed—he has had no ambition in that direction. He has always thought that for him, and others of his habits and tastes, "the post of honor is a private station." He possesses considerable practical knowledge of men and things, is full of reminiscences of the old mercantile days of Philadelphia, and is represented as a cordial, communicative companion. "Take him for all in all," he is a fine example of what ordinary talents for trade, honorably directed, can accomplish in the struggle for mercantile success.

CHARLES OAKFORD.

The story that the holy St. Clement, whilst performing a pious pilgrimage, eased his weary feet by placing loose fur in his shoes; that he discovered at the end of his journey that the hair had become felted into a regular cloth by the motion, heat and perspiration, and that from thence he deduced the inference that wool and furs might be felted into bodies—from which invention arose the art of making hats—was a legend of wide circulation among the early felt mongers. Even in our own time the Hatters' Society of Philadelphia bore upon its banner a painting of the pious St. Clement, with appropriate insignia and emblems. But the good St. Clement could never have imagined the revolution which the manufacturing of hats has experienced even within the memory of many now living. The fur hat, the castor, the roram, the light beaver, have disappeared. The dress hat is now a pasted article, the most ornamental part of which is not produced by the beast, but by the worm. The silk hat has totally exterminated the fur hat for dress and fashionable wear. The cutting knife, the hurl, the bow, the plank and kettle, and the coloring kettle, are exchanged for the scissors, the pot of shellac, the iron and the brush. Dress hats are glued, not made; and were it not that the popular mind inclines to the soft Kossuth and slouch hat for business and pleasure wear, the art of hating, as it existed when Charles Oakford commenced business for himself, would be totally lost.

The capital with which this young hatter set up as a "boss," on the twenty-seventh of September, 1827, was merely six years and ten months experience, gained during his apprenticeship, and five dollars and thirty-seven and a-half cents in cash. When it was known among his acquaintances that the young hatter was thus about to try his luck in trade, there were fortunately a few friends who were ready to give him orders. On the first day that he set up for himself he received orders for four hats, at four dollars each. They were to be made with wool bodies, napped with muskrat and coney fur. He purchased for his first manufacture six muskrat skins, at thirty-seven and a-half cents each, four Saxony wool bodies, at fifty cents each, and a quarter of an ounce of coney fur, for seventy-five cents. Thus five dollars of his small capital was already employed. With the balance he bought an apron, knife and whetstone. Having thus invested all he had in the world upon the faith of the sixteen dollars which he was to receive for his work, he made a contract with John Gillingham, who carried on business in Front below Spruce street, to stiffen the bodies, for one dollar and ten cents each—making his investment in material and credit nine dollars and seventy-seven and a-half cents. Mr. John Land, in Second below Lombard street, offered to the young workman permission to use his shop in making up the hats. Oakford cut the fur from the skins with his crescent shaped knife, bowed it into a smooth felt, applied it to the bodies, and having secured the coloring and trimmings, took the finished hats home on the next Saturday night, receiving his sixteen dollars as the reward of his industry. After paying Mr. Gillingham four dollars and forty cents, and two dollars and fifty cents for his board, he had a balance of nine dollars and ten cents with which to commence business in his second week as a "boss." Fortune was more favorable to him than at first. He received orders for four hats at four dollars each and two hats at six dollars each, being the immense sum of twenty-eight dollars. He still had two ounces of muskrat fur, so that his expenditure for material was assisted by his economy. He applied himself diligently, and in due time had his hats finished, at a cost of six dollars and sixty cents. He was enabled again to pay his board, and had eighteen dollars and ninety cents left as clear capital.

This was the commencement of Charles Oakford's fortune, and as he was ambitious, faithful and not above his business, orders flocked in upon him, until it was impossible for him to make up, with his own hands, all the work that was offered him. It was necessary that he should have a workshop. The kindness of Mr. Land had been very great to him, but it was too much to desire a continuance of it, if it were possible for Oakford to relieve him. He, therefore, found his best friend where every honest and affectionate young man is sure to find it—in his mother. The old lady consented to give up her kitchen to be used as a hatter shop. Charles obtained a kettle and tools from his kind friend, Mr. Gillingham, and, with one workman, engaged in business more ardently than ever. But while he had his "plank shop," it was equally necessary that he should have a place for preparing his furs. He shortly afterwards hired a room at No. 35 Lombard street, where he put up his hurls and finishing benches, and was prepared to continue his business in all branches save one. This was the coloring—a peculiar, somewhat scientific and dirty part of the business. But there was no difficulty about this. David Jones, who for twenty-five or thirty years had been in business as a hatter, at the corner of Second street and the first alley above Race street, had an extensive shop, and devoted more attention to the coloring business than any other hatter of his time. He took in coloring work from the city hatters generally, and young Oakford had no difficulty in arranging with him for the coloring of the rough bodies.

Shortly afterwards he arrived at the dignity of what the hatters in those days called "a front shop." A shoemaker, who had occupied a little one story building, twelve feet front and eight feet deep, at No. 37 Lombard street, vacated the premises, and in this little "cubby hole" the future occupant of palatial stores, to be fitted up at the expense of thousands of dollars, opened his first shop. It was on the fifteenth of November, 1827, that the important sign—"CHARLES OAKFORD, HATTER"—was raised over this humble establishment, so that in six weeks the young manufacturer had prospered greatly, and witnessed many changes in his career.

Oakford was energetic and worthy. Such a thing as pride was foreign to his nature. He established for himself certain rules, by which he determined to conduct himself through life. One was never to be too big in self-importance to labor himself. Another was, to be strictly honest and faithful to his customers, and deserve, by the excellence of his goods, new patronage when the hats which he had made were worn out. He was not too proud to make, or finish, or to do anything necessary in the performance of his business. Hence, when it was necessary to convey a load of hats to David Jones, to be colored, he blocked them himself, secured the brims by stout cords, and then loading his wheelbarrow with the material, wheeled them to the coloring shop. By doing this he secured the delicate nap from being chafed and rubbed—disasters to which they were often subjected in the hands of careless porters or boys.

At No. 37 Lombard street Charles Oakford continued until August, 1828, when he removed to No. 30, on the opposite side of the street, in a larger and more secure place, where, upon taking an account of stock, he found himself worth $560, and entirely free from debt. He rented a factory and went into business more extensively. No. 30 Lombard street was perhaps as unpromising a location for a retail hatter as could have been selected. The street was dull, it was scarcely a thoroughfare, as it extended only to Front street. It was not opened to the wharf until several years after Oakford left it. Yet Oakford did, apparently, a thriving business there. He increased the number of his journeymen, and took two apprentices. When asked the secret of his success, he replied, " by making good hats, being attentive to my customers, and taking care not to forget the advice of the shoemaker from whom I rented my shop, who said, 'Charley, never hold a penny so close to your eyes as to lose sight of a dollar.'" These rules he carried out on an occasion, perhaps trivial in itself, but which evidenced the character of the man. A journeyman brought him one day a finished hat, which was slightly blemished; Mr. Oakford observed the defect. "Pooh," said the other, "not one man in a thousand would notice it." "Well, said Oakford, "let us have a hat for *that one man*, it may bring a thousand customers, which the little blemish, if detected, would certainly keep away."

After two years of industry, Mr. Oakford considered himself sufficiently well established to take unto him a partner—one of those fair and good creatures who make a man's home happy, and incite him to prudence and industry. He was married on the second of June, 1829, in a quiet, humble way, but he was able to stock his house plainly, but comfortably, with furniture suitable to his situation. He was free from debt, had a good custom business, and a name in trade constantly improving and extending. In the spring of 1830 he was surprised, and we need scarcely say delighted, by the reception of an order for $10,000 worth of hats from John Darrieux and Lewis Clapier, the one a next door neighbor, the other a merchant of the neighborhood, both of whom had watched the prudent and thrifty course of this young man, and formed a favorable estimate of his honesty and industry. These gentlemen had, by their commercial knowledge, discovered that there was an opening for a large exportation of hats to Mexico, and they took advantage of it. Oakford had, on the very day when Darrieux had apprised him of his intention to give him the order, accidentally invited him to walk in his shop and have his hat ironed. This little compliment settled the matter in the mind of his neighbor, who, while his hat was being ironed off, spoke of an order for one thousand hats. Clapier subsequently came into the contract with him. But these gentlemen were sensible that Oakford had not the credit to command the quantity of materials necessary to complete so large an order. They, therefore, proved to him the advantage of his previous well won character, by offering to go security for all his purchases; and furthermore, to advance him the money necessary to pay his hands; and this, without security from him of any kind but his own character. Oakford had six weeks to complete the contract. He put all his energies to work, and had it completed two days before the time, received his money, paid his bills, and on the last day of the contract took his dinner, with the certainty that all his debts had been paid, that he owed no man a dollar on account of the Darrieux and Clapier contract, and that he had the profits of his industry in his pocket. This happy adventure seemed to be a new lease upon Oakford's good fortune. He devoted himself faithfully to business, and although in as obscure a location as No. 30 Lombard street, by sharp attention to the improvements in his business elsewhere, he managed to make himself an oracle as to the novelties of the trade and a leader of fashion.

In 1833 he commenced making brush hats, of fine Russia fur, with all the nap brushed out of the body. These hats were light, peculiar in appearance, and calculated to strike the sensibilities of fashionable people. Oakford sold the first one to Frank Peters, who was at that time a young man looked upon as a leader. The brush hat became speedily "the ton," and Oakford reaped the advantage thereof in numerous orders. Black beaver bonnets for ladies were also an important manufacture with him at this time.

In the spring of 1835 Oakford removed from No. 30 Lombard street to No. 210 South Second street, opposite the new market. In March, 1839, he rented the store No. 78 South Third street, more in the centre of fashion, and kept up both establishments until 1840, when he relinquished the Second street store. In September, 1843, he removed to No. 104 Chestnut street, an old stand, which had been occupied since 1829 by A. Russel. In 1847, Oakford being stimulated by the effort of Beebe & Costar, of New York, to establish *the* fashionable hat store of Philadelphia, determined that native mechanics should not be outdone. Three thousand dollars were expended in fitting up his store in a splendor of style hitherto unattempted in the hatting business, and which was in remarkable contrast to the first Oakford store of 1827, at No. 35 Lombard street. His daring was well repaid, He took at once the cream of fashionable custom. "The Oakford hat" was a *sine qua non* at the West End, and after he opened his new store his business increased, in four months, fifteen thousand dollars over all previous figures.

In 1850 he went into the wholesale business, and soon sent his hats over the whole country. But the tide of business was going farther West; and when, after the burning of Barnum's Museum, Joshua Francis Fisher determined to erect upon the old Clymer and Harrison property the handsomest buildings of a business character, up to that time, built in Philadelphia, Charles Oakford, ever alive to improvement, contracted for one of them. He opened on this site the most elegant hat store ever seen in Philadelphia, on the eighth of June, 1853. At this place he remained until the contracts for the erection of the Continental Hotel, at Ninth and Chestnut streets, rendered it evident to his enterprising mind that he would be compelled to seek a location there. He opened two stores there, and it was obvious that hotel business was likely to be different from a strict hat business, he added to his stock such articles as were likely to be called for by the temporary sojourners of the Continental, who would most probably be his best customers.

His career of usefulness was cut short, however, in November, 1862, by death. He left to his sons a good name and a good business. They have shown their reverence for the first by keeping up the name of Charles Oakford as the principal one in the firm;

and as for the business, having had the advantage of the example of an honest, enterprising, industrious parent, to teach them how to walk through life, they will not forget the honorable lessons which they have learned from Charles Oakford.

Most men have two characters: one which distinguishes them in business, and another, sometimes widely different, which they have socially. We have in this sketch confined ourselves solely to Mr. Oakford's business character. He had a social reputation most popular and flattering. He was a genial, pleasant, witty man; accomplished and versatile, the life of a circle of friends, admired by all, and a hearty good fellow. But even in his pleasures, the prudence which distinguished him in business restrained him. He was never carried away by those who surrounded him into excess, and he avoided the rocks upon which too many men, fitted to adorn society, have struck.

DENNIS KELLY.

Of the thousands of emigrants who, from various causes, annually seek a home upon our shores, there are few, comparatively, of the whole number, who ever attain to any distinction. The principal cause of this is the propensity which most of them have to settle in, and do but little more than loiter about, large cities—the laboring man, like Micawber, vainly hoping that among so many people something will turn up whereby he may be benefited. Many of those who come with a little capital, trust by embarking in business to succeed, but find out, when too late, that they are dealing with a people of whose practices and manners they have but little knowledge. Their first efforts failing, they settle down into an apathy at once startling and pitiable—startling, that men remain idle in a country where untilled fields and ungathered harvests suffer for the want of helping hands; pitiable, because of the contentment with which they endure, or rather enjoy, hardships, which oftentimes amount to squalid misery, and which indicate that they have reached the goal of their ambition. This lack of an independent spirit and want of energy is one of the great reasons why the lists of crime are annually so fearfully swelled; yet the fault, in most instances, is hardly chargeable to the man—the difficulty lays in childhood's culture—for the spirit inculcated in early youth inevitably follows one through life. Happily, this picture has its relief. The proud and honorable position acquired by the few seems to atone for the fault of the many, and causes even the misanthrope to look with a more lenient eye upon the short-comings of the other, and no one has contributed in a larger degree to the accomplishment of this than the subject of our sketch.

Dennis Kelly was born in the county Donegal, Ireland, in the year 1779. At an early age death deprived him of his father; thus the mental culture and care of the boy devolved upon his mother, a woman in every way fitted to the charge. In his childhood days it was her care to instill into his mind the germs of those great truths and maxims which have become fully developed in the grown man. At a proper age she placed him in a linen manufactory, to learn the art of that peculiar trade, the county of Donegal being celebrated for the extent and fineness of its linen manufactures. After attaining his majority he married, and to support himself and wife worked at his trade. About this time the hand of death took from him his mother, who died breathing blessings upon a son who was always dutiful to her, and praying that He, before whom she was shortly to appear, would protect and guide her boy through the trials and vicissitudes of life.

In April, 1806, he left his native land and took passage for this country, arriving in Philadelphia on the eighteenth of the following June. It was his intention to go at once to the West—at least not to make his home this side of Pittsburg. In those days the two great cities of Pennsylvania were not bound together by the iron band which now unites them, and a journey to this point by the cumbersome Conestoga wagons, with their sturdy teams of horses, the remembrance of which is still vivid in the minds of our oldest citizens, was considered a momentous if not a perilous undertaking. It was mere chance that caused Mr. Kelly to alter his plans and cast his lot among us. The wagon in which he, with his wife and child, had taken passage, had gone but a few miles from the city, when Mrs. Kelly alighted and positively refused to go any further, upon account of the profanity of one of the men who was a passenger with them. All the promises of the driver to keep the man quiet, coupled with the expostulations of the remaining passengers, failed to induce her to alter her decision. This profanity, whilst positively disgusting to the lady, was no less unpleasing to her husband, who willingly acquiesced in her wishes, and the pair, with the infant in the mother's arms, retraced their steps. Night soon coming on, they were compelled to halt, and early next morning Mr. Kelly procured a place for his wife and succeeded in obtaining work on a milldam which was then in course of construction, and situated near where he now lives.

The loss of the price of his passage to the West was one he could ill afford, and presenting himself to the agent of the transportation company he stated the case to him, and demanded the restoration of his money. His request, however, was at first denied; but after some argument, in which Mr. Kelly convinced the manager that he could not spare so much money from his slender means, a compromise was effected, by which he received back one-half the amount paid. Going back, he rented an old house in Haverford township, which is still standing, and moved to it his family, with what few effects he had brought from the old country, and then industriously going to work, resolved for the time being to abide his fate. This job completed, he was not slow in procuring another; and thus for the next two years he honorably supported his family by the sweat of his brow. It is too often the case with day laborers that, when the day's work is over, they give themselves up to idleness, and care not for to-morrow; but not so with Dennis Kelly. He knew he had a great task before him; he appreciated fully that he was in a strange country, and that he was surrounded by people different in customs, in habits and avocations from those he had left. To study their character, to make himself conversant with their ways, now became the employment of his leisure moments. How he succeeded in this, after events will fully demonstrate. But here, let us state, as a remarkable fact—and one which we verily believe no other man can point to— that every spot which Dennis Kelly ever labored upon, after his arrival in this country, *he now owns.*

In 1808 there was a large demand in this country for the article known as bagging. Mr. Kelly having, by strict economy. saved a small sum, and by his knowledge of the manufacture of linen, felt himself competent to produce the article wanted. Beginning in a small way, his efforts were crowned with success; and the demand not only continuing, but increasing, he resolved to increase his facilities for its manufacture, but only to increase his business as his means accumulated, and always to keep within them. This resolution he steadily adhered to, and this, in a great measure, accounts for his success. During all the financial troubles with which the country has been convulsed from that day to this, Mr. Kelly was never in the least involved; so far from it, that he was always ready, and universally did, step forward to relieve his more unfortunate neighbors. In the manufacture of bagging Mr. Kelly was successful and with the capital thus accumulated he was en-' abled, upon the breaking out of the war of 1812, to materially assist the government, in manufacturing the much wanted and scantily produced goods for the clothing of the army. In this branch so faithfully and honestly did he perform his contracts, that his goods were in constant demand, and of the whole lot furnished by him, not one piece was ever rejected.

The war over, Mr. Kelly found his increase of capital far beyond his most sanguine expectations. But the wealth thus so quickly acquired, had not the effect upon him which it too often has upon others. He was not in the least elated, but to his friends he was the same Dennis Kelly still. Wealth gave to him one privilege, that of gratifying an elegant taste. He was always an ardent admirer of nature, and delighted in seeing nature's objects as near perfection as possible, and to make an improvement in this direction he now turned his attention. The horses in this section of the country were all of the heavy, ungainly appearance common at that day, and unfitted for anything but heavy draught. To improve the breed, and produce a horse equal to any of the famed animals of the old world, Mr. Kelly now set himself diligently to work, believing as he did, that the climate, the pasturage, and the common wants of society would warrant it. As an inaugurative step he imported the celebrated thorough-bred stallion "Daniel O'Connell," a horse noted alike for his beauty and high breeding. The great demand for the services of this fine animal proved conclusively that his owner had not been mistaken in his calculations. He was afterwards sold, at an unusually high figure, to a British officer then stationed in Canada.

This importation was followed by that of the no less renowned horse "Langford," a successful prize winner upon the English turf, and also by a number of high pedigreed brood mares. From the time Mr. Kelly took the first step to make these improvements, the value of the unwieldy horses began to depreciate, and they soon became out of date, while, in their stead sprung up a race of horses light built, strong and enduring; horses with which the farmer or teamster could do his days work, and on Sunday hitch them to the carriage and spin off to church at eight miles an hour with ease.

The business of raising horses was in those days an honorable profession, but beginning to fall into the hands of sharpers, and men akin to the modern jockies, Mr. Kelly relinquished a pursuit which, until then, was almost wholly confined to gentlemen of wealth and high personal character, of whom rare representatives may be found at the present day, prominent among them may be mentioned Mr. A. Maillaird, of New Jersey, and Mr. R. Atcheson Alexander, of Kentucky.

Not willing to give up wholly the breeding of cattle, by which the country of his adoption was so largely benefited, Mr. Kelly now turned his attention to beef cattle. Into this he entered with his usual spirit, and it was not long before he was surrounded by a herd of "short horns" that invariably carried of the first premium wherever exhibited. Many of our readers doubtless recollect the splendid bull of his importation, "Lord Barrington" (with his pedigree to the eighth generation), which has on several occasions been exhibited and admired at the Agricultural Fair at Powelton. Amongst his present herd may be found not only the descendants of this fine animal, but also many others of the finest blood in the country.

To gratify his tastes in this respect Mr. Kelly did not neglect his business as a manufacturer, but continued his *mills* even at seasons when producing cotton goods was far from being remunerative. He always was a man noted for his benevolence, and to stop in the dull season would deprive his operatives of work, and consequently entail distress upon them; this his kind heart could not endure; but at all times, let prices be high or low, he kept his mills running and his operatives employed. With a sagacity that would do credit to men deeply versed in the increase of the value of land, Mr. Kelly, rather than build up a gigantic business, which, to the best of calculators, oftentimes results in total ruin, preferred to invest his accruing wealth in real estate in his own neighborhood, which he felt assured would in a short time become of immense value. As his profits acumulated he bought land adjacent to him, until at present he owns in one tract upwards of *eight hundred acres*, and that, too, situated at from four to seven miles from Market street bridge, upon which no less than six cotton and woolen mills are erected, all now in the full tide of operation, and generally conducted by men whom his generosity has set afloat.

To the deserving Mr. Kelly has ever been a substantial friend, his liberality having established several young men in different branches of business, in Market street and other localities in this city, most of whom are now eminently successful. In all his dealings with his fellow-man he would never accept more than six per cent. for the use of his money, and the sums given as free gifts to those he wished to assist are almost incredible. There are sections of country in the West thickly populated by the recipients of his bounty, and there the name of Dennis Kelly is a sure passport to hospitality. It was always his delight to hunt up deserving men from his own country, and to counsel them as to the best means for their advancement, which, in his opinion, was to go West, settle, and grow up with the country. Those who had not the means to carry them there, he not only supplied with for traveling expenses, but also enough to start them in life after reaching their destination. Truly, to the needy and deserving he has always been a substantial friend, and there are hundreds at this day who mention the name of Dennis Kelly only to bless him, and to point him to their children and friends as a specimen of God's noblest work—an "honest man."

Mr. Kelly now sits, in the evening of life, surrounded by a large family of children, grand children and great-grand children; and as the shades of night thicken around him the gloom is dispelled by the consciousness of a well-spent life, while the pangs of approaching dissolution are mitigated by the knowledge that he has strictly complied with the divine decree, " Do unto others as you would be done by." And soothing to him, indeed, must be the reflection that the dying mother's prayer has ascended to the throne of Grace, that it has followed him through life, and will be attendant upon him at his death.

ALEXANDER YOUNG.

AMERICA owes to Ireland a large proportion of her physical and a very considerable part of her mental wealth. This is a fact which is tacitly acknowledged by every thinking mind, though prejudice may prevent its being boldly asserted as it ought.

Though we receive from the shores of the green isle thousands of men who are more useful for their muscle than for their intellectual quality; and though, like all other foreign nations, Ireland has sent us many non producers among her emigrants, yet still the truth remains, that the genius, energy and sturdy independence of Irishmen has added to the wealth of our republic. Poets, orators, scholars, merchants, manufacturers and capitalists of Irish descent are found in every city in the Union ; and in their genial sympathies for humanity, their love of progress and equality, the nation has found one of its strongest bulwarks. The proverbial warmth of Irish hearts is no less characteristic than Irish shrewdness and tact; and while in our almshouses we can find a due representation of the Celtic race, yet you will also find them high on the ladder of fortune, and prominent in all enterprises that help to roll the car of commerce and civilization along, and which assist in the great march of humanity as it moves on its ameliorating and triumphant progress. We can, therefore, give a cheer for Ireland, before proceeding to sketch the career of a son of Erin who has won "credit and renown" in the city of Brotherly Love.

Alexander Young, the subject of this sketch, is one of the many emigrants who prove how nobly America fosters her adopted sons, and encourages industry and enterprise. He can proudly claim the honorable title, a self-made man—one who, from the humblest fortune, has raised himself to wealth and position in the commercial community.

He was born in Donegal county, on the twenty-sixth of August, 1798, and landed in this country on the fifteenth of July, 1821, quite a youth, but one full of that energy and perseverance that will carve a way to fortune over any stumbling block. Having some knowledge of the malt distillery business, and desirous of learning the art of extracting whiskey from raw grain, he went into J. W. Dower's distillery, on the Schuylkill, between Race and Vine streets. He gave for this instruction fifty dollars in cash, and his services for many months. Having keen observation, with strong purpose, our young emigrant soon obtained a thorough knowledge of the details of the business, and determined to try his own fortune as a distiller. After working in a subordinate position for one year, he had saved money sufficient to purchase a small still, and commenced business for himself.

After keeping up his still for a year, Mr. Young went into partnership with John Maitland, and for two years they carried on together the business, producing a very pure and excellent kind of "malt whiskey," which to this day retains its then worthy celebrity. From molasses they also at one time distilled New England rum. They were the first firm that discovered the process by which an immense increase of spirit was obtained from the grain, having produced fourteen quarts of pure whiskey from fifty-six pounds of grain.

In 1825 there stood at the corner of Fourth and South streets a large building used as a "theatre;" but as the tide of population swept away towards the western and northern part of the city, it was closed for its original use and rented to Pat. Lyons, another distinguished Irishman, who used it for a hay press. In the fall of 1825 John Maitland took this building, and at a cost of twenty thousand dollars fitted it up for a distillery, and then, with Young as foreman, started on a larger scale than their former business. For twelve years they continued in this way, making important discoveries and improvements in the business, and founding, as it afterwards proved, one of the largest and richest establishments of our city.

In 1837 John Maitland's son, William J. Maitland, went into partnership with Mr. Young, and these two continued the business together until the death of Maitland, in 1847. Although successful, the business had not paid enough to make the deceased partner a man of wealth.

Upon the death of his partner Mr. Young bought out the establishment for twenty thousand dollars—the sum which John Maitland had first expended upon it. Ten years later the first partner also died, but he had not at that time any connection with Mr. Young. As soon as the establishment came entirely under the control of Mr. Young, he at once commenced to enlarge and improve it, spending in a few years over sixty thousand dollars on the building and machinery, and adding every improvement and extension that could add to the value of the establishment or the facilities for the business.

In the meantime the old distillery of J. W. Dower was changing hands. In 1828 the first owner died, and it was then purchased by John & Archibald Smith, and later by Samuel Smith, who sold it to Freeman & Co., from whose hands it passed into those of Z. Locke, its present occupant.

Mr. Young is, perhaps, the only distiller who can truly claim that he makes his whiskey from *pure, sound* grain. He purchases only the best rye, barley, corn and wheat—purchases and sells only for *cash*—and distills with hops and pure water. So careful is he about the latter article, that he has had an artesian well dug upon his premises, which throws up seventy gallons a minute of the purest water for distilling purposes.

On the eighth of October, 1822, Mr. Young married; and on the loss of his first wife was again married, June 8, 1830. His present family consists of five sons and two daughters, and he has lost one son and one daughter. He resided at the time of his first marriage within a square of his distillery, but in 1840 he removed from there to his present residence, No. 702 Passyunk road.

His present business is on the largest scale, as he annually turns out three hundred and eighty thousand gallons of pure liquor. On the first of September, 1862, he had on hand five thousand barrels of whiskey, valued at two hundred thousand dollars at least; and as this is about his average stock, and the article has since advanced more than one hundred per cent., the calculating mind will readily find out the value of his stock. Much of this liquor is kept for many years, but while it gains immensely in quality by time, the loss from evaporation is very heavy. An experiment was made by the late Robert Newlin, who nailed up a sixteen gallon cask. At the end of nine years, upon his son's majority, the cask was opened; only eight gallons of liquor was left, but the quality was remarkably fine.

Mr. Young is a man so indifferent in his dress, and so unassuming in his appearance, that but few, on a casual acquaintance, would believe him the founder of the large fortune he now possesses. His own energy and industry have carried him forward, in the country of his adoption, to wealth and position, and his honesty has made his staple celebrated as much for its purity as excellence in other respects.

The reader must not think that in sketching the career of Mr. Young, we are noticing an isolated case of this character. There are very many natives of Ireland who have begun at the wheelbarrow, and by perseverance, tact and shrewdness, have worked their way to positions of eminence and influence. We can at present recall, among cases of a somewhat similar character, the names of the following Philadelphians who have made their mark in the business world by their own force of character: James McHenry, Robert Steen, Hugh Craig, Dennis Kelly, Andrew C. Craig, Samuel Riddle, William Divine and John Macrae. If the varying fortunes of men like these could be told with the plain simplicity of truth, the reader would be amazed to see how much can be accomplished by pure intellect, accompanied by a stout heart, even if the adventitious influences by which other men rise are absent. There are lessons of honesty, encouragement and hope for the aspiring in such lives, which would do immense good in commercial, and, in fact, in all other circles where real merit is recognized, and where the value of a man consists in the intrinsic worth of his character, irrespective of the outward marks of station.

JOHN WELSH.

WHEN John Welsh, a lad of sixteen years of age, left his youthful home in Newcastle county, Delaware, and came to the great city to enter upon an *apprenticeship* to a merchant, he stepped upon the threshold of trade in her new mansion. The exhausting contest of the Revolution, some of the incidents of which young Welsh must have remembered, had prostrated commerce and annihilated credit. The successful management of business had passed in a degree from the hands of the merchants who had conducted it previous to 1775—new men had taken the helm, and new interests were springing into competition. The old colonial government had passed away. The confederacy was a bond which tied the the new states together, but did not unite them. Different rules and laws prevailed at different points upon the Atlantic seaboard, and foreign commerce was managed from Charleston to Boston by varied regulations and laws. Under circumstances like these, John Welsh, the country boy, entered upon his strange duties in the year 1786, in the counting-house of Joseph Russel, an eminent flour merchant, at the corner of Penn and Pine streets. Russel did a large and profitable shipping business, and the house was a most excellent one in mercantile character and standing. Here the young clerk obtained his first insight into the science of trade, and here he acquired his first lessons in those principles of mercantile honor which rendered his life useful to his fellow citizens, and a proud memory to his family.

In Mr. Russel's employment Welsh served faithfully, and after his indenture had expired he finished his education in the manner usual in those days, by a voyage as supercargo, which he made to Port au Prince. Returning to the United States, Mr. Welsh, an active young man of twenty-three years of age, entered, in the year 1793, the counting-house of Robert Ralston, at No. 90 South Front street. Here he took his final degree in mercantile proficiency. Clerks, in those days, were not like some of the present fast race of billiard-playing, whisky-drinking, horse-hiring, catfish-suppering upstarts who *adorn* our mercantile houses. They were modest, unobtrusive, honest young men, who were not above their business. Mr. Welsh frequently told the anecdote of his having been sent, with a quill behind his ear, from the counting-house to Mr. Ralston's farm, near where Spring Garden now intersects Tenth street, *to drive home the cows!* Think of that, young gentlemen who smoke cigars and indulge in profanity in the halls of the "Continental." Such was mercantile clerkship in the good old times.

In the year 1794 Mr. Welsh undertook to launch out in business on his own account, and established himself at No. 91 South Water street, near the drawbridge. Here success attended him. His ventures increased, his credit became established, and he was in good time a thriving merchant. His operations extended so much, that in three years he was compelled to seek a more suitable location for the shipping business, having a wharf front. He removed to the store No. 22 South Wharves, which extended through to South Water street, and then was numbered forty-seven. It may show how simple were the household tastes of those days when we relate that at this time Mr. Welsh lived in a modest brick house, at No. 31 Union street. Brown stone mansions and extravagance were not the follies of the business men of Philadelphia of the year 1797.

Whilst thus gradually rendering himself opulent, Mr. Welsh did not neglect his duties as a citizen. He was one of the projectors of the Philadelphia Bank. That institution was a voluntary association of subscribers, who undertook to carry on banking business as a partnership, and without a charter. The application to the Legislature for a charter was violently opposed by the Bank of Pennsylvania, the directors of which institution thought that the financial field was sufficiently occupied by the United States Bank, Bank of North America and itself. The Bank of Pennsylvania offered the Legislature two hundred thousand dollars if it would *refuse* the charter to the new rival. On the other hand, the Philadelphia Bank made various propositions beneficial to the state if it would grant the coveted authority. The Legislature of 1802 yielded to the influence of the old banks. The controversy was settled in 1804 by the passage of an act chartering the subscribers to the Philadelphia Bank, on the payment of one hundred and thirty-five thousand dollars in cash, and upon their undertaking to loan the state one hundred thousand dollars in cash whenever required, at five per cent. interest, for ten years. The Commonwealth was also to be allowed the privilege of subscribing to a large number of shares of the stock of the Philadelphia Bank at par. In this bank Mr. Welsh was elected a director, a position which he held until his death. The bank was opened at No. 104 Chestnut street, between Third and Fourth, with George Clymer as President. About the same time Mr. Welsh associated with Thomas Fitz-simons, Stephen Dutilh, Bohl Bolen, Samuel Meeker, Griffith Evans, and others, in establishing a new Insurance Company—the Delaware Insurance Company of Philadelphia. Of this institution Thomas Fitzsimons was President. He had long held a position in Philadelphia of influence and respectability, having been for many years a member of Congress, an office in those days of high honor, integrity and responsibility. In this company Mr. Welsh was elected a member of the first Board of Directors.

By industry, prudence and integrity, Mr. Welsh soon succeeded in establishing himself a name. His affairs were so prosperous, that in the year 1806 he was able to retire from business. Substantially he did withdraw, although he kept his counting-house at 22 South Wharves, and was interested in commercial questions. American commerce was very much restricted by the contending European powers, which were engaged in a gigantic struggle for the mastery. Decrees and orders in council, confiscation and seizures by the belligerents discouraged trade, and rendered the business of the American shipper extra hazardous. To these unfavorable influences the home policy of the United States Government added further discouragements, by frequent embargoes and measures which unsettled confidence. Mr. Welsh could afford to lay idly by during this season of depression. His counting-house received him during a portion of every day, but the greater part of his time was spent more agreeably at his residence, No. 42 South Sixth street, and at a later period at 146 Chestnut street.

After the war of 1812 had settled the relative positions of the

United States and England, and the fall of Napoleon gave peace to Europe, Mr. Welsh was ready to plunge deeply into business again. He was once more a large and widely respected shipping merchant. His vessels were well found and well manned, and his name was known and respected in many parts of the globe. During successive years Mr. Welsh prosecuted successfully his mercantile career. He was the soul of honor—and as a man he was a sincere Christian and a generous philanthropist. His hand and his purse were ever ready in assisting the needy, and by many who yet live he is remembered for his generous deeds.

Mr. Welsh, in the latter part of his life, gave up much of his business to his sons, but he kept up an interest in mercantile affairs until within a short time of his death. When the last hold upon business was relaxed, he said sadly to his aged wife, "now I have no ship." She replied, "and shortly you will have no wife." To which, in melancholy comment, he answered, "then soon I shall have no self." These words were prophetic. Within two weeks after the death of Mrs. Welsh her husband joined her in the unknown world beyond the grave: He died on the fifth of March, 1854, at the age of eighty-four years.

Mrs. Welsh was a Miss Maris, a sister of Richard and William Maris. One of these gentlemen was a member of the firm of Maris, Evans & Welsh, afterwards Maris & Evans, which house finally was merged in that of Joseph R. Evans & Co. The other brother was a member of the firm of Maris & Thompson. Mrs. Welsh was an exemplary woman—gentle, affectionate and benevolent; a kind mother and devoted wife. She was a communicant and a member of the Baptist Church, in which, for about a quarter of a century, she sat under the ministrations of Dr. William Staughton, Dr. Holcombe, and others. One of her daughters married Dr. William E. Horner, another David Lapsley, and a third Joseph H. Dulles.

The sons of John Welsh were brought up under his charge in a manner which insured them future usefulness and business qualifications. Gradually he relinquished to them interests in the business, thus insuring to them a correct guidance and a finished mercantile education. In 1834 these sons formed a new firm, under the title of Samuel & William Welsh, at No. 50 South Wharves. The present firm is composed of Samuel Welsh, John Welsh, and William Welsh, with whom was associated, February 1, 1857, John Welsh, Jr., a son of William Welsh. They are largely interested in the West India trade, importing for others on commission, but

EDMUND A SOUDER

not on their own account. They issue no paper; they pay a heavy amount of duties into the Custom House, perhaps more than any other firm in the city.

William Welsh gives freely for church matters, to "church extension" and other good objects. Samuel Welsh is a valuable citizen. His fondness for the fine arts renders him a useful member of the Pennsylvania Academy. John Welsh takes an active part in politics. He has been an active member of Councils, and a Commissioner of the Sinking Fund. All these brothers have been or are now bank directors, and they are ever to be found prominent in forwarding any enterprise which is for the benefit of the city of Philadelphia. Among our respected citizens, no family has more influence, or is more widely respected than the Welshes. Their aims are wise and intelligent, their actions beneficial and just.

EDMUND A. SOUDER.

THE coasting trade of our city has been developed upon a gigantic scale. The vast fleet which enter the Delaware from the various ports of the atlantic states, and bear away valuable cargoes of "black diamonds," and the vessels that bring hither lumber and other articles to exchange for our manufactures, and the produce which here finds a great central depot, fully compensate, in the estimation of many persons, for the absence of foreign ships. We are indebted for the rapid growth of this coastwise commerce, to the fact of this being the port of the coal regions, which are inexhaustible in wealth; and, in the second place, to the untiring efforts of commission merchants to promote intercourse with the seaboard states. The citizens of New England, especially, have been induced to enter into commercial relations with us, and the results have been an extensive and mutual profit. No man has labored more faithfully and successfully than the gentleman whose name forms the caption of this article. To Edmund A. Souder belongs the credit of opening the trade between this port and the towns of Eastport and Calais, Maine; and to his exertions also, we owe, in a great measure, the trade with St. Johns, New Brunswick.

Mr. Souder was born in Philadelphia in 1805. His father, Mr. Thomas M. Souder, was an energetic business man, but one whose free and generous disposition rendered him the victim of pretended friends. While in the heyday of prosperity the elder Souder resolved that Edmund should obtain the best education that the city could afford at that period, and accordingly the boy was sent to the academy, which then flourished under the tuition of Messrs. Wylie and Engles. But misfortune overtook the parent, and the son's studies were destined to be abruptly terminated.

A considerable estate was lost through the practice of rather indiscriminate endorsement, and Mr. Souder was induced to devote his energies to the transportation business, for the purpose of replenishing his purse. He opened a store at No. 312 Market street. It was in 1820, when only fifteen years of age, that young Souder entered this establishment, and was introduced to the arduous and exacting pursuits of trade. The change from the school to the counting-house is frequently trying to ambitious and energetic youth; but this lad appears to have had the faculty of concentrating his mind upon whatever duty he was called to perform. Throughout his career we find him self-reliant, confident of his own resources, and endeavoring to improve every opportunity presented, whether congenial to his tastes or otherwise. The elder Souder was engaged in trade with the interior and West. Transportation was then very expensive, the only facilities being conestoga wagons and the roughest roads. A year's experience in this business satisfied the son, and at the expiration of that time he succeeded in obtaining a situation in the shipping and commission house of Mr. John T. Hadaway, No. 29 South Wharves. Mr. Andrew C. Barclay occupied a portion of the same building, and it is a fact worthy of mention, as showing the industry and intelligence of young Souder, that he contrived to keep the books of BOTH firms at the same time. Two years afterwards Mr. Hadaway died; Mr. William Brown rented the same store, and Souder became the principal clerk and book-keeper for that gentleman. Here the young man completed his business education. He cultivated habits of precision, punctuality, unwearied industry, and strict integrity. He studied this particular department of trade with a determination to master all its details, and fit himself for future operations upon his own account. He labored to establish a reputation which would be the basis of future credit.

In 1828 Mr. Brown failed, and the clerk was appointed to wind up and settle the affairs of the house. This task was accomplished to the entire satisfaction of the creditors, and then Mr. Souder found himself adrift again, with small means, and no influential friends upon whom he could rely for assistance. It demanded considerable nerve to resolve to start business under such circumstances. Mr. Souder had no capital beyond the small amount of money he had saved during his clerkship. To this, however, he added the sum of two hundred dollars, which he succeeded in borrowing from a relative for twelve months without collateral security. Thus equipped, he determined to embark upon the great sea of trade on his own account. He commenced the commission business in the counting-room of No. 25 South Wharves, which was owned by the Messrs Pritchett. "Nothing is denied to well-directed industry." Mr. Souder was more successful than he had anticipated. Within a remarkably short period he had not only obtained the esteem and confidence of many merchants in this community, but of several houses in New York and Boston. In May, 1830, he formed a partnership with Mr. Abraham G. Walters, and under the title of Walters & Souder the firm transacted a heavy business at No. 23 South Water street. Mr. Souder's enterprise not only resulted in putting money in his own pockets, but was of permanent advantage to his native city. In 1833-34, he visited the Eastern States, and succeeded in opening the trade between Philadelphia and the towns of Eastport and Calais, Maine, which has continued to increase in value ever since. Taking his means into consideration, the young merchant could not suffer by comparison with any of the leading business men of that period.

Mr. Souder was strictly economical in the management of his affairs. It is stated that during the first three years of his business career he kept the books of the concern, and was frequently obliged to labor in the counting-house until two or three o'clock in the morning, in order to keep the accounts posted. No assistance was employed until the increasing prosperity of the firm was known to warrant the expenditure. Mr. Souder, it will therefore be seen, has discovered no royal road to fortune. Hard work, rigid economy and intelligent enterprise, were the agencies upon which he depended for ultimate success. The firm of Walter & Souder continued their business with satisfactory results at No. 23 South Water street until 1837, when the locality known as the "Drawbridge," on the North side of Dock street, near Delaware avenue, was improved by the erection of a block of commodious and substantial stores by the city, and the firm became the lessees of the store No. 3 Dock street. In this location the affairs of the house were managed with great skill, and it enjoyed uninterrupted prosperity. At length Mr. Walter's health declined. The burthen of the business fell upon Mr. Souder; but he was fully equal to the onerous task; and when, in 1848, his partner was compelled to retire, the concern continued as profitable and prosperous as ever.

In 1854 Mr. Archibald Getty was admitted to a partnership in the house; and in 1861 his son, Stephen T. Souder, was taken into the firm. The firm is now styled Edmund A. Souder & Co. As ship owners and commission merchants they have a reputation inferior to none in Philadelphia, and may be pointed out as worthy of the highest esteem for their modest pretensions, fidelity in all engagements, enterprise and public spirit. During the various financial panics that have occurred this house has never asked for the renewal of any obligation, large or small, and for many years past it has never requested any person to *call twice for a bill admitted to be due.* It is not good luck that explains the continued and substantial prosperity of the firm; it is able and sagacious management, for which the head of the concern has always been distinguishable.

Mr. Souder has been a politician; that is to say, he has held offices of public trust. In 1844 he was elected to a seat in the Common Council of the old city proper. That body included some of the most useful and respectable of our citizens—such as seldom consent to serve in that capacity at the present day. Mr. Souder took an active part in the discussion of municipal affairs; but was always more of a business man than a talker. Subsequently he was elevated to a seat in the Select Chamber, where he was admitted to be an influential member. He advocated and voted for the municipal subscription which ensured the completion of our great Central Railroad, and labored with much success to secure private subscriptions to the stock of that magnificent enterprise. Since the passage of the Act of Consolidation Mr. Souder has devoted his attention entirely to the business of the house which he founded and raised to an honorable position among the mercantile concerns of our city, and the different institutions of which he was called to serve as a director or manager.

The subject of this sketch is affluent. He has achieved fortune and social distinction by the practice of the virtues that mark the true merchant and the public spirited citizen; by relying upon his own resources; by toiling early and late; by the judicious economy of means; by the far-sighted extension of commercial operations; and, by rendering to every man his due. "Take him for all in all," we must regard Edmund A. Souder as one of those members of the mercantile community whom Philadelphia could illy afford to lose.

ARCHIBALD GETTY.

AGAIN on our list of honored merchants we find the name of one of Ireland's sons who has crossed the Atlantic to win his way to independence. The open arms extended by our country to all whose enterprise will tempt them from home and friends in the old world, clasp closely around their adopted son; and but rarely do we find the emigrant quitting his adopted residence for the land of his nativity. In the equal struggle—the broad, free arena—the many doors leading to wealth and position, the cordial welcome and helping hand so frankly extended, the wanderer sees his recompense for any homesick yearning or pain of parting; and, on the other hand, the hospitable refuge for Europe's overplus population meets the reward of her openhanded welcome in the honorable names swelling her lists of adopted sons—the stalwart heroes guarding her flag, and the wealth poured out by the liberal hands of her naturalized citizens upon her public works and institutions.

Archibald Getty, the subject of this sketch, was one of these emigrants whose name now stands high on the record of Philadelphia merchants. He was born near Belfast, in Ireland, in the year 1822, and eight years later emigrated and came to Philadelphia. Of his youth we have no record, save that he was educated in this city. In the year 1839, having to seek some means of livelihood, he went into the earthenware store of Samuel Asbury & Co., where he remained until 1844. During that year he entered the large china store of Tyndale & Mitchell, and was book-keeper there until August, 1848, when he again made a change to take a book-keeper's position in the establishment of E. A. Souder & Co.

This firm found the services of their book-keeper so valuable that, in 1852, he was taken into the concern as a partner, and still remains there. Being an active business man, and devoted to the interests of the firm, he has contributed largely to build up its coastwise and foreign shipping; the firm now being among the largest ship owners in the country.

During the progress of the present unhappy rebellion the firm of E. A. Souder & Co. have chartered more vessels to government than any other in the country, winning invariably the warmest commendations for the honorable and handsome manner in which they have fulfilled every engagement made in their contracts. When the country again resumes her peaceful avocations, the disgrace which must cover the dishonorable proceedings of those base speculators who have made mammoth fortunes by fraudulent filling of government contracts, will show out more clearly, by the strong light of contrast, the brightness of such honorable examples of patriotic efforts to aid the government by open and honorable proceedings, such as those of E. A. Souder & Co.

Mr. Getty is a member of the Presbyterian church; was at one time a Sunday-school teacher, (Hugh Craig was one of his pupils,) and in politics stands as an old line Whig.

·In his public capacity we find him connected for many years with the Reliance Insurance Coompany as one of its directors, and in 1862 acting as President of the Corn Exchange Association.

In 1845 Mr. Getty was married, and has now three children to inherit his wealth and honorable name. He is one of the bright examples of a self-made man, with which our country is filled; who, commencing business without a dollar, is now the owner of wealth, a well earned and honorable reputation; and by a steady course of untiring industry, social morality and unwavering integrity, has won for himself a proud position on the list of our Philadelphia merchants. Still in active business, occupying a responsible post in the Corn Exchange and other organizations, a valuable member of society, and a good man, we trust he may be long spared to our city.

THEODORE H. VETTERLEIN.

THE "History of Chestnut Street," in the goodly city of Philadelphia, has been written, and well written, by Casper Souder, Jr.,
assisted by those indefatigable local antiquarians and polished gentlemen, Messrs. John McAllister, John A. McAllister and Thomas
McAllister, the opticians, who have held so prominent a place on
that thoroughfare since 1796, when their business was established.
But we think the chronicles of Broad street would present a picture of Philadelphia of interest almost equally as varied. The
southern end of this wide and noble avenue begins at the Delaware
river, and passes at first through marshes, then comes a series of
truck gardens, which extend up to within sight of the Baltimore
Depot, at Broad and Prime streets, the truck fields gradually giving place to building lots and the Southern Boulevard. From
Prime street up we have railroad tracks along the street, and on
each side rise churches, express depots, coal yards and manufactories. At Locust street the splendid Academy of Music, built mainly
by our munificent merchants, rises; then comes the world famous
Academy of Natural Sciences, with its unparalleled collection of
animate and inanimate treasures; then we see one of the finest
hotels which has ever helped to draw trade to this city—the La
Pierre; then comes Harmer's, renowned for sociability; and Shinn's,
famous as a political head quarters. A little further up we see the
warehouses of Craig & Bellas, James Steel & Co., S. L. Witmer,
Baker & Hopkins, P. Stemad & Co., Jos. Bryan & Co., Allman &
Wenger, George Cookman, and others; then a railroad depot, now
turned into a huge military hospital. Then come another series
of railroad depots, coal yards, transportation and produce houses,
followed by a collection of foundries, planing mills, lumber yards,
and Baldwin's world famous locomotive factory. Where Ridge
avenue crosses Broad street diagonally, and Coates street also
intersects Broad, a large market house and Rowland & Ervien's
extensive flouring mill are the new features; and after this point
is reached Broad street changes its character. Palatial private
residences, inhabited by prominent merchants, are seen every
square or two. Among them are the residence of Mr. Anspach,

23

built by the late Mr. Stiles, who used his wealth to beautify this portion of the city (Green Hill) in the matter especially of shade trees. After Mr. Stiles' death this beautiful residence, standing white amid its statue adorned garden, was used as a school, the teachers being nuns. A Mr. Davis then purchased it; and it next fell into the hands of Mr. Anspach, who has added to its charms as a place of residence. Mr. Anspach "suspended," and the property was twice offered at auction, and we believe is now owned by J. Edgar Thompson, Esq., President of the Pennsylvania Railroad Company.

Crossing Poplar street, a large and striking looking house, at the southwest corner of Girard avenue, attracts the eye. It is built solidly of brick, with gables, bay windows, niches, and many peculiarities of architectural grotesqueness. It has fine grounds about it, and is luxuriously fitted up. It was built by Mr. J. S. Silver, coal dealer, and sold by him to its present occupant, Mr. T. B. Peterson, the famous publisher of Chestnut street. Crossing Girard avenue, and keeping along the western side, we once more enjoy a boulevard, whose well grown trees expand along the sides of the broad pavement, making a gothic arch above the head of the pedestrian.

On Sundays and holidays this boulevard is thronged by thousands of promenaders, who gaze with delight at the residences of the merchant princes along the street, and watch the flying vehicles of those who dash along on their way to "coffee and cakes" at the Falls, to the romantic drives along the Wissahickon, or to the beautiful lands around Germantown, for Broad street is a famous route to these attractive regions in summer, while in winter the sleigh bells never cease from daybreak to midnight. But we must "drive in" ourselves if we would reach the goal of the present article.

Just above Thompson street we see the brown stone fronts and the elegant iron fences enclosing the residences of Michael Bouvier and Edwin Forrest, the tragedian. The former erected his mansion for his own occupancy, while the latter purchased his from ex-sheriff Lelar, who erected it. The locality we are describing is quite prolific in mansions erected by former sheriffs of Philadelphia county. The splendid mansion, No. 1426 North Broad street, a square above Mr. Forrest's, was built by ex-sheriff Deal; it is now owned by Mr. Swain, of the Public Ledger, while Mr. Deal also built No. 1424, now owned and occupied by George Simons, the jewelry manufacturer; and ex-sheriff Magee erected the splendid residence No. 1422, which we are about to describe. It is owned and occupied by Theodore H. Vetterlein, one of the most extensive tobacco manufacturers and dealers in the country, and whose successful career is a marked example to enterprise, energy, tact and conservative power of retaining every advantage gained.

Mr. Vetterlein's beautiful mansion stands on Broad street, with a genial southerly exposure towards Master street, which serves to ripen the rich flowers and fruits in the grounds which lie on that side of the house. It was built in the year 1856, by ex-sheriff Magee, who designed it for his own use. The financial crisis of 1857, however, compelled Mr. Magee to retrench, and he wisely began with changing his residence to a less expensive mansion. When Mr. Vetterlein purchased this elegant house, he added to its already extensive garden twenty-five feet of adjoining ground, making a front of one hundred feet to a lot of one hundred and sixty feet deep. At an immense cost this was laid out in terraces and flower beds, filled with rare and beautiful plants. A large greenhouse and prettily ornamented carriage house and stable stand in the back ground, fronting on Carlisle street. The material of the house is finely cut brown stone, fronting East and South. It is three stories high, with basements and garrets. A heavy and highly ornamented balcony on the front meets a long flight of stone steps, leading to a deep arched-way entrance on Broad street. On the South side a broad bay window and a conservatory relieve the great mass of brown stone wall. The front room of the basement is Mr. Vetterlein's smoking and reception room, back of which are the larder and wine cellar. Over these is a very large parlor, furnished magnificently with rosewood, velvet and brocatelle, the piano forte inlaid with pearl and the walls covered with elegant paintings. Passing the conservatory through a grand, wide hall, we find the refreshment and dining room, fitted up conveniently and tastefully. On the second and third floors are sitting rooms and bed chambers luxuriously furnished, and over the garrets a large observatory completes the arrangements. It commands a view of the Delaware and Schuylkill rivers, and the blue outlines of Jersey, under some peculiar atmospheric influence, appear like chains of mountains, adding considerable to the fine easterly view. Mr. Vetterlein has spared no expense to make his family as happy as wealth can make them; and if carriages, sleighs, horses, goats, donkeys, music and flowers, and all that makes up the enjoyment of the wealthy, can satisfy them, then they have nothing to desire.

Mr. Vetterlein commenced business on his own account on the failure of Essenwein & Co., in whose house he had been a book-keeper. He then went into partnership with John A. Warner, about the year 1842, and they established themselves at Second and Callowhill streets; after a career of some four or five years they separated. Mr. Vetterlein then resumed business in Second street, below Callowhill, where he remained until 1864, when he opened the handsome warehouse, No. 111 Arch street, under the firm of Vetterlein & Co., with a branch in New York under the style of T. H. & B. Vetterlein & Co. His present partners are his brother, and Thos. Theirman, who manage the house in New York. By steady steps the business has been built up, and now, at the age of about fifty-four years, Mr. Vetterlein is in possession of an ample fortune, with a constantly increasing revenue. At the opening of his career he occupied a modest resi-dence in Lombard street, between Third and Fourth; he then moved to Callowhill street, between Front and Second; subse-quently he occupied a residence on Franklin above Coates, from whence he conveyed his household goods to the palatial mansion we have described on Broad street. He has shrewdly worked the amazing tobacco trade, which has been a source of inexhaustible wealth to thousands of prudent and enterprising merchants, as may readily be surmised when we remark the growth of this vast interest. The statistics prepared by the Secretary of the Treasury show that the *exports* of tobacco from the United States became *eight times* more valuab o in 1861 than they were forty years ago, when the record begins. In the former year 66,858 hogsheads, worth $12,341,901 were exported, while in 1861 the exports were valued at $94,866,736. Of this trade Philadelphia has had a very fair proportion, and the house of Vetterlein & Co. has built itself up in at least as rapid a ratio as the growth of the trade, and the basis of his future has at least as solid a foundation.

Mr. Vetterlein has a rather large family, with grace and beauty predominating on the female side, and a bright quick intelligence manifesting itself early among the boys. His eldest daughter, Bertha, a most estimable lady, married Mr. Stephen T. Souder, a young man of wealth and active enterprise, son and partner of the well known merchant, Edmund A. Souder, in the spring of

1862. The *fete* on that occasion, after the impressive wedding in Christ Church, gave a delightful idea of the hospitality of Mr. Vetterlein, and made, for that one rainy evening, a genial glow of good feeling; warmth, light, music and pleasure spread itself over the entire neighborhood.

It is now twenty-eight years since Mr. Vetterlein emigrated from Germany and entered upon his career in Philadelphia. He was without friends, without relatives, or any of those extraneous aids by which men climb to fortune, and had to rely on his own energy and perseverance for success. His stipend on entering the business house of Messrs. Essenwein & Co., was but four dollars per week, and from that basis he has accumulated the handsome competency which we trust he may long live to enjoy, and make others enjoy, by acts of liberality which are thoroughly characteristic of the man.

THOMAS P. COPE.

THE tenacity with which English families, and families of English descent, cling to ancestral honors, is well shown in the name of the subject of this sketch. Born in the year 1768, on the twenty-sixth of August, of Quaker parents, at a time, too, when middle names were uncommon, the pride of his mother in her stern old progenitor, the Cromwellian John Pym, led to the insertion of that patronymic between what were called the Christian and surnames of her son. His father, Caleb Cope, of Lancaster, was a descendant of Oliver Cope, one of the original emigrants to Pennsylvania, a respected Friend, whose non-combatant principles kept him quiet during the Revolution, even if his political bias had not done so. Perhaps it was a congeniality of views which made him the host of Captain John Andre, the afterward celebrated Major Andre, whilst the latter, in 1776, was a prisoner on parole, and in Lancaster. Andre and Despard, afterwards the Colonel Despard of the Gordon rebellion, shared the hospitalities of the Copes. While there, the artistic talent of John Cope, an elder brother of Thomas Pym Cope, attracted the attention of the accomplished English officer, and he gave him some instructions, and even offered to sell out his commission and take him to England to accomplish his education; an offer which was declined. At this time Thomas P. Cope was a boy of twelve years of age. He saw much of the versatile Andre, who occasionally condescended to wile away the tedious hours of a prisoner of war by participating in his boyish sports.

The education of the young Cope was very good for the time in which he lived. He was well instructed in English, and was proficient in German, and had even grounded himself in Latin to a degree which gave to his mind in future years a classic bent, and rendered him clear and tasteful in his thoughts and style. In the year 1786 Thomas P. Cope, then eighteen years of age, came from Lancaster to Philadelphia, to engage in the struggle of life. He entered the store of his uncle, Thomas Mendenhall, which was situated at Nos. 19 and 21 North Second street, at the corner of Pewter Platter alley, and opposite Christ Church. Mendenhall resided at No. 28 Strawberry alley, and in this humble mansion, as it would now be thought, Thomas P. Cope resided during the whole of a greater part of the time when he was an apprentice to his uncle. In four years he had not only thoroughly mastered the details of business, but had shown so much tact, activity and integrity, that his uncle took him into partnership. The firm of Mendenhall & Cope continued but a short time, and was dissolved after two years. Young Cope had not, up to this time, the dignity of being a householder; but we find him, in 1793, residing at No. 3 North Second street, a few doors below his store. The next year he removed his dwelling to No. 196 Arch street, where he resided for several years.

In 1798 came the first visitation of that dreadful scorge, the yellow fever, which the Philadelphians of that generation had ever experienced, and in the course of its baleful ravages Thomas P. Cope was prostrated by the epidemic. Having a sound constitution, uninjured by vice or excess, he succeeded in shaking off the fetters of the grim monster, and was restored to health in time to be of eminent service to those whose turn it was to become afflicted.

Mr. Cope went through a similar sad experience in 1797, at which time he was appointed, in conjunction with William Young, bookseller, to dispense the public charity, under the direction and authority of Hillary Baker, the Mayor of the city. Mr. Cope was at the time a member of the Board of Guardians of the Poor, and he was one of the few members of that body who did not in the season of danger desert their posts.

In 1803 we find Mr. Cope once more in partnership. The firm of Cope & Thomas held forth in the old stand, No. 19 North Second street, and were extending their business. The senior partner resided at No. 191 Walnut street, a situation which he soon exchanged for a better house, at No. 36 North Fourth street, in which he lived for many years.

Whilst thus engaged in the legitimate course of his business, he laid the foundation of that goodly line of packets to Europe, which have ever since been a feature of the commerce of Philadelphia. His first ship was built in 1807, not as a packet, but for the purpose of general freight business, on the account of himself and others. To this pioneer in *his* adventure in ocean trade he gave the name of "Lancaster," in honor of his native town. It was a small vessel of only two hundred and ninety tons, but it was a very successful and lucky ship, making good voyages and bringing in successful returns.

Mr. Cope, on one occasion, tested his faith in this vessel very remarkably. At the time of the breaking out of the war with Great Britain, in 1812, the Lancaster was upon the high seas, bound to Philadelphia, coming from Canton, with a very valuable cargo of teas, silks and India goods. The seas swarmed with British cruisers, and the underwriters asked full war risk premiums, even as high as seventy-five per cent. Mr. Cope did not feel disposed to pay so much, but his partner deemed that prudence was most advisable. Mr. Cope, satisfied that he could lose his entire interest without involving himself, gave to his partner permission to insure *his* half, whilst for the other Mr. Cope determined to take the risk himself. The result justified his judgment. His partner "made assurance doubly sure," but Mr. Cope took the risk, and was gratified shortly afterward by witnessing the Lancaster coming full sail up the Delaware, despite of the king's cruisers, her captain first hearing the news of the declaration of war when he came upon shore. This was probably the foundation of the well known policy of the Copes, never to insure their ships; they believing that from the savings of money which would go for premium they could realise enough to build more ships than they should lose. In the long course of their mercantile experience we believe that they have lost but one large ship; and that, after having by many years of prosperity saved enough, by non-payment of insurance premiums, to build half a dozen such vessels.

In 1810 Mr. Cope removed from No. 19 North Second street to

the Northwest corner of Walnut street and Delaware avenue, where the house has ever since been established. It was from this point that in 1821 sailed the first vessel of the first regular line of packets to Liverpool, of which line the lucky Lancaster was the pioneer ship. It was followed by the Alexander, Algonquin, Monongahela and Montezuma, all of which were small ships in comparison to those which have succeeded in the line. The Tuscarora, a later addition, was but 379 tons burthen. Mr. Cope always had a fancy for the preservation of the original Indian names, and as the line increased the ships Allegheny, Saranak, Wyoming, Tonawanda and others have been added; the only exception from this policy being the ship Thomas P. Cope, which, we presume, was named by his sons.

The success of this line of packet ships during the forty-two years that it has been in operation, has been very great. It has been a constant and certain means of intercourse between Philadelphia and Europe. It has outlived all competitors. The Welsh line of Liverpool packets, consisting of the ships Manchester, Sarah Ralston, Plato and Philadelphia, established soon after Cope's line, lasted but a few years. The Philadelphia, Liverpool and Savannah line, comprising the Florida, Julius Cæsar, Colossus, Courier and Delaware, when first established; and later, the Arab, Ann and John Wells, made a strong effort under Thos. E. Walker & Co., but the ships were eventually withdrawn. Cope's line of packets preceded all of them, and has succeeded all of them.

Mr. Cope held, during his life, many situations of public trust, commencing as a Guardian of the Poor. We find him, in about 1799 or 1800, in the City Councils, a promoter and advocate for the introduction of the Schuylkill water into the city—one of the most important measures for the health and prosperity of the citizens ever devised. In 1807 he was elected to the State Legislature, where he forwarded internal improvements and lent his voice and vote to every proper scheme for the advantage of Pennsylvania.

He was a strong advocate for the construction of the Delaware and Chesapeake Canal, which work he forwarded by all his influence, and had the happiness to witness its success. He was equally enthusiastic as a friend of the Pennsylvania Railroad Company, and foresaw the immense advantage that it would be to the state.

He was one of the founders and an active friend of the Mercantile Library Company, of which institution he was for many years President. He was also one of the first members of the Board of

Trade, its first President, and the only President of that institution until his death, a period of twenty-one years. He came into political life once more as a member of the convention to revise and amend the constitution of Pennsylvania, which met in 1837, and he was considered one of the most useful and intelligent members of that important body. Stephen Girard, who knew well his worth, made him one of the executors of his will; and subsequently he became the President of the Board of Commissioners of the Girard Estate and a Director of the Girard College for orphans.

On the twenty-second of November, 1854, this honorable merchant and good man died, leaving behind him an unspotted reputation attained during eighty-eight years of active life in Philadelphia, and extending over the memories of three generations. To the young merchant ambitious of an useful career, no better model for life and business character could be chosen than Thomas P. Cope.

The brothers of Thomas P. Cope—Israel Cope and Jasper Cope —came to Philadelphia from Lancaster shortly after him. They entered into business about the year 1800, and at one time were in Second street, above Market, nearly opposite the store of Thomas. They afterwards went into Market street, above Fourth, at No. 165, and remained in co-partnership together during their long mercantile career. They were in the silk business. A brother of Thomas Israel and Jasper resides in Lancaster county.

Israel and Jasper Cope were succeeded by Caleb Cope and Marmaduke C. Cope, which house finally was merged in that of Caleb Cope & Co., a firm which engaged largely in the dry goods trade. The difficulties in which this old established house were involved by some of the junior partners are well remembered.

Thomas P. Cope was twice married. One of his daughters—a most estimable lady—who married Job R. Tyson, is long since dead. John, a son, died before his father.

The business of Thomas P. Cope has descended to his grandsons, who conduct their affairs under the title of Cope Brothers. Francis Cope, the most active member of this firm, is a sterling business man—enterprising, energetic and liberal. He is an estimable citizen, whose hand and purse are alike ready to assist worthy objects and to alleviate the distressed.

THOMAS DRAKE.

THE mention of the name of Mr. Drake brings the entire history of the manufactures of the city of Philadelphia. He has been instrumental in adding greatly to its products in certain classes of textile fabrics, and he has seen its manufactures grow from a very small proportion of their present extent to their existing amount. Few persons are aware of the proportion of the capital and labor of this city which is invested in manufactures. The operations in that line are conducted quietly, without much flourish or parade, and the outside world knows little of the teeming wealth which is poured forth from the manufactories which make so marked a feature in the topography of the City of Brotherly Love. We say so marked a feature, and if the reader will go from Kensington to Moyamensing, from Southwark to the old District of Penn, and gaze at the tall buildings, and still taller chimneys which mark this class of establishments, he will be fully convinced of the truth of our remark. By the last reports which have come to hand we learn the following astonishing facts relative to the manufactures of this city. There are in this city :—

Manufacturing establishments,	6,244
Capital invested,	$74,486,791
Value of raw material,	$73,662,872
Males employed,	70,281
Females employed,	30,245
Value of productions,	$141,138,835

The extent to which water and steam power are used in manufacturing in Philadelphia is immense. We can give some idea of it by choosing out a table showing the power employed in the one article of textile fabrics. The table is as follows :—

STEAM ENGINES.

	Number.	Horse Power.
In city,	286	6,624
In vicinity,	71	2,362
Total,	357	8,986

WATER POWER.

	Number.	Horse Power.
In city,	52	1,074
In vicinity,	66	2,175
Total,	118	3,249

MACHINERY, LOOMS AND SPINDLES.

	Cotton Spindles.	Cotton Cards.	Wool Spindles.	Wool Cards.
In city,	155,533	737	64,482	419
In vicinity,	197,669	857	38,462	380
Total,	353,202	1,594	102,944	799

	Power Looms.	Hand Looms.
In city,	9,693	4,598
In vicinity,	5,923	153
Total,	15,616	4,751

Total cotton spindles,	. . . . .	353,202
Total wool spindles,	. . . . .	102,944
Total silk (in city), .	. . . .	12,750
Aggregate,	. . . . .	468,896

Of textile fabrics, the manufacture in the city of Philadelphia is classified as follows :—

Number of establishments,	525
Capital,	$8,795,226
Raw material,	$12,584,440
Males employed,	9,670
Females employed,	6,731
Value of products,	$23,561,568

In these tables no account is taken of the large number of factories in Delaware, Chester and Montgomery counties, Pennsylvania, and in New Jersey, whose products seek a market in Philadelphia. Were these establishments added, we could double the figures given in the foregoing exhibits. We could justly do so too, because, in a majority of instances, the owners reside in Philadelphia, and rely upon that city as the mart for the sale of their products.

But to return to the subject of our sketch. Mr. Thomas Drake is an Englishman by birth. After he came to this country he was employed in his youth in a factory at Steubenville, Ohio, where were manufactured the first lot of the goods called Kentucky jeans, which have since been so prominent in the trade reports of our cities. In the year 1837 Mr. Drake became ambitious of a wider sphere of action than that afforded by this western town, and he came to Philadelphia. Here he soon began business on his own account as a cotton manufacturer, and after a short period he built himself a small manufactory at Manayunk, where he turned out cotton jeans, and other similar goods. From the time he began business he was noted for making a superior article, and soon won for himself a reputation for integrity which was unsurpassed.

His goods also increased in favor among business men, and the lapse of years has rather added to than taken away from their good opinion. In a few years, by close economy, Mr. Drake amassed a sum which sufficed to build a factory at Naudain and Twenty-first streets, in this city, and here he continued to manufacture goods which commanded the very best prices up to the beginning of the present war. During the past ten years he had also taken advantage of his increase of means to build a large cotton factory at Twenty-first and Pine streets, where he manufactured in large quantities print cloths, an article which, up to this time, had been only manufactured in the New England States. This was a profitable branch of his business, and Mr. Drake vigorously prosecuted it until the opening of the war caused him to draw in his resources and see where he stood.

We may inform the reader, if he is ignorant, that Mr. Drake had at this time amassed a princely fortune, every dollar of which was won by his own unvarying efforts and undeviating energy.

Mr. Drake has been, up to his retirement, one of our most successful manufacturers. He had no trivial pretension; he has been strictly upright and fair in his dealings, and in every transaction he has evinced cool and unerring judgment. He never failed to meet an obligation, and prided himself on *never giving his note.* Since his retirement he has built himself a splendid mansion in Germantown, where his hospitality is as favorably known as his integrity has been in his innumerable past business transactions.

Mr. Drake was also extensively engaged in the manufacture of woolen goods, and a large portion of his princely fortune was made by fortunate investments in real estate and coal stocks. Although socially an agreeable man, he is singularly taciturn, and his great success is to be attributed to his devoted and untiring efforts in a single direction. The wealth of the subject of this sketch exceeds a million of dollars.

Mr. Drake was the first to commence the manufacture of jeans in this country. He was the pioneer in the business, just as Benjamin Bullock, Esq., was the pioneer in our immense wool trade. The first lot of wool sent from Ohio to the seaboard was transported from Pittsburg to Philadelphia in the old conestoga wagons, and consigned to Mr. Bullock. It was only a few hundred pounds —now we receive millions of pounds from the same state. Mr. Drake was the "leader" in the business. How many have accumulated fortunes by "following their leader?"

Among the most prominent of our cotton manufacturers we notice the names of William Divine, John P. Crozier, his son Samuel Crozier, Archibald Campbell, Charles Kelly, Thomas H. Craig, Samuel Riddle and David Trainor. The most of these men are rich, very rich, and in many instances built up their collosal fortunes from the smallest imaginable beginnings.

In a book entitled "Old Merchants of New York," is a good story of how the merchants of the olden time followed their leader. It is as follows:

"Thomas H. Smith, of New York, who did a business of millions annually, built an enormous tea store in South street, up by Dover. It extended through to Water, and was a hundred feet wide. It was the wonder of the city when it was built. The docks near it were named India wharf. Smith also built famous stores at Perth Amboy, and had his tea ships land their cargoes there. The travelers to Philadelphia by the old route must often have wondered what those immense brick stores were doing in such an insignificant place as Perth Amboy. Thomas H. Smith, besides being the greatest tea merchant of his day, was also the greatest *sprecite* of his day. He was the president of a club called 'The Fire Club.' It held its meetings in Franklin Square, on the corner of Dover street. Boys have a mode of amusement called 'Follow your leader.' This was adopted by the club of which Smith was president. Many men who are now aged and respected men, or dead, belonged to the 'Fire Club.' They gave grand suppers, and their entertainments were very expensive. They would invite a guest to these suppers, explain the rules, and if he refused to join, or could not carry out the idea, the fine was one dozen champagne. These fines were occasioned by a refusal to follow their leader. On one occasion a great cotton merchant from New Orleans was a guest. He agreed to all the conditions. It was late in the evening, in the dead of winter. The ice in the East River was floating up and down with every flood or ebb of the tide. 'Follow leader,' shouted Smith, and out of the warm luxurious club-rooms poured the members of the club. Out of the Square, around the corner into Dover street. 'Follow leader,' and on rushed Smith, the president of the club, with thirty men behind him, down Dover, past Water, past Front, into South, and thence on to the pier. One of Smith's ships lay at the dock. A lighter lay inside of the main wharf. The ice was loose and dashed up around the vessels.

'Follow leader,' exclaimed Smith, as he plunged from the dock into water. Some drew back, but others followed the leader, who succeeded in getting out of the ice water on to the lighter, and from thence to the dock; and shouting 'follow leader,' he led off with frozen clothes up Dover and into the room of the Club. Plunge, plunge, plunge, one after another, and so on until all had successfully accomplished the terrible and dangerous feat. The southern cotton merchant was last. Some of the regular club members remained until they saw him reach the dock again safely, and there they left him shivering. He did not remain long. As he walked up from the dock, he noticed a large store open in South street. He entered. It was a wholesale and retail ship store. 'I have met with an accident—give me a glass of cognac, hot, with sugar and water.' It was done, and he drank it. 'Do you keep gunpowder?' he asked. Receiving an affirmative reply, he bought and paid for half a keg, and then took his way to the club room. At the door were standing two members of the club, one of whom exclaimed, 'Brave southern stranger, you have passed the ordeal safely. You are now *leader*, and we are deputed to place the club under your command, if you choose to exercise your sacred privilege.'

"'Thanks, my friends, I shall do so, but I will not ask you to go out of the room this cold night. Let us drink!' and as he entered the room he sought a side closet where hung his cloak. There he placed the keg, and then returned and took a seat at the long solid mahogany table. President Smith called the club to order. The stewards for the night opened a dozen champagne amid shouts, calls and songs of the most stirring character. 'Order, come to order!' exclaimed President Smith. When order was partially restored, he said: 'members of the club, our guest has passed the icy ordeal. He has now the right of becoming leader for the balance of the night, or until a failure in our sacred rights. What says he?'

"The cotton merchant took from his bosom a bundle of tow, and laid it on the table. All eyes were fixed upon him. 'I accept the command. I will lead now. Wait until I give the word, and then do as you see me do.' By this time he had spun the tow into a a string, that would reach from the table to the grate. He placed a tumbler on one end of the tow, to hold it on the table, and then passed the other to the pan under the grate, and made that fast with a piece of coal from the coal scuttle. Not a word was spoken.

All felt that something unusual was to occur. Cotton merchant now deliberately went to the closet, and returning with the keg, took his seat. Then he went to work and removed the hoops until he could take out the head of the little keg. Not a soul moved. Then he took a very little of what appeared to be black sand in his hand, walked to the fire, and flung it in. The considerable explosion that followed started all. 'Powder, by Jupiter,' exclaimed Smith. Cotton merchant took the end of the tow line from the glass, and pushed it down deep into the powder in the keg, and then reseated himself. 'Now, Mr. President, and members of the club, I wish you to hear what I have to say.'

"'You have tried my pluck. I come from a hot climate, and you have made me go through an icy ordeal. It is my time now, but I will not be so cruel. I will give you a *firery ordeal* to go through. If you stand it you will never need more wine; and if you do not, the fines will amount to a small fortune, and you will have wine enough to last your club a year. Look at me.' He walked to the fire, kicked off the coal lump, and placed the other end of the tow-line in the red hot coals. Then he walked back, and as he brought his fist down upon the table, said in tones of thunder as he sat down, 'Keep your seats, and thus follow your leader.' The fire curled up in fitful spouts from the burning tow—it burnt over the grate pan, and began to crawl along the carpet. It had eighteen feet to go. Sixty and odd single eyes watched the burning train. One rose from his seat, then another; finally one exclaimed, 'we shall all be blown to old Nick,' and made for the door. The panic increased. Down stairs the club members plunged, like a flock of sheep. Even old Smith, the President, was among the first to bolt from the room. Before the tow-line had burned as far as the table all were gone but the cotton merchant. As soon as he saw that he was alone he placed his foot upon the burning tow, and extinguished it. Then he opened the window and emptied the keg into the snow, and again resumed his seat. He waited long for the return of the club members; one by one they did come back. There cotton sat, until Smith took his seat as president. 'Now call for the fines,' he said, and a severe lecture he gave them for their follies and real cowardice."

SAMUEL COATES.

AMONG the merchants of Philadelphia who united the traditions and experience of the ante-revolutionary period, with the stirring activity and commercial excitement which followed the establishment of peace, Samuel Coates for many reasons deserves mention. He was in some sense a representative man, who kept up during his life, in business matters, a full show of what commerce and business had been in Philadelphia, in the good old time. He represented that class of merchants, of whom there were in former times a large number in the city, who made business not only a means of support merely, but enabled them to contribute largely to objects of philanthropy and public benefit. After the signature of Samuel Coates might properly have been written "philanthropist and merchant." For although as a business man he was faithful and discreet, yet during many years of his life, business was with him of secondary importance to the prosecution of plans which were for the benefit of others.

The Coates' are an old Philadelphia family. Thomas Coates, the grandfather of the subject of this sketch, came to the city in 1684, from Leicestershire, England. As usual with the men of means of that day, he became a landholder in the infant colony. But being also of business education, he became a merchant, being cotemporary with Samuel Carpenter and other enterprising citizens of young Philadelphia. The father and mother of Samuel Coates died whilst he was yet a child, and they left but small means. But the boy found a friend in his uncle, John Reynell, and he was taken into his family. Under the generous care of this patron, he was carefully educated in the English branches, and received a very fair classic instruction, which controlled his tastes in after life. Reynell directed the thoughts of his protegee to mercantile pursuits, and he was secured an excellent business education. The confidence of Reynell in the solid qualities and prudence of Samuel Coates, was such, that in the year 1768, Samuel being then but nineteen years old, he was furnished with a small capital, and trusted to carry on business for himself. For three years this very young merchant conducted his own affairs. The experiment was in every way satisfactory, and in 1771 he was removed to a larger sphere, being taken by his friend Reynell as a partner. This connection was soon rendered of but little practical value by the events of the American Revolution, and after lingering through several dull years of the struggle, it was closed, in 1782, by the withdrawal of John Reynell, leaving Samuel Coates in possession of the business. A partnership of short duration was then formed by Samuel Coates with his brother, Josiah Langdale Coates, but the latter soon withdrew from the connection, and in 1785 we find that Samuel was in business alone in a building at the northwest corner of Front and Walnut streets, (still in existence,) and Josiah, as a grocer, in Church alley, between Second and Third streets. In 1791 Samuel was located as a merchant at 82 South Front street, at the corner of Walnut street, which was the place of his business for many years afterwards. He died in and was buried from this place.

After the close of the Revolution Mr. Coates devoted himself to the establishment of a business with New England. Newburyport, Mass., was at that time a place of active trade, and Coates opened a correspondence with Moses Brown, and the Bartlett brothers. Among other houses with which he had transactions, extending over many years, were Benjamin Willis of Portland, Maine, and John A. Curtis Bolton, of Savannah, Georgia.

The fearful epidemic of 1793 found Samuel Coates among the few citizens of means who remained in the city. He was appointed, together with Benjamin W. Morris and George Rutter, upon an assistant committee to the principal committee of citizens. It was the duty of this sub-committee to seek out and recommend suitable objects for relief. The boundaries of its jurisdiction was from the south side of Walnut street to the north side of Spruce street. During the continuance of the epidemic Mr. Coates was earnest, useful and faithful. His duties at this time seem to have directed his attention to matters of kindness and usefulness to his fellow men; although before that time he had become connected with some important institutions. He was elected a manager of the Pennsylvania Hospital, in 1785, in the place of George Mifflin, deceased. Of this institution he became an active and conscientious supporter, serving in various offices, devoting his time to its prosperity, and never failing in readiness to answer every demand for his assistance. His fellow managers testified their sense of his services, in 1812, by electing him President of the Board, which office he was afterwards compelled to resign, upon account of phy-

25

194

BIOGRAPHIES OF

sical infirmity, after forty-one years of unremitting attention to
the interests of the Hospital. His portrait, by Sully, is in the
possession of the institution, and honor well merited by his many
years of devotion to the interests of the afflicted.

A service nearly as long as that given to the hospital was extended by Samuel Coates to the body entitled "The Overseers of
the Public Schools, founded by charter in the town and county of
Philadelphia;" which body was the ruling authority managing
what were called "the Quaker Schools," so long located on Fourth
street, below Chestnut. Mr. Coates was nominated and appointed
to be an "Overseer" in 1786, and resigned his position in 1823,
after a service of thirty-seven years.

In 1800 he was elected a Director of the first Bank of the United
States, and served in the Board with Thos. Willing, the President,
Elias Boudinot, Samuel Breck, Archibald McCall, Wm. Bingham,
Robert Smith, Isaac Wharton, Thos. Ewing, Jeremiah Parker, and
others. The first Bank of the United States was managed on very
different principles from the second. It was one of the few banking corporations in the country which ever wound up successfully
on the expiration of the term for which it was chartered; all its
debts were paid; the stock was paid in full, and in the end—about
1811—every stockholder, beside his annual dividend, received
$197.42 for every $100 invested. Mr. Coates' ideas of banking
were prudent, and if followed at this day could not result in anything but a successful issue. His maxims on the subject were as
follows:

1. A bank cannot bear the shadow of suspicion.
2. A bank is created to facilitate *commerce,* and has nought to
exist for any other purpose. [When these opinions were uttered,
manufactures had not become as important as they now are. The
addition of "manufactures" to "commerce" would at this time
meet the theory of Mr. Coates.]
3. The proper check on the imprudent management of a bank
consists in a decline of the market value of its stock.
4. No reasonable man will give money for the stock of a bank
at any price at all, if it be used for any other purpose than faci-
litating commerce [or manufactures.]
5. Or if it be at a place that is not commercial [or a manufacturing centre].
6. Or if its capital is out of proportion to the business of the
place.

7. Or if it meddles with politics.

8. Or if there be a *politician* in the board of directors.

These apothegms were vindicated by Mr. Coates when the second bank of the United States was chartered. He refused to subscribe for its stock, and said that its capital, $35,000,000, was, in 1816, "out of all proportion to the business of the country, and out of all reason." He said "that nothing but trouble would come out of it," and history has shown that he understood exactly what he was endeavoring to impress upon others.

Mr. Coates was Treasurer of the Philadelphia Library Company from 1784 until 1824, when he withdrew, in consequence of age and infirmity.

His career as a merchant was influenced by his philanthropic exertions. His business, at one time prosperous, was neglected, and dwindled away; and when he finally gave up his affairs, he had but sufficient to pay his debts and leave a small competence, where he could have realized a handsome fortune, had he devoted to himself that attention and service which he gave to others.

Mr. Coates was married in 1775 to Lydia Saunders, by whom he had four children: John Reynell Coates, Hannah Coates, Joseph Saunders Coates, and Lydia Coates, and three who died in infancy. After a union of thirteen years his wife died, in 1789. In 1791 he married Amy Horner, by whom he had three children: Samuel Horner Coates, Benj. Horner Coates, and Reynell Coates—the two latter afterwards becoming physicians. B. H. Coates now resides at the northwest corner of Seventh and Spruce, and Reynell Coates resides at Camden, N. J.

Samuel Coates died June 4, 1830, at the age of eighty-one years, nine months and twenty-two days, after a life which was, perhaps, more useful as a citizen than as a merchant; but after a career which was honorable and useful in his public and private relations.

CHARLES S. BOKER.

THE business of banking is, in this country, an accidental pursuit, which rarely demands the attention of persons who are charged with financial trusts before they are inducted into positions which involve grave responsibilities. In Europe, the private banker is usualy brought up to his profession, and instructed in its doctrines and practices at an early age. He grows up to understand that banking is a science, and learns every day the important lesson that rash self-confidence cannot be permitted to control interests which are vast and important. But in the United States the prevalence of corporations, and the advantages to be gained from associate effort in the employment of capital, have made public banking all popular, and have, therefore, in a measure reduced the science of finance to an accomplishment which is to be acquired only when necessity actually arises. How much this system has contributed towards the instability of American banks; how many of the disasters which have in times past overwhelmed the banks and the community are to be ascribed to a policy which makes the most popular stockholder a director, and the most popular director president of the bank; how many blunders have been made by city bank officers who have come from the counting-house or factory into the director's room; and, how many serious and expensive mistakes have, in the country, been made by bank presidents who have left the plough to take their seats at the head of the board, we shall not stop to inquire. There have been serious losses by the loose system of bank organization which has been prevalent throughout the country; and yet, it is fair to say that there have been occasions when, among a number of stockholders there has been happily found one man by whom financial principles seemed to be perfectly well understood, and who has wielded the interests entrusted to him with care and success.

In presenting the name of Charles S. Boker, we shall instance a case in which one who had previously conducted commercial affairs, closed his life by a long and successful financial career at the head of one of our institutions, which by previous mismanagement had been brought to the verge of insolvency.

On the nineteenth of January, 1797, Charles S. Boker was born in the city of Philadelphia, at No. 98 South Water street, where his father, Aaron Boker, a tailor, carried on his business. When Charles was about four years old his father removed from Water street to No. 134 South Front, where he still pursued his sartorial occupation. This avocation was shortly after given up, and in 1807 Aaran Boker was an "iron monger" at No. 12 South Second street, and still later a general "merchant" at the same place.

The means of Aaron Boker were not extensive, and all that he could do for his children was to ensure them the rudiments of a good English education. To obtain this benefit Charles was sent, at a proper age, to "Benny Tucker," a schoolmaster well known to the people of the last generation, and still remembered by some who are yet living. Mr. Tucker had been a merchant before the year 1800, but having been unsuccessful in business, necessity made a teacher, an occupation which his fine acquirements rendered easy to him. At No. 98 Arch street Master Tucker governed his young pupils, and there young Boker obtained all the education which the schools ever gave him.

At the age of fifteen he was inducted into the busy scenes of active life, and he commenced his experience in his father's store. Three years later he assumed greater responsibilities in another establishment, and in consequence of the absence of the head of the house was entrusted with the sole management of the business. From the year 1815 until the year 1821, Mr. Boker directed the interests entrusted to him, and in that time he attained a promptitude of decision, and an excellence of judgment which were of the utmost importance to him in after years. He first went into business upon his own account at No. 32 Church alley, and there established a "domestic coffee warehouse." He tried that experiment for four years, and then relinquished the pursuit. In 1825 he was established at No. 12 North Fourth street, in a "leghorn store." In 1828 he was in the same business at No. 27 North Second street, and he remained there for nine years, by the end of which time, he added to the leghorn and straw hat business the shoe business, which now seems to be indissolubly united to the former. As his customers increased, and his profits accumulated, Mr. Boker made various investments from time to time. Among other enterprises to which he appropriated his money, the purchase of bank stock attracted his attention. To this circumstance is to be attributed his connection with the Girard Bank, which association afterwards became of vast importance to himself and to the institution. Holding a large quantity of stock, he was soon chosen by his fellow members to discharge the responsible duties of director. A faithful attention to the duties of that situation, and a close observation of the method in which business had been carried on in the bank gave him so many advantages, that in the hour of trouble he was considered by his associate directors the most proper person in the board to assume the management of its financial affairs.

We do not intend to write a history of the Girard Bank at this time. It is only necessary to say that its misfortunes dated from an early period after its charter. Its officers were either good natured or imprudent. They made large and injudicious loans, and in a few years the means of the institution was very much restricted. When, therefore, the extraordinary commercial revulsions happened which shook the firmest banks in the Union, the "Girard" had no strength of its own to resist the pressure. In the course of these financial troubles the bank had not only to suspend payment, but to make an assignment. It was at this period of gloom, when the stockholders had abandoned all hope, that Mr. Boker was called upon to pilot the shattered bank to some safe part of the strand, where, whilst abandoning ship and cargo, the crew might escape from the wreck. It was a forlorn hope that he undertook to lead. An entire recovery of the stock and capital was deemed impossible; all that was asked of the new president was that he should prevent the losses from increasing. It was a gloomy task which he undertook, but he resolved if possible to lighten the prospects of all who were interested. He applied himself assiduously to the business of the bank. He succeeded in extricating a portion of the capital. He managed to surmount the legal difficulties which surrounded the subject, and after the bank had been given up as irrevocably dead it was miraculously revived, and placed once more in the current of business.

Nor was this all. Under the steady management of Mr. Boker the bank regained gradually the confidence of the community. Business came back to it; its capital slowly increased, and still managed by the same care and fidelity, it has assumed as solid a position as many institutions which have had much better luck during their corporate existence.

On the tenth day of February, 1858, Mr. Boker died, surviving his beloved wife but five weeks. Grief for the loss of one who had been for many years his counsellor, companion and friend, hastened his last sickness, and sent him to rejoin the blessed one in another world.

THOMAS MIFFLIN.

In a period of general excitement, (June, 1863,) when the State of Pennsylvania is, for the first time in eighty-six years, made the scene of hostile invasion—upon a day, too, sacred to great memories—and a time when our own merchants are shouldering their muskets to meet the invaders of the soil, it will not be improper to slightly vary from the general plan of these papers, by a sketch of a Philadelphia merchant, who gave up the counting-room for the battle-field, laid down the pen and took up the sword, and after a series of eminent service in the field, became equally renowned in high position as a statesman.

Thomas Mifflin was a descendant of an old Philadelphia family which was attached to the society of Friends. At the time of his birth, in the year 1744, it could scarcely have been imagined that the quiet Quaker child, so straight laced and sedate, would ever become a Major General in an army, or the Governor of his native state. His parents designed him for the quiet pursuits of peaceful life, and they superintended the education which they supposed would be useful to him. After preliminary studies at the Quaker school, he was entered as a student at the College of Philadelphia, where he went through the usual course, acquiring a respectable knowledge of the classic languages, which accomplishment was of much importance to him in after life. At a proper age he was placed in the counting-house of William Coleman, of Philadelphia, a man whom Dr. Franklin said "had the coolest head, the best heart, and the *exactest* morals of almost any man he ever met with." At the age of twenty-one years young Mifflin, having fully accomplished himself in those mercantile principles and practices which were to be learned in Coleman's counting-house, was sent by his father to Europe, in order to improve his mind and enlarge his ideas, by the results of foreign travel.

On his return to Philadelphia, Mr. Mifflin entered into business with a brother, and put into practice the prudential maxims which he had learned in his boyhood. His bent of mind, however, was strongly turned toward public affairs, and his talent and manners recommended him to his fellow-citizens as a fit trustee of the public interests. He had taken some part in the discussions in regard to the policy of the British government, which were arousing the feelings of the colonists, and his efforts were always upon the patriotic side. His opinions entitled him to the respect of his fellow citizens, and accordingly, in 1772, he was elected a Burgess Representative of the city of Philadelphia, in the General Assembly of Pennsylvania. His course in the Legislature met with the approval of his constitents, and once more, in the succeeding year, he was again returned to represent the city, having a colleague in Dr. Benjamin Franklin. In 1774, his energy, eloquence and steadfast devotion to the rights of the people, were rewarded by his election to the first Continental Congress.

In April, 1775, news of the battle of Lexington was received in Philadelphia. There was great excitement—a town meeting was called in the State House yard—Mifflin was one of the principal speakers. His efforts were directed not only to rousing the feeling of the people, but to producing important consequences. He said, (and the advice might be repeated at the present day,) " Let us not be bold in declaration, and afterwards cold in action. Let not the patriotic feelings of to-day be forgotten to-morrow, nor have it said of Philadelphia that she passed noble resolutions and afterwards neglected them." This advice he followed up by suggesting the formation of companies and regiments, and the introduction of daily drills. His fellow citizens followed his advice, and the young Quaker was introduced to military life by being elected Major of one of the new regiments. But his active spirit was unsatisfied with the mere routine of the city militia. The seat of war was at that time distant from his home, but resolved upon active service, he sought the American camp at Boston. His first field service was at the skirmish at Lechmire's Point, where he had command of a party which repelled the British regulars with bravery and success.

After this, he took upon himself the discharge of the duties of the Quartermaster General's Department, which had been previously undertaken by General Stephen Moylan, but which, under the management of that officer, had become very much confused. It required a mercantile mind to properly conduct this important branch of the army organization, and, in General Mifflin, the right man for the place was found. He was soon after commissioned a Brigadier General.

In 1776, matters looked very gloomy throughout the United Colonies, and the patriot cause was so much despaired of, that calls upon the country for troops were answered coldly and unwillingly. The state of Pennsylvania was deficient in her quota, and as a means of rousing the people, Gen. Mifflin, with his fine manner and eloquent tongue, was sent through the state to address the people in town and county meetings, and to arouse their slumbering patriotism. In this mission he was very successful. He was enthusiastically received, and he accomplished much towards blowing up the dying embers into a blaze. For this service, and for his devotion to the cause, he received from Congress, in February, 1777, the commission of a Major General. He was still attached to the Quartermaster's Department, and, having a very responsible position, and the clashing interests of the States and Congress to harmonize, he fell under the censure which scarcely any occupant of this department can escape. Congress, for a time, withdrew its confidence from him. A committee of inquiry was appointed to examine his conduct in the Quartermaster's Department, a committee which made no inquiry or report, and the injustice of whose appointment was finally atoned for by the passage of a resolution of thanks, by Congress, in 1780, to Gen. Mifflin, for his " wise and salutary plans of retrenchment of the general expenses."

The greatest blot upon Gen. Mifflin's military career was the part which he took in the "Conway Cabal," to displace Gen. Washington, and appoint Gen. Gates Commander-in-Chief. This conspiracy failed in its object, and although Gen. Washington never liked those who were engaged in it, he generously stifled his own feelings, out of regard to the public interests, upon the subsequent employment, by Congress, of the officers conspicuous in the plot.

After the conclusion of the Revolutionary War, Gen. Mifflin was elected, in 1783, a member of Congress, and in November of that year he became the President of that body, and had the honor of receiving from Gen. Washington the resignation of the great power with which he had been invested. He was a member of the Pennsylvania Legislature in 1785, and in 1788 was a member of the Supreme Executive Council of Pennsylvania, of which important body he soon became President, and Governor *de facto* of the State. After that he was elected a member of the Convention to form the Federal Constitution, and took a leading part in that august body. Immediately afterwards he was appointed to the Convention to form a new Constitution for the state of Pennsylvania, and he was elected its President. To this succeeded his

26

highest civil honor.   He was the first Governor of Pennsylvania elected under the Constitution, and he held this seat by three successive elections, from 1790 until 1799, passing through, in that time, the anxieties of the epidemics of 1793, 1798 and 1799, the responsibilities thrown upon him by the "Whiskey Insurrection" of 1794, and also the war with France of 1799.   Having faithfully discharged these great duties, and having returned to private life, but few months were vouchsafed to him for that enjoyment.   He died at Lancaster, the twenty-fourth of January, 1800, being then a member of the Legislature of Pennsylvania.

He was the only merchant who in Pennsylvania ever attained to the glory of the epauletts or to high civil honors.   As such, his name is worthy of remembrance, and his example should at this time be considered a proud inheritance by those merchants and business men who are called upon to protect and defend their native state and native city.

SAMUEL BISPHAM.

WE only begin to appreciate the immense value of the trade of Philadelphia when we descend to details, and estimate the amount of each item that goes to swell the enormous aggregate.   When we find that of groceries alone our city now sells to the Western country about fifty millions of pounds per annum, and to the South many millions of pounds more, and consider that this is but a single wave of that great stream of internal commerce of which the busy metropolis is the fountain head, we gain a tolerable conception of the mighty interests involved, and the multiplied source of our wealth.   The wholesale grocers of Philadelphia now occupy a commanding position among the business men of the Union.   Taking advantage of the peculiar facilities enjoyed by this city for the concentration and distribution of the various articles that enter into this branch of trade, they have steadily widened the circle of their transactions, cultivated intimate relations with dealers in the most distant part of the country, and exhibited tact and energy that could not fail to ensure a large and very profitable traffic.

Among them may be found men of unsurpassed ability as merchants, and also public-spirited citizens, who manifest a lively interest in every project that promises to advance the prosperity and influence of the community in which they live. Several of our leading grocers furnish remarkable examples of indomitable industry, steady self-reliance and sagacious management, and we select one of their number as the subject of the ensuing biographical sketch.

Samuel Bispham is known to the majority of our business men as the head of the house of Samuel Bispham & Sons, wholesale grocers and commission merchants. But the antecedents of the successful merchant and respected citizen, may not be so familiar to those who are so ready to honor him on account of the high social station he has attained. He was born in the year 1796, in a house located on Market street, below Second. His father was a hatter, and in moderate circumstances. In 1798 Philadelphia was visited by that terrible scourge the yellow fever. A panic pervaded the city; all who could find means to leave the infected locality departed in haste, as if death were in pursuit. The elder Bispham took his family to a farm near Moorestown, New Jersey, where he remained until his demise in 1808. While yet a small child, young Samuel was sent to market with produce, and we are informed that it was while vending butter, eggs, &c., in the midst of the bustle of Market street, that he adopted a resolution to become a merchant. He seems to have possessed a natural aptness for trade. The death of his father threw the poor lad on his own resources, and in the year 1808, he succeeded in getting a situation as errand boy in the grocery store of Mr. William Carman, on Market street, above Front. There he remained until the year 1810, when he went to the grocery store of Mr. John Snyder, on Market street, below Ninth. At this period the trade between Philadelphia and the Western country commenced to assume importance. The traffic was carried on by means of the great lumbering conestoga wagons, and transportation was extremely slow and expensive. Among the prominent houses at that time were Henry Pratt, Simon & Hiram Gratz, Paul Beck, Levi Taylor, Guyer & Diehl, Clark & Greiner, Robert Fleming, Horner & Wilson, Matthew Baxter, Samuel & Aaron Denman, Hamilton & Wood, Robert Toland, and Peter Lex. Mr. Snyder was engaged in this trade, and young Bispham had ample opportunities for learning its mystery and appreciating its difficulties, while serving an apprenticeship as book-keeper and salesman. Always nursing his ambition to achieve to high position in the business world, the young man economized his earnings and cultivated habits of attention, promptitude and industry, so that when, in 1815, he determined to try his own wings, he had a small capital, excellent qualifications, and considerable experience to strengthen his confidence.

He chose for a partner Mr. Jacob Alter, a gentleman still living, and ranking as one of our most "solid" citizens. The firm opened a store at No. 825 Market street. They entered vigorously into the trade with the interior and the West, and were so successful that it was said there was scarcely a house upon the great road between Philadelphia and Pittsburg, in which the firm of Alter & Bispham was not known; their traffic even extended to some points beyond the western boundary of Pennsylvania. The young merchants were industriously pursuing the path of fortune, when a crisis in monetary affairs suddenly threatened to darken their prospects and overwhelm them with ruin. From 1819 until 1821 inclusive, the commercial depression was wide-spread and disastrous; the country customers of Messrs Alter & Bispham made but few payments. During this gloomy period, and while the affairs of the firm were in a desperate condition, Mr. Bispham determined to go upon a tour of collection in person. He was compelled to go upon horseback by the necessities of the time, and thus, alone, he journeyed as far as Pittsburg. The traveler who now accomplishes the same distance within twelve hours, will smile upon learning that Mr. Bispham did not reach his final destination until about three weeks after he left Philadelphia. But the result of this arduous tour were eminently satisfactory. Upon reaching Pittsburg Mr. Bispham found that he had collected a sum sufficient to meet all the obligations of the firm. The money was immediately forwarded to Philadelphia, and with this timely assistance the house was enabled to maintain a good standing, whilst almost every other firm on Market street was prostrated or totally ruined. Mr. Bispham's reputation for energy and business talent was greatly enhanced by this astonishing performance.

Alter & Bispham continued to prosper and to enlarge their sphere of business operations until 1830, when the senior partner retired, and Mr. Bispham took the business entirely under his own control. During the fifteen years of their association, these enterprising merchants were distinguished for their rigid fidelity to all engagements, successful management and liberal spirit. Mr. Alter subsequently became interested in coal lands, and from these he

now receives a very heavy income. In 1833 Mr. Bispham purchased the building now designated at No. 629 Market street, below Seventh, and moved his establishment to that structure, where
he has remained until the present day. In 1851 Mr. Samuel A.
and John S. Bispham was taken into partnership, and the style of
the firm was changed to Samuel Bispham & Sons, as it is still
known.

The subject of this sketch is now about sixty-eight years of age.
His life has been one of toil and intelligent enterprise. He is
the oldest grocer in Philadelphia, having been engaged in this
branch of trade about fifty-one years. Of all the grocery houses
that existed here at the time Mr. Bispham began business'upon his
own account, not one is left. Mr. Bispham is the patriarch, the
chief representative, and the luminous example in his department
of traffic. The dreams of the poor boy while selling Jersey produce in our commercial avenue have been more than realized.
Honest application, determined energy, skilful management, and
unswerving integrity have, in this instance, been duly honored and
largely rewarded.

Mr. Bispham has been too much absorbed in his private affairs
to allow of his participating actively in movements of public concern. He has never "dabbled in the dirty pool of politics,"
although he is careful to exercise the privilege of a freeman in support of what he conceives to be conservative principles and conservative men. He has been a Director of the Bank of Penn
Township, to which institution he was one of the original subscribers. He has also faithfully discharged his duties as a member of
the Board of Managers of the Schuylkill Navigation Company,
and a Director of the Reliance Insurance Company, in both of
which he is largely interested. But his modesty and retiring disposition have deterred him from accepting positions of public trust
which he could have commanded at any time, Religiously he is
tolerant, and free from any shade of sectarian bigotry. He is also
a generous and charitable man; one who gives to the poor with a
bountiful hand, without having his donations trumpeted in the
street, or glaring from the columns of the press. Socially, he is
very genial and pleasant, and his conversation evinces great practical sense, quick observation and cautious judgment. No Philadelphian's name has been current in business circles for a longer
series of years, and we know of none that can claim a greater degree of respect.

LAWRENCE PETERSON.

In certain characteristics which help to make up the character of a successful merchant, the late Lawrence Peterson stood prominent among his brethren, and at his death the community suffered a severe loss—a loss which has not yet been made good, so far as our experience extends. Mr. Peterson was a native of Philadelphia, and was born in 1816. In early years he struggled with pecuniary difficulties, and manly breasted the tide of life which seemed then to set against him. When a youth he entered the silk and dry goods establishment of John M. Whitall, in Market street, east of Third, near the site of the old Commercial Bank. Here he rose, as his abilities became tested, and formed associations which made him prominent and unusually successful in after life. Subsequently he became a member of the silk house of Yard, Gillmore & Co., taking the financial department of their extensive business, and managing it with great skill until his death in 1862. This firm was located for many years in Market street. Subsequently they removed to Third street, below Arch, where they remained until a few years since, when their warehouse was badly damaged by fire. They then removed to their present location, in one of Dr Jayne's beautiful marble-fronted stores on the north side of Chestnut street, above Sixth. They were the first wholesale silk firm which moved into Chestnut street. Mr. Peterson had the arrangement of the new Chestnut street store made under his own eye; but the firm had hardly got into the successful tide of their operations there before Mr. Peterson was carried away by consumption, his death taking place at midnight of April 1, 1862. Since that period Mr. Gillmore, another partner of the same firm, has also deceased.

Mr. Peterson's talents as a financier were remarkable. They enabled him to outride all financial storms, and would have qualified him for success in public life, if his taste had led him in that direction. Few men were so intelligent and comprehensive in regard to everything which entered into the questions which are ever settling themselves in regard to the business of the whole country. He never confused one with whom he was conversing on these subjects with the technics of political economy; but with a singularly transparent clearness he would state all that any one knew touching the principles and facts of the whole matter, and frankly point out the precise point where his information stopped. We have known him, months before a given result in regard to business occurred, clearly to state it as the inevitable development of causes then in operation. We have known him to state the minute as well as general principles that would regulate the business of a fall or spring season not yet reached. He had, in short, a thorough business talent; a judgment singularly sound, and an acuteness that saw through all false appearances to the bottom of the actual facts of every case. While industrious to a fault, over-tasking his delicate constitution, and thoroughly attentive to his business, Mr. Peterson was unambitious beyond that point. Never was anything more orderly and even elegant than his store, his house, his grounds, and everything with which he was concerned. But beyond this he seemed disinclined to go. He took but little part in politics, in public institutions or entertainments, and even confined his social life to within a limited circle. Yet he was well qualified for enjoyment and success in all these ways. Of a rather slight build, elegant figure, with a keen eye, a bright mind and a kindling intellect, he was one never seen without attracting attention. His opinion carried weight with it. His presence had in it a peculiar charm. Mr. Peterson was a singularly brave man; in the entire battle of life his moral courage was most conspicuous. He "took the responsibility," habitually, and in the fine language of an English writer, "seized the purposes of others and threw them forward in his own direction." Nobody ever dreamed, after knowing him even for a short time, that Lawrence Peterson would flinch from anything, and when his mind was made up, no one that knew him well ever thought of trying to alter it.

For a number of years, Mr. Peterson contended with the disease which finally carried him off; but he fought it so resolutely that his friends hardly thought he would ground arms to it at last. Nearly a score of years since, he went in company with a robust and hearty friend to have his life insured. The insurance agent declined to take the risk of Mr. Peterson's life, but insured his robust friend. Within a year the latter died, while Mr. Peterson lived to tell the story eighteen years afterwards, in the parlor of his elegant residence on Girard avenue. In religion he was a Presbyterian. He connected himself with the Presbyterian Church in

Arch street, then under the care of Dr. Skinner, from which he went to the Clinton street church, under Drs. Todd, Parker and Darling; and at last, settling himself in a beautiful place on Green Hill, he joined the latter congregation. His piety was not demonstrative. He abhorred—the word is not too strong—all cant; he could bear no shadow of humbug; he could listen to nothing but the truth on all subjects, theoretical and practical. He was the same in his religion, which he supported not only in sentiment but by liberal and frequent pecuniary contributions to all objects connected with the denomination to which he was attached. At his death he was sincerely mourned by the entire neighborhood, and at his funeral, at Laural Hill, four distinguished clergymen themselves lowered the coffin into the grave, to testify their deep respect for his memory.

Lawrence Peterson was a brother of Charles J. Peterson, the accomplished author and editor of *Peterson's Magazine*. Theophilus B. Peterson, the head of the publishing house of T. B. Peterson & Brothers, and a most estimable gentleman, is also his brother, the firm having originally consisted of T. B., George, (since deceased), and Thomas. The entire family possesses business talents of the first order, and have been remarkably successful. The volumes issued by T. B. Peterson & Brothers, are known and read in every household in the land, and their business seems to increase with each year. They issue not only light literature, but editions of standard works which adorn thousands of libraries in all parts of the country; and in analyzing the characteristics of Lawrence Peterson, we think we give a very fair idea of the peculiarities of the entire family. Having been mainly the architects of their own fortunes, the bold, strong traits of their disposition have been brought into clear relief, and we confess that we like to describe those robust mental traits by which men rise to eminence in any walk of life.

We cannot close this notice without referring to Mr. Whitall, who is a most successful merchant. He was born near Woodbury, N. J., and was formerly captain of the ship "New Jersey," owned by the late Whitton Evens, engaged in the West India and East India shipping business. Mr. Evans failed, and died in rather indigent circumstances. Mr. Whitall afterwards engaged in mercantile pursuits, and is said to be quite wealthy. He is now of the firm of Whittall & Tatum, Nos. 408 and 410 Race street, largely engaged in the glassware trade, and have extensive glassworks in New Jersey.

BENJAMIN W. RICHARDS.

In the long succession of Mayors of the City of Philadelphia, extending from the year 1701 until 1863, the proportion of merchants is small. Before the Revolution, when men of business talents were required, and the Recorder was the law officer of the city, there were many mercantile men who were elected to the office of Mayor. Among them may be specified Richard Hill, Mayor in 1709, William Fishbourne in 1721, Clement Plumstead in 1736 and 1750, and Thomas Willing, elected in 1765. For the last forty years the lawyers seem to have preference in the Mayoralty, there being during that time but three Mayors not lawyers by profession, viz:—Robert Wharton, Joseph Watson, and Benjamin W. Richards. It is manifest that in these times a good lawyer is better suited for the Mayoralty than a civilian, who, whatever his administrative capacity, must be ignorant of many legal doctrines which, in the conduct of municipal affairs, need frequent and prompt application.

Benjamin W. Richards was the last merchant Mayor of the city of Philadelphia, and to the very successful public and private career of that gentleman we shall devote this sketch. Mr. Richards had the advantage of being born to the possession of wealth, which placed him, at the proper time, in position to use his talents to advantage. He first saw the light at Batsto Iron Works, Burlington county, New Jersey, in the year 1797. His father, William Richards, was the proprietor of the extensive furnace and forges at that place. He was a man of wealth and social influence in New Jersey, and an extensive land owner. He had the means to ensure to his son a splendid education, and the natural aptitude of young Benjamin enabled him to make rapid progress in his studies. He was sent in his early boyhood to New Brunswick, where he was placed under the charge of the Rev. Mr. Dunham. He progressed rapidly under the instructions of that gentleman, and was at the Freshman age perfectly qualified for admission to the college at Princeton. Here he was an earnest student, and graduated with all the honors when he was nineteen years old. At that time he was distinguished by his religious principles, his interest in that subject having been awakened by the preaching and instruction of the Rev. Dr. Alexander. He was desirous of studying for the ministry, and was ready to prepare himself for the important office. But his health being delicate it was considered important that he should take means to recruit his constitution. His sedentary life had weakened his strength, and traveling was prescribed as the best restorative. He accordingly left Batsto for the Southern states. Through this region of country he traveled extensively on horseback, stopping at towns and partaking of the hospitalities of the planters. From the South he struck towards the West, and he traversed many parts of the country which were then wild and uncultivated, but which are now the garden spots of the Union. When he returned to his home. in the year 1818, he had thoroughly renovated his health, and his body had assumed those splendid proportions which in after years distinguished him as one of the finest looking men in our city. It was then determined that he should embark in mercantile pursuits; and although he had never had the experience or training deemed necessary for the successful business man, he had capital sufficient to command a connection with those who had acquired a full knowledge of the principles of trade by patient service.

Upon his coming to this city the opportunity was not long wanting. He formed a partnership with Jesse Godley in the year 1819, and the firm of Godley & Richards was established at No. 53 Market street, at which place Mr. Godley had been previously located. In this firm Mr. Richards continued for about three years. How much longer he would have remained with Mr. Godley it is not now necessary to enquire. His course of life was altered by one of those important events which exercise a great influence upon the destinies of every man. In his social intercourse with the best society in the city, he met with a beautiful and amiable young lady, the daughter af Joshua Lippincott, of the firm of J. & W. Lippincott & Co., auctioneers and commission merchants. He was fortunate in winning the esteem and love of this lady, and his marriage soon afterwards brought him into a situation which induced him to change his business interests. He was admitted a member of the firm of Lippincott & Co. about the year 1823.

This house was at that time one of the largest and most successful auction and commission establishments of Philadelphia, and as that business has a history, some allusion to it will be interesting. Before the American Revolution the office of " Venduo Master" of the city of Philadelphia was considered a proprietary franchise, which was conferred by the executive authority of the colony upon special favorites. When the opposition to Great Britain had assumed such formidable proportions that the proprietary authority was abolished, there were numerous persons who were ready to avail themselves of the absence of all laws regulating auctions and auctioneers. It was soon discovered that these voluntary vendue masters were injurious to the public interests. Being under no restraint they were convenient means for the disposal of stolen goods, and the frequency of their sales was considered an evil by shopkeepers and merchants, whose customers were attracted from the regular course of trade to the vendue rooms. This evil was in due time repressed by the re-establishment of regulations for the license of vendue masters, and at a later time, when peace was re-established, laws were passed providing for the licensing of a certain number of auctioneers in the city and county of Philadelphia. Later legislation has thrown the business open to any one who will pay for the license and engage to make faithful returns of the commissions on sales which were exacted by the state. The firm of J. & W. Lippincott, which was superceeded by Lippincott & Richards, was in direct *descent*, if we may use that term in a business sense, from the oldest of these post-revolutionary auction houses. In the year 1797 Peter Benson was a regularly licensed vendue master of the city of Philadelphia, established at No. 74 South Third street. In 1799 Samuel Yorke, who had been brought up by Richard Footman, a famous vendue master in his day, went into partnership with Benson as auctioneers, and the firm was Benson & Yorke. They were established at 39 North Front street. When Mr. Benson retired from business, about 1802, Joshua Lippincott became a partner with Samuel Yorke, and Yorke & Lippincott continued the business at No. 51 North Front street. Mr. Yorke made money in this connection, and the fine row of houses—considered very splendid in their time—extending from Washington Square to Eighth street, on the south side of Walnut street, and still called "Yorke Row," was built from his profits in this business. When Mr. Yorke died, Joshua Humes succeeded to his place in the firm, and Humes & Lippincott was established.

In 1822 Joshua & William Lippincott carried on the business at No. 34 South Front street. About the year 1823, Benjamin W. Richards became a member of the company, and shortly afterward, by the retirement of William Lippincott, the firm became Lippin-

cott & Richards—being composed of Joshua Lippincott, and his
son-in-law Benjamin W. Richards. When the senior member of
the firm retired from business, Mr. Richards associated with him
Joseph Bispham, about the year 1836, and the firm of Richards &
Bispham was kept up until the death of Benjamin W. Richards in
1852. His son, Benjamin W. Richards, Jr., succeeded him, and
shortly afterward the firm of Richards & Miller was established.
The latter has since been dissolved, and Samuel C. Cook carries on
a business which has been continued and transferred from the time
of Peter Benson until the present period, during the changes of
sixty-six years.

Mr. Richards having had a fine education, and possessing strong
natural talent, soon became distinguished in public affairs. He
was nominated for the Legislature as early as 1821, upon an independent ticket, but was defeated. He was, however, a few years
afterwards, elected to the State Senate from the city, and in 1827
to the House of Representatives of Pennsylvania by the Democratic party. His care, attention and talent in these positions attracted the confidence of his constituents; and, in 1829, when the
office of Mayor was made vacant by the resignation of George M.
Dallas, he was elected to fill the vacancy. Mr. Millnor succeeded
him for the official year 1829-30. Mr. Richards was elected for
the full term 1830-31.

He was so far successful that an association was formed by Nathan Dunn, John J. Smith, Frederick Brown, Isaac Collins, and
himself. They bought the beautiful country seat at Laurel Hill,
which had last been occupied by John J. Rodriguez, and established there the celebrated "Laurel Hill Cemetery," which, as a piece
of property, now divides an immense revenue among its very few
owners.

As a member and Manager of the Deaf and Dumb Asylum, and
as one of the founders of the Blind Asylum, Benjamin W. Richards
has proved his benevolence of heart.

In literary institutions he was equally active. He was a member
of the American Philosophical Society, and a Trustee of the University of Pennsylvania, and he was one of the first Directors of
the Girard College elected by the City Councils.

The Girard Life and Trust Company was an institution of which
Mr. Richards had a large share in developing the system and policy. This company was in some respects a novelty. Life insurance had been well understood, and concerning that branch of the

business there was little to be settled beyond the exercise of that prudence and promptitude which are necessary at all times for success. But there was engrafted upon this corporation, by the exertions of Mr. Richards, something new in corporations, a power to execute trusts and act as fiduciary agents, a sort of confidence which before that time could only be conferred by individuals upon individuals. A corporation trustee was a novelty, but the success in establishing this company, the integrity of its management, and the promptitude and satisfactory method employed in its business soon drew towards it a large interest. The Judges of the Orphans' Court, Common Pleas, and District Court of Philadelphia county were satisfied with the honesty and fairness of this corporation, of which Mr. Richards was President, from the time of its organization until his death. Large sums of money in the jurisdiction of the Court were ordered to the care of the Company. These vast and important trusts have been faithfully performed during the lifetime of Mr. Richards, and since, under the excellent management of Thomas Ridgway, Esq., and the " Girard Life and Trust Company" remains amid the wreck of mushroom rivals, solid, profitable and enduring.

BENJAMIN BULLOCK.

The wool trade in Philadelphia, from very small beginnings, has increased to a magnitude of the first importance. Fifty years ago, it had scarcely an existence as a separate branch of business—now the annual sales in this city alone are counted by millions of pounds. The money value of this product has also advanced immensely. Common wool, which before the commencement of the rebellion never brought more than from thirty-three to thirty-five cents per pound, now sells readily at eighty cents per pound. The simple addition of the sum, in the transactions of a leading wool house, reaches an aggregate which is to be computed by millions of dollars. As a pioneer in this branch of business, the career of Benjamin Bullock will furnish some useful details, and serve to demonstrate the value of perseverance and steady industry.

Benjamin Bullock was born at Yeadon, near Bradford, in England, in the year 1796. His parents were poor, and he enjoyed but limited opportunities in acquiring an education during his youth. At an early age he was placed as an apprentice with a grocer, at Bradford, and served his time faithfully. Upon arriving at full age, unlike most young men, he determined to remain in the old shop. He continued there under small wages, and had no opportunity to accumulate savings of any great amount. For twelve years he served faithfully his employer, and continued with him until the latter died. This event happened about the year 1818, and as testimony of his satisfaction with his faithful assistant, his master left him a legacy of *twenty pounds*. This small sum was the commencement of the fortune of Benjamin Bullock. It placed him in possession of a larger amount of money than he had ever had before, and it enabled him to put into execution a plan which it may be reasonably supposed he had long meditated, viz.: emigration to the United States.

In the year 1815, this young Englishman, then about nineteen years of age, left the land of his nativity, to seek his fortunes in a strange country. He was accompanied by Mr. John Hurstler, who afterwards opened a wool store at No. 36 Church alley. They were recommended to the care and attention of Joshua Longstreth, then in fair standing as a merchant in this city. The latter kindly favored the emigrants with his advice and services. Mr. Hurstler went into business, as we have said; he had capital. But Benjamin Bullock, after paying his passage money, had but little left for business purposes. He resolved to labor and to wait. A situation was procured for him with Henry Korn, then in business as a weaver of woolen laces and fringes, and a manufacturer of military goods, on Third street, above Market. Mr. Bullock commenced his career of industry in the United States in Mr. Korn's establishment as a wool-comber. His experience as a grocer in England could not have assisted him much in this occupation, but he was ingenious and observant, and soon became proficient in all the details of his new calling. So well did he profit by his practical lessons, that having saved some money, he felt encouraged in undertaking another branch of the wool business, in a small way.

In 1822, Benjamin Bullock and Anthony Davis associated themselves in partnership, as Bullock & Davis, and commenced the business of wool pulling, in Front street, above Poplar. Their success in this enterprise was so great, that, in 1823, they were encouraged to take the store No. 32 North Third street, where they established themselves as dealers in wool, in connection with M. Barker, Esq., as agent at Pittsburg, still maintaining their own wool pulling factory in Front street. Their first invoice from the West was a lot of three hundred pounds, and their whole sales, for the first year of their business, was about five thousand pounds. The *first consignment* of wool from the West was sent to this house. The extraordinary manner in which this traffic has increased, may be imagined from the fact that the successors of Benjamin Bullock have alone received, used and sold, during eight months of the present year, (1864,) five millions of pounds of wool.

When Bullock & Davis commenced as wool dealers, in 1822–3, the principal manufacturers of woolen goods in Philadelphia and its vicinity, were Dennis Kelly; William Fisher, of Germantown; James Kershaw, of Blockley; James Schofield, of Delaware county; Jos. Brook, at Rockhill, near Manayunk; and Bethuel Moore, at Conshohocken. All of these, except Dennis Kelly, are now dead.

By a transition which seems natural, Bullock & Davis, from buying and selling wool, became manufacturers of woolen goods. They entered upon this branch of business, in the year 1837, keeping in operation at the same time their wool pulling factory, on Front street, and their warehouse on Third street. They worked the "Spruce Street Factory," near the Schuylkill river, which establishment is now owned and run by William Divine, who was the foreman of Bullock & Davis at this mill. Mr. Divine has since become wealthy, as a mill owner and manufacturer, and now owns and runs two of the finest mills in the southwestern part of the city. After the firm of Bullock & Davis relinquished the "Spruce Street Factory," they transferred their work to the "William Penn Factory," at Spruce street wharf, on the Schuylkill, about the year 1840.

In 1841 or 1842, Bullock, Davis & Co., dissolved partnership, George Simpson being at that time a member of the firm, having been previously admitted. Mr. Anthony Davis, the retiring partner, lived in honor and respect until 1862, in which year he died.

In 1842, the firm met with its first misfortune. It was obliged to temporarily suspend payment, in consequence of the failure of Bancroft & Co., which was indebted to it about $100,000. The energy of Mr. Bullock enabled him to surmount this misfortune, and make such arrangements as enabled the house to continue in business. Fortunately for all interested, the failure of the Bancrofts and others was not a permanent one. They recovered from it, and subsequently paid every dollar of their indebtedness, and are now quite rich.

In 1842, Charles W. Croasdale was associated with Mr. B. Bullock, although he was not generally known as a partner until 1851. In the latter year, George Bullock, a son, was admitted to the firm, which was continued as Benjamin Bullock & Co. In 1855, there was a dissolution of partnership, caused by the misconduct of Mr. Croasdale, who had used the name of the firm for his own purposes, and been guilty of other irregularities. Mr. Croasdale afterwards became insane, and died in 1856.

A new firm was now formed, consisting of the father and his two sons, George and Benjamin Bullock, Jr. In the meanwhile, the manufacturing business of the house was extended. Mr. Bullock bought the "Franklin Mill," in Haydock street, near Front, and afterwards established a very large factory at Conshohocken, Montgomery county, which is the largest but one in Pennsylvania, employing at the present time over two hundred hands.

On the fourth of June, 1859, Mr. Benjamin Bullock died, in the sixty-third year of his age, having been an occupant of the store No. 32 North Third street for more than thirty-seven years. He was an excellent and highly respected citizen, a man of probity and influence, whose career is a striking example of the advantages of our institutions. Arriving here at an age which to many who have not succeeded before, seems hopeless for the commencement of new enterprises, he was enabled by persevering industry and good management, notwithstanding his losses in business, to leave to his children a handsome sum, and the more precious legacy of a good name.

The surviving sons, members of the old firm, wound up their business, and in time were ready to form a new combination. The firm of Benjamin Bullock Sons, established in March, 1863, is composed of Benjamin Bullock, George Bullock, Joseph Bullock, William Bullock, and James Bullock. The only remaining son, Anthony D. Bullock, has been in business in Cincinnati, Ohio, for nineteen years, but has no interest in the Philadelphia house. Benjamin Bullock Sons now occupy the extensive warehouses Nos. 40 and 42 South Front street, and No. 9 Letitia court.

Benjamin Bullock Sons have, since the commencement of the rebellion, been largely engaged in manufacturing woolen goods. The Conshohocken and Haydock street factories are worked by them to their full capacity. They make fifty thousand yards of government kerseys per week. Since the beginning of the war they have furnished the United States three millions of yards of kerseys—*enough to reach to England*—also an immense number of blankets, and three hundred and fifty thousand yards of blue cloths. Prices have naturally advanced considerably since 1861; 3-4 kerseys, which formerly brought 69 cents per yard, are now selling at $1.17; army blankets, formerly worth $2 and $2.25 each, now bring $3.45.

The firm has the advantage of succeeding to a large capital accumulated by the father, but they have also made much money during the war—not by extraordinary prices, not by defrauding the government or the soldiers—but by fair profits, which upon a small business would not show, but which upon transactions of the magnitude of those of Bullock Sons, rapidly swell to thousands upon thousands of dollars. Whilst it is true that they have made largely by the war, it is also true that they have given freely. Every charity which has been projected for the benefit of the sick, wounded and suffering soldiers, has been benefited largely by their contributions. Every effort to equip troops has been responded to liberally by them with their voices, their influence, and their donations. What they have made they have used as trustees to be liberally paid back to every cause which is for the benefit of the country and the perpetuity of the Union.

JOHN B. AUSTIN.

IT is the boast of our country that it has more self-made men than any other land. In the War of Independence, the voice most potential in our national councils was that of the shoemaker of Connecticut, Roger Sherman. The mere clerk of the West Indies became the organizer of our government, and the founder of our financial system, in the person of Alexander Hamilton. Since that period the greatest and best of our statesmen and generals, the men who have possessed the largest share of the public confidence, have been those who have toiled upwards from the school of adversity, and have made themselves famous by dint of honorable exertion. Look at the mill boy of the Slasher, and the factory boy in the person of Millard Fillmore; and now we have to chronicle the career of a man, who, from humble beginning, has made himself one of the most eminent and successful financiers in Philadelphia.

John B. Austin is now the President of the Southwark Bank. He was born in this city. Being of an adventurous disposition, he went to sea, for the purpose of finding excitement for his restless spirit, and seeing foreign lands. His ability, as illustrated in a number of voyages, soon won him the position as second mate of a vessel. Indeed, it was evident in his case, as it has been in many others, that those who are born to command or counsel, will not long remain a hand in the ranks of any service.

Austin returned to this city while yet a minor. He had managed to acquire a thorough knowledge of book-keeping during his varied experiences, and he now obtained a situation in the Southwark Bank, as assistant book-keeper. In this position his character for fidelity, industry and talent, was so far established that he was promoted to the post of discount clerk; from this situation of responsibility he was elevated successively to the offices of general book-keeper and cashier's clerk. In all these positions he was remarkable for identifying himself with the interests of the bank, and laboring strenuously for the advancement of its rank among the monied institutions in the public esteem. While Mr. Austin held the position of cashier's clerk, he was offered more lucrative offices in other banks, whose directors had a high appreciation of his abilities; but he had a thorough understanding of the old proverb, that a "rolling stone gathers no moss," and was so intensely devoted to the prosperity of the "old ship," that he could not be persuaded to leave the institution. Some misunderstanding having occured, in which Mr. Smith came in conflict with Mr. J. Sparks, the President, that gentleman was induced to resign, so that the subject of this sketch might be retained, and he was then promoted to the responsible position of cashier. Mr. Smith, the former cashier, having been elevated to the presidency of the bank. Not long afterwards Mr. Smith "shuffled off this mortal coil," and the directors, with a wisdom that might have been emulated in other instances without disadvantage, promoted the cashier, Mr. Austin, to the presidency. During the general excitement attending the run upon the banks, a week or two before the suspension of the Bank of Pennsylvania, Mr. Austin's firm and decided course secured for him the esteem and admiration of our bank officials, many of whom were older in years and experience.

At a meeting of the cashiers, held to consider the condition of the Allibone institution, he boldly, and in unequivocal language, demonstrated the rottenness of that concern. This opinion was delivered at the time when a number of the oldest banking institutions were straining every sinew, so to speak, to maintain the credit of the Bank of Pennsylvania. Mr. Austin's course may have made him enemies among the corrupt supporters of the fraudulent institution, but it won him a high place in the general esteem, and subsequent developments proved the truth of every assertion he had made. It had been well for the cashiers if they had adopted his advice, and resolved upon some decisive action, to prevent the disastrous consequences of the explosion.

The bank over which Mr. Austin presided has the entire confidence of the people of the lower portion of the city, as well as of the community generally. It is conceded, we believe, that the prosperity of the institution is due to the energy, sagacity, prudence and firmness of its president. A thoroughly self-made man, educated in the harsh school of adversity, rising from post to post by sheer force of merit, he is the best ideal of what a bank president ought to be. Mr. Austin is still a young man, comparatively, but he may be proud of the position he has already achieved in the public esteem, and we expect from him still more brilliant things. Socially, he is a man whose company is always desirable. Politeness comes to him as a natural trait, which he displays to everybody who has any connection with him, either in the way of business, or in the affairs of private life. Such a man is an honor to the city in which he resides.

One of the prominent features of the management of this truly successful institution, has been the determination on the part of its president and directors to discount for that class of our community who most need it; for instance, a mechanic's note received for services rendered, or materials furnished, placed before them, has invariably received attention, to the exclusion of other parties better able to dispense with accommodation. The working class, particularly, have been benefitted by this admirable arrangement. The capital of this bank is $250,000. The salary of the president is $2,500 per annum.

There is another feature in this institution; one which might be introduced into other banks with equal profit to all concerned. It is the division of a portion of the surplus profits of the institution among its officers. We understand that if the profits of this bank, at the expiration of every six months, exceeds ten per cent. upon the capital stock, every officer in the institution receives for that term an increase of twenty per cent. on the amount. This course operates as an incentive to cashiers, tellers and clerks, to devote their entire time and individual energies to advance the best interests of the concern. The cashier of the Southwark Bank is Mr. Frank Steele. He is still a young man, but one of much experience. After having been employed in the Farmers' and Mechanics' Bank for a period sufficiently long to acquire a considerable knowledge of finance, he was elected to the position he now holds on account of his genuine ability and urbanity of bearing. Mr. Steele is calculated to become a very popular cashier. He has hosts of friends, and is generally esteemed and admired by all persons who come in contact with him in transacting business at the bank. It may be well to mention here, that Mr. Steele is a graduate of the Central High School. He is one of many brilliant young men who have been educated by our admirable system of public schools, and who are now making a prominent figure in the community, shedding lustre upon their education, and bearing testimony to the wisdom of the system itself. Mr. Steele is a gentleman of real ability in financial matters, and a worthy associate of Mr. Austin in the management of the affairs of the Southwark Bank. The numerous manufacturers, master mechanics, and others, who have their men to pay every Saturday, have spoken in praise of his anxiety to extend to them every accommodation. Even during the crisis, those who were pushed for cash obtained it at this institution, in consideration of their being regular depositors or customers. As long as the bank has such officers, it must enjoy a deserved popularity.

HORATIO A. FITZGERALD.

THE provision trade of Philadelphia does not occupy that rank in the general estimation which its importance entitles it to hold. Few of our citizens seem to be aware of the enormous development attained by this branch of the business, and even many prominent merchants and financiers, whose position should lead them to display a degree of interest in the matter, are lamentably ignorant of the statistics of the trade. It is a remarkable fact that there has been but one failure among the provision dealers within the past ten years, and yet the paper of these houses does not rank as high, and will not sell as well as the notes of dry goods houses which have not one-fourth of their capital, and which are often exposed to much greater risks. When we consider the extent of the trade in provisions, and learn that most of the sales are made for cash, with only occasional transactions upon a credit of from thirty to sixty days, we confess that we can offer no other explanation of such a singular distinction than that of a lack of information in reference to this department of commerce. A few figures will show that the provision business is one of our most important interests, and one that promises to add very largely to the wealth of the city. The following is a statement of the amount of salted meats and lard received here from Pittsburg by the Pennsylvania Central Railroad during the past five years :—

					Salted Meats.	*Lard and Lard Oil.*
In 1854,	-	-	-	-	35,099,277 lbs.	9,363,167 lbs.
1855,	-	-	-	-	32,417,180 "	7,984,457 "
1856,	-	-	-	-	24,560,670 "	10,126,195 "
1857,	-	-	-	-	34,704,577 "	7,155,977 "
1858,	-	-	-	-	39,360,027 "	10,752,224 "

This table includes only the amount received from Pittsburg DIRECT. In addition, the receipts from way stations on the same route, as well as from Baltimore and various points in the interior of our own state, by the Reading and North Pennsylvania Railroad, and the Schuylkill and Delaware divisions of the Pennsylvania canals, were very heavy. The receipts of cattle during the past ten years were as follows:—

	Beeves.	Cows.	Hogs.	Sheep.	Total.
In 1854, - - - -	73,300	13,350	78,000	61,000	227,750
1855, - - - -	55,200	11,530	60,300	132,500	264,530
1856, - - - -	61,978	12,930	103,350	240,700	418,928
1857, - - - -	62,400	14,700	95,700	342,000	514,800
1858, - - - -	81,990	17,125	166,600	277,600	543,315
1859, - - - -	87,555	11,153	115,226	272,168	486,102
1860, - - - -	99,845	10,575	127,964	324,500	562,944
1861, - - - -	82,365	4,214	199,179	269,020	554,778
1862, - - - -	87,520	4,650	206,000	229,300	572,470
1863, - - - -	103,150	6,950	174,370	275,100	559,525

Notwithstanding the immense business indicated by these figures, we have strong reason to believe that this branch of our trade is still in its infancy, and that many years will not elapse before it is doubled in value.

One of the most striking consequences of the growing prosperity of all interests in Philadelphia, is the influx of enterprising men from New England and New York. While we have full confidence in the energy and ability of our native merchants and manufacturers, we think an occasional "infusion of fresh blood" has a wholesome tendency. The gentleman whose name forms the caption of this article is a native of the Empire State. Mr. Fitzgerald was born in Orange county, the garden district of New York, in 1816. Although still comparatively a young man, and possessed of ample means, he began life in an humble way, and owes his fortune entirely to his own indomitable industry and peculiar talents for trade. Having received a fair education, he entered a grocery store in New York in the capacity of clerk, being then but seventeen years of age. The courage and self-reliance of the youth were exhibited in a remarkable manner only a year afterwards, when he bought out the concern and set up for himself. But he only continued in this business a single year, at the expiration of which time the pursuit of health induced him to seek the fresh air of the country.

It was in 1837 that Mr. Fitzgerald returned to New York, where he accepted a situation as clerk in the house of Ely, Hoppock & Co., provision packers and dealers, located on Sullivan street. Here he began to acquire that experience which laid the foundation of his future fortune. Circumstances led Mr. Fitzgerald to quit this firm, and he entered a dry goods house, but his talents, character and services were so highly valued by his former employers that they solicited him to return, and he complied, resuming his previous position as clerk. He appears to have advanced rapidly, in knowledge of the business, for in 1841 he was admitted to a partnership in the firm. In 1844 the firm was dissolved, and Mr. Fitzgerald came to this city. At that period the provision trade of Philadelphia was not very extensive. The receipts of pork, bacon and lard from the West were trifling. Our railroad connections was incomplete, and the bulk of the products of the Western states went to New York. But Mr. Fitzgerald had sufficient sagacity to perceive that such a state of things could not endure. He saw that a new spirit of enterprise was awakened here, and rightly calculated that those who were first in the field to take advantage of the creation of a particular branch of trade in a new locality, would be able to take at the flood that tide which is sure to lead on to fortune. He was equipped with an ample stock of experience, and was confident in his own resources. The opening was attractive, and Mr. Fitzgerald was the man to improve the opportunity. He formed a partnership with Mr. T. Van Brunt, and the firm was known as Van Brunt & Fitzgerald. The store was located at No. 6 South Water street, but the greater portion of the business was transacted at the smoking and packing establishment, on Front street, below the Germantown road.

The firm was eminently successful. Their exertions contributed to raise the reputation of our city for curing and packing provisions, and gave an extraordinary stimulus to that department of trade.

In 1854 the partnership was dissolved, Mr. Fitzgerald having purchased the interest of Mr. Van Brunt; but the business was continued with constantly increasing profit until March, 1858, when Mr. Fitzgerald, having accumulated sufficient wealth to satisfy even a greedy ambition, and feeling the necessity of repose and relaxation, withdrew entirely from active pursuits of trade. The energetic man did not limit himself to the opportunities of a single house while advancing with rapid strides upon the road to worldly independence.

It is only inferior characters who can "have too many irons in the fire." The man of steady nerve and active intellect can manage a host of things without diminishing the care bestowed upon any one of the number. For three years Mr. Fitzgerald was the silent partner in the house of J. H. Michener & Co., and for eight years he had an interest in the establishment of J. Van Brunt. All of his investments proved profitable, and Mr. Fitzgerald was enabled to retire from business at the age of forty-two years, with ample means of rendering his leisure easy and luxurious. Very few men in this country have more reason to be proud of their success in life than Mr. Fitzgerald.

It is his boast that he began his career without a cent, and that he realized by steady industry and sagacious management a liberal fortune by the time that the majority of other men are still struggling with the cards of trade, and uncertain whether they will ever reach the goal of fortune. The character of this achievement indicates the qualities that distinguish the man. He appears to have adopted in early life the scriptural council—"Whatever thy hand findeth to do, do with all thy might." Having determined to rise, the poor clerk kept his eye steadily fixed upon the object to be attained. Choosing a particular branch of business, he devoted his energies to obtaining a complete mastery of it, in all its ramifications. Opportunities are seldom wanting to him whose vigilance is sleepless. Mr. Fitzgerald was quick to see where a good field for his abilities was presented, and prompt to take advantage of the occasion. Indefatigable labor, studious care, and courageous enterprise accomplished the rest. Mr. Fitzgerald resides in an imposing mansion of brown stone, situated on Broad street, in the midst of a locality which promises to be the centre of wealth, fashion, and splendor. Not all of those who occupy such palaces have as good a claim upon a luxurious existence. Riches are only honorable when earned by the toil of thought or the sweat of the brow, and those who are born to "the golden spoon" are often but little more worthy of respect than the ass whose "back is with ingots bowed." The citizen that knows he has nothing but what has come to him through his own exertions, is the man who can truly appreciate the surroundings of comfort and magnificence. By his labor he has won the privilege of rest and recreation. By his efforts to develope a particular department of trade, he has conferred a vast advantage upon the city of his birth or adoption. By the nobility of his example, he has stimulated hundreds to strive to do likewise. Few envy such a man the possession of wealth; all are glad of his success, for the obvious reason that he has deserved to be successful.

Mr. Fitzgerald is a man of varied information, liberal heart, and amiable manners. He has every quality essential to the adornment of the social position he has so proudly achieved. If New

York has any more such contributions to make to our stock of self-made men, we shall welcome them most cordially to the city of Brotherly Love.

JOHN TRUCKS.

THE daily newspapers of May 1, 1863, in Philadelphia, contained the following announcement in the notices of deaths:—

TRUCKS.—On the evening of the 30th ult., after a short illness, JOHN TRUCKS, in the fifty-ninth year of his age.

The relatives and friends of the family are respectfully invited to attend his funeral, from his late residence, No. 12 North Seventh street, this (Tuesday) afternoon, fifth inst., at three o'clock. To proceed to Woodlands Cemetery.

The career of John Trucks is another example to be added to those already given in these sketches, which shows how honor and competence may be won by those whose origin is humble, if they have the great qualities of integrity and industry to guide them aright.

John Trucks was born in Easton, Northampton county, Pennsylvania, in the year 1804. His father died while he was very young, and he was the only child by the first marriage. His mother was in comfortable circumstances until her second marriage, eight years afterwards. Becoming reduced she removed to Philadelphia, about 1815. When but a boy, about twelve years of age, he entered the grocery store of Allen & McCartney, at No. 10 North Fifth street, to learn the business. No. 10 North Fifth street was near Market street, and not far from the Sorrel Horse Tavern, on the opposite side, an inn which did a large country business, and which furnished to Allen & McCartney many valuable customers.

In the year 1823, John Trucks having reached the age nineteen, determined to try his fortunes in the great West. He went to Pittsburg, where, not finding any encouragement, he engaged passage on a flat-boat, and so floated slowly down the Ohio and Mississippi until he reached New Orleans. In that great city he was without friends or acquaintances, and after vainly seeking for employment for some days, he determined to return to Philadelphia. He engaged passage on a homeward bound ship, but when a few days out of port, was stricken down with the yellow fever. He received but little attention, his presence on board being considered an omen of ill-luck, and the heartless captain, desirous to get rid of him, put into Norfolk. He was taken to the hospital, where he remained until he recovered sufficient strength to write Mr. Allen, the surviving partner of the firm of Allen & McCartney. On his return to Philadelphia Mr. Trucks found himself poorer than when he had left the city. The day of his arrival was marked by the burial of Mr. Allen. He then managed the business for the widow for one year. About this time, Mr. William Adams purchased the store, who having a high opinion of the integrity and business capacity of Mr. Trucks, took him in partnership. This copartnership was very successful, and made money rapidly. Mr. Adams declared that he never achieved good fortune until he took Mr. Trucks in with him.

In 1833 Mr. Adams relinquished business, and John Trucks continued it alone. Mr. Adams retired to his country residence in Mantua village, where he lived for some years, dying at the ripe age of eighty-two. Mr. Trucks carried on both the retail and wholesale business until 1848, when he relinquished the former entirely. In the meanwhile there were various changes in North Fifth street. Mr. Trucks purchased No. 17, on the opposite side of the way, and removed thereto. Commerce street had been cut through the sorrel horse property to Fourth street, and large stores were built upon the street. By these changes Mr. Trucks became located at the Southeast corner of Fifth and Commerce streets.

In 1847, Mr. Trucks associated in partnership with him Wm. L. Boggs. The latter came into the store on the nineteenth of June, 1833, as an apprentice.

The firm of John Trucks & Co. was enlarged in 1853 by the admission of a son of Mr. Trucks, and it became Trucks, Son & Boggs. In 1855 Mr. Boggs withdrew, and the firm was continued as John Trucks & Son, until 1857, when the senior partner retired. The business has since been conducted by William Trucks, John Trucks, Jr., and Joseph Parker, the latter a nephew of Mr. Trucks, under the style of William Trucks & Co.

Mr. Trucks was an old line Whig, and first became a member of the City Councils from Locust Ward, in 1841. Previous to that period he was a Trustee of the Philadelphia Gas Works, and was a strenuous advocate of the reduction of the price of gas from $3.50 per thousand cubic feet to $2. He declared that the city could afford to sell at $1 per thousand and make money. In Councils he was earnest and attentive, a valuable member of committees, and independent in his views and votes. He was one of the very few councilmen who sided with Charles Gilpin in the strong opposition he made to the city subscription to the stock of the Pennsylvania Railroad Company.

He was for some years a Director of the Commercial Bank, and for one year of the Schuylkill Bank. He was a man of sound judgment, keen and thrifty, but very prudent. He kept out of wild speculations, and made his money by careful and judicious investments.

Mr. Trucks married Eliza, daughter of Thomas Brown, of Philadelphia. He was a faithful, affectionate husband, and devotedly attached to his family. He was ever a fond and dutiful son to his mother, who still survives him. His large circle of friends and acquaintances mourn the loss of one who was ever valued and loved for his industrious habits, and high principles of honor.

CHARLES MASSEY, JR., AND MANUEL EYRE.

THE firm of Eyre & Massey, for more than forty years, commanded in Philadelphia the respect and confidence of persons in business, and of citizens generally. It occupied during that time a very prominent situation among our largest mercantile houses, and it was in the development of the shipping interests of our port one of our most important commercial firms.

This eminent establishment sprang from the house of Pratt & Kintzing, in which Charles Massey, Jr., and Manuel Eyre were both clerks. After they had fully accomplished themselves in the principles and practices of trade, it was natural that they should determine to try the adventurous course of business themselves, and it is not surprising that these graduates of the same house finally united in partnership, as they must have had by frequent intercourse and association an intimate knowledge of each other. It was some years, however, before this union was effected, and the separate history of each partner has its own story.

Charles Massey, Jr., was the son of Samuel Massey, an old Philadelphia merchant, and he was born April 14, 1778, in the City of Philadelphia. His uncle, Charles Massey, was, at the time of his birth, and for many years afterward, a biscuit baker at No. 19 South wharves. His nephew, the subject of our sketch, was named in compliment to him, and in order to distinguish the uncle and nephew, the name of Charles Massey, Jr., which he preserved during life, was kept up by the subject of our sketch long after his uncle had sought "that undiscovered country from whose bourne no traveller returns."

Charles Massey, Jr., was a great-grandson of Samuel Massey, an Irish Quaker, who emigrated to Pennsylvania in 1699, before the death of William Penn. Samuel Massey devoted his attention to the commerce of the infant colony, and was a shipping merchant in a good business for the time. His son, Wight Massey, succeeded him, and during what may be called the middle period of the colony of Pennsylvania, while yet strictly under colonial impediments, he did as large a business as a merchant as the jealous restrictions of British statutes would permit. He was successful in accumulating property. Among other curious matters, it may be noted that he owned the lot of ground Northwest corner of Arch and Broad streets, ninety-nine feet on Arch street, and three hundred and six feet on Broad street. Cherry street now passes through the lot. This somewhat extensive piece of ground was leased by Mr. Massey, in 1749, to Robert Paxon, for seven years, at the annual rent of $10.67 per annum.

Samuel Massey and Charles Massey were sons of Wight Massey. The former was the father of Charles Massey, Jr. He was educated at the Quaker school in Philadelphia, and at a proper age was placed in the counting-house of Pratt & Kintzing shortly after that partnership was formed. He remained in that establishment from 1795 to 1799. In the latter year he formed a partnership with his brother, William Massey, and Thomas Shoemaker, under the firm of Massey & Shoemaker. They were located at No. 24 South wharves, but shortly afterwards removed to the storehouse of Charles Massey, Sr., at No. 19 South wharves. Here they remained until 1803, at which time the firm of Massey & Shoemaker was dissolved, and the firm of Eyre & Massey was formed. The new firm remained here for about three years, when they removed to No. 25 South wharves, a building numbered afterwards by the changes on the river front, No. 28, and latterly No. 27.

Manuel Eyre was a son of Colonel Manuel Eyre, of revolutionary memory, a resident of Kensington, and an active patriot during "the times that tried men's souls." Mr. Eyre, Sr., was a ship-builder. During the Revolution he built ships and galleys for the State of Pennsylvania, and was patriotic in field service. His son inherited splendid physical powers and determined energy. He was a fine-looking man, being fully six feet in height, well proportioned, and of a dignified carriage. He was somewhat distinguished in public life during the continuance of the firm of Eyre & Massey, having been a member of the City Councils and a Director of the United States Bank in 1816, and again of the Pennsylvania Bank of the United States in 1836. He died in 1845, and by his decease the old firm of Eyre & Massey was dissolved.

Eyre & Massey were engaged extensively in the shipping business. They owned twenty vessels, and did a large trade, foreign and domestic. One of their ships, "The Globe," made twenty-nine voyages in twenty years, eight of them being to China, and many of them being more than a year in duration. Their vessels were known in almost every principal port of Europe and Asia, besides the United States and West India islands. The firm had business with the following extensive list of foreign ports: Archangel, Tonningen, Hamburg, Amsterdam, Antwerp, Havre, Bordeau, Bayonne, Lisbon, St. Ubes, Oporto, Cadiz, St. Lucas, St. Sebastian, Gibraltar, Malaga, Barcelona, Corruna, Marseilles, Island of Sardinia, Genoa, Leghorn, Palermo, Cette, London, Liverpool, Londonderry, Plymouth, Falmouth, Madeira, Teneriff, Cape de Verde islands, Vera Cruz, Alvarado, Jamaica, St. Jago de Cuba, Havana, New Providence, St. Domingo, St. Thomas, Guadaloupe, St. Croix, Curacoa, Laguayra, Maracaibo, Cayenne, Pernambuco, Bahia, Rio de Janeiro, Santos, Rio Grande, Paraguay, Buenos Ayres, Montevideo, Valparaiso, Irico, Coquimbo, Copiapo, Lima, Guayaquil, Panama, Sandwich Islands, Java, Sumatra, Manilla, Canton, Calcutta, and Madras. This extensive list of ports embraces the names of very many with which the merchants of our day have no intercourse. Added to these the home ports of the United States with which they traded, would show that the firm of Eyre & Massey held extensive mercantile intercourse with all parts of the world. This splendid commerce was prosecuted with a continued course of good fortune. Eyre & Massey never lost a vessel, and all they suffered from the perils of the sea during the forty-two years was a few partial losses of cargoes. They were equally lucky as insurers, having made underwriting a part of the business of the house. This they frequently did without restriction as to the ports to be visited, insuring certain vessels *by the year*, whatever voyages they might make.

Mr. Massey was a public spirited citizen, largely trusted in our civic affairs. He was a member of the Select and Common Council during several years. He was Chairman of the Committee of Councils which regulated the opening of Delaware avenue in 1834, according to the provisions of the will of Stephen Girard.

The business of Eyre & Massey was suffered to decline after the death of Mr. Eyre, in 1845, but it was nominally kept up by Mr. Massey for some years afterwards. He has, however, long since retired from business, and in his eighty-ninth year may be considered almost the only living memorial of the merchants of Philadelphia when our port was the principal shipping mart of the United States.

ELLISTON PEROT AND JOHN PEROT.

To unite in one sketch the biography of two brothers would be in many cases a difficult task. Even in the same family the tastes of the children frequently vary so widely, that, except in the common tie of parentage, there is no sympathy between them. The sons grow up to separate in the journey of life; whilst one may be a sedate clergyman, another will turn out a rough, adventurous sailor; whilst one becomes a merchant, another never rises above the condition of a carter. Up to a certain point, a sketch of the career of one child may answer for all, but beyond that there is a wide divergence. But in the course of life of the founders of the Perot family there are not such difficulties. Elliston Perot and John Perot endured their longest separation, and went through their most stirring adventures in boyhood. Manhood brought them together, and for sixty-two years they trod the pathway of life side by side, whilst they had the satisfaction of beholding their children and their children's children marching with them.

Elliston Perot, the elder of these brothers, was born in the island of Bermuda, on the sixteenth of March, 1747. John Perot was born in the same island on the third of May, 1749. At the age of seven years, for the advantage of a better education than the West Indies afforded at that time, the young Elliston was sent to New York, where, under the guardianship of his uncle, Elliston Perot, then Controller of His Majesty's customs, it was hoped that he would gain the benefits of liberal instruction. He was sent to school at New Rochelle, but before he had completed the course of studies appointed for him, his uncle died, and he was sent back to Bermuda. In that island he remained until he was of age. In the meanwhile he had placed his hopes upon success in a mercantile career, and hoping for a wider sphere of usefulness, he revisited New York, and commenced business there.

In the meanwhile John Perot had grown up in Bermuda, being advanced as far in his education as the limited means of that island allowed. In 1769 he made his first foreign voyage in a trip to Virginia, where, with his uncle John Mallory, in Isle of Wight county, he spent nearly three years, making voyages, meanwhile, to the West Indies. In the year 1772 he made his first voyage from Bermuda to Philadelphia, and saw in this city a very desirable place of residence, the advantages of which must have made an impression upon his mind. He returned to Dominica with a vessel well loaded with choice merchandise. Up to this time the interests of the two brothers had been divided, but now they were about to be united, with the most important consequences to both.

In the year 1772 they entered into partnership under the firm of Elliston & John Perot, in the island of Dominica. For six years they carried on business there, but finding that the profits were not as extensive as they expected, they were induced to remove to St. Christopher. At that place they found trade dull, and in a short time they transferred their interests to the Dutch island of St. Eustatius. For three years they tested the mercantile advantages of that location. In 1781 a British fleet and army, under command of Admiral Rodney and General Vaughan surprised and took possession of the island, to the astonishment of the inhabitants, who were ignorant of the existence of hostilities between Great Britain and Holland. Among the victims of these summary proceedings Elliston & John Perot were severe sufferers. They were seized as prisoners of war, and all their property was taken, confiscated and sold. They were detained under guard some months. When they were liberated, John Perot came to Philadelphia, where he arrived in the year 1781. Here he soon was admitted to the best society, and was so well received and appre-

ciated, that in 1783 he led to the alter Mary Tybout, daughter of
Andrew Tybout, hatter, a well-known and highly respectable citizen, a resident of Chestnut street, above Second.

Meanwhile Elliston Perot had gone to England in the hope of
obtaining satisfaction and reparation for the outrages of Rodney
and Vaughan. We need hardly say that British justice towards
British subjects was, in those days, a matter depending not upon
right, but upon Court favors. The Perots had been unjustly de-
spoiled in St. Eustatius by both naval and army officers, but they
never recovered anything from the Government. Elliston was
trifled with during three years of endeavor, during which he
visited Holland, Ireland and France, but he did not effect a resti-
tution from the English ministry. Growing tired of the injustice
of the English officials, he left London, in 1784, and repaired to
Philadelphia. Here he met his brother, and upon consultation they
resolved to try their fortunes here. They were not entirely penni-
less. They still had means; and accordingly the second firm of
Elliston & John Perot was established in property bought by
themselves at No. 41 North Wharves, below Arch street, and
alongside of an alley running out to what was called Perot's wharf.

John Perot, possibly by virtue of his wife's influence, was an
Episcopalian, and a member of St. Paul's church; but Elliston
saw reasons for favoring the principles of the Society of Friends.
He was admitted a member of Meeting in 1786, and on the ninth
of January, 1787, he married Hannah Sansom, only daughter of
Samuel and Hannah Sansom, at the Bank Meeting House, North
Front street. He established himself in his dwelling house at No.
45 North Front street, nearly opposite the Water street store. In
1789 Elliston built for himself a handsome residence at No. 299
Market street, but John remained with his family at No. 108 Arch
street until the year 1795, when he removed to No. 279 Market
street, ten doors below his brother's house. In 1803 he again removed to No. 251 Market street, but two years afterward he obtained a location at No. 297 Market street, adjoining the house of
his brother, in which affectionate proximity the brothers and
partners remained with their families until death separated them.

The business of Elliston & John Perot was extensive. They
enjoyed unlimited confidence abroad; their correspondents were
numerous and their consignments valuable.

After many years of successful venture, they were gratified by
the advent of their children and their gradual engagement in

mercantile careers. About the year 1816 Sansom Perot, the son of Elliston, engaged in business with Mr. Ridgway, at No. 39½ North Water street, next door to his father's and uncle's store; and Perot & Williams, of which James Perot, a son of John Perot, was senior partner, was established in the old store at No. 41 North Water street. The firms of Perot & Ridgway, and Perot & Williams were soon dissolved, and the cousins, James & Sansom Perot, formed a partnership and occupied the greater part of the store No. 41 North Water street, the old gentlemen confining themselves to the settlement of former business, not seeking for new customers. At the same time, it may be proper to note in this family history, that Francis Perot, son of Elliston Perot, became a brewer, and with his brother, William S. Perot, carried on for many years the extensive brewery at No. 120 Vine street and No. 107 New street. About 1820 there were added to the active members of the Perot family Charles and Edward, sons of John; and Joseph, son of Elliston. Joseph and Charles established themselves as merchants at No. 39 North Water street, under the firm of C. & J. Perot.

The business of the old firm of Elliston & John Perot was finally closed, in 1834, November 28, when Elliston Perot died. His aged brother withdrew from business, leaving the management of affairs to the young people. He survived his brother nearly seven years, dying January 8, 1841, in the ninety-second year of his age, full of honor and universally respected, having by himself, his brother and children, illustrated, from the Revolutionary times almost to the present era, the advantages of probity and attention to business.

As time advanced the Perot family was enlarged by the appearance of new members in the mercantile world. Elliston Perot, the second, established himself as a merchant in Church alley, in 1847. James P. Perot, senior partner of Perot & Hoffman, located at No. 41 North Wharves. He is the only fighting member of the family. He was wounded and taken prisoner in the battle at Sheppardstown, while acting Adjutant of the Corn Exchange Regiment, and was Lieutenant-Colonel of the 49th Regiment, called out for the emergency in 1862. T. Morris Perot, dealer in drugs, was established, about 1850, at No. 19 North Fourth street. Perot & Hoffman were succeeded by James P. Perot & Brother. Perot & Senat were in business, in 1856, at No. 80 Chestnut street, and J. S. & E. L. Perot are now at No. 36 North Delaware avenue. The latter are young and energetic men, enjoying the confidence and esteem of the mercantile community generally.

ROBERT MORRIS.

THE start upon a voyage in the midst of a storm may not be in accordance with our notions of ordinary prudence. We call such a step rather foolhardy than demonstrative of courage. But when such a start is made, and we observe the daring navigator breast the fearful gale and foaming waves, ride out the storm and move safely out upon the smooth untroubled seas, we cannot restrain our admiration; and so is it when it is proposed to begin a new business, or inaugurate a new enterprize, at a period of financial difficulty. The mass sneer at the proposition, speak of the projectors as lacking judgment, and prophesy a disastrous failure. But when the thing is accomplished, when the managers of the new concern have succeeded in proving their ability to surmount all trials and ride out the storm, the reluctant lips are constrained to utter praise. Such an enterprize was the Commonwealth Bank, and such a financial navigator is Robert Morris.

The name of Robert Morris is intimately associated with the financial history of this country. But it is not the great purse-holder of the war of independence who will now claim our attention. Bearing the same name, we have a genial, upright and able gentleman, long a prominent member of the editorial fraternity, and now President of the Commonwealth Bank.

Mr. Morris was born in Philadelphia, and while he was yet in his minority he became attached to the Pennsylvania Inquirer in an editorial capacity. In this position Mr. Morris soon won for himself a high reputation and a very numerous circle of friends. His graceful and elegant leading articles, and his many essays upon solid subjects, gave the Inquirer the character it has ever since maintained—that of a calm, conservative and pure-toned family newspaper, which, while keeping square with the progress of the age, is not absorbed in one idea, or misled into radicalism of any description. A number of the essays which have appeared in the Inquirer were recently collected and published in handsome style, under the title of "Courtship and Matrimony, with other Sketches from Scenes and Experiences in Social Life." Without being a work of genius, calculated to dazzle the public mind, this volume possesses merits which will secure for it a cordial reception in many a household. It may not fascinate, but it cannot fail to improve the heart and instil truth into the mind. It is the crowning work of Mr. Morris' very useful and commendable career as an editor, which has extended over a quarter of a century.

As the editor of a Whig and American newspaper, Mr. Morris was naturally something of a politician; but as it was impossible for him to descend to the low arts and associations which are now-a-days essential to success in the political arena, he has never been a very prominent figure there, and, we believe, has never but once been fortunate enough to taste the sweets of office. He has contented himself with the vindication and advocacy of his partizan rights in the columns of the Inquirer. This he has accomplished without the slightest touch of rancor, and with a firmness in the treatment of his opponents which is worthy of general imitation among politicians.

We now come to Mr. Morris' financial career. Though brief, it has been uncommonly brilliant and satisfactory. The institution over which he was chosen to preside went into operation in November, 1857, in the midst of a crisis and suspension of specie payments. The movements of the new concern were watched with much anxiety. Many, even among its friends, anticipated a speedy failure. Mr. Morris certainly had a grave responsibility resting upon his shoulders. He was expected to navigate a new institution into the safe haven of the public confidence, at a time when a financial hurricane was sweeping over the country, and the popular mind was filled with apprehensions of still further disasters. The President bent all his energies to the difficult task. The policy he adopted excited much astonishment. During those days of trouble the bank received nothing but specie on deposit, and issued none but their own notes, so that at that period it was the only banking institution paying coin. The bank passed through the crisis successfully, and the worthy President was warmly congratulated upon the sagacious management he had displayed. The new institution has always secured the public confidence, and is considered in a thoroughly reliable condition. Its Directors are among our most intelligent, reliable and popular citizens.

Few literary men succeed as financiers. The combination of practical sagacity with a talent for elegant expression is rarely found; but Mr. Morris unites to an agreeable fancy and a fine flow of language, a practical line of thought which can turn with ease from the editorial desk to the calculation of the counting-house. He has already demonstrated that he combines tact and talent to an extraordinary extent; and, we need scarcely observe, that when these qualities are joined in the same individual, he is sure of success in almost every walk of life.

Socially Mr. Morris is a very amiable and agreeable gentleman. Affable, courteous and unostentatious, he is calculated to win friends wherever he goes. His conversation is always pleasing and instructive, abounding with that wisdom which has been gained by a long and varied experience, during which the best faculties of a solid mind have been endeavoring to improve his fellow man. As an editor, no man connected with the Philadelphia press was more accessible or more unpretending. As a politician, no one within the limit of our acquaintance was more generous towards opponents, or more modest in the maintenance of his convictions. As a financier he has already made his mark by the exhibition of extraordinary skill under the most difficult circumstances. In all the relations of private life he is an exemplary gentleman. To those who are not acquainted with Mr. Morris this may seem the language of unmitigated eulogy; but the truth will not allow us to alter a word.

Although not now connected with any public journal, the disposition for literary pursuits still exists, and within a short time Mr. Morris has written a domestic play, entitled "Temptation," and a series of Songs for the Loyal, which way be seen at the well-known music store of Messrs. Lee & .Walker, of this city. The play which we have read is beautifully written, and the songs are equal in poetic spirit and enkindling patriotism to anything of the kind that has been produced since the commencement of the Southern Rebellion. Among the most stirring and exciting are "Gettysburgh," and "The Christian Commission." "My Love is on the Battle Field" is quite a gem, and is deservedly a popular favorite. With our best wishes for the continued health and prosperity of our esteemed friend, we close this brief sketch, not for lack of material, but because the subject of our notice is too well known in this community to require any elaborate biography or eulogy at our hands.

RODNEY FISHER.

"It is with sincere regret," says the *Commercial List* of September 20, 1863, "that we record the death, in this city, on the thirteenth instant, in his sixty-sixth year, of Rodney Fisher, a very well known and highly respected citizen of Philadelphia, who was in truth, to use the words of a cotemporary, 'a relic of a past generation, identified with many business and fiscal movements of importance here.'" By every family tie and early association, the deceased was also closely and honorably connected with the history of our country, being a grandnephew of Cæsar Rodney, the signer of the Declaration of Independence, and grandson of Colonel Thomas Rodney, who, during the Revolutionary War, led the van in the famous march from Trenton to Princeton, on "the awful night," January 1, 1777, when he was wounded. The subject of our sketch was son of John Fisher, late United States District Judge, of the State of Delaware, at Dover, where he died, April 23, 1823.

In early life, Mr. Rodney Fisher, who was born at Dover, Delaware, in 1798, entered the navy as midshipman, but being more attracted by commerce, for which his mind was peculiarly adapted, soon left the service and entered the employ of the well known Edward Thompson, of Philadelphia, who was at that time at the head of "the China trade" in this country. He was, subsequently, for a long time, in the Bank of the United States, and in its service resided for nearly a year in England, in company with the well known Samuel Judson, having previously traveled extensively as agent for that institution in this country, conducting for it many highly important negotiations.

Returning to China, Mr. Fisher became partner with "McVicar & Co.," one of the first English firms in Canton. He resided, at different periods, many years in the East, and was, both in China and India, connected with some of the leading commercial transactions of his time, and intimately acquainted with many of the first men, both natives and foreigners, who distinguished themselves in the important series of diplomatic and military events which attended the opening of China to the world. Having remarkably varied powers of observation, and a very retentive memory, Mr. Fisher retained a fund of anecdote and description, drawn from his extensive travels, such as few men possess. He had known China and its trade as they were in "the old time," in "the days of the Hong Merchants," when life in every respect was more strongly marked than at present, and while the laws and strange customs of the East maintained a vigorous struggle with those of Europe. In addition to what he learned from observation, Mr. Fisher also possessed an extensive fund of very valuable knowledge relative to the history of the Revolution, which he had drawn from his many relatives who had taken a prominent part in the war, and the diplomacy of our Republic, while it was yet young; and this knowledge he had cultivated by much reading of what had been written on the subject.

He returned to the United States and to his family in the year 1845, and resided in Philadelphia to the day of his death. He had married many years before his return a daughter of Thomas Callender, a well known merchant of this city. Of his children, one daughter is at present the wife of Mr. Charles Godfrey Leland, while another, who died at Paris, in France, but little over three years ago, was married to Mr. Edward Robbins, of this city.

The loss of this child was, unfortunately, not the only bereavement which Mr. Fisher was called on to mourn, since but a few weeks before his death, his already rapidly failing health received a shock from hearing that his only son, Cæsar Rodney, First Lieutenant in the United States regular service, First Cavalry, had been mortally wounded at the battle of Aldie, Va. We may be pardoned for stating in this connection, in the words of his captain, R. S. Lord, "that Lieutenant Fisher fell while doing his duty in the bravest and most gallant style." "He acted," said an eyewitness, "most heroically, leading his company in a charge which has not, I believe, been equalled during this war." Unfortunately, the first news received by Mr. Fisher relative to his son was to the effect that he would soon be cured of his wounds, and it was while waiting for his return that the father suddenly learned the sad truth of the death.

Mr. Fisher had been many years a Director in the Bank of Commerce, in this city, and was, for some time previous to his death, its Vice President. On receiving intelligence of his decease, the following resolutions were passed by its Board of Directors:

BANK OF COMMERCE, PHILADELPHIA, *September* 15, 1863.

At a special meeting of the Board of Directors, held this day, the President communicated to the Board the decease of Rodney Fisher, Esq., late Vice President of this Bank.

On motion, the following was adopted:

Whereas, This Board has learned with deep regret of the death of their late fellow-member, Rodney Fisher, Esq.,

Resolved, That we have sustained in him the loss of a worthy and amiable member, who has been connected with this institution as Director, and lately as Vice President of the same.

Resolved, That, as a mark of our deep regard and respect for his memory, we will attend his funeral, and that a copy of these resolutions be transmitted to his family with the sincere condolence of this Board.

The above is a copy from the minutes.

J. A. LEWIS, *Cashier*.

Such is the brief sketch of an honorable merchant of the old school, who flourished during a period when the world's truest history was, in a great measure, embraced in the lives of its men of business, and who was personally connected with many of the first commercial transactions of the time, or with the men who managed them. It should not be forgotten that in every relation of private life Rodney Fisher was a man of more than ordinary merit, and that he will long be remembered in a wide circle of friends, as one whose kind and honest heart formed the true basis of all the courtesy and refinement of a true gentleman.

JOSEPH B. SHEWELL.

JOSEPH B. SHEWELL was a son of Thomas Shewell, a prominent merchant of this city, by his second wife, Hannah Brown, and he was born in Philadelphia, October 13, 1822. He was educated at the famous academy of John H. Willitts, at Carpenters' Hall. His first introduction to business was in 1840, when he entered the hardware house of Carr & Keim, Commerce street. After a trial of a year he found the business did not suit him and he became a clerk in the house of Sperry & Wright, produce dealers, in South Water street. Here he remained until 1843, the firm having changed in the meanwhile to Sperry & Randolph. At the dissolution of the firm of Sperry & Randolph he was gladly engaged as a clerk by Mr. Nathaniel Potts, of No. 30 North Water street, and subsequently by Earp & Young. With this latter firm he remained until May, 1847. At this period he was in his twenty-fifth year, and he had an ambition to try his own fortunes in the world. He therefore leased the second story of the store No. 3 South Water street, occupied in the first story by William Newell. He opened his office there as a merchandise broker. The first year of this experiment was a trying one to him, and the second was but little better. But as his business prospects became brighter, which they did during the third year, he was compelled to secure other accommodations for his customers. He rented a large office at No. 21 South Water street, where he remained until he entered into partnership with John D. Tustin, on the twelfth of February, 1849. They established themselves at No. 21 South Water street, in the second story of George M. Fleming's store. From this location they removed, in less than a year, to No. 24 South Water street, where they remained until 1855, and then changed their headquarters to No. 34 South Water street. In the year 1860 Tustin and Shewell removed to No. 126 North Front street; from which situation they again changed their location, at the commencement of the year 1862, to No. 206 Market street. On the ninth of July, 1863, the firm was amicably dissolved, Mr. Shewell retaining the stand, and Mr. Tustin removing to Front street, below Market.

The dissolution with John D. Tustin was premonitory of the final cessation of the interest of Joseph B. Shewell in worldly affairs. He was at the time of closing the partnership in ill health, having contracted a heavy cold, in November, 1862, while upon a visit to New York. This misfortune developed the latent seeds of pulmonary consumption, which finally removed him from this world of trouble on the twenty-eighth of January, A. D. 1864. He died at his residence in Germantown, and was buried in the German Baptist (generally known as the "Keyser Burial Ground,") on Monday, February 1.

Mr. Shewell married, October 1, 1850, Catharine Clemens Backus, daughter of Frederick R. Backus, Esq., a most amiable lady, who, with four children, mourn the loss of a kind husband and affectionate father.

Mr. Shewell was endeared to a large circle of friends by his noble traits of character. He was the soul of honor, and in all things endeavored to act up to the golden rule. In religion, although a member of the Protestant Episcopal Church, he was a firm believer in the final restoration of all men from sin to holiness. He was a warm admirer of the writings of the late Elhanan Winchester, whose name was so widely known as a preacher of this doctrine. In business matters, Mr. Shewell enjoyed a general popularity for his good judgment in matters connected with his own department of trade. There was no better judge of the quality of provisions in Philadelphia. His opinion was appealed to frequently in matters of dispute upon such topics, even by the oldest and most experienced produce merchants. His well known integrity and experience were guarantees that his decision would be fair and satisfactory. For punctuality in keeping his engagements Mr. Shewell was particularly noted. A short time before his death he told a friend that he had only once in his lifetime been too late for the cars.

During the present troubles of our country the heart and hopes of Mr. Shewell were earnestly given to the patriot cause. He sustained the Union by his voice, and his purse according to his means, and in September, 1862, he volunteered for the *defence* of the State, and partook of the fatigues and dangers of the Corn Exchange Regiment.

As a member of the Masonic Order Mr. Shewell was noted as a bright brother, having taken the highest degrees. He paid much attention to Masonic history, and had made it his study during many years.

As a merchant and gentleman, as a friend and citizen, Mr. Shewell was a model man. He leaves behind him, as a legacy to his children, a reputation honorable and commendable, unspotted by any vice, a reputation such as it is, is the hope of the true Christian, that he may leave to his posterity.

- - - —— ——

PERSONAL PROSPERITY OF MERCHANTS.

WE propose in this article to take a general view, in a moral aspect, of the objects and end of mercantile pursuits, as affecting the personal condition of the individual. The great aim of mercantile life is wealth. In most other pursuits fame—a desire to be

31

distinguished in political, literary, or the scientific walks of life, is the main object, and wealth only incidental and collateral. But with the merchant getting money is the chief object of his pursuits, and fame is incidental to his wealth and talents, and the grand sum total of all his *labors* finally result in financial success or failure. The countless vicissitudes of trade which regulate commercial life are so intricately interwoven with all the relations and ramifications of society—depending on so many contingencies and nice dependencies, that financial success or failure may be truly said to be the result of surrounding, collateral, unforeseen and unavoidable causes, rather than the mere personal efforts, misfortunes or faults of the individual. It is energy and attention to business which almost universally secures success, but it is not always the absence of these essential qualities which induce failure. It has been wisely said by the great moralist, Dr. Johnson, " That with due submission to Providence, a man of genius has been seldom ruined but by himself." This is true as regards the physical *status* and personal character of the man, for these being founded upon moral principles, correct deportment, attention to health, and innate rectitude of purpose, depend on the man himself, and not on those circumstances and contingencies of trade which follow fortune's smiles—

"Forever changing like the changeful moon."

But bankruptcy, or in common parlance, financial failure, is not the worst fate that can overtake the merchant. This is a condition which may result, as it does almost universally, (the contrary, we are happy to say, for the honor of Philadelphia merchants, as a class, is the exception to the general rule,) from entirely innocent, unavoidable, and, very frequently, meritorious causes. This is a common fate, however remote it may be, ever possible to overtake the merchant whose business requires him to trust to the success or failure of others, who, in turn depend on

"A mighty stream of tendency,"

Ever changing with the ceaseless ebb and flow of trade in the wants and caprices of society.

It is well known in mercantile circles that with but few exceptions, success rarely follows more than the first or second generation of the families engaged in the pursuits of commerce. If the first generation is successful, an ample patrimony renders the second generation either unfit, through the soft appliances of luxury, for such arduous pursuits, or gives them ample means for elegant leisure, or of following some other occupation more congenial to the tastes of the pampered pets of affluence, who may be—

"Though equal to all things, for all things unfit—
Too wise for a *merchant,* too proud for a wit."

Hence it is that the mercantile ranks are continually changing in the *personnel,* as well as in the various alternations in the lights and shades of fortune's smiles and frowns.

If we look at the leading commercial houses in our large cities, we will find, as a general rule, that the most successful and prominent merchants of the day were recruited into the ranks of commerce from some quiet village or farm in the country. They came to the city from their native hills and valleys, with robust frames, vigorous constitutions and active intelligent minds, with hearts filled with the teachings and precepts of rural life, and the simple rustic manners of their country home. Many of them with no patrimony but a parent's blessing, and the Bible—a mother's keepsake—to guide them from the snares and temptations which beset the unwary in the untried paths of city life. Boldly pushing their little bark out on the stream—

"The shot of accident, and the dart of chance,"

puts them in the ranks of the ancient and honorable "guild of ye merchants companie."

Success rarely fails to attend men who commence life from such beginnings in large cities, where the field for enterprise is so various and extensive. Whilst they maintain that greatest of all earthly blessings, "a sound mind in a sound body,"

"They bear a charmed life, and must not yield."

But while such men as these succeed, whose

"Joys are lodg'd beyond the reach of fate,"

there are thousands who, though they commence life under the same auspices, with the same hopes, the same determination and equal talents, yet fail to reach that fortunate goal of their youthful ambition.

But their failure may not be bankruptcy, to which, through the various currents in the whirl of trade, they are rendered

"Subject to all the skyey influences;"

but it may be of a more melancholy nature, in the loss of health and even of reason itself. Assiduous toil, unremitting cares, and an inordinate grasping avarice, may disappoint their cherished hopes and precipitate them into an untimely grave, or drive them into the yawning jaws of that living tomb, the mad house, over whose sombre hopeless portal are inscribed those dreadful words :

"All hope abandon, ye who enter here."

This is no fancy sketch. Would to heaven, for the sake of humanity and all the buried hopes of the victims of self-immolation on Mammon's golden altar, it were only such. But, alas ! it is too true, many who entered the race of mercantile life with the brightest hopes and presaged the fairest promise, are now inmates of the mad house, or hopelessly demented through over-taxed exertion of the brain in the single, selfish, inordinate pursuit of speedy wealth Melancholy instances of this kind may be found in our midst, of men almost yet

"In the morn and liquid dew of life,"

victims and maniacs to the love of gold. Men who come from the country to the city, where their industrial talents soon raised them by degrees from subordinate positions to be partners or heads of firms, and with the opening prospect of wealth before them and within their grasp, the fatal appetite for gold, as soon as fairly tasted, seized upon them with inexorable power, devouring every other impulse of better nature, and dragging within its insatiable vortex health, happiness, and even reason itself.

In the Insane Asylum in this county there are inmates bereft of their reason, or languishing in hopeless imbecility, whose malady was brought on by extreme labor to become speedily rich. Constant labor, night and day, with the mind continually strained to its highest tension, brooding with ceaseless anxiety over anticipated profits or conjectured losses, with no rest or relaxation, must sooner or later wear out the body and affect the mind. And these effects are soonest felt by those of the most active and nervous temperaments, very many of whom, to feed the unnatural excitement of the brain, and to keep the body for the time up to the work, are compelled to resort to stimulating drink, and a controlling appetite, through an apparent necessity to support their labor, being acquired, they escape the Scylla of the mad-house to be wrecked in the Charybdis of the pot-house.

This inordinate striving in our day and country for speedy wealth is a great moral evil—like a canker-worm destroying the fruit of fairest promise, it cuts off its votary ere half his days are run, or clouds his life with mental darkness—"the heaviest stone which melancholy can throw at a man." Or, if the victim live and tottering reason maintain a place in his sordid brain, his heart becomes obdurate, hardening like the idol of his worship, and forever brooding o'er his heaps, his days and nights

> "With av'rice, painful vigils keep;
> Still unenjoy'd the present store,
> Still endless sighs are breath'd for more."

Man's destiny has a higher and nobler aim and end than seeking wealth at the sacrifice of health and reason.

Dr. Johnson said, that "there are few ways in which a man can be more innocently employed than in getting money"; and Strahan, his friend, remarks, that "the more one thinks of this the juster it will appear." But this, however deep the philosophy may be, must mean that just and reasonable pursuit, which should be subject to the proper demands of nature and society for the necessary and rational enjoyments and duties of life. The same high authority says, in speaking of the vanity of wealth—

> "Oh, quit the shadow, catch the prize,
> ——— which gold could never buy,
> The peaceful slumber, self-approving day,
> Unsullied fame and conscience ever gay."

www.ingramcontent.com/pod-product-compliance
Lightning Source LLC
Chambersburg PA
CBHW020056030728
47498CB00006B/1811